Strung

E-book: 979-8-9856810-0-0
B&W Paperback: 979-8-9856810-7-9
Full-color Paperback: 979-8-9856810-5-5
Full-color Hardback: 979-8-9856810-9-3

ζ

Published by the Conceptual Chronicler of Time
RoskeChronicler@gmail.com

AUTHOR'S PREAMBLE

Strung sits at the center of a Venn diagram lapping science-fantasy and literary historical romance to explore the question: "If there's a reason folklore shares so many elements across disparate cultures, what forms could that reason take?"

I've always gravitated towards authors who display faith in my intelligence as a reader, and I've tried to emulate that approach in writing Strung while staying faithful to its origins as a decades-long paracosm. Everything you need to know is there on the page—but usually without direct hand-holding, allowing you to knit Strung's deeper narrative threads together on your own.

Provided you don't blink too often, no question should go unanswered.

Trigger warnings include mild self-harm, off-screen abuse, and brief on-screen violence.

Special thanks to Trevor, Katie, and Oliver the Cat.

Musical Terms

ADAGIO
Tempo: stately, leisurely; 60-80 bpm.

BRIDGE
Musical passage which connects two sections of a song.

CODA
Ending passage to a movement or piece whose themes are separate to the larger work.

CODETTA
Small ending passage to a movement or piece.

DOWNBEAT
The downward stroke of a conductor's arm indicating the first or accented beat of a measure.

GRAVE
Tempo: very slow and solemn; 30-50 bpm.

FERMATA
Musical notation indicating the prolonging of a note.

INTERLUDE
An intervening or interruptive musical composition inserted between the parts of a larger composition.

OVERTURE
A composition introducing a musical work

PRESTO
Tempo: fast and lively; 160-200 bpm.

REPRISE
Repetition or reiteration of a composition's prior material.

SEGUE
To continue at once with the next musical section.

SONATA

Movement I
Exposition phase wherein the primary thematic material is presented.

Movement II
Development phase wherein Expository themes are further explored. Often carries greater tonal, harmonic, and rhythmic instability.

Movement III
Recapitulation phase wherein Expository themes are repeated and altered.

TACET
Musical notation indicating a voice or instrument does not play.

Table of Contents

TUNE-UP

a̰'ḭa͡ ꞯa, the people's Keening takes root in the soil.

Blue shells are crushed and woven into earth; their color seeps into roots of the giant-trees.
When giant-trees are cut into vessels, they sit blue against blue on the horizon.

a̰'ḭa͡ ꞯa, the people's Keening is forged in the fire.

a̰y͡ ꞯa is forged to bind the seams of vessels, to make fins which carry the vessels forward.
When a̰y͡ ꞯa is welded to vessels, they sit gleaming on the horizon.

a̰'ḭa͡ ꞯa, the people's Keening is woven in the cloth.

Blue cloth is woven to cover the a̰y͡ ꞯa of vessels, to mute their shine with colors of the sea.
When the sun reaches zenith over blue vessels on blue waters,
peeking a̰y͡ ꞯa winks to hunters sitting hungry on the horizon.

a̰'ḭa͡ ꞯa, the people's Keening is voiced in the song.

a̰y͡ ꞯa fins of the vessels propel the voyage; their articulation is sung in Ʂm'a̰ḛꞯ.
When the people must move quickly, the strongest Ʂm'a̰ḛꞯ sits low on ʔTh̰ḛa̰m's horizon.

a̰'ḭa͡ ꞯa, the people's Keening begins on the vessel.

The strongest Ʂm'a̰ḛꞯ of ʔTh̰ḛa̰m cannot be willed.
The strongest Ʂm'a̰ḛꞯ of ʔTh̰ḛa̰m sits at dusk; the only path forward is darkness.
When ꝣd̰a'h̰ḛ͡ ꞯa is offered, the Ʂm'a̰ḛꞯ of a̰'ḭa͡ ꞯa sends the people's vessel over the horizon.

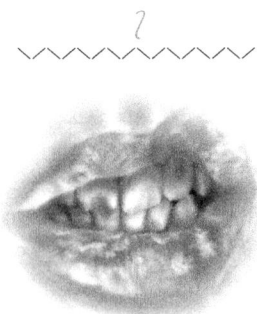

Captain Ibalis returns the ocean's salt from his mouth and hikes the top of his chapped lip in satisfaction. For five months, they've been making sweeps along the edge of The Brine—the uncharted expanse of sea surrounding Iodesh's pangea—half-heartedly carrying out their contract.

Some scat-brained Earl had approached Ibalis with a deal last Spring: capture a Faye and keep the crew quiet. Ibalis had laughed in his face. Only quill-snapper-sages and bad-rum-sailors[1] believe in the Faye. Besides, Fayetales say they're shapeshifters who can move objects by looking at them. How's anyone supposed to capture something like that?

But the Earl was set on bedding a Haywood, and the Lady in question was a Faye-nutter herself: "A gesture this grand would guarantee the marriage seal, *and* earn My Lady's deepest appreciation. I flatter myself, it's fool-proof!"

Fool's errand, rather, though Ibalis wouldn't have risked shattering the Earl's delusion by saying so. Better to be free on the high seas than to have your ship and crew commandeered for the Kingswar, after all, and better still with a fool volunteering to fund your truancy. Ibalis had ordered his men to sign the Earl's ridiculous writ of silence and they'd left within a week. Today, their contract came to an unexpected end.

After the midday sun erected too-tall columns under the hold's grate, Ibalis had altered course for a resupply. That's when the crow's nest saw it: a brief sparkle on the horizon. The same sparkle reported in every sea encounter with the Faye. It'd taken the entire day to catch up to the slippery bastards, and now...

Uproarious cheers from his crew pulse outward from the deck, riding dusk-lit waves below. Ibalis eyes the lone scow drifting towards him as the larger, stranger, blue vessel behind it gains an impressive burst of speed.

He'll be rich. The Faye are real, and they'd willingly given up one of their own.

First thing he'll do is threaten to talk. The Earl wants all the glory, but his writ of silence failed to include provisions for disembarking. Ibalis should be able to squeeze the dolt for enough to buy a title. Then maybe he'd call on the Haywood mare himself.

Cheers reach a fever pitch as the scow scrapes along the side of his ship. Shadows of empty lifeboat hooks slither down grimy wooden planks—crooked rust stretching for water. Ibalis' sneer expands to a grin.

No, first he'll find out just how many Fayetales are true.

---

[1] *An Avon idiom of three parts. Respectively: adamant philosophizing from behind one's desk, those who succumb to maritime superstition, and altogether, any lot particularly inclined to figment.*

Sky-blue silk rises and falls with Lysbeth Haywood's sigh; her matching eyes re-read the message held taut in her hands:

> *...how I pined over Spring Equinox. You spoke of your childhood fascination with Faye, and in the course of your speaking, the shapes of your mouth transfixed me. Ever hot did my yearni—*

Ignoring the drivel on either end:

> *...a pigeon arrived from their ship. They have done it, My Lady! They have captured a being wrapped in silver! Not in five-hundred years has this been accomplished, if we are to believe the tales!*
> *They have been instructed to dock at Limingten, where I will examine the cargo personally. If it is acceptable, I shall hasten to Lindenholt Manor with every intention of gifting this very rare creature. I will not attempt to hide my desire, sweet Lady, that this offering might induce your passions for me...*

The parchment wrinkles in Lysbeth's grip as her gaze returns to the window of her sitting room.

Hers is a leisurely life, if somewhat dull. All the duller now, as most men of gentry and peerage are occupied with the Kingswar to the North. Unfortunately for Lysbeth, one gentleman was given leave from the fighting.

The Earl of Dorsit, referred to simply as Dorsit, had been preening and panting over her for the better part of a year, though he was hardly first. Lysbeth's height—nearing six feet—pleasing features, and polished mannerisms lend her an air of elusive refinement uncommon to those of twenty-three. Before the Kingswar, Avonleigh Lords with questionable views on compliments had taken to calling her a "jewel of the court." She'd been sure to meet their expectations: sitting pretty and silent in her setting, pointedly cold to their advances.

Dorsit is no exception. Lysbeth finds his personality as disagreeable as his attentions, but her opinion matters little, as he's never cared to acknowledge it, and her refined sense of propriety prevents her from dismissing him outright. Over Spring Equinox, the Earl had called on Lysbeth and her brother, Isaac, Marquess of Edenshire. Though she'd taken great pains to be civil, Dorsit's company was difficult to tolerate, and she'd soon fallen back on a subject which offered her repose from several disquieting events throughout her life: the debated existence of beings known to her countrymen as Faye.

As topics go, it was an unfashionable choice. Any Avon of good breeding would tell you the Faye belong to children and half-mad carousers. Thus, Lysbeth was sure to make an overzealous presentation, and Dorsit's premature departure suggested her plan had worked to put him off. Now she realizes her liveliness had spurred his affections instead.

She folds his ink and turns to a young woman reading in the middle of the room. "Anything?"

Elane closes the book in her lap. Its spine reads, *Evidence for the Faye: A Collection of Accounts from the Dawn of Man.* "No, the most recent records are the Spencish galleon and the burning of Corburg. Nothing we would've forgotten."

Resigned, Lysbeth joins her cousin on the couch. The veracity of Dorsit's far-fetched claims can't be determined until his arrival in two weeks. She'd, rather pointlessly, hoped something in the book might provide her with the truth now, sparing her the need for patience.

Though appearances of Faye are scattered across ages[2] of historical record, their existence is disputed for two reasons: the outlandish descriptions of their physical appearance and abilities, and the frustrating peripheral events which always seem to accompany the main accounts—leaving just enough room to question their authenticity.

The encounters Elane has just mentioned are prime examples of the latter.

Five-hundred years ago, the seafaring nation of Corburg proudly claimed the capture of a Faye—or Syren, as the Corburgish called them. Within a month, a devastating fire swept across the capital where the Syren was said to reside. Corburg's much larger neighbor took advantage of the chaos and invaded before the ashes settled, ensuring the loss of any singed primary records through the ravages of their brief and brutal occupation.

Two centuries later, a Spencish patrol galleon set after a sparkle at the edge of Spencish waters. After hours of slow gains, the sparkle took the form of an unfamiliar vessel and deposited a small craft into the water. Despite the mothership's unanticipated surge of speed, the Spencish galleon pursued it for a time, returning later to find no sign of the scow. Though specifics of the account matched others before it, the report was largely discredited due to additional claims of a dragon's silhouette in the clouds.

Lysbeth bites her cheek.

"Please don't fret, Lys. Dorsit must be teasing you," Elane says, placing *Evidence* on an end table.

"I would agree, but then what could give him cause to so openly state his intentions?" She scans the message again and runs her thumb over the referenced line. "Here, 'that this offering might induce your passions for me,' he writes. You see? He seeks to extort my sense of obligation."

"Well, Dorsit is hardly a beacon of wit. Perhaps he's been fooled by his hired sailors? Or perhaps his men believe they've caught a Faye but in truth they..." Elane's brow knits.

"Precisely. How is one meant to mistake a Faye for anything else?" Lysbeth asks, waving the parchment. "Alder's descriptions were quite clear."

Were it not for Alder, the Haywood family's peculiar progenitor, it's unlikely any

---

[2] *Two-thousand years. Calendar years reset at the end of each age.*

Haywood would've given the Faye much thought. After all, such rare and undependable accounts left little else to be said about Faye which hadn't already been said over millennia. Alder's own account, however, begged pardon from this rule.

Three centuries ago, Alder rose from Earl to Marquess, bringing the Haywoods into Avonleigh's elite peerage. Given the southern county of Edenshire and a new residence at Castle Lindenholt, his dutiful approach to Sovereign and soil was regrettably short-lived when, after his supposed loss at sea, Lindenholt passed to his wife until his young son came of age. Even today, such tragedies are common enough, though less common is the return of the lost decades later.

Thirty-four years after Alder's disappearance, he'd reappeared on Lindenholt's stone court offering vague explanations for his fated voyage and blaming his protracted return on a bout of amnesia. Rejoicing Lindenholt residents chose to muzzle the gift horse rather than pry its mouth, and the remaining nine years of Alder's life were merrily spent. It was a happy piece of Haywood family trivia, and would have remained so, had the letter Alder composed in secret not been found by his son after his death.

In truth, according to Alder, a Faye ship had spirited his own away to their homeland—where he'd lived in bliss until the desire to see his child once more compelled his return to Avonleigh. Alarmed by nearly every passage of the letter, Alder's son assumed his father's madness and kept the document a family secret. So it happened this account of the Faye—by far the most detailed—remains unknown to the world at large, passed down through generations of Haywoods as a source of great debate and whimsy among them.

"Yes, but Dorsit's sailors aren't privy to Alder's letter. His descriptions of Faye were humanlike, but *they'd* be searching for something from a Fayetale." Elane tilts her head to *Evidence*. "Something intelligent but *in*human, like a chimera or a shapeshifting demon."

"Aye, but the captured wears some manner of silver attire, just as Alder said," Lysbeth counters. Satisfied Elane's confoundment has reached suitable levels at last, she skims the message again. "'...examine the cargo personally.' Whatever they've found, Dorsit considers it more debris than intelligent being." She returns the letter to her lap indignantly. "Why should I be made to accept such a man? Even supposing his claim is true, would Father really secure a *person* as my price?"

"Considering tradition, he may not have a choice. And Isaac is liable to take Dorsit's view on personhood regardless." Elane cups her cousin's flexing fingers. "We'll find a way out if it comes to it, Lys, but we won't know anything for certain until Dorsit arrives."

———————————————

—————————

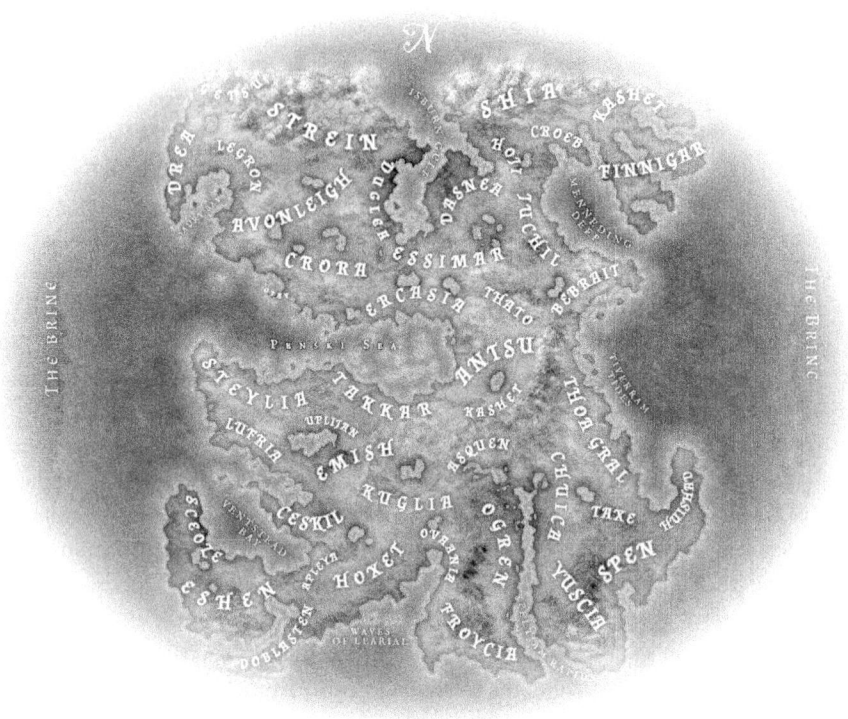

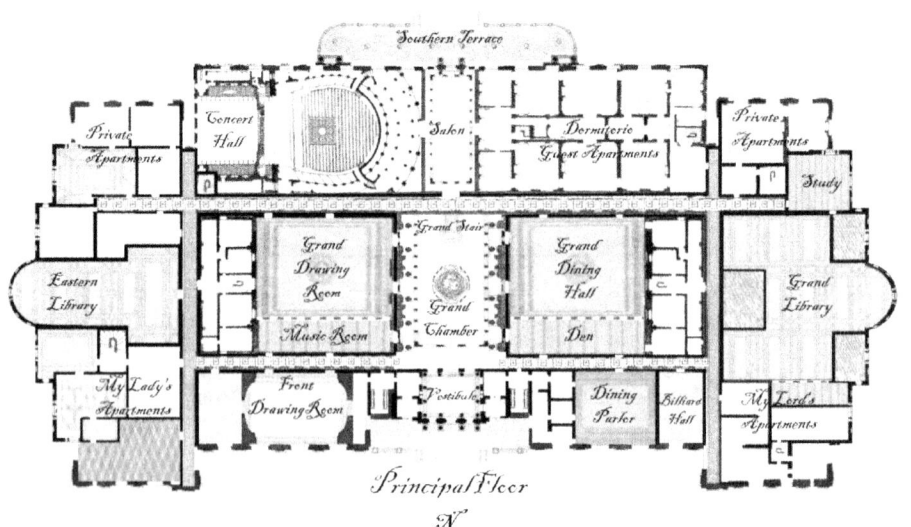

Principal Floor

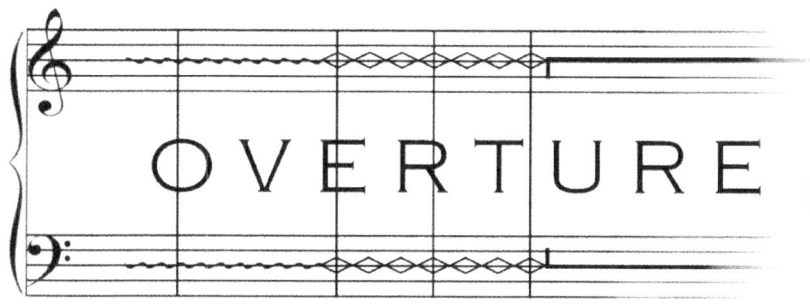

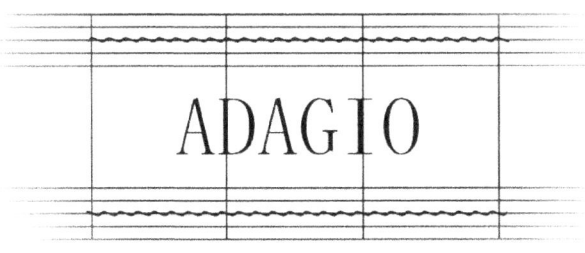

ADAGIO

I write to you, here at the end of my life, regarding the matter of the legendary people known variously as Elvs, Syrens, and Faye: to confirm their existence, and to beg that we of the broader world abide by their wish for solitude.
-Alder Haywood-

Lysbeth pretends to admire the prospect of her morning room's corner view. Before her, Lindenholt's stately drive empties into an imposing stone court from the north—framed by a handsome stable block to the east and an identical kitchen block to the west. It's a grand sight, and she'd be enjoying it, were her mind not previously engaged.

Four others litter the room behind her, conversing intermittently as the minutes stream long. Elane reads on a couch. Gina and Marium, bored Ladies from surrounding Houses, needlepoint on the couch opposite. Lysbeth's brother, Isaac, leans against a corner table, radiating scorn over the potential imposition of a Faye.

The last fortnight had been an exercise in speculation. Lysbeth agreed with her brother and cousin that Dorsit's claims were unlikely, but she couldn't help leaving a crack in the door. The Faye had been the centerpiece of her childhood daydreams, and now the shade of the girl she'd once been won't allow her the comfort of hopelessness.

She runs her fingers along the lace curtain as her eyes glaze. The agony of waiting increases the closer she draws to waiting's end. Her thoughts meander, entertaining fanciful outcomes for the day, until movement far along Lindenholt's drive pulls them forward and into focus. Two triangles of fog appear on the pane under her nose as she leans in. Forthcoming forms clear: a rider's progress on the path is continually thwarted by the fierce opposition of the horse he strings behind.

"Someone's come with a bit of trouble," she says, misting words on the glass.

The Ladies rise and join her.

Gina sways. "Surely that's not the Faye?"

"An interesting ponderance, Gina." Elane flicks cagey, hazel eyes to her cousin. "Horse? Or Faye?"

"Finnigarian Faye are said to shapeshift into horses, you know," Marium offers as the rider drags the horse to the stable block.

Lysbeth grins. "The Finnigar refer to Faye as Nykur[3], but unless Nykur prefer the stable, I believe we've just acquired a horse." Spying a stable boy's sprint towards Lindenholt's servant's entrance, she stays at the window as the Ladies trundle back to their seats. Soon there's a knock at her door. "Come!"

Ani enters and walks briskly across the room. "Message for you, My Lady."

"Thank you." Lysbeth takes the folded parchment from her maid's outstretched hand. Dorsit's seal sits on the reverse. Her thumb breaks the wax—the rest of her fingers wait for Ani's exit to unfold the note. She reads aloud:

> *Dearest Lady Lysbeth,*
> *I write to assure you my efforts have been fruitful, indeed, and to warn you—most seriously—of the being's shocking attire. Whatever qualities these creatures possess, modesty is not among them. Please accept the fine horse accompanying this letter as an additional token of my esteem on this historic day. You are unlikely to find its equal in power or beauty.*
> > *You may expect us before sunset,*
> > *Dorsit*

The room absorbs the Earl's words—further confirmation of his claims.

Lysbeth takes a deep breath to quell the gnawing in her chest. "He sounds earnest, but it simply doesn't seem real," she says, turning to place the letter on her writing desk. "He's correct, though. The occasion would be historic. Are we expected to inform Sovereign Henri and the peerage? Few could call with the Kingswa—"

"Being saddled with its living expenses is enough," Isaac interrupts. "I won't risk its introduction to royalty until it's proven itself civil company. Nor will I abide the expense of hosting gawking nobles until I'm certain it will be of some use to us." He tugs his jacket sharply. "And it had better be of some use since it's to be lain on our doorstep."

Women on the couches exchange a meaningful glance; the woman at the desk eyes her brother. There's an Avon adage concerning the worldviews of people: *Some cats see only laps, some see only dogs, some see only water, and some see only mice.* Isaac belongs to a fifth worldview: one that sees four ways to skin cats—pointless creatures whose lives might finally find meaning in his amusement as he collects a new coat. Having learned long ago to curate her battles with the Marquess, Lysbeth nods in his direction.

"I'm going to have a look," he says, covering his dark hair with a fine hat.

Glad for a distraction, the Ladies follow. A bouquet of carriage polish and manure builds as they step through the stable block's large, arched gate to an active inner-courtyard. Stable boys deliver tack and hay, a farrier works on a grey dapple's shoe, houndsmen test commands near the kennel, and a gruff, middle-aged man limps near.

---

[3] *Shapeshifting water spirits often taking the form of horses or dragons.*

"Greetings, My Lord. My Ladies," he says.

"Marshal." Lysbeth smiles.

From its origins as a castle fortification, Lindenholt has undergone slow renovations to become today's grand estate. The title of Marshal has been kept over the centuries as one who oversees the horses and guards. Previously a tenant of Lysbeth's father, the Duke of Edenshire, Marshal Brom earned the position after his heroics last Kingswar. Such advancement is rare, and much to his credit.

"We understand you've a new charge?" she asks.

Brom motions to a gate opposite the one they'd entered. "I do, My Lady. To his displeasure."

The group passes through the second arch onto a lane dividing corrals. As they collect near a fence, frenzied shouts erupt behind the stable wall. A door bursts open, and a dazzling creature emerges.

The body and legs of the horse are tall and slender, but from the deep creases of its muscles, very powerful. Its coat is black from nose to tail, but reflects light unusually, like the sheen of an oil slick. A long mane and tail flow freely, and behind the ankles are small tufts of matching hair. Its face and head are nearly dainty and seem at odds with the furor exhibited as it darts around the enclosure.

It halts abruptly and turns to Isaac, bowing its head like a bull ready to charge. The Marquess leans forward on the fence, returning its scrutiny with amusement. After a tense moment, it rights and trots away with high knees.

"Fickle, isn't he?" Isaac smirks.

Brom grunts. He has his work cut out for him.

After draining a well of observations on the gelding's unusual coat and agility, the Ladies return to the morning room to amuse themselves with cards. One eye trained on the window, Lysbeth has cost her partner two games by the time the gatehouse bell rings.

Servants assemble on the front terrace as the Ladies proceed to the Grand Chamber. The extravagant marble hall is a central intersection to Lindenholt's equally extravagant entryway, Grand Drawing Room, and Grand Dining Hall. Ornate frescoes on the vaulted ceiling peer over the floor's polished, crystalline veins. Clerestory windows cast warm, westerly light on the railing of a second story mezzanine. Behind the gathered Ladies, a series of ornate columns guard the Grand Stair at the room's end.

"Moment of truth." Isaac frowns, sauntering to the group from his den.

"Yes." Lysbeth's throat constricts as Mr. Tenson, Lindenholt's head butler, takes up his position at the seam of two mahogany doors. She squeezes Elane's hand and straightens, finding courage in well-stacked vertebrae.

They wait.

A muffled hum swells from the terrace. Mr. Tenson clutches brass at his hips and peeps through the door's sliding window. His back stiffens; he clears his throat. Carved mahogany swings wide, pulling sharpened murmurs into the room on a puff of cool air.

"Announcing The Right Honorable, The Earl of Dorsit... and guest," he declares, following the door's swivel to the Chamber's inner walls.

Dorsit, a man of fair build and looks—and upon whose features pretension finds permanent accommodation—stands alert in the entryway as mahogany knocks against marble. Beyond him, curious glints of light move into the vestibule's shade and dull. Lysbeth's squint reverses course. They're horns. Thin, silver, and affixed by some means to the head of a taller person behind the Earl.

"Your esteemed Lordship. My Ladies," Dorsit simpers, removing his hat to perform an exaggerated bow. A gasp emits from the greeting party. Dorsit's bow has revealed the figure at his back.

Thin tubes of silver alloy run over a lithe torso. Beginning at either temple, two jet-black, fishtail plaits lead to an exceptionally long ponytail decorated with thin chain. Diagonally above each ear are not one, but three horns stacked in a gentle downward arc. Though a silver mask covers the lower face, large eyes, fine brows, and the beginnings of a tall nose give the impression of great beauty.

Gina pulls a smelling-salt pouch from her bliaut-bodice and tilts against Marium for a huff. In turn, Marium tilts on Elane, who releases her cousin's slackened hand to shoulder her friend's daze.

Lysbeth takes in as many details as possible, drawing a sharp breath as her gaze climbs. The eyes. They'd been aimed at the vestibule's ceiling, now they look into the Chamber. Their striking shade of green—or is it blue? —leaps from the landscape of black, sterling, and tan that comprise the face they inhabit. The rattling in her chest threatens to topple her carefully constructed spine. Dorsit had written truthfully.

Arising from his bow, the Earl blocks the stranger again. "I hope the evening finds you well, Lady Lysbeth."

"Indeed, thank you, Sir," she manages a steady voice, "though we've been quite anxious for your arrival."

"*M'yeees*? How delightful." Dorsit purses his lips and swallows. "Eh, before I present the Faye specimen, allow me to allay any fears of ferality. My men addressed him as Evyn and assured me he's a docile sort, though I'm afraid his appearance may shock the sensibilities of one so delicate and virginal as you, My Lady."

"We're all equally shocked by the magnitude of your good fortune in this endeavor, I'm sure," Lysbeth responds in fruitcake: dry, but with enough scattered moisture to be given the benefit of the doubt.

Dorsit puffs and moves to the side. Fully visible now, the room eagerly regards the Faye again.

He touches the doorframe with long, graceful fingers as he steps into the Chamber. Willowy, tall-waisted, and extremely lean, hems of musculature tailor his body. An elegant filigree[4] of resplendent silver—which leaves little to the imagination—journeys across his physique, hiding at times beneath thin plates along the inner and outer planes of his appendages. A rectangle of snake-chain hangs like a loincloth from his hips. Above it, a narrow path of panels climbs the center of his abdomen. Eight lines of silver wrap around his torso and converge under a slightly convex, diamond-shaped cover against his heart.

Lysbeth's gaze skitters across him. As she reaches his face again, she finds he's looking at her, too. Aquamarine eyes trace her frame as Evyn takes several steps forward. When he stops, he gestures with hand and fist.

Uncertain, Lysbeth entrusts the easing of her stupor to formalities, watching Evyn's head cock slightly as she speaks, "Welcome to Lindenholt, Evyn. I am Lady Lysbeth Haywood. Allow me to introduce my brother, his Lordship, Marquess of Edenshire," she says, holding an upturned hand to each wide-eyed person beside her. "Our cousin, Lady Elane Futhord. Our friends, Lady Gina Lesterfield and Lady Marium Reedly."

The Ladies dip their heads as their names are called—motions born of muscle memory rather than true salutation, as their current astonishment prevents their full presence of mind.

Lysbeth folds her hands and smiles; movement under Evyn's eyes suggests he's doing the same. "I confess, we weren't sure what to expect, but here you are," she adds.

He drags his palms from chest to waist, then splays his hands over the floor. An affirmation: Here I am.

"You understand Vonish, then?"

The Faye trails a gracile finger up his throat. When it arcs away from his chin, he makes a fist and taps his ear and forehead: voice, ear, mind.

"I-I see. Well, that should make things easier. Truly, I have so many questions." She pauses to raise her chin and drop her shoulders. "Forgive my rudeness. I hope your journey was pleasant?"

⟨Evyn remains still.

"Perhaps you need some time to settle in? Have you any things? Luggage or—"

"Yes, My Lady," Dorsit interjects, kneading the air with clawed fingers. "In fact, he arrived with a rather large, erm, configuration of metal straps and bars?"

---

[4] *A pattern or design of openwork metal.*

"Very well, Lord Dorsit," Mr. Tenson says, "I'll have it taken to the stateroom." The butler steps awkwardly around the Faye and exits through the vestibule.

Evyn keeps his eyes on Lysbeth. His silence perplexes the room and seems to amplify his presence. Moving closer, he repeats his very first gesture: hands run down the sides of his head, like hair. One arm continues on to bend over his stomach. Anchored at the elbow, he raises his fist in an arc. Though Lysbeth is unsure what to make of his proximity or gestures, her fascination exempts her from discomfort.

Isaac's jaw flexes. "Stop this nonsense. Speak."

Evyn reproduces his throat gesture.

The Marquess blinks. "Dorsit, you seem to have confused gift and burden. What are we to do with a naked mute?"

"I'm sure you'll find some use for him yet, My Lord. Perhaps he could replace one of your armor displays here," Dorsit titters, pointing to a gilded suit in a Chamber niche.

"That would require finding the view agreeable," the Marquess says flatly.

Mr. Tenson reappears in the vestibule. "The crate is on its way to the White Room, My Lord. Shall I show our guest the way?"

"I care not, Tenson," Isaac moans.

Tightening the grip on her hands, Lysbeth slips through the crack: "Well, after the day's wait, I feel in need of exercise. Come, Ladies, let's show Evyn to his quarters." She spins and begins a hasty gait to the Grand Stair. Her group soon follows, with Mr. Tenson stepping lively to the rear.

"His incivility will not be tolerated," Isaac calls after her. "The dining parlor only seats those dignified in dress and manner."

"As you like, Sir!" she lilts, quickening her pace.

"Well, well." Isaac strolls to the Earl as the group departs. "It seems your cargo has outshined you, Dorsit."

"Quite right, I'm afraid," he grumbles and fidgets with his sleeve. "I'm not accustomed to my hunting trophies receiving so much attention. I find I'm rather put out."

The Marquess' feet come to a stop; his glower narrows over the shrinking man. "And I find we have that in common."

~~~~~~~~~~~~~~~~~~~~~~~

Clicking shoes trail Lysbeth's wake as she cuts west across the second-floor landing to a wide hallway. Runners dampen the party's steps between a series of stateroom doors and richly-dressed windows facing Lindenholt's stone court. Now well out of her brother's range, her pace slows. Evyn joins at her side, glancing at portraits and busts as they pass.

"Our ancestors. Lindenholt has been in the family for over three centuries," she says, pointing to a portrait further down the hall. "Jeni Haywood, the first Duchess of Edenshire after her husband was raised from Marquess. She encouraged the construction of the western wing and scrivery. They say she's also responsible for introducing headstrong women and red hair into the family," she adds, grinning.

Evyn repeats his hair-like gesture and arcs his fist at the elbow. When he fails to be understood, he points to Lysbeth's head and then to the setting sun beyond a hall window.

"Oh, the sun? My hair is like the sun?" The Ladies behind her giggle as Evyn nods. Allowing herself a reserved grin, she slows near the White Room's door.

Eager to avoid the more unpleasant implications of Dorsit's gifted person, Lysbeth and Elane had entreated Isaac to place any potential Faye in a stateroom instead of servant's quarters—arguing that, as Sovereigns of antiquity were considered God-Kings, persons of Myth and persons of State must share a similar claim to proper guest-hood. More pestered than convinced, Isaac agreed to the room of lowest status, furthest from the Grand Stair.

"This is where we've put you. Though I don't see your things?"

"Yes, it may take a moment, My Lady. The crate is quite unwieldy," Mr. Tenson explains.

"I see, thank you." She glances at Evyn's mask. "Might we hear you speak this evening?"

Grabbing the air between them, Evyn brings his fist to his ear and shakes his head.

"But you are *able* to speak, are you not?"

He arcs his fist three times.

"Three suns... in a few days then? Is this silence a Faye tradition of sorts?" When his head tilts noncommittally, she continues, "Well I look forward to its conclusion, though I may need a reminder to piecemeal my questions. Surely your going hoarse so soon after speaking would only inflame my appetite for answers."

Happy eyes and deepening abdominal grooves imply a silent chuckle.

Lysbeth smiles. "We'll be dining soon, but Lord Edenshire prefers conversation at the table, and of course your attire would not be quite appropriate." She folds her hands as another round of giggles pelt her back. "I'll have someone fetch you after supper. I expect his Lordship and Dorsit will have plenty to discuss on their own."

Evyn dips his head.

As the Ladies begin back down the hall, commotion in the servant's stairwell past Evyn's room pulls their attention. The door opens to a struggle between several sweaty footmen and a large metallic tumbleweed. When the footmen succeed in getting it to the hallway, Evyn approaches and lays hands on protuberances spaced across the thickest cylindrical band. He twists and pulls gently. After a few faint clicks, layers of silver peel back and up—a series of fists spreading their fingers—until the jumble stands as a tall, flat pine tree with the thickest band as its trunk. Freed of its cage, a handsome chest sits smugly on the floor beside it.

Heavily breathing footmen stare at the Faye. Evyn lowers his head apologetically and carries the metal tree to his room. Returning to the chest, he places his wrists against two small protuberances jutting from silver piping on either side. After more faint clicks, he lifts and carries it to the White Room, stopping to regard Lysbeth at the doorway.

Her eyes flick from tree to chest and land on the Faye with puzzled awe. Smiling, he nods to her group and crosses the threshold.

~~~~~~~~~~~~~~~~~~~~~~~

After supper, the Ladies adjourn to the front drawing room, and to Lysbeth's disappointment, the Lords follow. Unable to call for Evyn due to her brother's mounting vexation, she settles at the end of a couch and turns her attention to the Earl, who's been prattling since the eastern gallery.

"I'm afraid I still don't understand, My Lord. Why not invite your peers to meet the Faye? His attire is unsuitable for everyday wear, I grant you, but would surely be acceptable for an introduction—an homage to the rare. *And* proof of his origins." It's clear to his audience the Earl wants word of his accomplishment to spread as quickly as possible, but he won't risk the Marquess' ire. He's seeking permission.

"If rare objects of distant origin were enough to garner favor among the peerage, Lindenholt's collection of Ogren vases would've earned our inclusion in the royal succession a century ago," Isaac says, pacing in front of a fireplace.

Determined to make a good show of his deference, Dorsit studiously lowers to a chair.

"I believe such collections are better sold than maintained at one's own cost," the Marquess continues, peering at Lysbeth, "though *some* may find wonderment in their cultural motifs, unless they offer a tangible benefit to *us* at *present*, I see no point in them."

Gina shrugs and sips her sherry. "Well, they say there's no accounting for taste."

"It's hardly a matter of taste." He scoffs. "Enough pretense. We can't know the Faye's true worth or the viability of his manner in polite society until he speaks. Announcing him before determining either increases our exposure to reproof. He's a risk at present. And a drain on our hospitality. Nothing more."

If any disagree, none risk arguing. Isaac is not a man to be gainsaid.

~~~~~~~~~~~~~~~~~~~~~~~
~~~~~~~~~~~~~~~~~~~~~~~

presto

◇◇◇◇◇◇◇◇◇◇◇

The Called are those we have named Faye in our ignorance: that is to say, those who
have appeared in our histories over the ages—those left adrift at sea as bait for
pursuing ships so that their own ship might escape.
-Alder Haywood-

◇◇◇◇◇◇◇◇◇◇◇

Ani finishes a plait.

"Have you seen him this morning?" Lysbeth asks, offering her maid a hairpin.

"Not personally, My Lady, but Brom saw him near the water gardens after breakfast."

"How is the Marshal? His leg seemed quite sore yesterday."

"I'd venture he's a little better, though he's too stoic to know for sure." Ani smiles and plunges the pin. In Avonleigh, masking is a highly regarded social convention. Referring to one as stoic is lofty praise, indeed.

"Right you are. Though I know he must resent remaining here while there's fighting to be done. The new horse should help keep his mind from it." Lysbeth flicks her eyes to the mirror. "That's enough, Ani. I'd like to find Evyn before his Lordship bears fangs."

"Shall I notify Lady Elane that you're up and about?"

"Good idea."

Lysbeth stands as Ani exits the dressing room to her bedchamber. Moving through the door opposite, Lysbeth follows a continuous line of vanities to her sitting room's corner writing desk—which she's relieved to find empty of correspondence requiring her attention. An antsy pace along the northern windows begins as she waits for her cousin.

Having lost their mothers within a year of each other, Elane and Lysbeth grew close as girls. Elane's mother, the Duke of Edenshire's sister, had been married off to a man of lesser rank and even lesser financial acumen. Though rich in fondness for his family, he'd left his widow and child with little more than his gambling debts. By the time Lindenholt took Elane in, she'd had nothing left to cover her expenses.

To reduce her upkeep, the Duke arranged for his niece and daughter to share Ani until Lysbeth was presented at court—and to alleviate both girls' grief, he'd converted the private dining room of his late wife's apartments, now belonging to Lysbeth, into a bedchamber for Elane. When the time came, Elane was offered her own room and Lady's maid, but the cousins jointly refused. Both had bonded with Ani, and neither wanted to give up the advantages of their adjoining bedchambers—which allow for morning conversation as they dress and late-night chats after bedtime.

Ani appears in the dressing room's doorway wearing a recently donned smile. "Lady Elane says to go on ahead. She knows you're anxious to see him."

Lysbeth grins and moves to the hallway. Turning down the eastern gallery to the Grand Chamber, she questions a footman who relays Evyn's last known location: the southern gardens. She makes her way to the southern wing, crossing the Grand Gallery to the Salon. Large windows on the back wall frame a stone terrace and a pretty landscape beyond.

As a fortification, the spot chosen for Lindenholt was the best vantage the area had to offer—the only feature to resemble a hill for miles of otherwise lazily-waving earth. The incline itself is so gradual the manor's stately drive can be viewed end-to-end, and there'd been no need to flatten the hill's summit to accommodate construction.

A footman opens the door and Lysbeth trots to the terrace railing. Gravel paths wind through manicured hedgerows to a marble fountain at the garden's heart. The tallest spout releases chromatic mist into a crisp breeze, and beside it, a figure in silver looks to the horizon. Taking in the rolling Autumn scenery, Lysbeth descends the steps and crunches through evergreen funnels.

Evyn turns as she approaches. Sad eyes above his silver mask brighten at her smile.

"Good morning," she says, "I'm sorry I couldn't call for you last night. I thought I might make amends with a tour."

Three fine chains draped between his ornamental horns and left ear sway gently as he nods. They begin their morning ramble with the western water gardens. Lysbeth provides history lessons where applicable, and while Evyn's silence and attire unnerve most observers, she seems largely at ease. Re-entering the manor, they're joined by Elane, Marium, and Gina, and the five make a merry party journeying through the eastern wing. By midafternoon, they arrive at the front drawing room for tea, where Isaac is quick to send the Faye away. After a prolonged farewell to Gina, Lysbeth finds Evyn again while Elane keeps Marium occupied.

Continuing her tour with the western wing, she saves the most impressive room, the Grand Library, for last. It was here—as her mother lay dying from the delivery of her sister, Corah—Lysbeth was first introduced to Alder Haywood's letter.

On seeing the state of her eldest granddaughter, Avrella Haywood, Dowager Duchess of Edenshire, brought Lysbeth to a very old and very fine desk tucked away in the library's corner. There, she'd retrieved the document from a false panel drawer, gingerly laid its pages across the desk, and stepped back—observing the genesis of Lysbeth's fascination with the Faye from a respectful distance.

Avrella had taken both Corah and the document to the family's Walstead estate some years ago, but Lysbeth finds the current setting appropriate, considering the subject she wishes to broach.

The massive room bathes in rich, eventide hues and pleasing scents of leather and stale parchment. As they step, Evyn occasionally bends to examine books lining tall, walnut shelves. Each time he lingers, Lysbeth studies more of the metal he wears.

There are two layers—a simpler filigree lattice under the first—and five intricate divots climb the stalk of silver on his spine. All lines of the frame, even delicate ones on his hands and feet, eventually connect to the spine over one path or another. When he bends, the metal retracts into itself where needed by telescoping, articulated plates, or groove-and-tongue slotting.

As he stands again, Lysbeth shifts her gaze to his mask and begins her query, "I know it's early, but I've been anxious to ask you about an ancestor of ours. He left a letter—a confession, really—claiming an association with the Faye. In fact, he claimed to have spent a great many years among your people after an incident at sea."

Evyn's feet plant. Eyelids and brows pulled away in disbelief soon re-constrict in aggrievement. Lysbeth takes a few steps before noticing his lull and stops. His expression softens as she continues.

"He wrote at length of how beaut—" She reconsiders. "Of how idyllic your culture is. He said he fell in love with someone in your position; one of those trained to be offered to pursuers to ensure your vessels aren't followed or captured."

Evyn extends no confirmation beyond slightly harried lungs. Lysbeth turns towards panes leaking sunset on the far wall and idly caresses the velvet couch-back at her waist.

"He meant for it to be seen by the world; a plea to leave the Faye in peace. We never made it public. Perhaps if we had..." she trails, ashamed by how liberally her younger self doles out giddiness. Dorsit may as well have delivered a unicorn. Only, unicorns aren't people, she chides herself. Frowning, she looks to Evyn. He's studying her intently. "His name was Alder Haywood. Did your people know him? Was he telling the truth?"

Evyn remains still for several moments. Finally, he makes one distinctive nod.

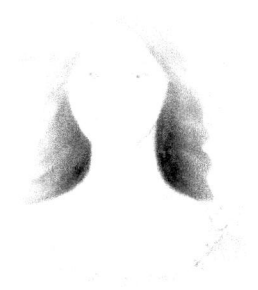

Her eyes close over a long exhalation. "I knew it," she whispers. A wave of invigoration forces her eyelids apart. "He said the sexes are treated equally. Is it true?"

A smile accompanies his nod.

"And the birds?" She grins.

He hesitates before nodding again.

"And the library of languages?" Her hand trails the

couch as she moves closer.

He takes an exaggerated look around the room and nods matter-of-factly.

Lysbeth's eyes sparkle above a soft laugh. "Well, I would ask more, but it's been so long since I've read the letter, and with all the excitement I feel it's run from my head." She beams. "Thank you, truly."

Smiling gaze tilted, something in the tenderness of Evyn's look gives the impression of thoughts formalizing.

The nearest double-doors swing open. "Your party is gathering for supper, My Lady." Mr. Tenson's pupils comb the pair before jumping to a footman at the room's end. The butler is happy to see his mistress so pleased, but if she were found alone with the scantily clad stranger, the resulting whispers would not be kind.

While Avonleigh Lords are free to explore their desires with any class or sex—so long as his affairs are discrete, and his wife has already produced a son—it's another matter entirely for Avonleigh Ladies.

From the day of her birth, the focus of a Lady's life is to marry well and bear heirs for her husband. To increase her odds, she learns to speak, dress, and gesture favorably, is taught arts pleasing to a wide array of suitors, is educated just enough to keep her husband's house, and is kept a virgin through keen eyes, looming threats of social ruin, and the ever-present, noxious cloud of shame generated by the supposed-inferiority of her gender.

Mr. Tenson has Lysbeth's best interests at heart.

She levels her grin. "Thank you, I'll be along in a moment."

Neck curved in acquiescence, the butler leaves the doors open as he withdraws.

"I suppose our day has come to an end. Do you have everything you need?" she asks.

Evyn nods.

"Good. Please let me know if you find that you don't."

He nods again, slower this time.

Unable to prolong the exchange, she bids him good night and treks across the manor to the front drawing room—where a nagging silence bands her entry and tracks her migration to a chair. She sends Elane a giddy look before reapplying her mask and sitting. After an awkward beat, the Lords begin a clamoring refrain of grievances: Evyn's disrespectful silence, inappropriate dress, and apparent indolence.

Isaac concludes the anthem with a verse on the demeritorious nature of indulgence and sycophancy, training a dangerously placid expression on his sister.

"... everything. He confirmed it all directly!" Lysbeth crosses her bedchamber. "You can't imagine my excitement."

"Oh, I think I can." Elane's smile grows as Lysbeth nears. "We should write to Granmama again tomorrow."

Lysbeth takes a spot on the bed's edge. "She'll be buried in messages within the week."

"She'll be thrilled. Do you suppose she'll ask to meet him over Solstice?"

"Demand, I should think." Lysbeth reaches for her brush and begins on a section of hair. "How do you suppose the Faye bear Winter's chill wearing only silver?"

"Perhaps they exchange it for cloth during the season?" Elane posits.

"Or perhaps their homeland remains temperate through the year? I hope your guess is correct, though. Isaac seems bent on finding any excuse to rebuff Evyn. Were he not afforded the hospitality of a guest, I expect Isaac would pry the metal away himself."

"That would only increase Evyn's exposure." Elane chuckles. "The silver is quite striking, Lys, but you must admit it's rather indecent for Avonleigh." She positions her eyebrow in upward insinuation. "He's fortunate one Lindenholt resident doesn't seem to mind, at least."

Brush teeth halt in copper strands. "Elane! You think me a debauchee?"

"No!" She smiles innocently. "But don't you think fortune has favored him? Having been brought to one of very few Avons willing to accept his strangeness so easily?"

Lysbeth's eyes wander at the notion. "Perhaps I don't find him quite as shocking because I spent so many hours imagining Alder's descriptions as a child—Faye parity and appearance and the like." Her brush moves again as her eyes refocus. "Still, my admiration for Evyn's people is hardly enough to incite carnal desire. And as for fortune, despite his voluntary presence, let's not forget why he was brought here, Elane. I'm not his sole recipient."

Her arched brow returns its own insinuation.

GRAVE

After Marium's departure the next morning, those remaining gather in Lysbeth's sitting room—the Lords have conspired to keep the Faye away by occupying her here, where an invitation is needed. She would've found herself occupied for a time in any case, as she'd received a letter from her grandmother. Recounting the message to the room, she gives no indication of her tremendous relief at its contents.

"Granmama writes we're to leave early for WinterSol this year, as Father's furlough will see him at Walstead by late Nuver. Furthermore, once the festivities conclude, she has decided Corah will return to Lindenholt with Elane and myself, and relays word that the Marquess will accompany our father to the front."

Isaac says nothing from his spot at a window—an ominous portent. When the Marquess simmers, the whole estate feels it, and when he erupts, you'd best find cover. His current silence is smoke.

Lysbeth shifts. "I've had reports Marshal Brom is still experiencing trouble with the gelding. Might we know the breeder, Sir?"

"My dear Lady," Dorsit coos from a couch, "if I were to reveal my sources, even to one so seductively charming as you, then everyone could obtain such a creature, rendering yours all the less valuable for it. We couldn't have that now, could we?"

"But surely there's a pedigree or some—"

"Hush-hush, now, My Lady. I'm sure it will be broken soon enough."

The Earl's voice tallows Lysbeth in greasy, stubborn condescension. She un-grits her teeth as the door raps. "Come."

Ani enters. "My Lady, Evyn's come around. I think he's looking for you. What shall I tell him?"

"The impertinence!" Dorsit scoffs. "A Lady's sitting room is for invited guests only."

Isaac redirects his scowl to the maid.

Lysbeth takes inventory.

A few of her childhood musings had resurfaced after yesterday's confirmation of Faye egalitarianism. While she doesn't expect the same respect or opportunities afforded to Avonleigh Lords, morning room invitations are one of the very few privileges afforded to Avonleigh Ladies. The least she can expect of herself is the upholding of that right, even if it means flirting with a boundary of Decorum.

Resolute, she stands from her desk chair. "Surely, he can't be expected to know our rules of social engagement. Send him in, Ani, by my invitation."

Happy to escape the room's tension, Ani retreats to the hall as Dorsit readies a complaint with a glance to Isaac. At the Marquess' contemptuous expression, he thinks better of drawing attention to himself, but Lysbeth's protest has set him further on edge.

The practice of endowing rare gifts to secure marriage partners of a higher rank began four centuries ago when Count Erfeit forged and gifted a fabled Nottery manuscript to the Sovereign's daughter. Their engagement was broken two months later when the Earl of Bonafid found and gifted the genuine manuscript—thereby ensuring the precedent.

Confident a successful hunt would oblige the Haywoods to accept his proposal, Dorsit spent a small fortune on the voyage and its captain. Now the jagged doubts which formed on the night of his reception are bearing down and biting in. Lysbeth is meant to be grateful and indebted, not resistant and indifferent. The ease of her manner around the Faye is contentious in its own right. Would she risk the scandal of refusing him as well?

Lysbeth clears her throat and steps towards the vanities along the wall to her dressing room. Whether by the thrill of righteous opposition or the turbulence of mounting apprehension, the looping in her stomach accelerates as Evyn's lean frame appears in the doorway.

A miniature version of the chest he'd arrived with sits in the nook of his arm. Looking around the room, he makes brief eye contact with each occupant before stepping in and crossing to Lysbeth.

She swallows as he nears. "Good morning, Evyn. Have you brought something to show us?"

He nods and moves behind her to place the box on a vanity. Long, chrome-trimmed fingers linger thoughtfully on its surface as he turns back. Eyes on the floor, he takes a slow breath, steps beside Lysbeth, and makes his gesture for hair. It ends with an open palm: a request. Bright teal blinks from the floorboards to her face.

Lysbeth feels the room's eyes as she teeters over Decorum's ledge.

Her curiosity provides the push.

She pulls forward a copper wave and lays it in Evyn's hand. Eyes grinning, he quickly offers a section of his ponytail. Not wanting to offend, she takes it. Huffing, Dorsit stands. The display is too great an insult to bear.

Evyn inspects her lock, smoothing and weaving it between long fingers. Lysbeth stifles a smile and monkeys him. "Oh, it smells of something sweet," she says, fanning his ends, "though I don't recognize the fragrance. A Faye perfume?"

Under Evyn's nod, his left hand rises. To the side, Dorsit's resentful steps close in—fingers reaching for the line of jet hooking Lysbeth. The Faye's hand veers from its upward course and knocks the Earl's wrist aside.

The Avons freeze. In the hierarchy of transgressions against an Avon Lord's pride, refusal is second only to unsolicited contact—even, or perhaps especially, contact in self-defense. Evyn has just performed all.

Dorsit's reddening cheeks vibrate.

Lysbeth inhales. "I'm sure he didn—"

"You've a talent for contriving excuses on his behalf, Lady Lysbeth, truly," Isaac says, "but I'd rather hoped you would not seek to insult us with an attempt to excuse this as well." The evenness of his enmity saturates the room with dread. He motions to the door. "You are dismissed, Faye. Allow me to show you out."

Evyn's eyebrows wave with apologetic confusion as Lysbeth struggles to mask her panic. Avon convention demands retribution for his action; whatever the Marquess has planned, resisting him will only make it worse.

She nods for him to go.

With a glance to the vanity, he gingerly lowers her hair, grips a wrist behind his back, and follows Isaac from the room.

———————

While Marshal Brom sees to the stables and the retinue of guards employed by the Duke, the Marquess spends a portion of his yearly allowance on two private guards for personal security—and personal activities. As they exit to the hall of Lysbeth's apartments, Isaac motions to the waiting men on his payroll. The group of four continue to the servant's stairwell and descend two levels. Reaching the bottom step, the front guard takes a lantern from the wall. Isaac's pace grows urgent as they wind through increasingly dark, quiet halls.

Though Lindenholt has seen extensive renovation and additions, the prison of its original castle had been left largely untouched—Isaac discovered the area while exploring the basement as a boy, and saddened by its neglect, put it to use straight away.

When the group nears an iron door at the center of Lindenholt's substructure, Isaac digs out a necklace from his collar. Slipping the chain over his head, he nearly drops it in his excitement to bring its keys to the lock. Hinges groan. Isaac waits for those behind him to pass before walking through and swiveling the latch.

A decrepit hallway looms. He leads the group to the door at its end and repeats the ritual: unlock, wait, close, swivel. On the other side, the guard passes the lantern to Isaac, who begins an illuminating stroll along a short path of braziers.

Feeling the prison's atmosphere could not be properly appreciated in the confined space, Isaac eventually ordered all but three cells dismantled. The result is an oppressively bleak room interrupted on occasion by the few load-bearing walls that couldn't be removed. A fine chair stands out among what little, rundown furniture there is. Unpleasant looking instruments line a repurposed display case. Heavy chains dangle from a pulley system in the ceiling. Beneath it, chains peek from cutouts on the surface of a short table. The guards release Evyn beside it and move to a counter on the far wall.

Isaac hangs the lantern on the door. "Take off that ridiculous contraption," he says, tugging on leather gloves.

Under an apprehensive nod, Evyn's left hand rises to his mask. The silver branches hooking behind his ears swivel down towards his shoulders and up again to end flush against his jaw. He pulls the cover from his face and snaps it to his left shoulder—where it looks something like a topless epaulette, and matches a similar crescent on his right.

Seeing Evyn's face, the Marquess chuckles. High cheekbones, a narrow chin, and pleasant lips. The Faye is beautiful, and defacement is only really satisfying when the effects are profound. He'll enjoy their time together.

The guards appear beside Isaac. One delivers a glass of spirit, the other holds a roll of cloth. The Marquess sits in his chair and takes a long sip, watching as Evyn pulls his horns forward. As they come away, short, pronged strips at their bases emerge from his fishtail plaits. He snaps them to the alloy over his collarbones and points his right toes. Silver lines unfurl from his body as he alternates his feet—right heel flat, left toes pointed—until a metal lattice stands at his back.

Isaac exchanges his empty tumbler for the guard's bundle and ambles to the Faye, shoving the rolled prisoner's garb into his naked chest.

"Wear it."

Evyn complies.

"Stand there."

Evyn obeys.

Isaac smiles.

———————————

The Marquess doesn't reappear until early evening. After whispering to his guards, he summons a scribe to the study and dictates the following:

> Baron,
> A foreigner said to be Faye requires elucidation. Discover his abilities and teach him our manners. If he is stone, deliver me clay. Smooth. You will receive him tomorrow, sundown.
> - Edenshire

A pigeon is sent. Isaac stands and sighs contentedly.

Sauntering to the drawing room, he approaches the Earl and holds forward a lock of jet hair bound in silver chain. "Here you are, Sir. You may inspect it at your leisure."

Dorsit takes the long tress with priggish amusement.

Elane turns away; Lysbeth feels ill.

The Marquess struts to the fireplace. "Lady Lysbeth, you were right. The Faye cannot be expected to know our customs. It is therefore imperative the whole of his ignorance be swiftly and unconditionally rectified—lest we risk a repeat of today's reprehensible assault on poor Dorsit." Laying a hand on the mantle, he toes soot into the hearth and turns. "I will not see him bring Lindenholt's ruin. Tomorrow his education in civilized conduct and social station will begin. He's sure to find the Baron's instruction edifying."

The room sits stunned.

A prison Warden of notoriously cruel tactics, the Baron made a name for himself among gentlemen of a less-than-gentle nature. Not truly a Baron, rather, the name he's made for himself derives from the infamous Baron Schiefer who, a century ago, earned a reputation as the most sadistic judge the county of Edenshire had ever known.

"I see." Lysbeth maintains her composure. There are few paths of resistance available to Lysbeth where Isaac is concerned, but a convincing mask can, at least, deny him the lecherous satisfaction of observing the effects of his torments. "And what's the expected duration of his stay?"

"He will stay until I'm convinced he's been properly enlightened and the true extent of his worth has been determined."

"And when you're dispatched to the Kingswar?" she presses.

His nostrils flare. "The Baron will keep me informed."

Lysbeth knows there's nothing to be done. She may have taken over her mother's role as Lady of the House, but she'd only become a Duchess through marrying a Duke. The Marquess' rank far exceeds her own.

She pairs her brother's stare. "He should be left unmarred."

There's a moment of chilling silence as Isaac closes the space between them.

"Do not take me for a fool," he hisses. "*I* am the pragmatist, *you* are the credulous doe, and if *he* is not an avenue upon which the Haywood name might advance, he will be ground under my heel and remade until he *is*."

Time hangs. No one dares move.

Avonleigh's social interactions rely on the principles of catch and toss. An action is performed, received, and returned. Actions too ungainly to receive—such as unfettered passion—are discouraged as a matter of course, as they are often discomforting to witness and leave one with no means of rebounding.

The border of discomfort is far behind the expedition now, though, as they settle deeply in trepidation's territory.

A cheerful Mr. Tenson rounds the doorway. "Dinner is served!"

The Lords tug their jackets and proceed to the dining parlor. The Ladies linger.

"I've a sudden headache, Mr. Tenson. Make my excuses, would you?" Lysbeth mutters.

"Oh dear, shall I fetch Doctor Howe?"

"No, thank you." She stands. "I'm sure it will pass soon."

Elane takes her arm. "I'll look after her until then."

"Very well, my Ladies. I'll have your meals sent," the butler says, setting off briskly.

"Don't let Isaac snare you, Lys," Elane whispers as they walk.

Lysbeth strives to follow the advice, but doubts tangle her progress. Once safely in her sitting room, she lowers to a couch and unspools her thoughts.

While she wouldn't describe her current self as one easily lifted by flights of fancy, perhaps the remnants of her juvenile musings had swayed her more than she'd realized—and if already swaying, surely the tangible reality of Evyn's presence had only increased the motion. Though his mythological associations could be a prized asset, prosaically, he's a foreigner with no recognizable title or standing. His gifting to the family must be understood as a transaction; her own wishes and reservations are irrelevant.

Her brow creases over wringing hands. "It's only, I was awed by him, Elane. I'd scarcely considered the ramifications of taking him in—as a permanent guest, no less. If he offers nothing substantial to us in return for our hospitality, we'll be taken for fools. More so now that he's caused such offense. How could I have been so naïve? I don't know what I expected to come of all this, of him, and yet Isaac saw the pitfalls so clearly."

"You mustn't be so hard on yourself, Lys, we were all awed. Evyn's being here is a miraculous thing." Elane lowers her head to catch her cousin's eyes. "But if the practical implications are your main concern, think of it this way: the differences in our peoples being what they are, he was bound to cause offense eventually. Better it be now, early, and with Dorsit rather than someone of greater import. What's more, with Evyn's carelessness known, he'll never be accepted as payment for your hand. You'll be spared Dorsit's proposal."

Lysbeth takes a slow breath. "Yes, perhaps there's some good to come of this. But what of Evyn? The *Baron*, Elane."

Both women fall silent. They've heard gruesome tales.

———————————

The following morning, Lindenholt's sixty-four servants and thirty-three guards gather on the stone court. Few things give the Marquess greater pleasure than making an exhibition of those who've earned his disdain, but gratification isn't his only consideration. The assemblage for Evyn's departure will be understood as a show of mock respect, and all present will think twice before performing an act of rebelliousness—no matter how small.

Lording on the front terrace, Isaac nods to his guards in the vestibule. They move outside dragging the Faye between. Bruises splatter Evyn's face and neck above rust-colored stains on his prisoner's garb. Head shaven, what hair remains is bristled between small patches of bare scalp and scattered cuts. A silver chain he'd worn in plaits now binds his wrists behind his back, and along his parade route to the prisoner wagon, a series of pulls and shoves sees him favoring his right leg.

The court's murmuring grows. Though there are no laws against beating one's servants, Evyn had been received as a guest. The truth of the matter is clarifying now, though: guests aren't usually gifted between nobles as one might gift a painting or jewelry.

Watching sorrowfully from her morning room window, Lysbeth turns his black and silver box over in her hands.

TACET

My Lord Marquess of Edenshire,   9 Nuver 1514 III

I am pleased to know My Lord and I are of one mind in our judgment that the process must not be rushed, and I have begun my work using the techniques approved by Your Lordship.

Of note: the specimen's tongue has a three-inch divide rendering it, instead, two tongues. Each tongue is pierced several times by silver filament. The specimen does not respond to queries.

I thank Your Lordship again for the rare opportunity to study such an elusive species.

I remain,

-B

My Lord Marquess,   19 Nuver 1514 III

I regret to inform My Lord that the specimen remains recalcitrant. I suspect previous conditioning to resist physical discomfort.

Of note: the specimen possesses an unusual joint laxity and tensile bone strength which has rendered several of my mechanisms ineffectual.

As always, Your Lordship's interest in my work flatters me greatly, and it is thanks to the additional information My Lord has provided that a possible solution might be reached should my usual methods continue to fail.

I remain,

-B

My Lord Marquess,   2 Dicter 1514 III

As per Your Lordship's request:

My hypothesis arose from the information My Lord provided regarding the specimen's role as a self-sacrificial member of its population. I believe the correct application of pressure on this aspect of its nature will lead to its break.

I began evaluation of this theory by inviting the specimen to witness my work on other individuals. The disturbances observed in the specimen are promising, and I have acquired two souls to further aid in this endeavor.

I shall keep Your Lordship apprised of any developments.

I remain,

-B

My Lord Marquess of Edenshire,   13 Dicter 1514 III

I write with an update which I hope will please Your Lordship.

Four days ago, the Earl of Dorsit appeared in my offices bent on obtaining coordinates of the specimen's homeland. I used this opportunity to test my hypothesis and brought forth one of the souls mentioned in my previous memorandum.

After several trials, I am gratified to report a successful conclusion to the experiment: The specimen has fully broken, and the remaining soul has already proven a powerful motivator. His Lordship was satisfied with the information gathered, and the payment remitted for extraction has been applied to the discrete disposal of remains so as not to inconvenience My Lord.

I remain,

-B

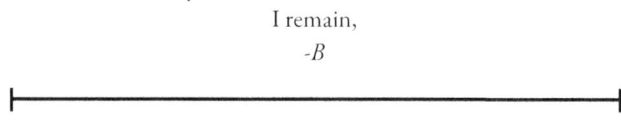

My Lord Marquess of Edenshire,   20 Dicter 1514 III

As per Your Lordship's request:

The specimen spoke upon breaking and continues to speak where appropriate.

My agreement with the Earl called for my absence after the break, and so I regret to inform My Lord I know not what was said—though I must assume his Lordship safeguards the information to ensure he is the only beneficiary of its potential returns. A writ of silence preventing questions of a similar nature while the specimen is under my care is also in effect.

Of note: I have ascertained that the unusual arrangement of the specimen's tongues results from a series of modifications valued among its kind.

Pleasant Solstice,

-B

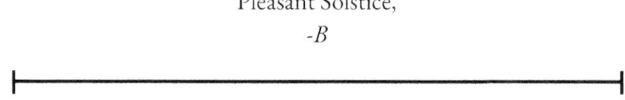

My Lord Marquess,   5 Jonun 1515 III

As per Your Lordship's request:

I have determined the specimen possesses a foundational understanding of fourteen languages. The specimen credits this to training in memory techniques, though it is my belief the species also has preternatural recollection.

I regret to inform My Lord the species' musical capabilities—as purported by the first Marquess of Edenshire—cannot be confirmed in this specimen. A range of instruments and incentives have been provided. However, as even calculated damage to the remaining soul has yielded no results, I must conclude the specimen was trained in language rather than music.

Out of consideration for the approaching delay in correspondence due to Your Lordship's brave service in the north, I humbly request that my payment be reduced to one fortnight's fee per month while I await My Lord's instruction.

I remain,

-B

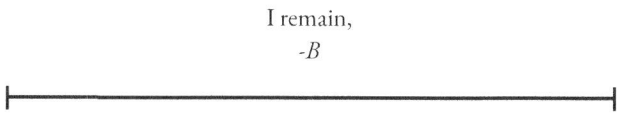

My Lord Marquess,   30 Jonun 1515 III
Further exploration of the specimen's linguistic capabilities has revealed exceptional skill in scribal recording and scene illustration. The specimen presents ambidextrously with remarkably refined motor skills and the ability to accurately reproduce imagery which has long since passed from view.

However, I must caution My Lord against advertising this ability, as the duplication of sensitive material could be deleterious to more than just myself.

Of note: The specimen alludes to unusual associations between the senses: projective spatial recollection, chromatic orthography, and palpable acoustics.

I hope My Lord finds comfort in knowing the specimen has proven useful in at least one respect.

I remain,

-B

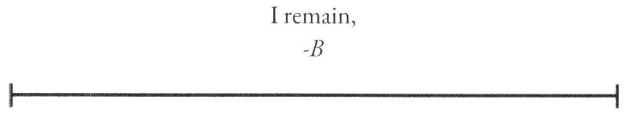

My Lord Marquess,   24 Febar 1515 III
As per Your Lordship's request:

The specimen takes my dictation so My Lord might view its hand. Enclosed is the specimen's illustration of an anatomical exploration performed with its assistance this afternoon.

I am pleased to report I have finished administering the lessons in social decorum My Lord was kind enough to suggest.

I remain,

-B

My Lord Marquess of Edenshire,   21 Mara 1515 III
As per Your Lordship's request:

The specimen confirmed the purpose of its spinal fixtures as joining sockets for the suits of metal My Lord has described. Though the information was freely given, I felt Your Lordship's suggested experiments should not go to waste. Results follow:

Each fixture attaches sub-dermally to spinous processes of the lumbar and thoracic pine. They are firmly appended, vary in ferromagnetism, and are composed of an unidentified alloy. I beg My Lord will accept my full consolatory assurance that the alloy's composition is also unknown to the specimen.

Of note: The specimen presents with an additional thoracic vertebra. The parcel accompanying this letter contains additional notes, molds, and specimen illustrations which I believe Your Lordship will find satisfactory.

Pleasant Equinox,

-B

My Lord Marquess,   16 Arel 1515 III

Given his established levels of competency, news of Lord Dorsit's loss at sea is not wholly unexpected and is likely unrelated to information compelled from the specimen.

I therefore agree with My Lord's assessment that the specimen is well under control and may be returned to Lindenholt Manor. I will arrange for its delivery within the week.

It has been my very great pleasure to serve Your Lordship again.

I remain,

-B

Dear Lady Lysbeth of Edenshire,   19 Arel 1515 III

I wish to express my condolences regarding news of Lord Dorsit. Though I only had the pleasure of meeting his Lordship on two occasions, he spoke quite highly of you, and I am sure his company will be missed.

Lord Edenshire believes Evyn is ready to be returned to Lindenholt, therefore I would like to take this opportunity to recommend his placement as a translator under Your Ladyship's scriveners.

If his work is found wanting, or if My Lady wishes to free herself of his burden, I would be pleased to relieve Your Ladyship at no additional cost.

I remain your humble servant,

-Warden Ian Wescott-

DOWNBEAT

Lindenholt's music room finds itself occupied.

Upon the bench of its pianoforte sits a sullen girl with strawberry blonde hair. Behind her, a man with long features delivers a long lecture on the importance of daily practice—even for instruments of accompaniment—and on its chaise lounge sit Lysbeth Haywood and Elane Futhord, who listen amusedly while making apathetic progress on their needlepoints. Another enters and clicks across the room.

"A message has come for you, My Lady," Mr. Tenson says, passing the note.

"Thank you." Lysbeth draws up on noticing the Baron's seal. Her eyes catch Elane's.

It's been six months since they'd last seen Evyn. Isaac demanded the household's silence, and so effectively instilled was Lindenholt's fear of him that no servant spoke openly of last Autumn's events—even after the Marquess' departure to the north.

Lysbeth longed to discuss the matter with her grandmother, Avrella, who shares Lysbeth's affinity for the world described by Alder. Unfortunately, Isaac's specious retelling of events over Winter Solstice left little ground for debate or discussion among the family. All agreed Isaac had been very prudent to nip the bud of social peril—and though perhaps he didn't need to raze the stem and salt the roots as well, when tasked with upholding the proper modes of civility, it's better to be viewed as a family of austerity than leniency.

Having grown deeply ashamed of her own lack of foresight and good judgement, Lysbeth took to avoiding the subject all together. However, as this shame was an integer in Isaac's calculations, she'd managed to shake it after several weeks spared his company.

Now, finally, here is word.

She breaks the seal and reads, returning her eyes to Elane a moment later. "I must attend to something. Mr. Spantier, please continue the lesson." She stands with her cousin and sends a look of caution to her eleven-year-old sister, Corah. "I'm sure there will be no trouble."

The Ladies march to the morning room. When the door shuts, Lysbeth hands Elane the letter and moves to her desk. "What do you make of it?" she asks, arranging her writing utensils.

Elane presses a knuckle into her chin. "Perhaps Isaac told him of Dorsit. Though I can't imagine when they would've met."

"Yes, odd, isn't it? What of the rest?" Lysbeth sits and dips a quill.

Elane re-reads. "Oh, he suggests Evyn be placed *under* the scriveners. A buffer?"

"That was my thought as well. A peon of the scribes to avoid interacting with the family directly." She dips her quill again and shakes her head. "It must be Isaac's doing."

"The Warden's offer to take Evyn on again..."

Lysbeth scoffs and blots the parchment. "A paragon of charity."

Seeing the message is ready, Elane summons a footman from the hall. Lysbeth seals the note and crosses to him. "Tell the Coop Master this requires immediate dispatchment to Rhodyn. You mustn't delay, Temus."

"Yes, My Lady!" Temus pinches the scroll and begins an unseemly jog to the gallery.

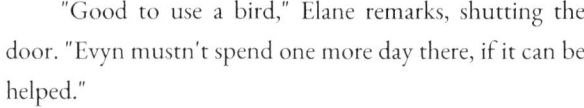

"Good to use a bird," Elane remarks, shutting the door. "Evyn mustn't spend one more day there, if it can be helped."

"No, not one." Lysbeth folds her arms and strolls aside the windowed wall. "Now, where's he to stay? The staterooms are off-limits."

"The attic should suffice until the scrivery dorm makes arrangements."

"Agreed, assuming the Baron's recommendation finds merit. But placing him in the attic would make him a servant. Officially, I mean." Stopping at her corner window, she turns to her cousin. "Is that what we're meant to do with a Faye?"

"I'm sure I haven't the slightest idea what we're *meant* to do with him, Lys, but after what transpired, his return is fortunate enough. His standing is immaterial."

"Yes. And surely the attic is more appealing than the Baron's anyhow." Lysbeth sighs and steps to the shiny black box on her vanity. "We should visit the family plot tomorrow."

"Really?" Elane puzzles. "If you like, but why?"

"Maintenance." Lysbeth runs fingers over silver piping. "Alder must've toppled his cairn by now."

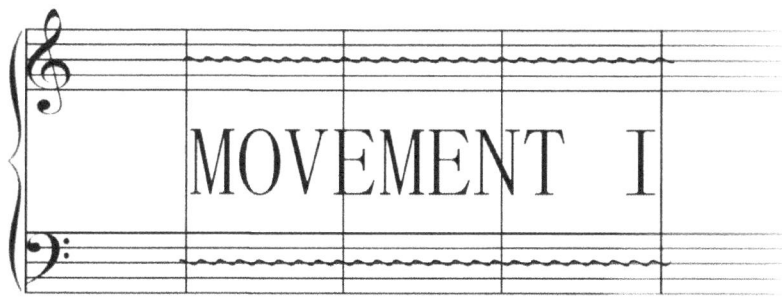

SPRING

*For it was only through knowing the Faye that the true depths of man were
revealed to me: his spitefulness, his fragile pride, and his sadism.*
-Alder Haywood-

After an anxious day and a half, Lysbeth assumes her perch at the sitting room window. Shortly before sundown, a worn cart follows a fine carriage up the drive, and the Ladies move to the front drawing room for the Baron's reception. Though impressively sized for an informal space, the room's fireplaces and décor make it feel cozy. They stand in a broad aisle between two mirrored rows of seating as Mr. Tenson opens the door.

"Mr. Westcott for you, My Lady."

"And Evyn?" Lysbeth asks.

"I understand he's gone around to the servant's entrance."

"I see." She glances at Elane. "Please call for him. We'll see the Warden now."

The butler returns to the gallery once a trim, older man moves into the room.

"Lady Lysbeth, it is an honor." The Baron leans an ornately carved cherrywood cane outwards as he bows. His words and movements are smooth and deliberate.

"Warden Wescott, welcome." Her voice is stiff. "May I present my cousin, Lady Elane Futhord."

The Baron bows again. "A pleasure."

He seems a man assured of his hold on any situation.

Lysbeth swallows. "I trust the journey was not too taxing?"

The Baron rises. A viscous gait emerges.

"No, My Lady." His dispassion is irregular. "In fact, I've recently had the good fortune of upgrading my carriage." Uncanny, even. "I was made quite comfortable."

The Baron pours deeper into the room—tar from a barrel—his measured pace building anticipation. Apprehension.

"Yes, it appeared quite handsome." Lysbeth's hands clasp over her stomach. Her pulse knocks on her palms. Elane inches closer. "Thank you for your condolences regarding Dorsit."

"Of course." His tone and step are daunting. "A tragedy."

The Baron's leaden advance hems in.

"Indeed." The room is small. "I wonder, how did you make his acquaintance?"

He stops in front of Lysbeth. Some primal urge wills her to escape.

"My services bring a great many people to my door, Your Ladyship." His eyes demand her attention as he lowers the tip of his cane to the floor.

The drawing room door opens.

"Evyn, My Lady." Before standing aside, Mr. Tenson locks Lysbeth's eyes and lowers his chin: a signal to prepare herself.

A black fitted tunic and black trousers stretch over a thin, pale figure in the doorway. Eyes down, Evyn's features retain the fundamentals of beauty, but his face is gaunt and racked with trepidation. His hair is still short enough to see the scars of Isaac's carelessness and the knuckles of his right hand are white from their grip on his left elbow. The turbulence of his ambulation stands in stark contrast to the Baron's as he roils diagonally behind the imposing man—who continues to examine Lysbeth.

Rap

The Ladies jump as the Baron's cane strikes the floor.

A second crack echoes as Evyn drops to his knees, flinching as he lands.

Rap

Evyn's hips fall to his heels.

Rap

Evyn's palms and forehead meet with floorboards.

The Baron's cane switches hands; the Baron's eyes remain on Lysbeth.

Rap

A strained voice reflects off woodgrain, "Please forgive my insolence, Your Ladyship."

The women look on with alarm. The abject motions of Warden and ward had been so efficient the performance took only a moment. The implications are bleak. This introduction to Evyn's voice stains them bleaker.

Spying an opportunity, Lysbeth draws herself up to match the Baron's five-foot-ten height. "You're forgiven, Evyn. Thank you for delivering him, Mr. Wescott. It was a pleasure to make your acquaintance, I'm sure."

The Baron's expression doesn't change, but his hesitation is enough to reveal his surprise: he'd expected to be received as a guest for the night—as he'd been once, long ago.

Still, when he speaks again his voice is placid, "The pleasure was mine, Your Ladyship. And please remember my offer." He peers at Evyn. "I rarely waive my fee, but then, I rarely find my work to be quite so gratifying."

"Very gracious of you, Mr. Wescott. We'll be sure to keep it in mind. Good evening."

"Good evening."

The Baron bows and turns, walking precariously close to the huddled mass on the floor. A disquieted butler extends an arm to the gallery. Lysbeth waits for their steps to fade before speaking.

"You needn't prostrate yourself, Evyn. We're pleased to see you."

At length, Evyn's torso inclines and curls—a wilted stalk planted in wood. His hand returns to grip his elbow, and to Lysbeth's disappointment, his eyes remain on the floor.

"Mr. Wescott mentioned you might be interested in scribal work?"

His breath quickens. Shaky fingers dig into his arm. "If it please Your Ladyship." A whispered distortion in pitch anchors his voice to a mild, unplaceable accent.

Elane flashes an uncomfortable look to Lysbeth, who folds her hands and crosses the room to direct a footman in the gallery. Orders relayed, she returns to a couch near Evyn's position. Elane follows suit, moving to a couch opposite.

"Would you care to sit?" Lysbeth offers.

Evyn digs.

The women exchange another unsettled glance and slowly sit themselves.

"Is something the matter with your arm?" Elane asks.

Evyn's fingers exchange digging for a tight clamp. "I am sorry," he whispers. Water weaves through long lashes. He lowers his head and rolls his shoulders, tucking himself away.

The Ladies' masks falter again; his behavior is extremely unfamiliar. In Avonleigh, one endeavors to conceal inconvenient emotions, but here are Evyn's on full display—and so easily interpreted, the women are forced to recognize them: anxiety, anguish, abasement. Unsure how to navigate the situation, they join in his silence for what feels like an interminable length of time. Finally, the door opens.

"Your tea, My Lady!" Ani's chipperness lances the room. Rounding the first couch, she stops short. "Oh, I didn't—er, pardon me." She steps around Evyn and continues to a table beside Lysbeth.

Under cover of rattling porcelain and silver, Evyn carefully pushes himself before an empty chair. The Ladies thumb their teacup deliveries and pretend not to notice. He folds inward again as Ani returns to the tray and flicks her eyes between Faye and pot.

"Join us, Ani," Lysbeth says, hoping the addition of a fourth party—if Evyn could be called a third—will lessen the awkwardness of the wait.

"With pleasure, My Lady." Ani daintily lowers to a chair—regretting the invitation as the silence drags on. Fortunately, the jolly voice of Lindenholt's head scribe, Mr. Sandel, soon comes from the hall.

Mr. Sandel Sr. Sr. Sr. had worked with Jeni Haywood, Lysbeth's redheaded forebear, in planning the Grand Library and scribal workshop. Thanks to their efforts, the scope of

Lindenholt's book collection gained notoriety, and nobles began placing orders for copies of its tomes and replications of their own shopworn favorites. Eventually, the Haywoods donated older books to surrounding villages as they were replaced. Edenshire's populace became rather well-read, and the county flourished.

A cheery face appears. "Your Ladyships! Have I the pleasure of an evening dictation?"

Lysbeth smiles in spite of herself. "No, Mr. Sandel. I was hoping you might evaluate the skills of a potential scribe?"

"Well of course! I'd be quite happy to, My Lady. You know I always say we can never have enough scritchers!" He chortles and holds a wooden box forward. "Shall I prepare the case while we wait for the candidate?"

"You're free to prepare it, Mr. Sandel, but the candidate, Evyn, is already present." She nods to the floor.

"Oh?" He shuffles around the first couch. "Oh! So he is. Well, I had better get started!" Oblivious to the tension he's just disrupted, he plomps down behind Evyn.

The Faye scoots to the vacant couch seat between Lysbeth and the scribe's annexed chair while Mr. Sandel pulls a side table around and opens the case flat atop.

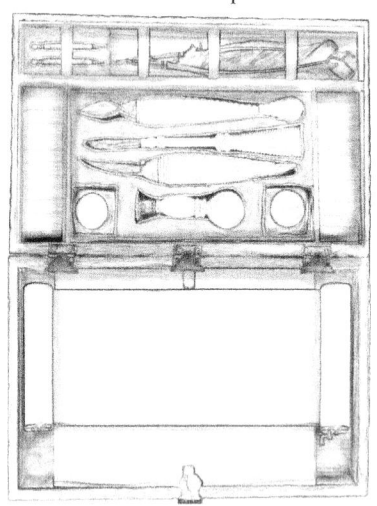

Removing a wooden plate from the upper lid reveals all the standard tools of a scribe: inkwells, quills, wax, blotter, and lead styli. A second plate covers the lower lid's hollow to support the scroll of parchment stretched across it. Noticing smears, Mr. Sandel turns a small roller to reel in fresh paper.

"There we are, no fuss about it," he says, exchanging an inkwell's cap for a quill. "Now then, what shall we copy? Ah, I know! Nothing so challenging as a client address book!" Grinning, he opens a leather booklet from his jacket and fastens it to a clip along the case's inner seam. "How does a three-page trial sound?"

Evyn lifts his eyes to the table as Mr. Sandel rotates it towards him.

"That will do fine," Lysbeth answers.

At her voice, Evyn quickly looks down again. Her lips purse.

"All scribes have their eccentricities, My Lady," Mr. Sandal assures. "We're a strange lot, that's why we're squirreled away in scriveries!" He guffaws and pushes the table directly in front of Evyn. "There. Now, take your time. Speed may be improved upon, but legibility is set by the ink!"

Another moment passes before slender, faltering hands release the booklet from its clip. After staring at the first two double-sided pages, Evyn sets it down on the table and winces as he returns to his knees. One hand draws the quill from the well while the other finds and dips a second quill from the case. Though perplexed, the women stay silent to avoid frightening him off. Mr. Sandel stays silent because he's seen stranger behavior from other scribes.

Evyn brings the quills to the top of the parchment and begins two columns of characters. Reaching the bottom, two new columns begin from the bottom up. Elane and Ani move closer for a better look. The parchment is double the height of the booklet, and it soon becomes clear the columns—quartered by perpendicular lines of negative space—belong to four distinct pages. After two minutes, Evyn lays the quills on the wooden plate and sits back on his heels, eyes fixed on his lap.

The four onlookers gawk at dense rows of addresses. Mr. Sandel slowly reopens the booklet for comparison. His handwriting, his mistakes, and the size of the pages are exacting. Marginally out of breath, he lunges for the blotter in the upper lid. Evyn flinches and renews the digging of his left forearm.

"I'm sorry, Evyn, I didn't mean to startle you. This is—It's—I simply must see more!" Mr. Sandel exclaims, passing the booklet to Lysbeth and blotting the scroll.

Lysbeth's pupils dance between page and box as she stands. "It's a perfect match. All of it, look!" She hands off the booklet and moves to a text on the nearby table.

Elane and Ani huddle, chins pivoting over ink.

"Amazing!" The maid's grin fades with a glance to Evyn's tense digging. Her eyes pass to Lysbeth, now flipping through, *A Heathen Philosopher's Treatise on Life.*[5]

"Are you able to write in Croran or Spencish, Evyn?" Lysbeth asks. His head lowers further. Determined to push through his discomforting behavior, she places the open book on his table and continues her request, "Please translate this page."

"Ambidextrous *and* bilingual? My Lady, you've outdone yourself!" Mr. Sandel proclaims, dabbing his face with a handkerchief.

"I rejoice to say I take no credit," she mutters, watching Evyn's unsteady closing of the cover.

Careful to keep his eyes low, Evyn rises to his knees and begins two new columns on the scroll. Then two more. By the third pair, Elane's bewildered expression compels the rest closer. The parchment is split—Croran left columns and Spencish right. Lysbeth retrieves the book.

---

[5] *Philosophers who despise the vanity of dress and often refuse it on principle.*

Eight columns. Ten.

"Astonishing," she whispers, numbly passing the tome to Elane.

A few moments later, a stupefied Elane deposits the text into Mr. Sandel's awaiting palms. The anesthetized circuit continues as the translations progress. Though some words and syntax are old-fashioned, the feat before them is remarkable. Finished, Evyn replaces the quills and shrinks to his heels under blank stares.

Mr. Sandel gulps and dabs his brow. Two dizzy, backward steps return him, slumped, to his seat. "When might he start at the scrivery, Your Ladyship?" he manages.

~~~~~~~~~~~~~~~~~~~~~~~

Lysbeth's foot dangles over the bed. "There was always very little chance of him coming back unchanged, but this? He's nearly unrecognizable, Elane."

"Is it any wonder? Keeping the company of that odious man for months on end? I nearly fainted from his look."

"Yes, it turns my stomach to think of him. That cane..." Lysbeth trails, lowering her brush to her lap. "We should've called for Doctor Howe."

"Oh, you're right. His arm must be in a sorry state," Elane says gloomily.

"And his knees. It must've been truly wretched."

"Perhaps he'll improve now he's come back?"

"Perhaps. I certainly hope so." Lysbeth tosses her brush. "As it stands, he's not fit to be seen."

"Lys! Don't be so unkind."

"I don't mean it unkindly, Elane, but surely you saw his recoiling? What are we to do with him? He's too terrified to speak or move." She sends her hands this way and that, tone softening after a moment. "Of me in particular, apparently."

"Yes, I noticed," Elane confirms. "Agreeing to consider the Warden's offer must play a part. I doubt Evyn's lessons included much in the way of social charades."

Lysbeth's rumination plucks her vocal cords, "Hmm. Do you suppose I ought to clarify my position?"

"It couldn't hurt."

After a pause, Lysbeth groans and tips over. "If only I hadn't invited him in that day!" Well-acquainted with the proclamation, her cousin looks on with solemn amusement. "It could all be so different. Surely he'd know much more about the way things are done if he'd learnt from us instead?"

"Yes." Elane stretches her neck and exhales. "It's safe to say education was never truly Isaac's intention."

"Impervious, more like. Isaac would never knowingly act in a manner benefiting another." Lysbeth rises and smooths the blanket, frowning as a thought arrives. "Did the Baron claim Dorsit had been a *client*?"

"Truthfully, I was so overcome I can hardly recall." Elane peers earnestly. "I hope to never see that man or his cane again, Lys."

"Nor do I. Mother's aversion doesn't seem so unreasonable now."

"Aunt Lily knew him?"

"Not exactly. They were introduced when Father appointed him Warden and she flatly refused to host him again afterwards. That was years before I came along, mind, but I recall one or two contentious occasions around it."

Elane's brow creases. "Then his unpleasantness proceeded his appointment? Somehow I prefer the other way around."

The cousins fall taciturn revisiting the Baron's likeness. He'd been in the drawing room no more than a few minutes, but his afterimage would linger for many weeks to come. Lysbeth clears her head with a wiggle and glances at the book on her nightstand.

"Mr. Sandel's affability should be a boon, at least. Evyn's skill is truly extraordinary."

"Aye. I wonder how quickly he could translate *The Takkar-Ercasian Saga*?"

"Elane! You're the last person I'd expect to abuse his talents... though I'd guess no more than a week." Lysbeth's chiding grin dims. "Are we simply to lock him in a closet for an eternity of book translation?"

Elane smiles gently. "There are worse fates. Give it time, Lys."

~~~~~~~~~~~~~~~~~~

Ani plunges a pin.

"Oh, he was a sight at breakfast, My Lady. He hardly ate a bite, and I don't think he slept a wink. After he'd gone off to the scrivery, Brom confided he'd seen a similar bearing in those driven mad by the fighting and prisons last Kingswar."

"Mad?" Lysbeth repeats, staring at her maid in the mirror. "Did he say what's to be done? Is there a cure?"

"He didn't mention one, but I hope there is. I've already heard some of the others complaining."

Knowing the news will spur Lysbeth, Elane pins her own hair up from the adjacent vanity's chair. "What do they say?"

"That his manner makes them uncomfortable, mostly. But I think it's just as likely they can't see past last Autumn." Ani plunges another pin. "All they remember is a speechless, half-naked, metal man who angered his Lordship."

Lysbeth sighs. "Yes, likely both. Thank you, Ani."

She stands and moves to the hall with Elane, relaying summons to a footman before entering the front drawing room. As her cousin sits, Lysbeth paces in short bursts. Her eyes wind to the floor. Cracks of cane and caps reecho in memory. Soon regretting her choice of venue, she spins to alter her summons on the point of Evyn's arrival. He enters, head low, arm gripped, and looking altogether unwell.

"Oh, good morning, Evyn." Lysbeth motions to the couch. "Please."

He glimpses her gesture with a look near her feet. Stammering legs pitch him to the couch, and after a promising point of sail, throw his knees down in front of it. On impact, his cringe holds—a wreathing thread binding his frame.

Lysbeth expels a startled breath. "Please don't do that, Evyn. It's unnecessary, and unseemly. And it can't be good for—" Her reproach breaks on his escalating panic.

Elane mimes a rap under wide eyes. Lysbeth nods and folds her hands, moving beside Evyn to allow herself a gander. Fingertips deepen their efforts in his arm as she lowers to the couch. Distended cheek and brow bones tauten pale skin, red-lined eyelids float on inky semi-circles, and he shivers with seemingly-endless foreboding.

He's a wreck, there's no denying, but the fairest ship wrecked still claims the fairest wreckage.

"I only say it to help, and I'm quite resolved that none of us should see the Warden again," she explains. "I don't know why he taught you this, but it's not something we do."

Cowed, Evyn's rapid breathing gives way to a whisper, "I am sorry."

Lysbeth takes air to reply as a footman announces Doctor Howe. She sighs through flaring nostrils and waves in an older, well-assembled man.

Doctor Howe has been the Haywood's physician for thirty years. When Lysbeth expressed an interest in anatomy after reading Alder's letter—finding descriptions of long waists and fingers peculiar—Doctor Howe had given her a text. It's not often a man encourages a woman's curiosity, let alone a girl's, and she returns the kindness by ignoring his occasional patronizing.

"Good morning, Your Ladyship. Up early, are we?"

"Yes, I suppose so." Lysbeth ejects a short sigh and stands. "I've a patient for you, Doctor. Evyn is a new scribe with us. If you've no prior engagements, please see to an examination."

Doctor Howe's perplexed gaze falls on the kneeling scribe. "Shall I return him here?"

"Please do." She hesitates, adding, "Perhaps you ought to know there are a few differences between our peoples."

"Our peop—?" Doctor Howe's eyebrows rise to support a weighted realization. Residing in his own cottage on-grounds, he's only privy to servant gossip with waves large enough to splash his patients in the nearby village. He'd heard vague rumors of a Faye last Autumn, but they'd faded just as quickly as they'd begun.

"Yes, I assume some may be obvious," she continues, "for instance, much less, and finer, hair below the brow."

The Doctor smooths his vest. "Well, how curious. Come along, Evyn."

Jaw straining, the Faye stands and follows his newest keeper to the hall as Brom arrives for his own summons.

Elane eyes his dusty jacket. "More trouble with the gelding, Marshal?"

"Afraid so, My Lady." He grunts as he takes the offered chair. "Can't get close for long—determined thing."

"Your match then?" Lysbeth smiles. "Truth be told, I'd hoped you might be able to help with our *other* new occupant as well." Her head tilts to the door. "Ani mentioned you'd seen soldiers with Evyn's troubles last Kingswar?"

"Yes, I did."

"Go on, Brom." Lysbeth knows the Marshal is a man of few words who occasionally requires additional nudging. He's playing second fiddle to Evyn now, though.

"A few seemed to lose themselves after the fighting. Soul-rot, soldiers called it. Prone to despair. Nightmares. That sort of thing."

"What was the cause?" Elane asks.

"Not sure. Some said it was a man's nature—a lack of fortitude. But those who said it were usually those kept furthest from the fighting."

When no more is offered, Lysbeth probes further, "What does one's proximity to the fight have to do with it, Marshal?"

"Nothing, formally. But I observed those most affected were those caught in the worst of the fighting." He crosses his arms. "And the worse the fighting, the more occasions you'd like to forget, but can't."

"I see. What was done for them?"

"Nothing I'm aware of."

"Well, what became of them, then?" Lysbeth asks with growing concern.

"I'd heard of one or two who'd recovered after a while. Not fully, but close. As for the others…" His head slants in inference.

Elane straightens. "Would you mind looking after Evyn for a while, Marshal? You seem to know more about his condition than anyone."

Lacing his fingers and tapping his thumbs, Brom mulls the request over a long silence. Finally, he nods. "I can keep you informed, Lady Elane. Lady Lysbeth. But I can't promise any fixes, as I haven't any."

"Thank you, Brom. You're still in the kitchen block double?" Lysbeth asks.

Brom grunts affirmatively as he stands. Out of respect for his leg, he was given accommodations closer to the stable rather than the barracks halfway to the gatehouse. Lysbeth walks him to the door with a grateful smile. "Then I'll have his things sent, and him, too."

The Ladies spend the rest of the morning awaiting Doctor Howe, who returns with the Faye just before noon. Afraid to risk his knees, Lysbeth permits Evyn to remain by the door as Doctor Howe sits to deliver his report.

"The arm's lesions have been cleaned and bandaged. I strongly recommend three days' bedrest for the knees. I'll reassess the damage once the swelling reduces, but I'm afraid only time will resolve the remaining injuries."

"Remaining?" Elane asks.

"Yes, rather severe contusions across the appendages and torso, My Lady. They appear to be markings left by a restraint of some kind, though I find myself at a loss where the spine is concerned." At the women's quizzical looks, he continues, "There are five metal discs embedded along the vertebrae. Atypical bruising issues from them. Both the discs and the contusions are unfamiliar to me. In fact, my tardiness is due to an unsuccessful foray into my medical library." He turns to glance at the Faye. "As you can imagine, my patient was not very forthcoming."

Recalling the five divots on Evyn's filigree last Autumn, Lysbeth glances too.

Evyn remains still.

"I'll check up in three days," Doctor Howe adds, "but I've done all I can, for now."

~~~~~~~~~~~~~~~~

The eastern gallery's floorboards groan unevenly under Marshal Brom's pacing.

Other than his accurate prediction of Evyn's nightmares and Doctor Howe's work clearance three weeks ago, there's been little to report. He knows Lysbeth's been disappointed by the lack of progress, but he's sure today's update won't mollify her either. He looks up from the scroll in his hands as she appears in the music room's doorway.

"You asked to see me, Marshal?"

"Yes, Your Ladyship. I've something to show you." He hesitates. "It might best be viewed privately."

Lysbeth's fingers twitch as she glimpses the scroll. Lidding her curiosity, she motions him to follow her down the gallery. "You do seem rather distressed," she remarks of the faint, downward tug on his mouth.

"Yes, I find I am." When they reach her morning room, he accepts a couch seat beside a low table and holds the scroll up in her direction. "I went to change for a late lunch. This was drying on the dresser. I must warn you, it's a very troubling image."

"And you believe it belongs to Evyn?"

"It must. I've never seen an illustration like it."

"A scrivery order, surely?"

"No, Your Ladyship, no book would have it. It's... a study of two children, but one is beyond recognizing."

Lysbeth's eyebrows skew. "Beyond recognizing? Do you know them?"

"No, I— Recognition. One is beyond recognition. As a child."

"I'm not sure what you mean, Brom. How can you know it's a child if it can't be recognized as one?" The curve of her smile levels on revisiting his expression.

"It's a series. Stages. Beginning, middle, end."

"Perhaps you'd better show me," she says, moving to his couch.

He grunts. "I'll go slowly."

Laying the parchment on the table, he anchors the scroll's edge and unreels four inches of an exceptionally realistic ink sketch. Lysbeth sits and leans forward. Huddled against the wall of a stone room, two very young and very frightened children return her gaze from the page.

Her mouth slackens. "How can it be so lifelike?"

In lieu of an answer, Brom unrolls the next image. The background repeats, but the younger child now hugs her knees against the wall alone. Lysbeth follows her gaze to the second child—a boy of about three—who's tightly bound to a stool further in. Above him, two weighted, iron-spiked panels form a peak of precariously opposed angles. Lysbeth turns wide eyes on Brom. He meets them and unrolls another inch—just enough to reveal the wall and girl splattered with...

She stands. Brom quickly rewinds the parchment.

Using the corner view as a mainstay, Lysbeth strides to her window, and rests a hand on the sill, steadying herself over a long breath. The pregnant pause births her query: "Marshal, are these vile fabrications commonplace among afflicted soldiers?"

"No, Your Ladyship. Most are preoccupied with troubling memories."

Lysbeth rounds to deliver a long, meaningful look. "You're suggesting a depiction?"

He inhales deeply. "I'm suggesting the possibility."

"That is very difficult for me to accept, Brom."

He nods at the scroll revolving in his hands. "The murder of a child should be difficult to accept, My Lady." The scroll stills as his eyes lift. "That's why I'm suggesting it."

Her breath quickens. Unable to match his gaze, she turns back to the window and falls silent for several moments.

"Alright." She twists. "Can your lunch wait?"

Reappearing in the gallery, they slow to summon Evyn before continuing across the Grand Chamber—as Lysbeth's drawing room-aversion has driven her to the western wing. Arriving at the study, they approach a heavy wooden desk with a large bay window at its back. Brom stops between the two chairs facing it, passing the parchment to Lysbeth as she moves to the other side. Taking burnished pebbles from a dish, she weighs the scroll and leans over the first scene. "The detail is truly staggering." She peers at Brom across the desk. "Have you met the Baron?"

"Once. I had orders to deliver a group of prisoners to him last Kingswar." He shifts to his good leg. "I found him off-putting."

"A generous assessment," she mutters. "He's barbarous, to be sure, but do you really think him capable of this?"

"Wescott's popularity among peerage relies on his ability to get results." He tilts his head to the scroll. "If this were required to get results, I believe him capable."

Lysbeth straightens and crosses her arms. "If he is, making it known would certainly damage his reputation. Though it would likely damage the reputation of his patrons as well." She frowns. The Haywoods are among his patrons thanks to Isaac.

"He's had a long career, Lady Lysbeth. With the information he must hold over the peerage, he's likely very well protected, too."

They look to the door as a footman opens it. Head down, Evyn gives a wide berth to his announcer and stops midway through the room. He wears one of the tunics Lysbeth had ordered for him—verdigris, to match what she remembered of his eyes—and holds a scribal case close. Acclimated to his habit of remaining as distant as possible, Lysbeth has taken to directing his position.

"Come in, Evyn," she says, motioning to the desk's left.

He walks forward, roving the scribal case's latch with long, assumptive fingers. As he nears, his eyes trip on the scroll and fall to the floor. Shallow breath accompanies the forced termination of a reflexive, rearward step. He hugs the case tightly. Floundering feet sow. Strain locks his face.

At Lysbeth's nod, Brom sinks the liver[6]: "This was on the dresser."

His tone is question, statement, and verdict. Evyn folds beneath it. Sinking slowly to his knees, constricting dread wrings faint words from his throat, "I am sorry."

His inquisitors exchange looks—it's the most direct answer they've come to expect. Lysbeth brings a hand to her hip and moves around the desk. "Is this illustration an event you witnessed at Wescott's prison, Evyn?" The overwrought figure offers no response. Continuing with the supposition, she tries again, "Did the girl meet with the same fate?"

To her surprise, wet eyes briefly jump to her elbow. Evyn curls forward and shakes his head. Progress.

"Is she alive?"

A tremor fidgets with his whisper, "I am uncertain."

"She was alive when you left?" Lysbeth offers.

"Please, she—" A choked sob throttles.

Lysbeth feels his anguish like a barb in her gut. "Brom, take as many men as you need. Your unannounced arrival should prevent Wescott's disposing of her, if she lives. Where was the girl kept, Evyn?"

---

[6] *A blacksmithing idiom deriving from an old Avon belief that a weapon's strength increased if plunged into a Kingswar prisoner's liver: "a requisite action of questionable gain."*

"The... wall." His ink-speckled fingers push the air and bend sharply at the top joint.

Brom sends his confusion on a glance. Raising an eyebrow, Lysbeth forwards it to the scroll. "Please draw it for us," she says.

The Marshal guards a smile. "I'll gather the Keepers."

"Send Mikael in on your way out. He'll deliver the drawing before you leave." As Brom departs, Lysbeth pats the desk's chair. "Sit here, Evyn."

She wouldn't normally be so blunt, but rooming with Brom had revealed another subject on the Baron's syllabus: verbatim commands. Politely offered accommodation was too ambiguous. Without clear instruction, Evyn would stand or kneel indefinitely. Ani's guess that he hadn't slept a wink the night of his return was accurate. He'd been shown an attic room, but not told to sleep.

Evyn stands, and to avoid Lysbeth, takes the longest way around the desk. Holding back a sigh, she returns the paperweights to their dish and pushes the scroll aside. He squeezes into the chair and quietly unlatches the case in his lap.

"Silverpoint, please."

A sheet of ground parchment flutters to the desk; tremulous hands bring two lead styli over it. Evyn holds his breath as the points lower, and when they connect, each hand seems to grow sentience. Nimble textures deepen as Evyn picks up speed, and his anxiety soon gives way to a nearly trance-like vacancy. Before long, lead hashes and arcs merge into a square of linenfold paneling with a well-concealed latch in its pleat. Evyn's hands flip abruptly. His eyes escort them to his lap.

"Remarkable." Lysbeth brings the image closer to her face. "I'd never guess such detail could be achieved through such speed." A footman moves in the doorway. She waves him over and hands off the square. "Mikael, please have Ms. Makensi pack Brom lunch and deliver it to him along with this. Thank you."

As the door shuts, she glances at Evyn. In cases of tragedy, Decorum advises an expression of condolence, but Lysbeth can't seem to recall its recommendation for cases of apotheotic atrocity.

She steps to the bay window on uneven footing, opting for the firmer ground of Decorum's third fork: the distancing mask of stratum. "Evyn, I'm not sure if you were told, but scribal materials belong to the scrivery. Please only use them when instructed in the future."

A hushed reply follows a brief pause, "I am sorry."

She sighs at the water gardens beyond the panes. "And I'm partial to appeasement." As she watches the splashes and ripples of Lindenholt's pools, a thought buoys. "Did you happen to see his Lordship's key to the basement room?"

"Yes, Ladyship."

She turns, smiling slightly at the address. Evyn has made a habit of dropping her title's determiner. "Are you able to draw it?"

He tilts his head forward.

"Please do. Silverpoint again. Every angle you recall."

Evyn lays another square of ground parchment. The vacancy comes faster, and within minutes, the sheet is covered in detailed angles of two distinct keys. When his hands flip and retreat to his lap, Lysbeth picks up the image.

"Thank you. While you're here, I could use your ink."

Over the last fortnight, she'd occasionally summoned Evyn for dictation to check on his progress for herself. While she'd been disheartened by his bearing, his recording skills had far surpassed her expectations. His regularly alternating hands keep the quills wet and his scratching constant, his superior dexterity keeps his tidy letters uniform, and his accurate word predictions often leave Lysbeth behind.

She opens a drawer and produces a booklet. As she begins to leaf, Evyn prepares vellum, an inkwell, and two quills. Once Lysbeth finds her page, he draws a quill from the well and steadies his fingers.

> *Dear Mr. Tuttle,*
> *Please reference the enclosed illustration for an order of two keys to be*
> *delivered to Lindenholt at your convenience.*
> *Regards,*

He rotates the sheet and she adds her signature. In turn, she points to an address in the booklet, which Evyn adds to the page's lower corner.

"Let it air, I've another, please."

He slides the message to the side and draws a quill. Lysbeth begins:

> *Dearest Duchess,*
> *I write seeking your advice on a matter of some delicacy. I have in my*
> *possession evidence of a heinous act committed by Warden Ian Wescott:*
> *the murder of a child. I do not know how or why such a man came to be the*
> *child's custodi—*

Evyn's scratching stops. Lysbeth checks the note to see if he's fallen behind, but he's already begun the next word. A glance to his face is greeted by silent, rolling tears. For the first time since his return, Evyn's eyes meet her own—and in them, she finds only the vivid engravings of Westcott's rings around his soul.

"Because of me," he whispers.

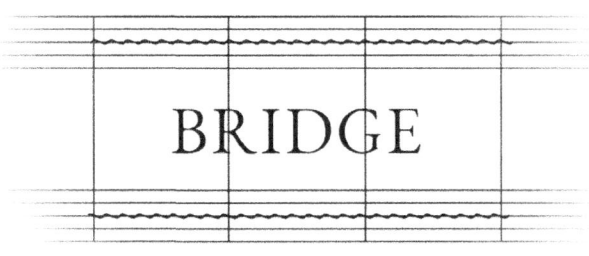

BRIDGE

...the great devotion and love shown among them—for each other and
for the land—is the quiet wish of every nation of man.
-Alder Haywood-

Sixteen days ago, Marshal Brom returned from his excursion to the Baron's prison with a very fragile parcel: the young, terrified girl introduced to Lindenholt through Evyn's illustrations. Brom deduced the children were obtained through an orphanage, and as is tradition for anonymous children, Lindenholt has called her Jonun—after the month which sees the greatest increase in orphans. As Jonun was acquired for the sole purpose of breaking Evyn, Lysbeth felt obliged to take the girl under her own rapidly crowding wing. She receives regular reports on the pair these days, and their dreariness has begun to wear on her.

Evyn's nightmares and anxieties keep him shuttered—a state worsened, Ani reports, by less sympathetic servants who make a point of disparaging him and Jonun within his range of hearing. Though a nurse has been employed, the severity of Jonun's distress has proven even more challenging than Evyn's. Doctor Howe attributes her mutism and temperament—which fluctuates between listless despondency and frenzied, violent episodes—to mental strain.

Unfortunately, there is little legal recourse. Children share a similar status to women, and in the eyes of the law, damaging one's own property is not a crime. Knowing this, Avrella Haywood has cautiously approved her granddaughters' request to spread rumors of the Warden's misdeeds to a select list of Ladies. Lysbeth and Elane have finalized the letter, but though Evyn's skill perfectly befits message copy, feel his involvement is best avoided. Lindenholt is host to a war of attrition for the souls of Wescott's victims, and every battle counts.

Therefore, the task will fall to scrivery while Lysbeth, Elane, and Ani attend the annual Summer Solstice Promenade. Their furlough will last six weeks, and they've nearly filled their trunks for tomorrow's departure.

Lysbeth lifts a jeweled brooch in the shape of a sparrow and turns from her trinket-covered vanity. "What of this one for the yellow dress?"

"It's a bit..." Elane tosses her hands.

Lysbeth translates: gaudy. "Agreed. But most here are."

A large portion of her jewelry was inherited from Haywood Ladies whose fashions were very much a product of their eras. Looking over the pile, Lysbeth spies Evyn's box under a carelessly thrown scarf.

Its silver feet squeak gently as she pulls it forward. In a nearly subliminal ritual, she examines it again. The silver tendrils piped over its shiny black wood act as a cage preventing further exploration. On top, three fine chains spoke out from a small disc affixed to the filigree. No hinges are seen.

"I bet that has some nice treasures, My Lady," Ani says, folding the scarf.

Half-present, Lysbeth slowly spins the box around. "Perhaps, though the mystery is treasure enough for me."

"Is there a keyhole?"

"Not that I'm aware of. See how these creases stack along the silver? Here, and here, too? They suggest it opens down the sides, but where are the hinges? And this configuration of chains, I'm certain I saw something similar on Evyn's horns when he arrived."

Ani giggles. "I'm sorry, My Lady. It's not often I hear mention of horns."

"Aye, true—" They start as a loud crash comes from the hall.

Being closest to the door, Elane hastens over and peeks out. A child's scream is followed shortly by a woman's. She twists to Lysbeth and Ani in alarm, and the three make a quick exit. Rounding the gallery's corner, servants in the music room's doorway hint at an ongoing disruption within. On the gallery floor behind them, Jonun's nurse sits holding her arm, and nobly, holding back tears.

Elane increases her step. "Ms. Pinley, whatever happened?"

"I thought Jonun might like to hear Lady Corah play when they come for her lesson, m'Lady. But soon as we were in, she started kickin' and screamin'. I tried to carry her out. She bit me clean through!" She blows into a handkerchief.

"Fetch Doctor Howe instead of gawking, please," Lysbeth quietly chides a footman, who moves away chagrined. "Where is the child now, Ms. Pinley?"

"She ran under the table, m'Lady, and won't let anyone close! I fear there's nothin' to be done for the tot. That Baron's run her through the h-heart," she wails.

Elane and Ani tend her while Lysbeth joins Mr. Tenson in clearing the doorway of curious servants. She peeks in. A partition dividing the music and Grand Drawing Rooms serves as a backdrop for a footman and maid. Soft whimpering comes from a table at their shins.

The footman scratches his head. "We could move it?"

"And?" The maid flashes angry welts on her hand. "Then what?"

Lysbeth enters as a panel across the room slides away. Evyn stands among the small group of servants on the other side, carrying a book, a scribal case, and an alert expression. Stepping through the partition, dimming chatter and scornful looks force his eyes to his feet and his feet to the floor. He stills, arrested in an awkward lull until Jonun's whimper uproots him.

Compelled forward, he places his items on the table and kneels beside to peer beneath. At Jonun's yelp, he sits up for reassessment. The footman sniggers. Seeing he's about to remark, Lysbeth moves to catch his eye when the deep rumble of a shoved table jolts her.

Evyn follows the furniture's lurch with a swift reach for Jonun's scream, and a partially hidden struggle ensues. The girl soon emerges tossing her weight—and ensuring Evyn's participation by way of her teeth and claws. He makes no attempts to defend or retaliate against her ferocity, instead using his surrendered arm as the frayed lead of her ushering.

Once in his lap, he folds her into a kneel matching his own, and leans his chest against her back to keep her contained. Panicked and frustrated by her inability to move, she lets loose one last scream before falling into sobs. Evyn's own eyes brim as he strokes her hair— offering patient comfort while her tears yield to sniffles, and her sniffles to peaceful torpor.

~~~~~~~~~~~~~~~~~~~

Lysbeth sighs and locks her trunk.

The previous evening had been a whirlwind of negotiations. Ms. Pinley agreed to stay on with a small raise and a promise that Evyn would attend to Jonun's eruptions. Corah, ever cognizant of opportunities to harry her piano instructor, Mr. Spantier, insisted the day's theatrics were proof of music's malignancy on society. Mr. Spantier agreed to stay on provided his student apologize—which, naturally, required additional negotiations with Corah, from whom a convincingly sincere apology was eventually wrested.

Tucking the trunk's key into her bliaut-bodice, Lysbeth moves aside for footmen to carry it out. Her departure feels negligent, but PromSol is not an event from which one is generally excused, and she needs the respite. Marshal Brom knows to send a bird if there's an emergency, Corah's governess has been paid a seven-week advance, and Mr. Sandel has promised to write with an update on Evyn and Jonun.

Adding a pin to her traveling crespine, Lysbeth stops in the hall to view the portrait of her mother opposite the sitting room's door.

"No judgments, please. I haven't a choice," she mutters.

Lily Haywood smiles serenely at her daughter.

"Much obliged." Lysbeth arches an eyebrow and turns down the passage.

~~~~~~~~~~~~~~~~~~~

~~~~~~~~~~~~~~~~~~~

SUMMER

...there is nothing like the beauty of their speech. Each utterance is unto a note—and when not a note, a chord—so that each word is a musical motif, and each sentence a musical phrase. I shall die wishing to hear it one last time.

-Alder Haywood-

Dear Lady Lysbeth,   *29 Jyn 1515 III*

I hope you are having a most marvelous time at the Proms-Solstice extravaganza, My Lady! Oh, I do look forward to Lindenholt's hosting again two years hence. The last event was sensational, though I must admit my memory becomes fuzzy after the concert. How the spirits did flow!

Marshal Brom sends his regards and mentioned to me in passing that the gelding has calmed rather steadily—now a whole four weeks without causing injury. I suggested that he open an equine finishing school, but I don't think he took my meaning. In any case, I took the opportunity to throw a little celebration during our Solstice festivities in honor of the occasion—though I may have offended some stable workers with my choice of cake décor: trousers marked with a horse-shoe! Oh, how they hooted, My Lady! Ms. Makensi was quite the sport for agreeing to make it!

Now, to the meat of the matter: I am of course delighted to keep you updated on our timid acquaintances. Evyn has formed a tender attachment with the child, whom he has taken to calling Erem, and much of their time is spent together in the kitchen gardens. The girl is still jumpy—as is the boy! —but Erem's outbursts have lessened. I am sorry to pass along reports, however, that Evyn's night terrors are little improved.

I was pondering the matter recently and—if My Lady permit my musings—despite the slow progress, I believe Evyn despairs somewhat less now that Erem has given him duty. Sometimes a kindred spirit is all one truly needs. As I must regularly remind my colleagues, the scribal arts are not the answer to every affliction!

And on the subject, Evyn's work continues to be invaluable. We have had several new orders for illuminated scripts now that members of our recently effectuated constituency have sung our new scribe's praises. Indeed, I think that you will be quite happy with the funds produced this month!

Incidentally, My Lady, that is why I hope you will not mind too terribly that I have given Evyn a sheet of parchment twice now as thanks for his excellent work. He always seems a little better after draining his mind of the images therein, and I know that you and I share the hope that he be better-much and not just better-little, eventually. Every better-bit must count! Please do let me know if I can be of any further assistance, My Lady. If I hear not from you, I shall look forward to our meeting again three weeks hence!

Your devoted friend and scribe,
Benthor Sandel

Three weeks hence, Edenshire's Ladies return from their reprieve, pleased to discover Lindenholt in good working order. After settling a few mishaps with Corah's instructors, Lysbeth catches up on estate accounts, finding her locksmith order has been fulfilled, and that Mr. Sandel had not exaggerated the profitability of the previous month. Evyn is able to produce high quality copies in a very short time, and as word of the workshop's new employee grows, so too do the orders.

Fortunately, Gina and Marium—the Ladies present during Evyn's arrival—have honored their promises of discretion, and the rumor mill seems ignorant of his origins. Though Lysbeth enjoys hostessing, any nobles come calling to meet a Faye would be sorely disappointed in the result. She glimpses the view from her desk and stretches.

"I think I'd like a walk."

"Good idea." Elane returns another piece of jewelry to its vanity box and smiles to Ani. "I'll stay on to help unpack."

Lysbeth journeys to the kitchen block and veers towards the inner court's scrivery entrance. One foot through the door, a merry voice rings out.

"My Lady! How wonderful to see you!" Mr. Sandel stands from a large desk and wipes his hands on a rag. "How was the host this year? Still can't hold a candle to Lindenholt, I presume?"

"A short wick, perhaps." She smiles.

2

Last century, it was decided Proms and Summer Solstice should coincide to spare pampered nobles additional travel, and there had been much debate on where the merged event should take place. Eventually the matter was settled by upholding Prom's tradition of rotating yearly hosts—tradition, of course, being the safest response to change.

Since that time, highly ranked nobles are expected to have a concert hall on-ground, with some keeping entire orchestras in-residence to trot out when important guests need impressing. Retaining a moderate ensemble in the nearby village and a quintet on the estate, the Haywood's less extravagant approach is offset by the favoritism Lindenholt enjoys as a PromSol venue.

When opened, the manor's core is uniquely situated as a loop of door-less Grand Rooms around the Grand Stair—and as every event location is readily accessible, Haywood ancestors seem nearly prophetic in their architectural planning. In truth, Lindenholt's arrangement was fated on Alder's return. Inspired by the Faye's massive, open-air rooms, he'd commissioned blueprints for future alterations in their aesthetic, and subsequent generations simply carried out his wishes.

2

"It was very pleasant, Mr. Sandel, thank you." Noting Evyn's absence from the room, Lysbeth leans in. "Did the Baron's messages make it out?"

Mr. Sandel lowers his voice, "Yes, My Lady. Quite vile business, I must say. Very wise to remain vague on all the details. I was sure to keep the project from Evyn, as you recommended. Rather an easy task given how quickly he finishes his work. I've already increased his quota but as you see." He nods to an empty desk.

"Well, after examining the accounts, I won't complain if you won't."

"Indeed, I surely shall not, My Lady!" Mr. Sandel chortles. "If you're looking for him, I suggest the kitchen gardens."

"Thank you."

Lysbeth exchanges pleasantries with other scribes as she strolls through the workshop to the adjoining greenhouse—an unfortunate neighbor for a scrivery, but most storage issues were solved by a cellar, and though they'd never admit it, the scribes benefit from proximate nature.

Verdant humidity greets her in the next room. To her left, fragrant eddies reach in from the kitchen garden's doorway. Among the densely packed herbs, vegetables, and fruit trees, Ms. Pinley knits on a stone bench beside the Faye and fawn-like child. A bee's lavender-guzzling holds the girl's attention as Evyn kneels to tie a white ribbon in her light-blonde hair.

Mr. Sandel's letter had been equally accurate in its descriptions of the troubled pair. The child seems far more at ease than Lysbeth's memory of her six weeks prior, and Evyn's attentive doting seems to distract his anxiety. After taking a few moments to steel herself, Lysbeth moves to the garden's gravel path. The three faces turning in her direction quickly reduce to one.

Ms. Pinley smiles as she nears. "Hullo, m'Lady. Welcome home."

"Thank you, Ms. Pinley. You're looking rather peaceful."

"Oh yes, we're just enjoyin' the weather and the green. What can we do for you, m'Lady?"

"I've come to speak with Evyn, if you'll pardon the interruption."

The girl clings to the Faye's arm as he moves to stand, and his reluctance to leave her is clear. Hoping to avoid alarm, Lysbeth joins Ms. Pinley on the bench as the child climbs into Evyn's lap.

"Evyn, Lady Corah's had some trouble with her instructors, and I thought transcriptions of the lessons might be beneficial. Will you come to the music room tomorrow at two for recording, please?"

At mention of the room, the child tenses and buries her face in Evyn's chest. He lays a slender hand across her head and leans close. "o'ed k'me-nar ̄ni k-un'ia-it ̄er'em ̄a ̄ik-ey ̄ine."

Lysbeth's jaw lowers. Though she can't be expected to know the language, she has reasonable expectations for the spectrum of sounds available to human speech—the sounds Evyn has just produced fall widely outside of this expectancy.

"It's somethin', innit, m'Lady?" Ms. Pinley regards the two sweetly. "I nearly keeled over the first I heard it."

"Y-yes, Ms. Pinley. It's..." Lysbeth trails as a passage from Alder's letter surfaces:

Each utterance is unto a note—and when not a note, a chord.

As a girl, she'd spent days imagining a language to match the account. The later troubles of adolescence and the dreary monotony of adulthood had since buried such playful thoughts. Now they spring forward.

"Alder wrote of it. I'd forgotten." She looks to Evyn, who, on realizing he's drawn her full attention, has grown very still. "Would you mind repeating it?"

After a moment, Evyn brings his other arm around the girl and echoes, *"o'ęd k'me-nar͡ ni k-un'ia-it ͡ʒer'em͡ a̜'ik-ey ͡ine."*

Lysbeth listens intently. Within his vocalizations rise and fall up to three separate, simultaneous pitches. Three distinct voices. Articulations stay forward in his mouth as dressings over smooth, unbroken tones from his throat. It was just as described: each utterance a note, and by the inclusion of another pitch or two, more often a chord.

"It's quite lovely," she says. "I'd always wondered what Alder meant by musical chords. I think I'd settled on humming while speaking." She tucks a hand under her chin and smiles slightly. "Polyphonics never occurred to me, though I suppose I wasn't so very, very far off."

Evyn remains still.

Lysbeth nods to the enfolded child. "Mr. Sandel said you've taken to calling her Ear-eem. May I ask what it means?"

He blinks at gravel. "*ʒer'em, Erem*: flicker of light in darkness. Hope, Ladyship." Readjusting Erem's ribbon, his gaze moves to the shadow of Lysbeth's feet. "Firefly, also," he adds quietly.

A syrupy warmth spreads in Lysbeth's chest.

Ms. Pinley gives a little laugh. "Which is she, dear?"

Evyn's eyes shift to the small, expectant face in his lap.

A faint smile crosses his lips.

"Both."

~~~~~~~~~~~~~~~~~~~

Lindenholt's richly adorned dining parlor gazes upon its occupants with regal detachment.

"I wish you'd been there, Elane," Lysbeth says, collecting a variety of morsels on her fork. "It was so unexpected, truly. He must be teaching the girl."

Corah straightens in her chair. "What about me? I'm sure I'd like to hear it."

"Yes, Corah, I'm sure you would." Lysbeth sighs.

Amused, Elane reaches for her wine glass, "It sounds otherworldly. What did he say?"

"I didn't think to ask. I was too swept up in the shock of it."

"We should call on him to demonstrate after supper," Corah states directly. "You can ask him then."

Lysbeth smirks. "Oh yes, I'm sure that would go over quite happily."

"You haven't met him, Corah," Elane explains, "He's far too meek to make an exhibition of or to call on for our own diversion."

"I don't see what meekness has to do with it, so long as he answers the question and does as he's told."

Lysbeth rests her utensils on the edge of the plate. "It isn't that simple. Evyn and Erem must be given extra consideration," she says, sharing a glance with Elane.

Corah's willful and precocious nature often leads to skirmishes with those foolish enough to presume authority over her, but when she hints at relishing her own position over others, Lysbeth can't help but think of Isaac. She worries after her sister and who she might become.

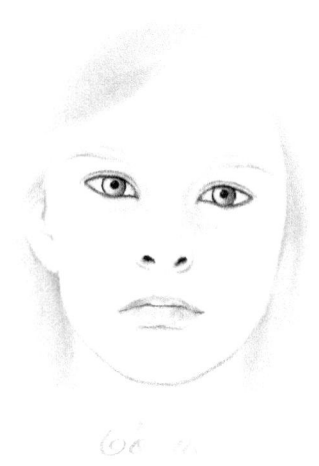

"I don't see why you should be making excuses for him, Lys. He struck Lord Dorsit," Corah retorts.

It would appear Isaac's revisionism is still in effect. Lysbeth forces her shoulders down. "Dorsit wasn't *struck*, Corah. Only his pride was injured, and it was repaid one-hundred-fold." Her tone softens. "You must promise to be kind tomorrow. Please."

The young girl studies her sister. Unsure which portrayal of the Faye's character is true, she resolves to judge for herself.

"I shan't promise to be kind," she says, raising her nose, "but I shall attempt to be impartial."

The next afternoon, a nervous Faye enters the music room ten minutes early for a two o'clock lesson. Mr. Spantier directs him to stand beside the pianoforte and use his scribal case as a desk on its cover.

At five-to-two, Lysbeth and Elane settle on the chaise longue with their needlework, and Corah, who wouldn't dream of arriving early for a music lesson, enters two minutes past two o'clock—which is to say, punctual enough to avoid a lecture on tardiness, but tardy enough to vex her reliably punctual instructor.

Corah remains aloof to Evyn's presence until the lesson begins in earnest. Unable to compete for her attention once the scribe's unusual mode of recording is established, Mr. Spantier moves Evyn to the low table near the chaise longue for the remainder. When the lesson concludes, Corah thanks Mr. Spantier—a social requirement which evens the playing field a bit—and parks herself at Evyn's side as he moves to stand.

Case securely held to chest, he freezes under her gaze.

"I've a dictation for you," Corah says.

"Corah," Lysbeth lilts disapproval.

"Yes?"

Lysbeth lowers her needlepoint and raises her brow.

Corah sighs. "I only want to see his hands go again. Once I'm satiated, he'll be able to record by the piano."

On further consideration, Lysbeth can't deny the reasoning. The transcriptions would be more helpful if Evyn were able to illustrate Mr. Spantier's references.

"Well, you might try asking politely," she piths.

"Fine. Would you *please* take my dictation?" Corah asks the Faye.

Without direct instruction, an uneasy moment passes before Evyn lowers the case to the table. Hesitant fingers trail to the latch. When no one voices their disapproval, he opens it and sets up. Training her eyes on his hands, Corah clears her throat and begins to pace.

To the Illustrious Alder Haywood,

The women on the chaise jar.

> *I believe it would interest you to know that a Faye now resides at Lindenholt and is currently taking my dictation. However, I regret to inform you that your descendant, Lady Lysbeth Haywood, has prevented me from requesting a demonstration of his native tongue despite your dying wish to hear it again.*
> *Condolences,*

Caught between stifled laughter and pink abashment, the older cousins watch quietly as Evyn's scratching starts again:

What would he have me say?

Corah peers over the table and resumes her pacing with a smug look to Lysbeth. "Hmm. How about... 'The Faye I loved had beautiful speech.'"

Evyn's hands and eyes move to his lap. Stacked, undulating pitches drain from his throat, "*ảo'j-re'n ̣ral'ya– ᴅda'he ͡na ͡j'at-ea.*"

Elane's eyes widen. Corah—having stopped her pacing once Evyn began—walks to him slowly now he's ceased.

Lysbeth keeps her wits. "Which is the word for Faye?"

"We do not have the word, Ladyship," he falters softly, "the one he loved was ̣ral'ya– ᴅda'he ͡na. *Ralya.*"

She bends forward on the chaise. "Is— are you saying you know the name of the Faye whom Alder loved? The one who orchestrated his return to Avonleigh?"

"The ᴐḍạ'hẹ‾ṇạ he loved was Ralya," he repeats, sinking lower.

Having developed an early fondness for Alder, Corah's interest is piqued. She follows her sister's example and leans over the table. "How do you know for certain? Was he famous?"

Four eyes now closing in, Evyn grips his left elbow. "The story is known."

"Alder did say he was the first to attempt to leave, it must've made an impression." Lysbeth brings her elbows to her knees. "What is said of them?"

"It is..." Evyn wavers, curling inward.

Throughout the Baron's tutelage were frequent, painful reminders to be neither seen nor heard, and the incongruity between prior drills and current attentions is daunting. The Baron's curriculum for interrogations, however, had been far more stringent. Evyn had earned top marks.

Pinching his arm, he swallows and tries again, "The actions of ᶻṛạl'ya–ᴐḍạ'hẹ‾ṇạ are not permitted, though the love is praised."

Elane sets down her needlepoint. "Is dah-he-nah what you call yourselves?"

"No, Your Ladyship." Evyn raises a shaky palm to his chest. "ᶻḍạ'hẹ‾ṇạ."

"He means the ones trained to be used as bait," Corah pontificates, standing from the table. "Why have you pronounced it differently?"

"Really, Corah!" Lysbeth admonishes. "*Bait*?"

"Yes, *really*! That's how Alder described them and he was among them thirty years!"

For a moment, the corners of Evyn's mouth lift.

"See?" Corah points. "He agrees."

Surprised by the development, Lysbeth leans to the side of the chaise in defeat.

"If you're quite finished?" Corah squints at her sister and returns to Evyn. "Why have you pronounced it differently?"

"Would you repeat it, Evyn? I didn't hear the difference," Elane asks.

"ᴐḍạ'hẹ‾ṇạ," he inflects, "ᶻḍạ'hẹ‾ṇạ."

"Oh, the first word began with a single voice," she says.

"There's a single voice in the second, too," Lysbeth adds, inclining slowly, "but it's difficult to discern exactly where."

"It's in the middle." Corah scoffs.

"ḥẹ."[7]

Corah's frown relaxes on viewing Evyn's expression—at least one among her current company is making an effort. Her tone lightens, "Yes. Why have you changed the pronunciation of beginning and middle if they're both the word for, 'those trained as bait'?"

Evyn attempts a concise explanation, "ᴐḍạ'hẹ‾ṇạ: beloved aria of the people.

---

[7] ˎ*One voice.* ˍ*Two voices.* ˌ*Three voices.*

ᶻ*da'he͡ na*: aegis of the people's hymn."

Corah strolls a pensive circle. "The number of voices varies the meaning?"

Evyn dips his head.

"Does the note of each voice vary the meaning, too?" she asks, pinching her chin.

He nods at his lap.

"Well?" Her hands drop. "You don't expect us to assemble it properly, do you?"

After a pause, Evyn shakes his head and parts his lips over a long breath. "The words nearby: *da*: strong-articulations: song; melody. *he*: nurtured-soul: cherish; wish." He touches his chest. "ᵛ*da'he͡ na*: a melody cherished by the people—the choir of voices who cared for us. The result of their efforts. This is our address once trained."

Elane and Lysbeth listen closely, it's the longest they've heard him speak. Brief, but noticeable, pauses between words give his cadence an unusual rhythm. Slight differences in pronunciation and inflection ripple across his mild accent. His timbre is dark and soft, and a fuzzy distortion rounds the edge of his words—most of which are produced from his throat and tongue, his lips move little.

"*da*: many-articulations: song; harmony, unity. *he*: bolstered-soul; protect, defend," he continues, briefly touching his chest again. "A nurtured voice who protected the others in turn. Who became ᶻ*da'he͡ na*: a shield for the people's harmony. This is our address at *a'ia͡ na*, the people's Keening." Foggy eyes settle near Corah's feet. "After we are Thread as bait."

The room is quiet.

Evyn was sent away so soon after his arrival, was absent for so long, and was so changed on his return. It had been easy for Elane and Lysbeth to overlook the subtext of his origins; to focus instead on the visible outcomes of the Baron's domination. It wasn't that they'd forgotten Evyn was Faye, rather, that his origins had been reduced to novel bits of trivia—perforations freckled across the Baron's looming shadow.

What they see now, through a crack in the marred surface of Evyn's shell, is a flicker of the pearl within—a soul lovingly cradled by its source, and a blunt reminder of the circumstances behind his presence: a desperate offering to Dorsit's ship in order to preserve the seclusion of Evyn's people. People who loved him and whom he loved.

People he would never see again.

The explanation given for Evyn's role is beautiful in its way, but the outcome kneeling before them is tragic. Few who saw it could question the Faye's wish for isolation. Seeing Corah is about to speak again—no doubt with further demands to be made of her new toy—Lysbeth takes pity.

"Corah, please review the notes." Ignoring her sister's pout, she continues, "Thank you for indulging us, Evyn. Corah's next lesson is two o'clock overmorrow."

Empty teacups bicker with their saucers as Ani tidies the sitting room. "I know he suffers, My Lady, but it isn't dignified," she says, placing porcelain on a tray.

"I'm afraid I agree, Lys." Elane turns to watch her cousin shuffle letters at the desk. "This is the fourth occurrence in as many weeks. He must mean to avoid tardiness."

Evyn was able to record by the pianoforte after Corah's satiation, and as his understanding of the terms and mechanisms grew, so did the succinctness of his notes. Observing some improvement in her sister's playing, Lysbeth expanded the transcriptions to subjects under the domain of Corah's governess. Though she doesn't normally monitor these lectures, she was incentivized to block Corah's Faye-solicitations after Brom reported an upswing in nightmares. Now early Aegur, servants have complained after finding Evyn napping in rooms near the lessons, and his usually neat hand has become sprawly.

Lysbeth sighs. "Alright. I'll ask Brom to speak with him next report. Surely a direct rebuff from us will only make things worse." She scans her notes and begins a wax melt. "Is there anything you'd like to send along to Granmama? I've finished Father's letter and have a few minutes before the Croran lesson."

After her grandmother's assistance with the Baron, Lysbeth felt confident enough to correct Isaac's version of last Autumn's events with her own. Avrella was receptive, and has since taken to asking after Evyn and Erem in her correspondence. Today's message arrived with an addition: a declaration of intent to meet the pair over WinterSol.

Avrella's seventy-seven-year-old joints tend to growl on long, jostling carriage rides. To avoid their barks, younger Haywoods make biannual visits to her residence at the family's Walstead estate. This year, however, as Duke and Marquess are to remain engaged in the Kingswar, Avrella's decided to grit her teeth all the way to Lindenholt.

"Have you already requested she bring Alder's letter?" Elane asks.

"Yes. I'm still angry with myself for not reading it last WinterSol."

"Don't be. Isaac is an accomplished conductor. In any event, it will be nice to have Granmama roaming Lindenholt again. It's been seven years at least."

"Nice for us, certainly. Perhaps less so for the servants." Lysbeth opens a drawer for her seal stamp and twists a devious smile on her maid. "Remind me to give you all raises."

Elane laughs. "Such a precedent would see us destitute by Spring."

"Well, you can save my raise." Ani grins as she carries the tea tray out. "I've always been quite fond of Her Grace."

Returning to the drawer, Lysbeth's gaze lands on the small packet containing Isaac's keys. Having had no clear reason to use them—and fearing what she might find if she did— she's kept them here. After sealing her messages, she replaces the stamp and pauses to push the keys further in and out of sight. As she passes the couch, Elane holds up a needlepointing basket.

"Good fortune, brave benefactress."

"Hardly." Lysbeth smiles and hooks an arm through the wicker handle.

Placing her letters on top, she moves to the hall door. A footman rounds the gallery corner as it opens. "My Lady, a bird's come."

"Oh, this one to Walstead, and this to the Kingswar Office, please," she says, exchanging notes. Leaning against the frame, she unfurls the delivered scroll and reads. Pale cheeks grow paler. "Elane." Large eyes turn to the couch. "We've an imp for AutumNox."

"You don't mean..." On her cousin's affirming cheep, Elane closes her book and sits up slowly. "I'll inform Mr. Tenson."

A wise decision. The imp in question is a foreigner of some infamy—one highly resistant to proper etiquette, and who will surely plant his nose squarely on Evyn's forehead.

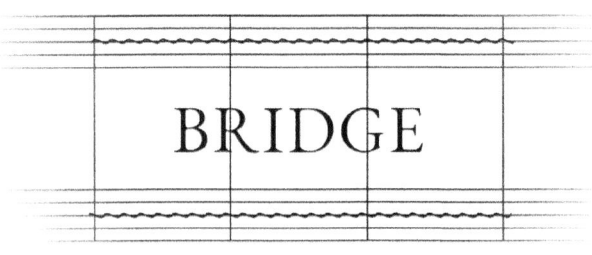

BRIDGE

*It is no wonder to me now that the Faye are referred to as Syrens by other nations, for
their deep respect of sound and music borders deification...*
-Alder Haywood-

The cousins have outlined accommodations since yesterday's news, and now head for another meeting with Mr. Tenson before Corah's music lesson.

"Temus," Lysbeth engages the footman as they traverse the eastern gallery, "please inform Marshal Brom I'd like his weekly report moved up to this afternoon. There are a few additional matters we need to discuss. And hav—" Elane's nudge interrupts.

Lysbeth follows her cousin's nod towards the Grand Chamber and pulls a draught of air through her nose. Sweaty, disheveled, and vacant, Evyn strides over marble to the gallery's parquet. The absence of an enveloped scribal case and the fore-leading of his glazed eyes have reimbursed all six-foot-four inches of his frame.

"Enjoying another snooze in the coat closet?" Temus sniggers.

Lysbeth relaxes her reproachful look before intercepting Evyn. "Good afternoo—" He brushes past the group and continues to the music room.

Unfreezing from the surprise and sting of his snub, Lysbeth spins in pursuit. She rounds the doorway as his march advances on Mr. Spantier—currently placing sheet music on the rack of the pianoforte. Confronted with the damp, brazenly-storming Faye, the instructor scoffs and retreats.

"Evyn?" Lysbeth's tone sharpens. "Evyn! Stop at once."

Evyn's left arm lifts.

Another step.

Evyn's fingers alight on the lower register.

One step more.

Evyn's weight depresses a violent chord.

He drops to the bench. Tumult erupts.

Long fingers diffuse as pale wisps on the board, weaving coarse textures on the loom of strings below the lid. The discordant cacophony collides with the refined stateliness of its setting: careening down glossy corridors to crash against carved silk couches, crisp lace curtains, and crown-molded coves.

Lysbeth's chase halts. Elane joins beside to amend her bewilderment. As Avons consider the pianoforte strictly an instrument of accompaniment, seeing it used in this way is nearly as shocking as the revelation of Evyn's ability. Soon servants amass in the gallery and bend around one another to see. Swallowing her pride, Corah pushes through the clog—trading an early arrival to her lesson for a better view as the instrument strains to keep pace with Evyn's fervor.

An exhaustive tempo persists through dissonant changes in pitch and timbre. The melody is heedless, though, much like its composer, the emotions it imparts are unambiguous to its audience: Rancor, aversion. Affliction, despair. Seven minutes of silent gawking and raucous playing pass before his fingers lift, suspending unresolved chords.

Beads of sweat on his brow threaten to dash themselves on the monochrome landscape below. Shaky and short of breath, he stares at the back of his ink-specked hands. The mist in his vision recedes—and accompanying the clarity is the realization of what he's done. His fingers curl into white knuckles. Jittering adrenaline is exchanged for trembling dread. Afraid to look up, he lowers his fists, and silently awaits his sentence.

Lindenholt's Ladies look to one another and back.

Evyn remains still.

Dropping her shoulders, Lysbeth walks to the chaise. Her voice is clear and calm as she sits, "Another, please."

Corah and Elane follow. On the way, a glance from the latter sends servants to open the room's partition. Mr. Spantier—once peeled from the wall—opens the pianoforte's cover and scurries to an ottoman.

⁊Evyn swallows as the commotion fades, returning unstrung fingers to the keys.

~~~~~~~~~~~~~~~~~~~~~~~

Brom wears a rare smile. Lysbeth strolls beside, watching stable boys prepare stalls for Lindenholt's guest. "If he's had a terror, it hasn't woken me in over a week. The playing seems to make a difference," the Marshal reports. "I hope he'll be allowed to continue, Your Ladyship."

A mild guilt chafes her ribs. On discovery of Evyn's pianism, she'd encouraged him to play in his free time. Once his diffidence yielded to her persistence, he began to play daily. The Faye's ambidextrousness and keen memory serve his compositions in much the same way as his recording—astounding speeds, precise clarity, and improvised arrangements that put Avonleigh's composers to shame. In her excitement, however, Lysbeth had failed to consider the draw his music would have on their upcoming visitor.

"I don't *want* to prevent his playing. Perhaps I'll explain my concerns and let him decide."

"Reasonable."

"High praise." She smiles. "Thank you for the update, Marshal."

Returning to the house, a hauntingly beautiful melody greets her in the vestibule. She slinks down the gallery to the music room's open door.

The melody stops. Lysbeth scowls at a squeaky floorboard.

Knowing he won't pick up again, she alters course from chaise to instrument. Evyn stands and holds a wrist behind his back, moving his eyes to the lower keyboard as she appears alongside.

"Evyn, next week the Duke of Gyenna will be coming through for a visit before his trip north. He's" —she searches for an appropriate word— "an eccentric."

The eccentric Duke, Jaques Vippon, is also the illegitimate prince of Crora: southern neighbor to Avonleigh, border-mate of Edenshire county, and whose populace the Haywoods are obliged to keep good relations.

Born to Crora's Sovereign and the widowed Duchess of Gyenna, social prescriptivism had declared Jaques' existence an affront before he'd been given the chance to earn the reputation for himself. Unable to forgive the slight, his revenge manifested as a performative personality—one guaranteed to increase his infamy with each open agitation of polite society. Lysbeth's father first arranged to meet the young Jaques when he'd come of age ten years ago. While he was not terribly impressed by the boy's antics, Lysbeth found them to be a pleasant change of pace.

"You see, he'll demand to meet you if he hears your playing, and I must warn, he can be quite" —she squints, thinking again— "assertive."

Evyn's head lowers.

"I'll leave the decision to you."

"Yes, Ladyship."

She moves to leave as a thought arrives. "I wonder, how quickly could you learn to play another instrument?"

His mouth opens and closes.

Well-acquainted with one-sided conversations, she answers herself, "Yes, I suppose it would depend on the instrument. There's someone I'd like you to meet."

After bustling to the door for a summons, she rejoins Evyn and takes a peek. Though he could still use a bit more filling, he's no longer gaunt. His hair has grown back to his ears, and the sleepless discoloration under his eyes has diminished. A marked improvement.

"I think you'll like Konja," she says, placing her hands on the pianoforte's lid. "He's our quintet leader, and quite knowledgeable regarding percussion and strings. I found him playing in an inn on our way to Walstead three years ago and hired him on the spot. Though I'm afraid his talents are largely kept to holidays." She glances at the row of chairs stacked against the far wall. A neglected harp in the corner echoes their vacancy. "In any case, he should find your compositional and performance techniques refreshing. Most music produced in Avonleigh has remained unchanged for many centuries."

¶In fact, most of the world's music—like most of the world—has seen little innovation.

"We seem to enjoy making a spectacle of music, but rarely encourage its progress."

¶Incidentally, the last major musical innovation arose from the small, sea-faring nation of Corburg Five-hundred years ago.

"Likely owing to our dependence on the comforts of tradition." She smirks.

¶The Corburg technique—a polyharmonic progression—enjoyed notable popularity just before the country's fall.

"Perhaps your being here might loosen the corner cobwebs."

Evyn remains still.

Before too long, a hop-skip comes from the gallery. A shorter man wearing a bright, wide grin pivots around the doorframe and stops.

"My Lady!" he blares, arms forward, fingers splayed.

"Konja." Lysbeth's chuckle pulls her chin down. "How are you?"

"I am well, My Lady!" He enters, flexing fingers in her direction. "Now that I see you!"

"Goodness. If your wellbeing relies on the sight of me, I'll be sure to call for you more often."

"Yes!" Konja hoots. "Please do, My Lady!"

Lysbeth shakes her head fondly. "Konja, I'd like to introduce you to Evyn. He's a new scribe with us. You may have heard of him?"

"Yes! I have, My Lady!" Konja steps lively to the pianoforte's free side and leans in to evaluate the tall, solemn figure. "Greetings! I am Konja!" After a beat, he brings a palm to his chest and bows slightly. "Of the nation of Antsu."

The Faye's head dips shyly to the upper register.

"Evyn shares your appreciation of music, though he's unfamiliar with some of our instruments." Lysbeth's smile widens at Konja's mounting excitement. "I hoped you might be willing to give him a few lessons in guitarra?"

Konja's grin attempts to escape the bounds of his face. "Yes!" he declares, tapping the piano with each syllable, "Of course! My Lady!"

"Wonderful, thank you. And Evyn, if Erem's aversion to instruments extends to guitarra, you're welcome to continue using the music room. Otherwise, the grounds are open to you, so long as there are no complaints."

Evyn pulls on his wrist. Tentative lips part under key-locked eyes. "Thank you, Ladyship."

The sincerity in his soft timbre catches Lysbeth flatfooted. As she sorts through responses in the lurch, Konja scoops the air with his arms.

"Come! Come! I have much to show you! And you, me!"

Lingering eyes brush Lysbeth's hand before Evyn trails the enthusiastic voice to the door.

"Do you know! My people have a tale of Mama Wati. She appeared as two water spirits wrapped in snakes of mirrors! Reflected women! And a beautiful guivre[8] between. They came to our shores on the back of a whale with silver wings..."

Lysbeth listens as Konja's voice fades from the gallery, slowly pulling the fallboard over the keys.

~~~~~~~~~~~~~~~~~~~
~~~~~~~~~~~~~~~~~

---

[8] *Mythical, wyvern-like creatures of conflicting temperament said to reside in bodies of water.*

AUTUMN

Of the land I will say only this: ...the utterly unique flora and
fauna it bore could not have come from any other scape...
-Alder Haywood-

Mr. Tenson holds forward two sheets of parchment as he clicks across the Grand Chamber to Lysbeth—whose plans to sneak out before supper have been waylaid in the vestibule.

"The Gold Room has been fully prepared for tomorrow evening, Your Ladyship. Here are the AutumNox menus and shopping lists for your final approval." He passes the pages and continues as she skims, "Ms. Makensi seemed to recall Lady Gina's trouble with leeks and has suggested an alternative. Additionally, Marshal Brom asks if the gelding is still to be placed in the forward pasture for His Grace's arrival."

She nods to the lists and returns them. "Yes, I think it will catch his eye well there."

Now that the gelding has calmed, Lysbeth hopes to sell it. Fortunately, the Duke's love of horses is second only to his love of spectacle—and as the gelding is both, he's sure to make a generous offer.

"Very good, My Lady. Another matter: the Duke's steward felt obliged to inform us that His Grace will be accompanied by ten servants, rather than the reported three. Shall I have the spare attic rooms arranged?"

Lysbeth smiles. "Yes, but let's put on a good show for him. You know he longs to catch us unaware."

"I'll have the scullery maids perform a few panicked laps around the court, My Lady."

"Thank you, Mr. Tenson." She folds her hands and nods in mock-earnestness.

Finally free, she makes her way to the kitchen block's court. A guitarra tune sharpens as she enters the greenhouse and peeks into the gardens. Ms. Pinley sits knitting on the stone bench. Erem sits in Evyn's cross-legged lap as he plays the guitarra like a cello against his shoulder. Konja sits on a crate, providing percussion and keeping impressive step with Evyn's frequent changes in color and tempo—which occur after gestures from Erem.

The Faye's long fingers reach over the fretboard with ease to maintain multiple layers of harmony, and the instrument's unusual positioning is accompanied by equally unusual utilizations: quickly twisting pegs to warp pitches of played chords, patting strings for tinny resonance, and adding complex percussion along the body and neck between notes. Though it's only been a short time, Konja has credited Evyn's masterful playing to an advanced knowledge of music which condensed his learning from years to days once he understood the structure of intervals between strings and frets.

Happy with the results of her introductions, and pleased to know Evyn will be spared unnecessary attention, Lysbeth quietly returns to the house.

~~~~~~~~~~~~~~~~~~~~~~~~~~

The following evening, Lindenholt's servants assemble on the north terrace for the Duke of Gyenna's arrival. Knowing he won't abide by a formal announcement from Mr. Tenson, the Edenshire Ladies await their guest just outside the vestibule entrance.

Loud muttering in Croran joins a quick succession of clicks on the steps. A few more clicks see a handsome young man with dark eyes and light hair hop to the landing.

"Ysbet. My family's jewels for the charger?" Jaques' performance begins with a new record: four rules of etiquette broken in only seven words.

Lysbeth stifles a smile and lifts her chin. "That depends. Have you brought them with you?"

"Oh, yes." Jaques sidles up to his hostess and thrusts his hips. "They are with me always." When the servant's assembly shuffles, he removes his glove to reveal heavily-jeweled fingers.

En Garde, Lysbeth retains her poise and motions to the vestibule. "We will certainly discuss it. Welcome to Lindenholt, *Your Grace, Most Noble Duke of Gyenna.*" When he draws breath to riposte, she swings her palms forward and parries, "I must address you properly at least once, Jaques."

Owning the hit, Jaques smirkles[9] and swaggers through the door. "Enson! Where is my welcome wine!?"

Past the vestibule, Mr. Tenson steps into view holding a tray. "Your Grace."

"Enson, you are a very good man. Why will you not come work for me, hm? I employ only the most beautiful maids," Jaques says, relieving the tray of its solitary glass. "Footmen, hounds, horses. Whatever you prefer." He sips and walks further into the Chamber.

Lysbeth enters with an apologetic smile to the stone-faced butler. "Jaques, will you allow us to fill your belly with something substantial? Or shall we move to the drawing room bar directly?"

The Duke begins a slow heel spin. "I will meet you halfway, Ysbet, and sit at your table

---

[9] *A friendly smile-smirk.*

to drink." When his spin points to the western gallery's dining parlor, he pushes off.

Lysbeth keeps her laugh to her nose and follows with Elane and Corah in tow. They arrive at the parlor to find the Duke has already acquainted himself with a chair—to the side of the table instead of the end—and is quickly draining his glass. Once the Ladies are seated, a parade of footmen and platters begins around the table.

"Save some for AutumnNox, Jaques," Elane ribs. "We're expecting Gina and Marium. They'll be put out if you empty the cellar before they're able to lend their aid."

"Only two guests? Why so few, hm?" Jaques tilts his head down. "I have heard of your little game. You want me for yourself, Lane?"

The game, Kiss or Tell, is something of a tradition among bored, young Ladies. Players are given a choice: answer any question truthfully, or kiss a third party—usually a footman sworn to secrecy. A win-win scenario, as the former ensures a healthy production line at the rumor mill, while the latter ensures your companions' diversion at the small cost of your own miserable time. Its secrecy isn't fool-proof—as most players are fools themselves—but on the few rare occasions word of the game has reached a father or brother's ears, its role as tradition has been its players' saving grace.

The truthful answer to Jaques' question is less salacious—Gina and Marium are the only people Lysbeth trusts to conceal Faye rumors from the Duke.

"Whatever you've heard is greatly exaggerated, I'm sure," Elane says, returning serving utensils to a footman's platter.

"Indeed. Certainly you're capable of recognizing a wanton bluster when you hear one, Jaques, having so refined the art of it yourself, that is." Lysbeth constricts a smile as Jaques' lips struggle to contain both amusement and wine. "We felt it appropriate to keep the festivities restrained, given news of our men remaining North for WinterSol this year."

Jaques swallows and groans. "Oh, this Kin'swar of yours. It's taking so long, no? It is exhausting to me, always having to hear of it. And now your Sovereign wants me to fund it." His face twists in revulsion, but quickly reverts to imbibe the remainder of his cup. "Look at me, I've become a carouser."

"Become?" Lysbeth quips, transferring a portion of meat to her plate. "The Kingswar has only been on seventeen months, Jaques. How do you explain the previous half-dozen years?"

"The previous?" Jaques smolders across the table. "Drink is the only balm for my long-suffered, unrequited love, Ysbet." He extends his glass to the footman behind him. The footman pours. When his arm remains, the footman pours again.

"Jaques," Lysbeth lilts.

"Yes, my darling?" He rolls his head above a precariously full glass.

"The cloud around you is evidence of your own intoxication, not the effect you are having on others." She smiles sweetly.

"Draught!" he cries. Leaning forward, he self-administers a slaking dose of salve. "Now, tell me." He pants. "How much for the horse, hm? What did you pay for it?"

Lysbeth sighs and cuts into her food. "It was a gift. One bestowed without a pedigree." Her utensils still beneath heavily-batting eyelashes. "I assume you don't mind?"

Corah pushes a green bean with her fork. "He's quite temperamental. When I first arrived, he caused weekly injury."

Elane drops her silverware to laugh in a napkin; Lysbeth's eyebrows arch innocently over a sudden captivation with her plate.

"Oh, for shame, Ysbet." Jaques' grin clucks. "Thank you, little one. I will have a closer look tonight."

~~~~~~~~~~~~~~~~~~~

Lysbeth and Elane wake early. As there aren't many fair-weather days left, and considering Jaques' state when they'd retired, the two decide to await their guest's emergence with a stroll. Moseying beneath the yellowing canopy of Lindenholt's oak drive, they look to the eastern pasture for the gelding. Unable to spot him, they step from the road and wind around shrubberies to the pasture fence—where they're confronted with an unexpected trinity lying in the center of the field.

Evyn sits against the gelding's belly and idly runs a hand over grass. Six feet across from him, Jaques lays on his side, fumbling with one of several empty bottles. The confounded Ladies make haste for the gate.

"*Ysbeeet, Laaane,*" Jaques intones as they approach. "Why did you hiding the Beauty? And *whyyy* did you trying to sell me a horse which is already being owned *hmm*?"

Lacking a cipher for his cryptic rambling, Lysbeth opts for the question most likely to receive a clear answer: "Jaques. Just how much wine have you poured down Evyn's throat?"

"No!" The Duke points—a flaccid indictment, as his wrist and palm disagree on how to get the job done. "You first, Ysbet."

Drawing a deep breath, Lysbeth motions for Evyn.

"*Nooo*! I must gaze on *heeem,*" Jaques mewls as the Faye wobbles to a kneel.

The gelding stands first and shoves his long snout under Evyn's arm. Half-hoisted, the Faye rises and nears with the assistance of his equine crutch.

"Please explain," Lysbeth says, ignoring whines from the grass.

"*ḳiʼḳyʼuṃ,*" he answers the ground softly.

Lysbeth straightens her smile and tries again, "Evyn, how have you come to be in this field with these two beasts?"

Rolling to his stomach, Jaques lifts his head and squints. "I came to see at the charger in the night and here was the Beauty. What else is it to say, hm?"

"This horse has vexed Marshal Brom for near-on eleven months, Jaques," Elane insists, "surely we're entitled to a more thorough explanation?"

Jaques starts a lunge in the Ladies' direction, landing prone again in short order. As he's closer to the group than where he'd started, he deems his locomotion a great success and celebrates by offering a thorough explanation through the dirt in his teeth.

"The Kiky was took from the Beauty"—his palm flops towards an Evyn-adjacent area—"and so here the Beauty comes at the nights to caress his secret Kiky," he mumbles, head lowering, rocking, and settling on the grass.

Evyn nods solemnly to the soil supporting Jaques' face.

The Ladies' hind-sighted stares meet: an unusual horse and a Faye had appeared at Lindenholt only hours apart. The leap was a short one. Lysbeth curses Dorsit again.

"I don't suppose you planned on telling us?" she asks.

Generally, Lysbeth doesn't pose questions to Evyn because she expects to receive a useful, or any, response. Rather, she feels the more times she swings the door, the more chances she gives Evyn to walk through. Now, with the assistance of Jaques' liver and Lindenholt's wine, the threshold is finally crossed.

"*k'uah ̄ni*." He strokes the horse's neck through a quiet reply, "I did not think the words could matter. Please forgive me, Ladyship."

Lysbeth fills her lungs and grins. "A fair assumption, all things considered. And I've nothing to forgive, though Brom might appreciate the gesture."

Evyn nods.

"Does the Duke know of your origins?"

"I am uncertain." He glances at the haphazard body. "The message might drown in the bottle."

The cousins exchange an amused look. "His name is Kie-key?" Elane asks.

"*ki'ky*. Kikyum, Your Ladyship."

Shortened to two syllables, the pronunciation resembles layered whistles, and as a full pronunciation requires three voices, Elane doesn't fret over getting it just right. "Hello, Kie-key-room. May I?"

Evyn performs a series of hand gestures to the horse before nodding at Elane's feet. She approaches extending a cautious hand. Kikyum presses his nose into it and inhales deeply.

"After learning Erem's name and your title I must ask, is there any special meaning to Kikyum?" Lysbeth probes.

"Yes, Ladyship. The words nearby are 'shadow-departed': *One so swift they have departed their shadow*." He strokes Kiky's mane as he lulls. "Occasionally, it is also: *One so unsavory their shadow departs them*. He can be both," he adds shyly.

Lysbeth laughs. "He certainly can."

Elane smiles at her reflection in Kikyum's dark eye.

Jaques snores.

Lysbeth peers at the drooling man. "How long had you two been sitting out?"

"I am uncertain. I came early-before the sun," he says, now petting Kikyum's withers.

"And you come every night?"

"No, Ladyship. Though, often. Just before the sun."

"At dawn? Isn't that your breakfast?" Elane asks, holding Kiky's face.

"Yes, Your Ladyship."

"I'm surprised no one has reported your absence from the servant's dining hall," Lysbeth remarks.

Evyn's posture quickly assumes the angles of abasement. Gasping, Elane hops away from the powerful hoof now striking earth.

An uncomfortable moment passes; Evyn's shaky hands come together on Kiky's coat. "This is because I am also *ki'ky'um*. Too... diff-errant." He wets his lips and pinches his fingers white in self-loathing. "When I am absent, they are spared me."

Lysbeth stiffens. She can't deny Evyn's transparency has made for several awkward exchanges—current exchange included. How is any reasonable person meant to rebound from such a blunt self-assessment? From such a willingness to acknowledge and reveal discomforting truths to others?

Unsure how to proceed, she watches the widening depression under Kikyum's hammer—earth and roots forcibly exposed, tamped, and drug out—while reexamining her questions.

Perhaps if unpleasant truths weren't buried so often, hearing them wouldn't be quite so jarring. Perhaps Evyn's transparency distresses others because it exposes the roots of their own fears—reminds them of their own precarious positions should they cross Isaac's sights. Reminds them of the Baron.

She holds out her hand. Kikyum's pawing slows as he scrutinizes her proposal. Rendering his judgment with a grunt, he drops his hoof and cups his nose with her palm. She smiles, moving closer to trace the shapes of his face with her fingertips.

"One so unsavory even their shadow departs from them," she mutters, spying the ground behind Evyn. "Curious. Yours seems quite securely fastened."

Evyn rotates slowly and lifts an arm; his grounded likeness proves its devotion.

"*ky rah*." He turns back, smiling faintly. "It is difficult to notice in the darkness."

~~~~~~~~~~~~

Jaques drops the remainder of a cucumber sandwich onto his plate. His hostesses were kind enough to serve him something tame, but a mild nausea persists despite thirty-three hours of recovery.

"I have already sworn my silence, Ysbet. If you do not call, I will wait by the charger."

Lysbeth sighs. "I'll send for Evyn if you insist, but you must promise to be gentle."

Jaques shakes his head affirmatively. "Anything for My Beauty."

She nods across the Grand Drawing Room.to an attentive Mr. Tenson.

"Also some spirit, Enson, okayplesetankyou!" Jaques cries.

"Already?" Elane tuts. "You've only just recovered."

"Milking from the cow, hm?" He leans back. "Why are you so frightened, Ysbet. You believe I cannot love you both?"

"Hair of the dog. I'm concerned, not frightened," she corrects, reaching for her tea. "And no, Jaques, I'm aware your love is boundless."

Jaques squints. "Why?"

"Why concerned? Because he's timid and you're a horseless carriage, ablaze and careening off the edge."

"No, why dog, hm? Cows have the beverage."

Elane smirks. "Would the answer change your drinking of it?"

As Jaques shrugs, the bar footman carries a tray before the Grand Chamber's archway. Under it, Evyn carries himself and a scribal box in Evyn's usual way.

Jaques points the footman to a side table. "Here to suckle the dog milk—"

Seeing Evyn, he stops and stands. Slowly, reverentially, he approaches the Faye with outstretched arms. Evyn does his best to maintain eye contact with the floor as Jaques gently lifts and guides his face to study the arcs of its sculpt in varying light.

"M-My Beauty," the Duke gasps with exaggerated awe.

"Grace," Evyn whispers.

"*Oh*! I *cannot* bear it!" Jaques throws his arms around tall shoulders and buries his face in Evyn's neck. "They tried to keep you away!" he wails.

Wearing a slight smile from the absurdity of Jaques' rolling nuzzles, Evyn remains still. Lysbeth laughs behind her hand at the Duke's well-received attentions; the pair are paradoxical.

Jaques straightens and squeezes Evyn's shoulders. "Come," he says, beginning a slow steer to the couch. "As a great admirer of art, I wish to gaze upon you from the best vantage. Sit, My Beauty. Don't be shy. I have promised to be gentle." He leans in, adding bass to his voice, "But do be a little shy, hm? It adds to your allure."

Hugging the scribal case, Evyn trains a sheepish expression on the floor and sinks to the couch's edge. Jaques hurries beside to pass recently poured dog milk from the tray.

Lysbeth suppresses her delight long enough to chide, "I doubt that's a necessary element of art appreciation."

"Then you do not properly appreciate the down of his voice, Ysbet." Noticing Evyn hasn't taken the glass, Jaques' free hand gently pulls on the scribal case. "He only speaks with drink."

Elane dons a coat of faux-concern. "Do you find art commonly speaks to you?"

"Of *cooourse*, Lane, all art speaks to me. Art speaks with the voice of its artist. If an object does not speak, it is not *aaart*," he drawls, hovering the seized scribal case over the floor and depositing the glass in Evyn's hands. "But My Beauty is *living* art, hm? And *living* art has the advantage of speaking for it*self*."

Eyebrows aloft, Jaques releases the case—a loud, clattering exclamation point on his perspective. He takes a spirit for himself and pulls the lip of Evyn's glass in pace with his own. Evyn looks to Lysbeth's feet as the drink reaches his chin. She waves her approval, and once the cups are empty, Jaques repeats the ritual. Satisfied, he returns the glasses and snuggles in the couch's corner to gaze at the exhibit.

The showpiece bashfully bites his lower lip.

"Yes." Jaques grins. "Just like this, hm?"

"It's a wonder you're permitted to leave the grounds of your own estate," Lysbeth manages through a chuckle.

"I'm charming," he purrs. "And unforgettable."

Elane rolls her eyes. "I'll grant the latter."

"Aye." Lysbeth sniffles and sets down her tea. "Is this how you spent your evening in the field? Leering at the fly in your web past dawn?"

Jaques vents a happy sigh. "We conversed as I gazed, though I do not remember most. Do you, My Beauty?"

"Some, Grace," he answers softly.

"*Oh*! The velvet!" Inhaling deeply, the Duke closes his eyes and brings a palm to his chest. "Go on, Beauty," he whispers.

"Now that you know Evyn's name it would be kind to use it," Elane scolds, taking a small dog milk for herself.

He opens an eye. "No. I cannot. The name does him no justice."

"You may be surprised. Faye names and titles are quite descriptive, from what we've heard of them." Lysbeth tucks a hand under her chin. "Though come to think of it, we've never asked after Evyn's."

"I am uncertain, Ladyship."

"Uncertain of your own name's meaning?" Elane puzzles. "But the others were so distinctive?"

"I am certain for my name, Your Ladyship." He grips his elbow. "Evyn is not..."

"W—" Lysbeth starts.

"Ah! As I say!" Jaques interjects, scrambling across the seat. "You must tell us the name that befits you," he urges, now nearly in the lap of his couch mate.

"I was addressed as ꞃerru⁀wyn–ꝁda'he⁀na." The Faye smiles as he's jostled further over the seat's edge. "Does Grace wish me lower?"

"No, I will not let you fall, my darling, come to me." Already joined at the hip, Jaques embraces his Beauty and pulls him in. "Once again?"

"ꞃerru⁀wyn. Erruwyn."

"Air-do-when," Jaques repeats along a lustful sigh.

Lysbeth scowls. "Why in heaven's name did Dorsit introduce you as Evyn?"

"I believe the name was given by those I greeted on the vessel, Ladyship," he says softly. "The sounds of celebration were too great."

"Animals." Jaques clucks. "Why did you not correct them, hm?"

"It was not known to me, Grace. I was not addressed. I learned at harbor, already with *ax'ni͡ rah*."

Elane straightens. "You were never spoken to on the ship?"

"Only occasions of command, Your Ladyship. Without address."

Jaques lays on Erruwyn's shoulder and rocks. "Beasties. Why not correct at land?"

"He didn't speak when he arrived," Lysbeth explains, swallowing the laugh in her throat.

Erruwyn smiles faintly as he's swayed. "*ax'ni͡ rah*. A time of silence to observe the Outland's words. To amend understanding before speech. To respect."

The Ladies share a glance—his earliest gestures suggested something similar, but confirmation puts the tired question to bed.

"Why not correct after you speak?" Jaques continues.

Erruwyn laces his fingers as a grate against the Baron's image. "It could not matter."

"Of course it matters," Elane says. "Would you repeat it? I'd like to get it right."

"Erruwyn."

"Ear-do-win?" Lysbeth tests. "Arrow-when?"

"It is that which you prefer, Ladyship."

Jaques slows his rocking embrace. "Now tell how it expands your beauty."

"Yes, Grace." He smiles at the floor. "*erru͡ wyn: a light-reflecting-mist of dusk*. A bridge of light appearing in mist. At dusk."

"Yes," Jaques whispers, returning to Erruwyn's shoulder, "yes."

"Bridge of light? A rainbow?" Lysbeth asks.

"When color is absent. White, only," he clarifies.

"A fogbow!" Elane sits up. "They're quite lovely. Uncommon, though. We've seen them at Walstead now and again, do you recall, Lysbeth?"

"Yes, of course! But the last must've been four years gone, at least." She presses a knuckle to her chin and finds her memory on the ceiling. "And it appeared some time shortly after noon. I distinctly recall because I had to change my dress for tea after stepping onto a muddy lane to view it. Do they only occur at dusk in your homeland, Erruwyn?"

"No, Ladyship. Dusk, *wyn*, because I prefer night's shelter. I am quiet, also." He lulls, watching his hands flex. "My twiceborn. Shared-soul. My sibling emerging with me."

"Twin?" Lysbeth suggests.

He nods in deference. "She is *erru͡ wan– da'he͡ na. Erruwan*. Light-reflecting-mist of dawn. She is as the waking day. Bright. Lively."

Jaques' neck erects. "There is another of you? A *woman!*?" he cries, grip tightening.

Erruwyn smiles, squished. "Yes. We are twins among the people, Grace."

"You mean, each of you has a twin? All the Faye?" Elane asks.

"Yes, only occasionally onceborn among us, Your Ladyship."

Jaques gasps and rolls his head on Erruwyn's shoulder, releasing a loud, protracted moan.

"*feu'n'en*," Erruwyn whispers, laughing silently through his nose.

~~~~~~~~~~~~~~~~~~

"Really, Jaques. It's only three days over Equinox," Lysbeth admonishes. "You've spent two weeks with him already."

"I am a Duke! How else to act?" Jaques tears a leaf from a bush as the two stroll along a wooded path on Lindenholt's grounds. "I already must wait for the scrivener and the recordings. Now you want to take my entire treat away. Of course I kick and scream."

"You've remarkable fortitude to endure such injustice." She smiles at the wildflower in her fingers. "You know I enjoy watching the two of you—you've had a positive effect, to my extreme astonishment—but Gina and Marium were present when Erruwyn arrived. They'll surely ask for an explanation once they see how he's changed. I'd prefer not to give one."

Jaques shrugs. "So do not give one."

"That's not the only reason. Erruwyn truly does get very anxious. You had the good fortune of becoming acquainted with him privately." Lysbeth glances with cheerful disapproval. "In my pasture. With my wine. It's different for the rest of us."

"You are like a mother, Ysbet."

"I suppose I am. I don't see why else I should be tolerating your tantrums."

She swings her arms and looks into the woods. The air is crisply scented with drying leaves. Tree roots burrow into earth across the forest floor—submersed stability clutching at life. The image returns her to Kikyum's hoof uprooting truths in the pasture. She'd side-stepped Jaques' meaning to keep her own discomforting truths buried.

Her gaze meanders back to Jaques. "Truth be told, I do feel responsible. I *am* responsible, at least partially, for his being here and for what's happened. It's only right that I should look after him properly."

"Mm. And what will become of Erruwyn when your brother returns?"

"I don't know. It seems so far away. Hopefully his workshop contributions will prevent Isaac's going after him."

"But Isaac does not truly need a reason, does he."

They continue in pensive silence.

Jaques learned of Isaac's nature while hosting the Haywood men at his estate seven years prior. His servants didn't whisper about the Marquess' behavior as their Lindenholt counterparts do. Instead, they'd gone directly to their young master—who'd hidden his knowledge to avoid diplomatic fallout, but taken inconspicuous measures to protect his people all the same.

He stops and turns to his hostess. "Ysbet, I have been thinking."

"Oh? What's the occasion?" she pokes, reclining against a tree.

His smile is brief. "These negotiations for aid in Avonleigh's Kin'swar. Before I meet with your Sovereign, I suspect your father and brother will attempt to sit on the scale—bribe me with your hand to ensure a favorable outcome for their liege."

Lysbeth stares at the chamomile in her fingers. She'd thought as much herself, but never expected she'd be given the opportunity to discuss it. Another uprooted truth, one leading to the next.

"And I was thinking also, if you felt this to be unacceptable, I could counter and ask to take Erruwyn away with me instead. For them, I think, one chattel is as good as any another, hm? They would not question too deeply." He clasps his hands behind his back and bends forward at the waist. "What is your opinion?"

Her stomach sinks. "Truthfully, I'd prefer you over most, Jaques. But once the fighting ceases, there's bound to be another suitor of amiable-enough disposition." She spins the flower slowly. "I don't *want* Erruwyn to go, mind, but your offer would be of significantly greater benefit to him—assuming you took Erem, too."

"Of course, I would not separate them." He turns to stroll again. "But if you feel this way, Ysbet, I might be able to secure all three of you with enough patience."

"You mean, decline me now to strengthen your position once Sovereign Hinri is more desperate?" she asks, moving from the tree.

"Yes, he was a fool to start this conflict. I will be summoned again before it ends. Another year, maybe?"

Lysbeth looks further down the path. "Then, on behalf of those here affected, I accept."

~~~~~~~~~~~~~~~~~~

The moment Gina and Marium depart, Duke, Faye, and gelding assemble on the stone court for a demonstration of Erruwyn's gestures. Lysbeth observes the trio from her morning room window as she fiddles with the black and silver box.

"I can't seem to tempt my mind away from Dorsit's ship," she says over her shoulder. "Can you imagine watching as your twin—a person you've known even before birth—is sacrificed to a hunting party?"

Elane joins her cousin from the couch. "It's difficult enough for me to imagine having a sibling, never mind a twin. You're the closest, Lys."

"I'm honored. Now, imagine me drifting towards a boat of cheering brutes never to be seen again."

"No, thank you."

"Precisely. They must have such conviction." Lysbeth hikes her brow. "Though if, '*Only male Dahena are offered to spare our sisters forced impregnation,*' doesn't stir your sense of conviction, I'm not sure what would."

"Yes." Elane laughs. "That was quite a shock to hear."

"Well, it's rather a ticklish subject, isn't it? Otherwise 'brood ewe' wouldn't need dressing up with 'wifely duty'."

"Aye. Their reasoning isn't flawed." Elane glimpses the box. "Will you ask Erruwyn about that now? He's more willing to discuss his home with Jaques around."

"With spirit around, you mean."

"They've slowed their guzzling, you know. And you must consider, Jaques grew up rebelling against our way of doing things, and Erruwyn grew up without knowing our way of doing things." Elane looks to the court and stretches her neck. "There's a large middle ground to meet on, I think, even if it began as an island in spirit's ocean."

Lysbeth regards her cousin fondly. "You may be right. As usual. After the Baron, I'm not sure anyone at Lindenholt could've reached Erruwyn the way Jaques has."

On the court, Kikyum responds to Erruwyn's gesture with an impressive, spinning buck. A dampened yelp reaches the Ladies as Jaques holds his temples and staggers a melodramatic circle around the Faye.

"Well, I hope you decide soon," Elane says, breathing a laugh. "Erruwyn might close off again once his Fe— what did Jaques say his new name was?"

"Fee-yoo-nen. He can't be trusted to relay an accurate translation, but something or other involving spikes."

"Well, once his Feunen departs."

"I suppose so. I'll think on it," she says, tapping the box's silver tendrils. Movement near the front steps draws her attention. "There's Corah. Shall we join?"

"Yes, let's."

The cousins make their way to the terrace where—after finger-wagging Corah's step-sitting—Lysbeth calls for chairs. Soon the Ladies are watching comfortably as Erruwyn turns away from Kikyum to show Jaques a gesture: laying thumb over palm and lowering his hand.

"He will bow. Offer a knee to mount," he explains.

Jaques jabs fingers upward. "Yes?"

"It is only one hand, flat, ¿*feu'n'en*?"

"This, hm?" He cups the air.

"Only... flat."

"Hm?" Jaques pumps his forearm back and forth.

Grinning, Erruwyn points to Kiky. "Yes, ¿*feu'n'en*."

Jaques turns sawing the air. Kikyum is on them in an instant—a prancing barrier keeping perfect step with the Duke's clumsy attempts to reach Erruwyn again.

"You've underestimated them!" Elane laughs.

Jaques waves her off through another failure to out-circle the steed and moves to tunnel beneath it. When four fetlock-ed bars realign to cage the way, Jaques grips his knees in defeat. Kikyum's high trot vaunts past.

"Please do not despair, ¿*feu'n'en*," Erruwyn says, bending beside. "Your mastery of grass and soil remains admirable."

He pants. "It took many years of bottles to harness my skill of the earth."

"Yes, the dedication is promising. You will match wits with fauna someday, also."

Jaques' haggard smirkle lengthens. "I think I prefer you quiet, hm?"

The Faye straightens and nods at stone.

"Well, I certainly don't." Lysbeth nears on a happy gait. "Keeping your pride contained is a taxing endeavor, Jaques, I'm grateful for the help. Have you learned anything useful?"

"No, but I didn't ask to learn, Ysbet. I asked because observing Erruwyn's hands gives me pleasure."

"I see." She juts her smile at Kikyum as he returns for nose pets. "I'd venture guitarra is a far less hazardous means of observance."

Jaques waggles his eyebrows. "Observing Kiky also gives me pleasure."

"Irredeemable. Granmama will be so disappointed to have missed you."

"Oh, Vrella. What a kitten, hm?" Jaques nudges Erruwyn. "She will love to sharpen her claws on you, I think."

"She can certainly scratch," Lysbeth mutters. "Have you shown the Marshal your gestures, Erruwyn?" she asks, seeing Brom appear from the stable block.

"Yes, Ladyship. Many *wox'ya*, the motions. I believe ¿*ki'ky'um* is forgiven."

"Indeed, he is. Lady Lysbeth, Your Grace," Brom greets on his approach. "Erruwyn, we're taking the hounds around. Northern pen?"

The Faye nods and instinctually parts his lips. Two distinct sounds exit: the squeaky hinge and clicking latch of the northern pen's gate. Ears swiveled forward, Kiky gives Erruwyn's chest a petulant shove before cantering down the drive. Erruwyn rebalances with amusement as he watches the horse's graceful leap into the pen.

"He is cross. He wished to stay," he says, returning to the group of feet on Lindenholt's court. The fixed stares of Jaques, Lysbeth, and Brom cast rigid shadows on stone. Their attention impacts—clapper to lip, chiming anxiety wrings around his chest.

"*Hm?*"

"I am sorry." Erruwyn swallows. "It is unfamiliar. Too diff-errant."

The Duke stirs the air. "*Hmmm?*"

"*aro'x*, Grace. The borrowed sounds."

"What else? What else to borrow?" Jaques' hands whisk his dumbfounded surprise into a froth of elation. "Do more, hm? More?"

"*aro'x* is any borrowed sound, *feu'n'en*. What do you wish to hear?"

"Any! Go, another!" Jaques exclaims.

"Any! Go, another!" Jaques' voice exclaims through Erruwyn's throat.

A laugh trails Lysbeth's gasp. A vague squint decorates Brom's face. Jaques' whisks unfreeze to palm Erruwyn's neck and pull him in.

Their noses bridge over a warm current of air from the Duke's lips.

"You are my waking dream," he whispers passionately.

~~~~~~~~~~~~~~~~~~~~

The party relaxes in the Grand Drawing Room on the Duke's final night, enjoying Erruwyn's guitarra composition as he plays on the floor.

A steady layering of *aro'x* emerges over the melody as Jaques—who feels the stress of a guest's demands should be inversely proportional to the remaining time of their visit—calls out animal and ambient sounds for Erruwyn to borrow. Noting a ceiling has been reached, Lysbeth ends the performance ahead of asphyxiation. Enthusiastic applause accompanies the Faye's trip to the guitarra case—and his bashful return to the couch, primed for another lunging embrace.

The Duke's gushings continue through his departure the following morning. Invited to join the servant's assembly, Erruwyn holds Erem beside the Ladies as Jaques bows to the terrace as an actor on a stage. Arising, he twines the Faye and whispers a promise to visit again before descending the steps.

A kiss pokes from Jaques compartment window as the caravan rolls north.

The assembly scatters.

Erem in his arms, Erruwyn remains still— watching the final vestiges of life drain from Lindenholt's drive.

~~~~~~~~~~~~~~~~~~~~
~~~~~~~~~~~~~~~~~~~~

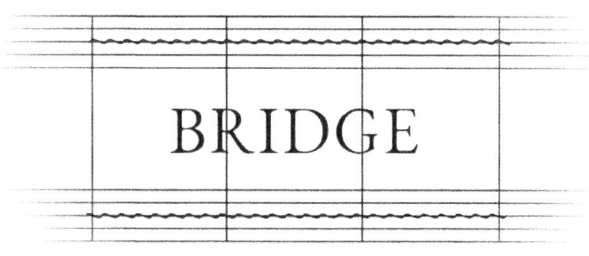

BRIDGE

I would soon come to learn of the special reverence they hold for
their hair, as below the brow they have none.
-Alder Haywood-

"It's decided. I'm going to ask about the box," Lysbeth declares to her dressing room reflection. "You'll recall we're surrounded by mirrors," she adds, catching Ani and Elane's cagey smile.

"I'm sorry, My Lady." Ani grins. "It's only I'd given up hope."

"Well, I'm quite resolved. It's been over a fortnight since Jaques' departure and Erruwyn hasn't reverted as we'd feared. Brom reports no terrors, and even Erem has been steady for the last month." She passes a hairpin. "In any event, if I've no answers for Granmama when she arrives next week, I'll never hear the end of it."

"And if you don't have an answer, *we'll* never hear the end of it," Elane says. "You'll find no arguments here, Lys. By all means, ask."

Lysbeth's nod slows and tilts. "But perhaps we haven't consider—" She blinks to Ani's giggle and then to Elane's suspended eyebrows. "Alright, you're welcome to hold me to it."

"Oh?" Elane brightens. "Then, shall we?"

Lysbeth blanches.

"Thank you, Ani!" Elane laughs, dragging Lysbeth to the gallery. Directing a summons to Temus, she continues to the front drawing room and nudges Lysbeth to a couch. "Now, it's been a year, Lys. I know you're concerned about dredging up the past, and I know you fear nothing in the box could satisfy you, but surely any answer is better than none— certainly better for those who must hear your repeated musings on the subject, in any case."

Lysbeth sits tall. "Yes. Agreed. And if he doesn't want to answer, we'll simply put the whole matter to bed and waste no more time on it," she assures herself, quite convincingly.

Agonizing minutes pass before Erruwyn and his scribal case arrive. Unable to think of a way to begin, Lysbeth knocks on her cousin's wrist for help as they stand. Unfortunately, she finds none, as Elane has recently learnt future dredging-of-the-past and present dredging-of-the-past are quite different prospects.

Lysbeth clears her throat. "Good morning, Erruwyn. I—That is, do you recall the box you brought to my sitting room?" She grimaces as the words slip; he'd recall in greater detail than she ever could.

He hugs the case. "Yes, Ladyship."

"Right. I suppose I meant, well, that I've kept it."

"It assists with the dressing of hair," he says, shifting his weight and eyeing the floor. "I will open it, if you wish, Ladyship."

Lysbeth blinks. Over the previous year, she'd imagined dozens of possible contents—built up and torn down a host of grand reveals—but Erruwyn has explained and offered before she'd even had to ask. She should've known he'd sweep the topsoil aside and deliver the truth, despite his obvious discomfort.

"Yes, if you don't mind?"

"I will open," he repeats faintly.

"Thank you," her response is nearly as faint. "Please, join us."

Leading the group down the gallery, Lysbeth trusses her thoughts as a frame of reference for her feelings. The box's contents had become secondary to its means of unlocking, yet Erruwyn's answer had evaporated the giddy anticipation of her curiosity. She revisits her first glimpse of the Faye's beautifully decorated hair. Two days later, he'd arrived at her apartments carrying a box—a hair dressing box. He'd held out his hand; she'd loosened a curl.

The sitting room door appears.

She rests her fingers on the handle and glances at Erruwyn. He looks sorrowful. Haunted. Her curiosity fell victim to his delivery, not his answer.

"Would you care to give us a demonstration?" she asks. "If your fingers fly over tresses as they do strings and parchment, I'm sure it's quite an event."

When a lighter expression nods to her feet, she smiles and ushers the group through the door. Hearing their entry from Lysbeth's bedchamber, Ani skitters to the dressing room for a clandestine view of the proceedings.

"I can't tell you how many times I've tried to solve its mysteries," Lysbeth says, pulling the box forward on the vanity. "And these chains atop—short, middle, long—converging on this disc. I'm sure you wore something like it between your ear and horn ornament."

"Yes, it is *>m-aen͡ hu'ay*: the mark of vocal mastery, Ladyship. We wear it as in your memory when *ᴜay'ena* is present." He covers his lower face with a palm. "Silver-plated mouth."

Elane leans against the vanity. "So, they're the same chains after all?"

"Yes, Your Ladyship." Erruwyn makes a move forward and hesitates. At Lysbeth's encouraging nod, he sets down the scribal case and lifts the center disc. After a slight resistance, it comes away with three attached chains—each ending in their own small disc. "Without *ᴜay'ena*, it is worn so."

He snaps *>m-aen͡ hu'ay*'s central disc to the cartilage guarding his left ear canal.

Lysbeth gasps. "A magnet?"

He nods, snapping the shortest chain to the end of his left eyebrow.

"Another? And their mates are beneath your skin?"

"Yes, Ladyship." The disc of the middle chain hops beside his nostril.

"How many are there?" Elane asks, bewildered.

"Many, Your Ladyship." The longest chain's disc springs under his bottom lip.

"Extraordinary." Lysbeth's eyes dart across his features. "I thought perhaps they were some kind of handle, but they're so fine I'd been afraid to pull them. Why had you placed them on the box?"

"They are used to articulate *ay͡na.*" Kneeling before the vanity, Erruwyn snaps >*m-aeṇ͡hu'ay*'s shortest chain to his throat and its longest chains to wide intersections of silver near the container's feet.

The women jump as the chain "Y" snugs in the air and the box's silver begins to animate—a serpentine crawl of tendrils telescoping into themselves at creases along their piping. As the metal retracts, four faces of shiny black wood are pulled away, and three onlooking faces gawk—Lysbeth's face the gawkiest of all.

After months of drafting mental blueprints, she'd concluded the lid's hinges were internal for security, but in fact there are no hinges of any kind. Each face is an independent panel, rooted with silver piping, and set into motion to materialize a handsome caddy.

The front face now rests at a forty-five-degree angle to the vanity, and a row of silver tools fasten neatly across it. The side faces, now swung out, host small drawers. The top face continues a vertical line with the back face and sports hooks from which dangle an assortment of chains and decorative items.

Lysbeth tempers her breath. "By what mechanism is this made possible?" she manages.

Erruwyn detaches >*m-aeṇ͡hu'ay* from its anchors. "Please forgive me, Ladyship. *ᵥda'he͡na* are permitted only to know the essentials of *ay͡na,* our silver." He trails the chains with a finger as he explains, "Primal pitches walk the silver path. Deliver their song to *ay͡na.*" His finger lands on an intersection at the box's base. "Vibrations[10] grow within. *ay͡na* resonates, articulates its response as anima."[11]

The room is silent.

Lysbeth brings a hand to her mouth and snorts.

"Lys!" Reserves of shock running low, Elane joins her cousin's laugh.

---

[10] *Acoustic energy; kinetic mechanical energy produced by sound waves.*
[11] *Vital, animating force.*

"I'm sorry!" She laughs harder. "I was so worried I'd be disappointed, or that I'd have missed something obvious. But naturally your people have *living silver*," she says, accepting a fresh handkerchief from Ani. Dabbing her eyes, she laughs again.

Erruwyn chews his smile.

"Do you mean to say your voice traveled along the chain, Erruwyn?" Elane asks.

When he nods, Lysbeth sniffles and checks with the others. "But we didn't hear you make any noise?"

"Yes, Ladyship. Outlanders cannot hear or sing Ʂm'aꬼn, the primal pitches of our song. Though Ʂm'aꬼn's texture can be felt with ay⌐na." He reattaches the short chain to his throat and hands the longer chains to Lysbeth.

After a pause, she gasps and drops them.

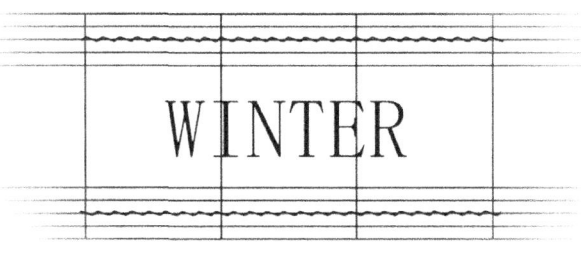

WINTER

*Physical affection, courting, and coupling are openly encouraged
and this, too, they say, brings harmony...*
-Alder Haywood-

Lysbeth holds a mirror behind her head to study her hair in a sitting room vanity. Volume added to her hairline flatters her attractive features, and a series of wide plaits weave together as elegant, self-supported knotwork at the back. The style is unique, but not so out of place as to cause alarm among Avonleigh's traditionalist populace.

She pivots her head again. "I'm sorry, Ani. After three days, it's no fluke. I'm afraid you've been surpassed."

"I can see that, My Lady." Folding arms behind her, Ani steps under Erruwyn and throws her head back. In such close proximity, he can't avoid looking at her without considerable effort. She'd discovered this over their last few mornings in the sitting room, and now delights in using his towering face as an awning for her petite frame. "Do all your people dress hair as you do, Erruwyn? Or are Dahena specifically trained to put Lady's maids out of work?"

He directs a shy smile to her chin. "Hair has meaning among the people, Ani. Growth of thought, dreams, experience. All celebrate with dressing."

"Well then I won't take offense," she says, sliding away to giggle at his bashful shifting.

Chuckling at the scene, Elane shoos her cousin away for her own turn. Lysbeth moves to the writing desk, opening a message from Avrella as she observes Erruwyn work. Learning of his ability to utilize sounds beyond her own people's range of hearing had been a remarkable revelation. Fayetales ascribe a number of outrageous abilities to the Faye, but variations of telekinesis are among the oldest common threads. While she still doesn't understand how vibrations and magnets animate metal, the demonstration grounded the myths in reality.

She smiles as he lifts a silver tool one might reasonably refer to as a comb—if combs had teeth on either edge, a pronged tip, and a collapsible handle—and parts Elane's light brown hair for a plait. Though less momentous, his dressings were another impressive discovery. He works with the confidence of an artist intimately familiar with their medium. If the statue is within the stone, Erruwyn's dressings are a matter of silhouette screens: he already saw the result, he simply needed to place the lock.

He finishes the plait with one hand and secures it in hair pulled taut against Elane's scalp. At the braid's satisfying conclusion, Lysbeth turns her attention to the unfolded message. A moment later, she gasps and clutches the rim of her bodice.

"Granmama reports Alder's letter missing! She writes her people will deliver it to Lindenholt by hand if it's found." She flips the page. "By the date, this was sent just before her departure from Walstead." Dropping both hands to her lap, she wheels her distress on Elane. "Didn't Isaac ask after it over WinterSol? Surely he'd have fussed if it were gone?"

Elane flicks her eyes to the desk. "Yes, I happened upon him copying passages from it in the study."

Fresh fuel catches on a flushed furnace. "To what end!?" Lysbeth flares. "Alder's story is unknown outside the family, and Isaac has never cared for any of it!"

Erruwyn's fingers stagnate. As Lysbeth eyes him, her anger over Isaac's copying reroutes to dismay over the copy's recipient. She rises and nears, smoothing the ruffles of her voice, "What knowledge did Isaac impart on the Warden, Erruwyn?"

His answer totters on labored breathing, "*ʒḏa'ḥę͡ ꞑa*, language. Music."

The cousins cross a queasy glance in the mirror: Alder's declaration of love for the Faye had aided in the brutalization of one. Evening her posture, Lysbeth tries to recall Alder's words on the given subjects. Those trained as bait, the library of languages, a deep respect for...

She inhales as images tumble forward—a kaleidoscope of moments landing and making way in quick succession: lesson notes on the cover of the pianoforte, the deep rumble of a pushed table, hands dissolving across keys, a white ribbon in blonde hair.

"Music," receding impressions leak past her tongue. "Erem's aversion to the music room." Her vision recenters on Erruwyn's grip around the comb's prongs. "What happened to her?"

He blinks water from lids fastened to Elane's chair. "My ignorance." His grip tightens. "I could not play. Baron thought me obstinate. He placed *ʒer'ęm* nearby a harp. He—" Deep, pronged indentations ride his palm as it rushes to defend his stomach from Guilt's blows.

Lacking a roadmap for proper procedure, the women plod through paralyzing ambivalence until, finally, Lysbeth dulls Decorum's droning enough to lay a hand on Erruwyn's. "Perhaps she'll join you at the pianoforte once the harp is removed from the room," she says quietly.

~~~~~~~~~~~~~~~~~~~~

Mr. Tenson barks caution to footmen as Lysbeth passes the gallery for Corah's lesson in the eastern library. She'd had a window of freedom from these lessons during Jaques' visit, but Erruwyn's sound-borrowing has been a difficult temptation to temper, and her buffering is required once again. She enters to find Erruwyn patiently ready at the front table while sister and governess, Ms. Leeve, settle at their desk further in. Greeting the group, she plunges into a deep chair and begins a two hours-long sigh at her needlework.

After a choppy lesson, Erruwyn carefully pushes a stack of notes to the desk's edge. Corah strides to the door and snatches them up before huffing to the hall.

"Sovereign grant me grace and patience," Ms. Leeve whispers as she follows.

Bringing the scribal case to his chest, Erruwyn eyes Lysbeth's feet as she tosses loose supplies from the chair into her basket. He stands and waits, hoping she'll notice his lingering and speak first. When she doesn't, he forces stale air from his lungs.

"Ladyship, may I please ask a second question after now?"

She rounds fiddling with spools. "Of course, Erruwyn."

"Thank you." He peeks at Corah's empty chair. "I wished to know if Ms. Leeve's language instruction is common."

"Yes, I would say so. Why do you ask?"

"I am uncertain. I had wondered..."

She sets her basket down on his table. "Wondered?"

"The teaching is different among us." He falls silent.

Lysbeth smiles fondly at his attempts, recognizing them as commendable. Given the explanation of his name, Erruwyn has always been somewhat shy—now natural shyness and Baron-inflicted anxiety each try to outpace the other for control.

"If you'd care to expand on the differences, I'd certainly like to hear them," she assures.

His voice and grip relax slightly. "Yes, Ladyship. Then, I had wondered of ≤m'aęn, the primal pitches."

"Your inaudible voices?"

He nods. "≤m'aęn are seeds of expression, existing in us always as sprouts. The seeds of ≈aęn, the voices you hear, sprout later. They require additional time. Additional dexterity within," he says, placing two fingertips on his throat. "To bring both seeds to bloom requires great effort, mastered only with diligent training."

Visualizing the space under his fingers, Lysbeth is momentarily lost to her old anatomy text. "I suppose polyphonics would require a good deal of fine motor control within the vocal tract."

"Yes." He curls his fingers down. "So. Before ≈aęn sprout, our language is woẋ'ụạ. The muted motions. woẋ'ụạ roots the Outland's branching tongues."

"I'm afraid I don't follow."

Erruwyn pauses to interpret her meaning. "I will attempt to pull the lead, Ladyship."

Lysbeth grins.

"We learn tongues through woẋ'ụạ. Always using motions under the words." He woẋ'ụạs. "*Table*." Speaking Croran, he repeats the motion, "*Kèch*." He makes the motion again, speaking Emish, "*Gestu*. The tongues branch. Diverge. *wox'ua* is rooted. The same, always."

"I see." Her head cocks. "The consistent association must be quite helpful."

He nods at the table. "Though I am not certain if this is true for those learning *wox'ua* at taller years of age, I wished to ask. To offer, Ladyship."

Lysbeth's mouth traps her surprise before it escapes. She clears her throat. "To offer to instruct Lady Corah?"

"If *wox'ua* could assist, I wondered. Though I do not wish to offend Ms. Leeve."

"If wokes-oo-ah could assist, Ms. Leeve would call for your Knighting. But surely you know Corah is not an easy project? Would you want to subject yourself?"

"I believe I am already as sour to Lady Corah as her instructors. Or nearby. Bitter, maybe."

Lysbeth smiles. "I think she's largely apathetic towards you personally, which is likely the safest place to be in Corah's estimation, but if you're sure, you have my support. I would join you to moderate, of course."

"Yes, Ladyship." He glimpses Corah's chair again. "May I— I am uncertain if observations are permitted."

Her eyebrow arches. "That generally depends on how inconvenient the observation is. For the time being, let's allow for all. Go on."

Erruwyn swallows. "Among the people, there is a special flame. *li'la⌢itet: dancer of the forge*. It is said, *li'la⌢itet* neglected will raze the world. Though, *li'la⌢itet* nurtured will exhale masterwork *ay⌢na*." He squeezes the case and lowers his head in preemptive apology.

Lysbeth exhales slowly. The entire exchange has been an unexpected and welcome surprise, but such a precise assessment of her sister's nature was wholly unforeseen.

"Quite so." She runs a hand along the table's edge and lifts her basket. "Are there many lie-lay-eye-tehts among your people?" she asks, leading him to the hall.

"Only enough in number for the flame to remain special, Ladyship."

"More than enough, then?"

"Yes," he says, pushing a soft laugh through his nose.

Lysbeth turns as they reach the gallery intersection. "Oh, Mr. Tenson saw to the removal of the harp a few hours ago. You're welcome to try bringing Erem along, but needn't feel obliged."

The carpet runner accepts his grateful smile. "Thank you, Ladyship."

"Of course. It hasn't been played in an age, anyway. An eye sore, really." She sighs happily. "Might we count on you for hair tomorrow?" His smile widens as he nods. "Wonderful, see you at ten."

The pair part ways.

As soon as she's out of sight, Lysbeth flings herself into the sitting room, throws herself onto a couch, and flops her cousin's book closed to recount the conversation.

"Really?" Elane asks, mouth agape.

"Yes, you look just as I felt. I'll have him introduce the idea to Corah himself tomorrow. If he survives the encounter, it may yet work."

"Let me know if he does, I would join those lessons." Elane reopens her book. "And Lys, seeing as he would never ask for himself, you might suggest he bring Erem along. He's been teaching her already."

~~~~~~~~~~~~~~~~~~~

Thanks to Corah's affinity for all things Alder, Erruwyn's proposal and trial lesson occur without injury. To Lysbeth's further relief, Erruwyn caters to Corah's personality while never truly yielding ground—outmaneuvering without pitting himself against her.

Over the next week of lessons, Lindenholt's Ladies find w̲o̲x̲'u̲a̲ to be a relatively painless language to learn. Though the unanticipated importance of facial expressions proved a small hurtle for Avon masks, the hand motions often make good, practical sense, and recollection comes easy.

Erruwyn's teaching is casual, with vocabulary expanded through walks around the manor and observing his conversations with Erem—whose sweetness the older Ladies have come to relish, and whose calming effect on Erruwyn has helped to open him up. After their second lesson, he'd even allowed himself a request: permission to sit on the floor. Despite Wescott's use of the floor as a tool of subjection, he'd explained sitting-furniture is uncommon among his people. They prefer the ground. *All together*, he'd said.

Currently, Corah's formal complaint is closing out the day's class in the front drawing room.

"I don't see why Mr. Spantier should be able to request sounds while I should not."

"Mr. Spantier asked Erruwyn for a flute to aid your music lesson, Corah," Lysbeth insists. "Surely you're aware that a bear's roar offers no discernible benefit to your education at present?"

Before Corah sparks the upholstery, Erruwyn dampens the room. "Forgive me. Though I have read of the animal, I do not know the sound. May I request a demonstration for my own education?"

Lysbeth fights a smile. As outmaneuverings go, Erruwyn's table-turning is a particularly effective strategy. "Very well. Corah, please proceed."

"Never mind, then." Corah slumps.

"Apologies, Erruwyn. I'm afraid the demonstration must be delayed until we find a safe means of granting you a firsthand account." Lysbeth pats her knees. "Well, I suppose we ought to ready ourselves for Granmama's arrival?"

"Yes, I'll need time for a bath." Corah stands and exchanges gestures of thanks with her instructor.

When the door shuts, Elane addresses Erruwyn. "How do you spin the fob so stealthily?"

"Fob. The reflection of wishes? As with the bear, Your Ladyship?" he asks, gesturing subliminally. As his eyes land closer to the Ladies' waistlines during lessons—a happy byproduct of speaking with hands—he sees Elane's nod and continues, "This path is used for those among the people who struggle to feel the others."

"Feel others as in sympathy? Or empathy?"

"Both, I believe, Your Ladyship. They resonate weakly. We strive to assist. Guide them to consider the reflection of their wishes—to feel their own demands as others do. In this way, they struggle less." Erem sits taller in his lap and _wox'ua_s when his eyes are on her. He laughs through his nose in the Ladies' direction. "Please forgive my muddy words. I did not intend 'reflection of their wishes' as the surface of a wishing pond."

"Oh, thank you, Erem," Elane plays along to great reward: Erem's precious grin and shy burrowing in Erruwyn's torso.

Lysbeth chuckles as he folds around her. "Growing up as we do here, it's difficult to ignore how freely you give affection."

His head lifts from the wiggling clump beneath it. "Yes, affection is shown differently among the people, Ladyship. _feu'n'en_ was nearby."

"Unsurprising." She smiles. "But it's not only the affection, you seem very at ease with children. Do you have a younger set of twin siblings?"

"Siblings. How to answer." Rubbing Erem's back, he looks across the room for a time. "Among the people, all emerge together under one moon. All raised together as siblings. All reared together among the people—as children of the people. In this way, I have excessive siblings and children next to Outlanders, Ladyship."

"You share a birth month? Every one of you?"

"Yes, Ladyship."

"_All?_ How can that be?"

Mr. Tenson opens the door. "Excuse me, Ladies, Ani has asked if you still wish to change for Her Grace's arrival," he says, passing a hint of disapproval at Erruwyn's location.

"Oh, yes." Lysbeth stands. "But I'd very much like to continue this discussion later, Erruwyn." Bringing the group to the gallery, she continues, "As the time has come, I want to be sure you're adequately warned: the Duchess' desire to make your acquaintance won't necessarily relieve you of her predisposition towards—"

"Soft nettling," Elane jumps in.

"Aye. To that end, a less formal introduction might benefit everyone, and I think your hair dressings could work well as the means."

Erruwyn boosts Erem on his hip and nods. "If that is your wish, Ladyship."

"It is. Come at nine tomorrow—just you." Lysbeth grins. "Hopefully she'll be too awed by your skill to take swipes."

~~~~~~~~~~~~~~~~

Two hours later, a sharply-dressed woman mounts Lindenholt's steps with a cane at one side and a fussing Lady's maid at the other. Halfway through her ascent, she turns and lowers her chin to better peer at the servant.

"Natty. If you do not cease, I shall cast myself down and you may continue your buzzing over my corpse."

Natty purses her lips and descends two steps—and when the climb resumes, raises her arms to break any falls, intentional or not. Reaching the terrace landing, Avrella takes several moments to straighten her form and sweeps the servants' assembly with hungry eyes.

She points her cane to a house maid and footman. "You there, and you, come forward." As they near, she rolls a thumb over her fingers and peers at each from top to bottom. "Why, do you suppose, have I called you forth?"

The servants glance at their clothing and pat their hair. Finding nothing amiss, they're forced to admit their ignorance.

"*Precisely*," clear and polished, Avrella's voice rings over the assembly, "for despite its air of foulness, ineptitude goes unheeded by those whose countenance bears it forth. Woe betide the halls of Walstead should the rank of Lindenholt's pollution find them."

She allows her words to settle before waving the two off. Similarly farcical exhibitions occur at every Avrella-arrival, regardless of locale, and are motivated by her long-held belief that slightly skittish servants are the most productive. However, as her faithless granddaughters had already warned the assembly of her antics, Lindenholt's productivity remains unchanged.

She continues her march. As is tradition, Lindenholt's vestibule doors remain open during family reception, and once her toes appear over the Chamber's threshold, Mr. Tenson booms.

"Announcing The Most Noble, The Dowager Duchess of Edenshire."

The three Edenshire Ladies and Duchess move towards one another until met.

Lysbeth clasps her grandmother's hand and loudly declares, "Lindenholt welcomes you warmly, Duchess." Under her breath, she adds, "Ineptitude is a foul look?"

"Thank you, Lady Lysbeth, I am thusly welcomed," Avrella proclaims. Lowering her voice, she responds, "Have you never seen a Sovereign?"

~~~~~~~~~~~~~~~~

Without the security of a scribal case, Erruwyn holds a wrist behind his back as he enters Lysbeth's sitting room the next morning. Avrella greets the room a short while later, and on seeing the tall figure claimed to be Faye, passes her cane to Ani and begins a steady stroll towards his spot near the vanities.

Erruwyn bows slightly as the bottom of Avrella's dress enters his field of vision, and

Lysbeth speaks from the side, "Duchess, allow me to introduce Dahena Erruwyn."

"Yes, thank you." Folding arms fore and aft, Arvella walks a scrutinizing circle, reflexively twitching her fingers as she scans. "He is quite good looking," she concludes, "though I do wish his appearance more closely resembled Alder's descriptions."

"Most of Alder's descriptions require less clothing to observe," Lysbeth piths.

"Yes, yes. *Where* is the metal?" Avrella asks, gesturing Erruwyn's length.

"I'm sure we told you; we assume Isaac sold everything off. Erruwyn's things were gone by the time Mr. Tenson went to collect them from the stateroom." She nods to the vanity. "The caddy I mentioned is all that remains."

"Foolish man. There had better be a substantial deposit in the accounts," Avrella mutters. After a silence she continues her assessment, "Alder failed to mention this categorical fascination with floorboards, though I suppose it must arise from the Faye's own lack of them—in which case, Alder would never have observed it to remark upon."

Her voice rides sardonic currents. Having fully informed their grandmother of Erruwyn's ordeals and what to expect of his demeanor, Lysbeth and Elane fidget. She pays them no heed.

"Look up, Erruwyn. I would like confirmation of sea-colored eyes."

He carefully lifts his gaze to her hand. Noting where he's landed, she raises her fingers to her neck. His gaze follows.

"Heavens, quite striking. Yes. I insist that you display them properly during my visit. Now then, we will converse while you work, and afterwards you may demonstrate the machinations of your bewitched caddy," Avrella says, claiming the desk and waving Lysbeth to the vanity. Once her orders are carried out, she begins again, "Lady Lysbeth has informed me the Faye populace share a month of birth. Explain how that is achieved."

Erruwyn answers softly as he parts Lysbeth's hair, "Yes, Your Grace. Each harvest, *ꝆRoske—*"

"Oh!" Avrella interrupts. "You were quite right about the chords, Lyssy. Begin again, Erruwyn."

"Yes, Your Grace. Each harvest, Chronicler weighs our numbers. The sum necessary for attunement—replenishment—is halved, as we are twiceborn. Twins. This number becomes the sum of next harvest's *me'ya ꞈitet*: dancers of primal life. Our mothers."

Considering the matter since yesterday, Lysbeth has her questions queued: "But how could you possibly control for both the number and precise timing of each pregnancy?"

"There is a record of those who wish to become *me'ya ꞈitet*, Ladyship. The number for attunement is taken from it." Erruwyn starts a half-plait. "During our celebration of life's pleasures, *me'ya ꞈitet* mate with those they have chosen."

Lysbeth's eyebrows climb. "*Those* they have chosen? More than one?"

"Yes. *me'ya ꞈitet* choose their mates. Often five or six."

"Do you abstain for the remainder of the year?" Elane asks, disbelieving, from a couch.

Erruwyn smiles. "No, Your Ladyship. We are very active. All year."

"Then how can such a system be ensured?" Lysbeth puzzles.

"*ne'ru'k*. Males begin formal training at fifteen years of age, Ladyship. Women accept only those who wear the mark of *ne'ru'k* mastery—of one who has mastered training."

"What manner of training?" Elane's brow furrows.

Avrella clears her throat. "My dear, let us follow where the hounds of inference lead."[12] She locks Elane's eyes until the first rays of realization form behind them. Returning to Erruwyn, she continues her inquiry, "You say these women have multiple mates. Am I to understand paternity is therefore unknown?"

"We do not share the Outland's Concept of Patrilineage, Your Grace. Children are raised among the people. It could not matter if *me'ya ˉitet* chose me as mate. All among the brood are my children."

"A happy thought, I'm sure. But it is rather one matter for your menfolk to claim parentage of children and quite another to participate in the rearing of them."

Erruwyn laughs softly as he finishes a plait. "Yes, Your Grace. We would not neglect our children. All participate."

Lysbeth peeks at his reflection. She knows conversation comes easier to him while working—which is why she'd wanted it for his introduction. Now she wonders if her grandmother reached the same conclusion within her first moments of knowing him.

Avrella cultivated her curmudgeonly reputation through years of blunt opinions delivered on a sharp tongue and takes care to maintain it by masking displays of her shrewdness and compassion. These traits become noticeable to those who spend a good deal of time in her company—as evidenced by the genuine devotion of her servants—but her true motivations can still be difficult to suss out, even for family. If her commentary on Erruwyn's eyes wasn't a moment of forgetfulness, the Duchess must have some design.

~~~~~~~~~~~~~~~~

Central to the Grand Drawing Room's sumptuous surroundings are keystone chairs belonging to the Duke and Duchess of Edenshire: a side table sits between, an aisle created by two white silk couches sits afore, a large space for servant passage sits behind, and flanking from a distance sit two of the room's four ostentatious fireplaces to chaperon the whole affair.

As per tradition, Edenshire's Ladies occupy the long couch to Avrella's right—and in traditional fashion, listen to her retort with amusement.

"My recollection flourishes, thank you. One should not presume a book of threadbare cover is equally bare of contents. Only books well-loved are well-worn, I daresay..."

"... and oft revisited for the wisdom contained therein," the couch rejoins.

---

[12] *Non-Ejaculatory Orgasm*

"Yes, well." Avrella lifts her saucer from the side table. "There are plenty of things I see without making a point of noticing, you know, but the boy's floor-gazing is highly irregular and ought to be checked. Once rumors of his presence are verified, society will pilgrimage to Lindenholt. He must be made fit for public audience before then." She peers at Lysbeth over her teacup. "Heavens, what an awkward expression. Do you disagree with my reasoning?"

Lysbeth—who felt quite sure she'd masked her disappointment in Avrella's answer—takes a breath to clear her mien. "No, Granmama, your reasoning is sound. I suppose I'd hoped you were trying to help because you'd made up your mind to like him, that's all."

"What in my reasoning suggests I dislike him?" Avrella chuckles. "Correcting these remnants of Warden Westcott is for his good as well as our own, Lyssy."

"Then you do like him, Granny?" Corah asks.

The Duchess returns her saucer to the table. "Yes, I think I must."

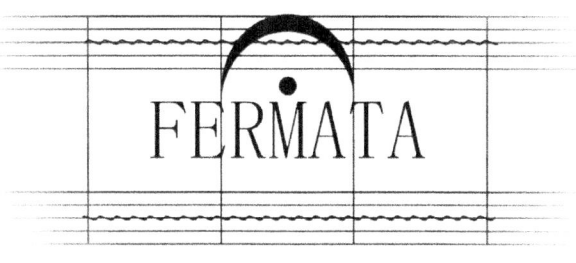

The vessel, its occupants, and the bird which heralded their arrival were incomparable to any other occurrence of nature, construct, or man.
-Alder Haywood-

Erruwyn and Avrella take a true shine to one another in the weeks that follow.

Though he still avoids direct eye contact, the Faye communicates openly with the Duchess, who dotes on him in turn. After learning of his preference for the floor, she's given him special permission to kneel beside her Grand Drawing Room chair—where he's summoned to play every night after supper, and often during afternoon tea. The retractable wall of the music room has been removed to better suit Avrella's rotating choice of instrument, and after testing Erem's reactions to the space, she permits the child's attendance as well.

Favorable outgrowths of Erruwyn's w͟o͟x͟'͟u͟a͟ lessons have also begun to emerge. Erem benefits from having a wider circle of people who understand her, and Corah's temperament has slowly drifted from those traits Lysbeth feared. The change is most apparent in Corah's protective treatment of Erruwyn—of whom she has recently requested a Faye name like Jaques'. Whether due to the coziness of the season, or the general improvements of its occupants, Lindenholt is experiencing a quiet optimism that would have seemed imprudent only a few months ago.

This morning, the Ladies and Duchess are busy in the sitting room drafting festive courtesies to extended family and sorting presents for Winter Solstice in two days. While most Avon servants may expect a large WinterSol meal, Lindenholt's servants are the fortunate inheritors of Alder's equitable EquiSol traditions: all dine together at a holiday buffet, and on WinterSol, staff receive small tokens from the family. This was less of an undertaking when Lindenholt was still a moderate estate. Now, however, the Ladies must oversee gifts and food for sixty-four servants, thirty-three guards, four scribes, and an orphan child—among a dozen other employees.

Feeling well-organized, the Ladies award themselves a proper hairdressing, and all but one voice extends salutations on Erruwyn's entrance. He repeats them quietly along his trek to the vanity before encountering a petite obstruction.

"Good morning, Erruwyn," Ani says, waiting expectantly at the base of his sternum for the shy smile and nod that conclude their daily ritual.

Erruwyn directs a shy smile and nod to her nose. "Good morning, *ȷanȷ*," he adds.

A squeak escapes the maid's dilating features as she's taken aback from his path—she'd been using his timidness to tease him for weeks. Today's counterattack has made him victor.

"That card cannot be replayed, you know," Avrella says, loosening white and copper-streaked hair as he nears.

"Have I shown it too early, Your Grace?"

"No. Better to shuffle expectations." She chuckles at Ani's abscondment. "Now you've come, I beg you explain one of the names you are given to dolling out."

Lysbeth looks up from her writing desk. "I'm still shocked you answered Corah's request faithfully, Erruwyn. More so that she didn't take offense."

"Naturally the girl would find pride in being a force of overwhelming potential, creative or otherwise," Avrella remarks. "And 'Lila' is rather pretty, I think. But I should like to know if the Brute-Duke of Gyenna received an equally accurate name during his stay, and no one here has been able to tell me."

"Jaques is hardly a brute," Elane says from a side vanity.

"Well. I am accustomed to being outnumbered in fondness for the man, so rest assured I do not begrudge your liking of him, Erruwyn." Avrella peers. "However, I am rather curious."

"Yes, Your Grace. I addressed him as *ȷfeu'ɳ'ɛn*," he explains, brushing her hair. "This is a phrase among the people: *follow the sting to honey*—shape irritation to advantage. Though *feu'ɳ'ɛn* is also: *one who lays a path of stingers*. In this way, it is one whose record of offenses grows so long it becomes a feat of admiration." He bites his lip and flicks his eyes to the mirror. Relieved to find Avrella smiling, he joins her.

"Quite accurate." Elane grins.

"Indeed. Have you a name in mind for me?" Avrella asks.

Erruwyn nods slowly.

"Let us hear, then."

"I address Your Grace as *ȝmɛ͡ɳa*, here," he says, briefly touching his head. "Beloved matriarch of the people. Named so by consensus." He begins a plait, softly adding, "My favored *ȝmɛ͡ɳa*, I am reminded."

"I see." Avrella turns in the chair. "Well, who could refuse such an honor?"

His surprise lands on her shoulder. "Your Grace wishes to be addressed as *ȝmɛ͡ɳa?*"

"By you, yes. I *am* a Haywood matriarch, last I checked the lineage. Lyssy?"

Lysbeth drops the back of her hand from her mouth—where it's been hiding the most conspicuous evidence of her laughter. "Erruwyn did say 'beloved' and 'by consensus.'"

Erruwyn motions to his chest. "Consensus of *the people*, Ladyship."

"Ah! Very good, yes, a consensus of one." Avrella taps her hands together.

"Unanimous."

The four continue their happy discourse through Erruwyn's quick work. After he leaves for the scrivery, a footman knocks with a message. Avrella reads on the couch. Lowering the page, a sharp throat-clearing regains her granddaughters' attention.

"Several weeks ago, I sent an inquiry to our solicitor, Mr. Venbry, regarding deposits made by the Marquess. I have here Mr. Venbry's report of no such activity within the last year and some." She peers. "I should like to know what has become of Erruwyn's metal. I submit our time is best spent on avenues bypassing the Marquess, as his word cannot be trusted where the boy is concerned."

Lysbeth frowns from her writing desk. "I looked over Lindenholt's accounts seeking similar evidence last Winter. Perhaps if we send my summary along, Mr. Venbry will notice something I've missed?" She opens a drawer and reaches in.

"Perhaps, but you're quite good with numbers, Lys," Elane says. "Could Isaac have pocketed the funds?"

"Improbable." Avrella refolds the message. "His Lordship knows to grow the honey, not sneak beads of it away. And if I am mistaken in that assessment, he certainly knows the wrath of the colony—and its queen—is better avoided."

As the Duchess speaks, Lysbeth's summary comes into view with small packet riding its back. Her hand withdraws to the drawer's lip. She'd forgotten, or rather, repressed, the existence of Isaac's keys. Their creation had been an act of quiet rebellion, but she'd been too frightened to use them—frightened that, once opened, doors barring the true extent of Isaac's sickness could never be fully closed to her again.

Her fingertips dip into the drawer's recess—Kikyum's hoof penetrating the earth.

Perhaps if discomforting truths were openly acknowledged, something could be done to change them. She lifts the packet and turns.

"There's still one among Lindenholt's rooms we've yet to search."

The Grand Chamber's abutting rooms have been opened. Three large archways frame the Grand Drawing Room on the left and three more frame the Grand Dining Hall on the right. With the additional space and perspective, the area's size and opulence is staggering.

The quintet—led by Konja and occasionally joined by Erruwyn—played through an afternoon of food, games, and gifts and have since joined Lindenholt's population for spirit and mingling under the Chamber's frescos. When light through the clerestory dims, employees queue to pay their formal respects to the family in the Grand Drawing Room. One-by-one, the party thins. When only a deliberate few remain—Ani, Konja, Brom, Mr. Sandel and Ms. Pinley—Avrella waves Erruwyn and Erem to the floor beside her chair and signals Mr. Tenson's exit.

"Well, what did you make of the day, Erruwyn?" she asks.

"It is a little like *da'ja͡na*, our longest night's celebration, *ʒme͡na*," he says, playing with Erem's hair. "Everyone, all together, exchanging favors. Though, no *me'ya͡itet*, or chosen. No"—he smiles and waves a hand—"excessive intimate activity among the people."

"The latter would certainly lower the fueling cost of these monstrosities." Avrella nods to a fireplace.

"Granmama!" Elane laughs.

"It is true, is it not?" she defends.

Curiosity keeps Lysbeth honed. "Longest night? Does your mating festival coincide with Winter Solstice?"

"Yes, Ladyship. Though *da'ja͡na* occurs over many days." He smiles again. "Among many other differences."

"That must be why Alder began the tradition of including everyone," Corah posits. "Don't you think so, Granny?"

As the wave of agreement settles, footmen appear in an archway carrying a large black and silver trunk, a strange metal tree, and a freestanding filigree. Under the direction of Mr. Tenson, they set the objects down at the end of Avrella's couch-aisle.

All present but the footmen have been watching Erruwyn closely. Were it not for misting eyes, they may have mistaken his blank expression and stillness for apathy. Concerned and lacking context, Erem monkeys what Erruwyn's response to her own tears has been, and gently wipes his cheeks with her thumbs. His hands unfreeze at her touch. He pulls her close, blank stare riveted to the filigree.

"We found them," Lysbeth says quietly.

Erruwyn remains still.

"Well?" Avrella leads.

He pushes the words, "For me, *ʒme͡na*?"

"Who else?" She chuckles.

His blink loosens freshly beaded tears. When he manages words again, they carry three tones: gratitude, sorrow, hope.

"*Thank you.*"

The chord is struck and felt through the room.

After adequate assurance the items are his to do with as he likes, Erruwyn stands and crosses the space. "Though I do hope you will consent to wearing your metal for the remainder of the evening. I would very much like to see the true image," Avrella requests.

"Yes *ʒme͡na*." Lifting the filigree he'd worn on arrival, Erruwyn follows Mr. Tenson to an empty room. Alone, tears snake past his smile as he traces the silver. Rolling back his tunic sleeve, he detaches *>m-aen͡hu'ay* from his wrist—where he's been wearing it as a bracelet—and places it on a table. After disrobing, he walks to the metal and spins a half circle. His right leg wraps around the filigree's base to plant his right sole on grounded foot-plates. His left sole drags flush against vertical foot-plates.

≶m'aen.

As he leans into the lattice of metal behind him, protrusions insert and snap to the five silver discs embedded along his vertebrae. Erruwyn's feet switch positions—left heel lowering, right heel rising—and a layer of filigree embraces him.

Slim, V-shaped tubules cradle each of his joints. Articulated plates wrap his groin and connect to a bisected belt at his hips. A long rectangle of snake-chain sways below it. His torso is largely untouched, save for a ladder of thin, flexible spinal cylinders astride his spine. Each ladder-rung attaches to subdermal magnets between spinal discs, and all metal of the frame—from fingers to toes—connects to it along one path or another.

His feet finish reversing.

≶m'aen.

The remaining, free-standing silver repeals his discs as he steps forward. Savoring the stability of metal, he rolls his shoulders and neck before returning to the filigree and positioning his soles against the final feet plates.

≶m'aen.

The protrusions attract his discs again, and once all are flush, click, turn, and lock. As he lowers his right foot and raises his left, a cage of casing folds around him, using the first layer of silver webbing as a base for its additions and thickening brace-points.

A sheathe of silver panels hide the ladder of his spine. Eight tubes reach out from it, bending around his torso to converge under a slightly convex, diamond-shaped cover on his heart. Tapered sheets grip piping on his forearms, thighs, and shins. Articulated plates cap his elbows, knees, and a narrow strip of abdomen. Three thin, horizontal lines climb his throat, and each shoulder bears a topless, crescent epaulette.

His feet finish alternating. Stepping forward, he detaches horns from silver along his collarbones and drags their pronged bases through shaggy, black hair. They snap, holding fast to magnetic implants on either side of his scalp.

He breathes.

On route to the Grand Drawing Room, servants stare as

Erruwyn drapes ⸢m-aęn⸣hu'ay across his face. When he'd first arrived, he didn't mind the looks. There had been enough to worry about, enough to mourn. Now their eyes burrow in channels left by Baron. Gaze low, he approaches the archway gripping a wrist behind his back, prepared to disappoint.

Those present erupt with coos and sighs on seeing him—despite stark changes to his demeanor, Erruwyn's form and silver are just as breathtaking as they'd been at his arrival. Avrella walks a stream of commentary around him, ignoring the Ladies' chiding of her suggestive turns of phrasing.

He grins.

Watching from the couch, Lysbeth is struck with memories of their first meeting—when his smile hid beneath the mask now residing on his left shoulder. Though she's seen his smile since, it's brighter at the moment.

Once the excitement calms, Erruwyn removes his left, middle horn and twists. The bottom opens, and a coil of chain falls out. As he unreels it, branches from the main line dangle their discs below. He attaches two to silver on his throat and four to silver intersections on the trunk.

Ṣm'aęn.

The container's tendrils animate. Black, glossy panels fan down its sides, pushing the trunk upwards as it unfolds. When a tall apothecary-style dresser forms, Erruwyn pulls items from drawers and passes them to Erem with gestures indicating their recipients. She delivers them dutifully: Ani receives a filigree cuff, Ms. Pinley an intricate ring, Konja a lattice earpiece, and Mr. Sandel a well of metallic ink.

Corah receives a thin chain dotted with small, pearlescent stones. At Erruwyn's suggestion, she palms it for a time, and her excitement triples as heat from her hands cause the stones to glow. Brom and Avrella are given quartz vials with conical, silver bases. Erruwyn twists and the cone detaches, dispensing a dose of liquid within—which he claims will lessen the pain of their joints.

Elane and Lysbeth are brought silver pins of flower buds. Both species of flower are unknown to them, but the unique folding and shapes of their petals are lovely. Erruwyn slowly turns the stem of one, and the Ladies watch with delight as the metal blooms and emits a faint, floral fragrance. The stems can be stopped at whichever stage of bloom they prefer, he explains, and more perfume can be added.

His gifting was unexpected, and after many rounds of thanks, most say goodnight. Before Brom helps footmen transport the trunk to their room, Erruwyn removes one last item and reseals the container. Alone with the family, he sits on the floor in the couch aisle, swings Erem to his lap, and holds the item forward: an eight-inch, silver figurine of a crane-like bird.

Its wide head sits on a tall, slender neck. Thick eyelashes outline large eyes above a hooked beak, groups of feathers on its skull arc like Erruwyn's horns, and a long, flared tail falls to its clawed feet. As Erruwyn swivels its legs, the figurine looks to fly—neck lowering, tail rising, wings unfolding—revealing the entire surface is comprised of tiny, individual feathers.

Lysbeth scoots up. "The birds Alder wrote of?"

"It is likely." Erruwyn's voices are richer in metal. He anchors his throat to the bird with ⇒*m-aęn͡hu'ąy* and continues, "*er'ǫǫ'ņ. Eroon.* The seeds of their expression change their form. *er'ǫǫ'ņ* is curious in this form. Feathers smooth. Beak forward. Nosy."

The Ladies grin over a pause for Erruwyn's inaudible ⩘*m'aęn*. The statue's head feathers spoke, the wings take on sharp angles, and the tail splays.

"*er'ǫǫ'ņ* is vengeful, affronted," he explains. "The feathers seek to cut."

⩘*m'aęn.*

The figurine's body and wings fluff. Head feathers separate into a wispy, delicate crown; tail feathers relax and curl elegantly upwards.

"*er'ǫǫ'ņ* is nurturing, content. The feathers embrace softly," he concludes, passing *er'ǫǫ'ņ* to Erem's awaiting arms.

Compliments to the smith begin a debate among the Ladies over which common items would benefit most from animated silver. If they land on any known to Erruwyn, he offers no confirmation, but listens to their thoughts with a quiet smile. By the time Elane begins nodding off, Avrella and Corah stand to retire. Seeing he's taken this as a suggestion to go, Lysbeth invites him to stay a little longer. He remains cross-legged on the floor, teaching Erem how to unfold the bird.

Cheek nestled in palm, Lysbeth observes through glassy eyes. She's touched by Erruwyn's generosity, heartened by his steady return to life, and dazed by the casual display of *er'ǫǫ'ņ*—which addressed musings she's had for years.

Despite her proximity, she speaks from a distance, "There was a time I might've been able to recite Alder's letter by heart. Now I can hardly recall half of the details. His descriptions of Eroon, though, I could never forget those. He said they stood taller than men and could speak in human tongue." She sighs. "I was hypnotized by those descriptions as a girl. I used to imagine one swooping down and carrying me off—telling me stories as we flew to your land."

Erruwyn listens, watching Erem grow sleepy as he strokes her hair. When Lysbeth's reminiscing fades, he leans back on a palm. His eyes trail the couch's arm to Lysbeth's elbow, her elbow to her cheek, and after a long moment, they find her eyes.

A giddy warmth expands in Lysbeth's belly. Afraid reacting will scare him off, she masks what elation she can as they hold a meaningful gaze—sea-green and sky-blue.

The fire's reflection in silver changes as Erruwyn takes a breath. "There was a time, many, many ages distant, when the people walked among Outlanders with _er'oo'n_ beside."

Lysbeth's cheek lifts from her palm.

"When _set'ne_, our voyages, were journeys of exploration. _er'oo'n_ flew above to lead us to your shores. The journeys became those of trade. _da'he⌒na_ emerged—trained as navigators, as speakers of many tongues to greet Outlanders, also. "

Her heart quickens.

"Our paths diverged. We withdrew. Outlanders forgot the friendship of _da'he⌒na_. Forgot _er'oo'n_. Created ideas to explain us. To hunt us."

Her throat tightens.

"Now our voyages are _set'ye_—journeys of desperation. _er'oo'n_ flies above to warn of Outland vessels. _da'he⌒na_ learn tongues of our hunters—no longer permitted skills of navigation so we cannot reveal the land of our people when Called and broken."

Burying internal disturbance, Lysbeth drops her shoulders and lifts her chin.

"It should not be so." Erruwyn smiles sadly. "Then you could meet _er'oo'n_."

~~~~~~~~~~~~~~~~~~

"Are you still out of sorts, Lys?" Elane asks.

"Oh, am I?" Lysbeth forces her return to the present—walking with the Ladies to the Grand Drawing Room after supper. "Apologies."

Solstice was weeks ago, but Lysbeth often finds herself revisiting the quiet evening. In the silence that followed Erruwyn's words, Elane woke from her doze. His eyes lowered again at her stirring, and the spell has remained broken.

Lysbeth's lingering questions act as intermissions to her daydreams—imagining an ancient world populated with friendly _er'oo'n_ and _da'he⌒na_. Who had they visited? Where do their voyages take them now? His version of history flew in the face of all known records, but had she overestimated its significance? The information felt momentous enough to assume its confidentiality, but while she hadn't expected him to broach it again directly, there'd been no acknowledgement of it whatsoever: no double-entendres, no subtle expressions during adjacent topics, no secret glances—albeit, the latter is challenging with an eye-averse partner.

The shifting scenery of the Grand Drawing Room corrals her thoughts. Kneeling beside Avrella's chair, Erruwyn moves Erem to collect the guitarra. Lysbeth eyes him as she sits. Tailored tunics and trousers still look well on him, but after that night, she can't deny she prefers the metal. It seemed a natural part of him, almost an extension; though a review of his physique certainly weighed her endorsement. He strums a melody, gradually adding vocal harmonies with impossible range across the rifts.

The Ladies sail on his flux for half an hour before capsizing on Corah's interjection, "He'll lose his voice carrying on for you. You'd make him mute if it meant your ears were satisfied first."

Erem's *wox'ua* elicits smiles from the Ladies.

"I ought to advertise for a Grand Drawing Room translator," Avrella says, holding out her sherry glass for tending. "Shall we offer our services to the Sovereign, do you think, Mr. Tenson? How does Lindenholt Embassy suit you?"

The butler shakes a solemn head over a small pour.

"Yes, quite right. We lack the opium port anyhow."

Lysbeth smiles. "Erem simply agreed with Corah, Granmama."

"We've invited you to join our lessons," Corah pipes.

"I am disinclined to learn any language that makes an exhibition of my feebleness."

"Come now, you're not truly feeble," Elane says.

"Yes, I can still waddle gracefully enough, thanks to Erruwyn's concoction. Though I do long for a dance now and again. I put on quite a few shows in my youth." Avrella glances at the pair on the floor. "Have you seen my younger portrait, Erruwyn?"

"Yes, ⸎me͡ na."

"And what is your impression?"

"It is pleasant. Though, I am uncertain of the accuracy in expression."

"I believe Granmama was after your impression of *her* as a young woman, not the skill of the artist," Lysbeth clarifies, exchanging a chuckle with her grandmother.

"Oh." Erruwyn ducks in apology. "Then, you are beautiful, ⸎me͡ na, as all here are."

Underlings are expected to polish the egos of their employers from time to time, but Erruwyn's words require no elbow grease—his sincerity is easily recognized.

"Singular. I cannot imagine why you would think so in my case, but I shall not argue a flattering opinion," Avrella says.

Erem *wox'ua*s again: hair sun.

Cheerful eyes return to Avrella's chin. "Though it is not the only reason I feel so, sol-hair is excessively uncommon among the people, ⸎me͡ na. It is greatly celebrated."

"I suppose that explains why your first woxua was a statement on my hair?" Lysbeth grins as he gnaws a sheepish smile.

"I had not expected it, Ladyship," he says softly.

"It is not terribly common among our own countrymen, you know," Avrella says. "However, I am infinitely more gratified by your appreciation of it than theirs, I assure you." She tips back her sherry and peers at the couch. "Before retiring I have a few announcements. The first is that I have decided to remain at Lindenholt for the foreseeable future, and the remainder are the reasons as to why." She taps the bottom of her glass with a finger. "Reason one: my nieces, Lady Regia Fernel and Lady Katrena Docenly, have been hounding for an invitation to Lindenholt and I have extended it. Now, you will recall they have a truly vulgar number of children between them. The men are north with ours, but five daughters and two sons will be in attendance ten days hence."

She raises a hand and the couch's chorus of complaints quits.

"The second reason: our Steward writes that Alder's letter has been found."

She raises a hand again and the couch's chorus of questions cut.

"I do not wish to make a copy of it, nor do I wish to risk its bearer's health in chill. Therefore, I have arranged for it to be brought from Walstead in the third week of Spring. There. Now. Whatever you have to say may be said to one other until tomorrow, as I must beg my pardon to retire."

Passing her glass to Mr. Tenson, Avrella begins her withdrawal—and as the Matriarch's departure must mark her own, Corah stands gesturing goodnight to Erruwyn.

"Goodnight, *lị'la*." He smiles, hands full of Erem.

The eldest and youngest gone, Lysbeth nudges Elane, who'd promised to give her a moment alone with Erruwyn next chance. When her cousin excuses herself, Lysbeth leans over the arm of the couch, keeping an eye on Mr. Tenson's glass-shuffling at the bar.

"Erruwyn," she whispers. "I have questions." Her glance is met with an amusedly arched eyebrow. "Before Jaques' arrival, I overheard Konja relaying a myth of twin women. Was that from the distant age you mentioned? Why did our paths diverge? Does Eroon speak?"

"It is likely. Aggression. Yes, recite," he answers softly and grins.

Lysbeth grins too.

Mr. Tenson clears his throat.

~~~~~~~~~~~~~~~~~~~
~~~~~~~~~~~~~~~~~~~

SEGUE

Avrella spears a dried apricot. "As I have said, they will depart before Equinox, Lyssy. If Erruwyn keeps his work to the scrivery and his playing to Konja, I fail to find issue."

"But surely his look is enough to draw attention," Lysbeth argues across the dining parlor's table. "Corah needs his lesson recordings and he won't go without notice on his way to and from. Particularly with that flock."

The five young women expected at Lindenholt in a few days have a penchant for improper activities—nothing guaranteed to result in scandal, but enough to flirt with the possibility.

"There is nothing to be done." The Matriarch rests her fork on the plate. "Even if I wished to deny them, they are already well on their way. Erruwyn's sociability is much improved. We do not need to hide *him,* only his origins—which, ideally, will be unveiled on our own terms." She peers. "And if the flock wishes to croon, let them, my dear. It will be good for the boy to prepare for the kinds of attentions he will receive en masse in the future." Final judgement rendered, she lifts her utensil.

Elane sighs. "I'll miss his dressings."

Corah frowns. "I'll miss his lessons."

"My word." Avrella chuckles. "You speak as if he's dying."

Lysbeth and Elane informed Erruwyn of the potential changes this morning. Though he was sad to hear it, he'd accepted the news better than they—partly because he had no choice, and partly due to his other optional activities.

Though he's still unpopular with the servants—as those who'd openly disparaged him early on gained allies in those jealous of his relationship with the family now—he's carved out other niches. He'd recently begun helping the kitchens with meal preparations, Konja extends frequent invitations to practice with the quintet, Mr. Sandel usually has extra scribal work, and of course there's Erem to look after.

The cousins' lives are comatose in comparison. Sitting out of direct sunlight is the only wholly-approved activity for Avon Ladies—though an allowance for tedious creative endeavors was eventually amended. Hostessing usually offers some measure of respite, new conversation at least, but they're currently resenting the interruption. Erruwyn's music is entertaining, his wox'ya lessons educational. Morning dressings have become a favorite part of their routine, and every now and then, he softly mentions something fascinating from home. In short, he'd spared them insufferable boredom.

Now, they'll be stuck needlepointing for an age.

~~~~~~~~~~~~~~~~~~~~~~~~

A smattering of young women read and embroider in the front drawing room. One sits sandwiched between a window and a silhouette screen for another to trace her shadow with charcoal. Elane and Lysbeth smile subtly over their canvas hoops—if only their relatives could see Erruwyn's illustrations.

"Have you heard? They say the Marquess of Chadum was badly injured," Bell, second eldest, reports.

Elane lowers her canvas. "No, we hadn't. Will he recover?"

"Haven't a clue." Bell shrugs.

"He had better," Kitti, second youngest, remarks. "Chadum is to host PromSol this year."

"Yes, too late to change it now," middle-of-five, Indra, says.

Elane tuts, "If the worst occurs, would you have them host through his mourning?"

"They must do, if it comes to it," Kitti insists, rapidly turning pages of a book she isn't reading.

"Yes," Bell agrees. "Can you imagine being the first house to cancel?"

Indra gasps. "The Marchioness would die of shame."

"Let's hope she serves well as his motivation to carry on, then," Lysbeth spouts dryly.

Quiet footsteps come from the eastern gallery.

"Ssh!" Feobe, youngest at sixteen, rises.

Four move to spots with a view of the hall as Jemine, eldest, opens the door. A moment later, Erruwyn moves across frame.

"Good afternoon," Jemine lilts as he stops.

"Good afternoon, My Lady," he says quietly.

"Did Lady Corah find you useful today?"

"I hope, My Lady."

He flicks eyes to Lysbeth, who's stifling a laugh over the back of her couch. She'd asked him to borrow Avonleigh's accent in front of their guests and—ridiculous attentions of their relatives aside—hearing him speak so differently tickles Lindenholt's Ladies through.

Bell romps over to nudge Jemine away. "Croran or arithmetic?"

"Croran."

"How did you come to know it so fluently?" she asks, draping the doorframe. "My pronunciation isn't half so smooth. Perhaps you might tutor me while I'm here?"

"I learned the essentials early, My Lady." He bites his lip at Lysbeth's curbed snort.

"Though your praise is kind, I must not burden your stay with lectures."

Erruwyn wades patiently through a door of revolving Ladies until the depletion of inane questions grants his pardon.

"Ohh!" Feobe whines as the handle latches. "I need a proper dictation for him, Lys! Why are you so contrary? Even a nibble would do."

"Perhaps she hopes to cook for herself," Kitti gripes.

"Only virtuous porridge." Lysbeth pulls her needle. "I told you we've little insight to give. He's a private sort of person."

The eldest three guests spin a web of glances and saunter back to their seats to catch a fly. Indra clears her throat and locks on Bell. "Did I mention mother had news of Jaques Vippon this morning?"

"Oh, Indra, we weren't meant to repeat it," Bell says, turning to Jemine. "Seeing as it involves Lysbeth."

"Well now it would be rude not to repeat it, Bell." Jemine moves her gaze to Lysbeth. "But only if we're asked properly."

The Flock giggles.

~~~~~~~~~~~~~~~~~

Lysbeth's chin inclines defiantly as she moves to a large, low chair.

To her right is a side table, a minute timer, a strip of black cloth, and an amused Ladies maid. On the bar behind, a half-full bottle of elderflower cordial makes soldiers of the Ladies to her left. Straight ahead is the only entry to their battleground—the Grand Library's partitioned den—and on every side, the drums of Kiss or Tell resound.

Lysbeth asked after Jaques on Indra's last turn and was relieved to learn nothing new: he'd turned down her hand as they'd discussed in Autumn. However, her lack of surprise at the answer had ruffled The Flock's feathers as much as their unanswered questions regarding Erruwyn's sweethearts. They whisper attack strategies to the side, and Jemine soon turns.

"What's the true reason for Jaques Vippon's refusal?"

"Kiss," Lysbeth answers steadfast.

The thought of lying hadn't occurred to her. Kiss or Tell is as much a game of honor as it is of gossip, and in revealing she knows the truth, she's invigorated Avonleigh's Ladies-only rumor mill. Kept in the company of confined Ladies, a worthy rumor's lifespan can surpass even generous estimates.

The battalion squeals into action.

Elane hops to the bar. The Flock roosts near the partition. Ani—trusted referee since the cousin's first introduction to the game at sixteen—arms herself with cloth and timer and marches from the room. Lysbeth accepts Elane's offered cordial and downs half on her way to the partition. Peeking through a panel, she watches her maid crack the library's nearest double-doors. Footmen were dismissed from the hall and western gallery for the game's purposes; whoever comes along next is Ani's target.

A few minutes later, the maid waves over her shoulder to the den. Temus, a footman usually posted in the eastern gallery, has appeared in the hall from the study. As he nears the Grand Library's far entrance, the servants' stairwell across from it opens.

Ani bounces on her toes—the scrivery has an errand.

Erruwyn enters the Grand Library as Temus takes his place in the stairwell. Lysbeth drains her glass and whirls on Elane's titter. The Flock pushes them aside, and a stack of five faces peek through the panel as Ani beckons Erruwyn over. Jealous warbling scores his journey across the library and Lysbeth's dumbfounded return to the chair. The partition crack seals as he nears Ani's spot.

"I've an offer for you, Erruwyn," she says. "You see, there's a game—a tradition really—the Ladies sometimes observe when they're together. Occasionally it requires a third party." Her spritely eyes dance. "Your people are comfortable with affection, aren't they?"

Eyebrows trenched, he nods.

Ani lowers her voice, "This is only for the game, understand, but one of the players needs a kiss." She wiggles the timer. "A kiss lasting this long."

His eyebrows reverse course, climbing in surprise.

"To protect the Ladies' reputations, your partner will remain anonymous," she says, swinging the cloth strip, "and you'll need to swear your silence, but really, you've got quite good luck to be the one who plays." She holds the strip up with taut expectation.

"I am uncert—"

"Oh, do wear your Avonleigh voice," she insists. "Come forward, let me tie this 'round."

Unsure, Erruwyn defaults to doing as he's told and bends down for the petite maid to cover his eyes.

"You'll kneel before your partner," she explains as she ties. "*She'll* initiate the kiss—you mustn't touch her, well except to kiss her, naturally." Blindfold secure, she drags him to the partition. "I'll bring you back out afterwards. Remember, never speak of it."

Not waiting for acknowledgment, she pulls him through the door. The room's now-seated Ladies stifle a bout of giggles as he's brought to Lysbeth's chair.

"Here please," Ani directs.

Feeling acutely vulnerable, Erruwyn kneels tall.

"Once your partner begins, I'll flip the timer."

He nods and waits. The room's hushed amusement grows as Lysbeth's fits of tipsy, silent laughter continually inhibit her participation.

After an uncomfortable length of time, he sits back on his heels and grips his elbow. "Ani, Mr. Sandel is waiting," he says softly.

Mr. Sandel *is* waiting, but hounding fears have begun to yip. The situation presented is not, in fact, the luck to which he has grown accustomed, and his mind is forming grand rationalizations in search of the truth: a room of servants, not Ladies, with another derisive prank like the frequent hair in his food. A trick—laugh as he kisses something taboo, then censure. He'll be traded back to the Baron, just as Baron said.

Heeding his anxiety, Ani motions a reversal to Lysbeth, who shrugs under a wide grin. "You'll need to initiate, Erruwyn, but I'll give you the timer as a show of faith. Left hand, please." Spurring his hesitant compliance, Ani pulls his wrist to the table and wraps his palm around the timer. "And your right?" She connects long fingers to Lysbeth's chin. "There, as you like."

Fears receding, Erruwyn carefully explores his partner's jaw and cheek. She's grinning, and quiet laughter pulses her frame. He bites a faint smile and rises to his knees. "I believe my teammate suffers a tremor. Landing accurately will be challenging."

"Give it a go, anyhow," Ani says over the room's giggles.

"Then, may I share a kiss with you, teammate?" he asks.

After taking several deep breaths to dull her laughter, Lysbeth closes her eyes and nods. With her consent, Erruwyn lightly traces the seam of her mouth with his thumb. On its return journey, he leans forward to trail it with his lips.

Lysbeth's smile relaxes further at his grazing. His fingertips guide her chin closer to the warmth of his exhale, and a brush of his tongue parts her lips—an unexpected development for the Avon—as he flips the timer.

Their kiss begins tentatively, softly skimming mouths mingling breath—his scented with the medlars he'd recently split with Kiky, hers with the cordial she'd recently imbibed. The bouquet quickens their draw, each pass venturing further until the scene and arrangement of their choreography is set—a heady dance of foretasting lips locking, lingering, and pulling away, only to flit for the palate again.

Their giggling audience quiets.

The game has seen many kisses. Most were tedious, all were awkward: tight lips pressed together for an agonizing minute, or partners who mistook bigger for better and resolved to prove it across an unfortunate Lady's face. Surely no kiss had been a source of envy; no kiss had bordered passion. Until now.

Sensing the minute is nearly up, Erruwyn discreetly lays the glass across his bed of fingers. As enraptured by the kiss as the rest of the room, Ani only notices his trickery after several moments have passed.

"Erruwyn!" she exclaims. "You can't stop the timer!"

The kiss ceases. Struggling with woozy eyelids, Lysbeth grins at the scene awaiting her on the tabletop. The upsurge of her cheek elicits a thin smile from Erruwyn.

"Forgive me," he says quietly. "We must begin again?"

Ani catches the beginning of Lysbeth's laugh and spreads it. "No! That's not how the game works."

"Oh. Though certainly we have a little more time?"

"Well, I *can't* know for certain since you've stopped the sand, can I?"

"Mm. Yes, you are right. We must have an accurate count." The corner of his mouth climbs as long fingers rotate the imprisoned minute. Ani yelps with exaggerated offense and seizes the glass; his fingers remain in place. "You are displeased, Ani. You did not expect we would win your game so easily?"

"It isn't a game you can win!"

Erruwyn raises an eyebrow. "Do you hear her desperation, Teammate? She is threatened by our skill."

Lysbeth nods through giddy glances to her maid and cousin.

"You're needed in the scrivery," Ani says, choking back a giggle and pulling on his arm.

"Mr. Sandel will wait." He smiles.

Yielding to her grunt prompts a hasty lug to the door—where, before complete removal, he turns a broad grin on the chair behind.

"Do not despair, Teammate, we will claim our rightful victory!"

<hr>

Another hairpin joins the vanity's pile.

"I didn't think he was capable of such cheek, My Lady!" Ani giggles.

"Or such impishness," Elane agrees from her chair. "And you looked to be enjoying yourself, Lys."

"Indeed, there were many surprises in that encounter." She fans her face and grins. "I don't have much by way of comparison, other than prior game kisses, really, but it was certainly the most pleasant of those."

Ani loosens another pin. "It really isn't fair, is it? The poor flock."

The Flock agreed, it really wasn't fair. They bemoaned their luck through the remainder of their stay, and many attempts were made to tempt Lysbeth into playing again—she denied them all the way to their departure.

Though the kissed footman became nervous around Ani for a decent stretch, she reported no change in Erruwyn. This was good news for the Lindenholt cousins, who'd been concerned his transparency would arouse suspicion. In the end—and for reasons she'd been unable to decipher—it was Lysbeth who feared she'd give herself away, and she was thankful The Flock kept Erruwyn at wing's length for another fortnight while she'd pulled herself together.

Now, one week after The Flock's migration, a Walstead has come bearing a sealed, leather scroll case. Summoned to Avrella's Grand Gallery apartments, Lindenholt's Ladies stand a respectful distance away as the Duchess reverently unfurls the heirloom across her—

previously Alder's—writing desk.

The ritual completes when each page lays in order and carefully weighed. She motions her granddaughters near. Four faces lean over the parchment.

===

To the World at Large,

From a Citizen Within it

I write to you, here at the end of my life, regarding the legendary people known variously as Elvs, Syrens, and Faye: to confirm their existence, and to beg that we of the broader world abide by their wish for solitude. Though I will remain vague in many respects, lest I reveal information of import that might risk their discovery, I vow on the honor of my esteemed lineage every word conveyed herein is true and appropriate.

Heed them well.

YEAR 1197, AGE III: the dawn of my extraordinary journey. I departed Lindenholt Castle in Spring, traveling by carriage to the port of Limington to meet with the merchant ship upon which I had arranged passage—and whose destination I shall not here recount. At the middle point of our lengthy voyage, a storm of rare voracity set upon us and lead our vessel far astray our charted course. To our great shock we found ourselves run aground on a long shelf of sand—though precisely how long, I know not—surrounded by the deep waters of The Brine. There we lamented for many days, our craft marooned and our supplies wearing thin.

Then, lo! From the horizon came a sparkle, and upon the sand beneath the shallow waters was cast an enormous shadow—exacting in its approximation of the dragons depicted in Nottery's illuminated manuscripts. As we watched, the sparkle upon the horizon took the form of a ship, and the creature producing the shadow—once passed from the line of the sun whereupon our eyes could bear the brightness of the naked sky—was revealed to be not a dragon, but a bird of grand proportions.

The ship anchored well and nimbly against the bank that was our prison, and there began a procession of the people known to my countrymen as Faye. The vessel, its occupants, and the bird which heralded their arrival were incomparable to any other occurrence of nature, construct, or man.

Of their visage: exquisite. Flowing, dark hair. Elongated fingers and waists. Vivid eyes every shade of the sea. In the features of their faces were found such a delicate balance of angles that determining the sex of an individual was rendered near impossible. Upon their bodies—which stood tall, unusually lithe, and sinewy—and in their hair was an assemblage of smooth, lustrous metal. I would soon come to learn of the special reverence they held for hair, as below the brow they had none.

The ethereal grace and beauty of their bearing overwhelmed me. A poor fellow by the name of Gorge, convinced our thirst and exposure to the sun had taken his mind, grew inconsolable at their arrival. When at length the bird—who stood six feet by its shoulder and ten by its head—reproduced the speech of a human tongue unknown to us, Gorge fled into the sea and sank quickly beneath the waves.

Through ingenious machinations, our boat was freed from the bar and fixed to their own with a long chain of considerable strength despite its fineness. Our crew was shepherded aboard their craft—whose interior and amenities were luxurious in comparison to our own—and we soon embarked for the land of the Faye.

On arrival we were given shared accommodation and once settled were besieged with questions about the world: our lives, our cultures, our scientific advancements, and our languages. Where my crewmates concealed the truth, the Faye detected falsehood. Eventually the true character of each wayfarer was determined and those who read vile or destructive were winnowed out. I know not what became of the unworthy, and—I flatter myself—as the judgments of the Faye matched my own, I was not inclined to seek the answer. Six and myself were all that remained of our company by the first fortnight's end... and there I remained for thirty years more.

Of the land I will say only this: she, the land, is herself a living record of the people, for no part of her has gone untouched by previous generations. The utterly unique flora and fauna she bore could not have come from any other scape, as no other could match the dazzling formations, vistas, and atmosphere required to produce them.

Of the people: the great devotion and love shown among them—for each other and for the land—is the quiet wish of every nation of man. Women and men wander all facets of society together effortlessly, and it is this trait to which the Faye credit their considerable technological advancements and general harmony. We have handicapped our own development and thrown our world into discord with our division of the sexes, they say—for if only half a people can live and contribute freely, progress will take twice-long and taste twice-bitter. Physical affection, courting, and coupling are openly encouraged and this, too, they say brings harmony—though males must learn to stay their seed if they desire the attentions of women.

It is no wonder to me now that the Faye are referred to as Syrens by other nations, for their deep respect of sound and music borders deification, and much attention is paid to its study and creation. In my twenty-third year as their guest, I was honored with a tour of their Library of Language. Their vast collection spanned epochs, and extant languages are carefully updated each time a ship is retrieved from the shelf. They exhibited an incessant desire to expand their use of sound, and phrases from other languages are commonly incorporated into their conversations. A tragedy, in my own opinion, for on this subject it must be said: there is nothing like the beauty of their speech. Each utterance is unto a note—and when not a note, a chord—so that each word is a musical motif and each sentence a musical phrase. I shall die wishing to hear it one last time.

Of their social arrangement: A lack of personal property and ownership results in the absence of theft and poverty. A lack of prescriptive institutions, such as marriage, results in the absence of adultery and possessive treatment of partners. A low population results in a surplus of basic needs and children, the elderly, and the infirm are well cared for by everyone. All are sheltered, educated, fed, and cherished.

I once asked what of their laws compelled this and was astonished to learn they had none. Codified laws, they claim, are only a means through which to enforce the concepts we have created and shackled ourselves to. Instead, they rely on an oral tradition of social taboos, whose merit is based on a sense of equilibrium they call the Attuning Will of the People.

Such equilibrium is said to be disrupted when a citizen assaults another being, for instance, though it should be noted that all forms of assault are extraordinarily rare. In my thirty-four years among them, I heard of not one. When these disruptions occur—it was explained to me—the population partakes in a series of protracted, introspective debates to determine their failure in rearing. Other notable proscriptions included any disregard for their highly regulated system of procreation or attempts by The Called to return home.

The Called are those we have named Faye in our ignorance: that is to say, those who have appeared in our histories over the ages—those left adrift at sea as bait for pursuing ships so that their own ship might escape. These individuals are tremendously respected, but once taken are expected to honor the exchange, never to return.

The Called, it was said, must consent to follow the Will of the Outlanders' Sovereign—the laws of our nations. Alongside our laws, The Called follow a third, enigmatic Will known as the Will of the Wayfinder. As I understood it, this Will belongs to one chosen by The Called and whose relationship thereof is deemed essential.

I fell deeply in love with one of those trained for sacrifice during my time among the Faye. It was he who organized my return to the land of man, though it had never been attempted or requested—for their world is a paradise offering profound contentment. However, as the years passed, I was beset with longing to see my son once more. I assured my beloved I would not reveal the truth of my whereabouts—a promise my conscience will never again afford me the peace of holding as I break it now—but I must speak as one of them, as the only one who can, to implore the world to let them alone.

For it was only through knowing the Faye that the true depths of man were revealed to me: his spitefulness, his fragile pride, and his sadism. The thought of my Dearest, or any Faye, being subjected to his laws and whims racks me with anguish. Surely the prestige gained by a Faye's capture is nothing next to the loss of one's soul through obtaining them?

Perhaps if we cure ourselves of the wickedness inherent to our kind, the Faye will come forward and meet us willingly. It is my most fervent wish that this might one day come to pass.

Until then, I beseech you, let the Faye fade into legend. Take no more of our children away.

The Most Hon'ble, The Marquess of Edenshire
~Alder Haywood~

===

Erruwyn smiles at the rattling bell above his scrivery desk. He's been expecting a summons since mid-morning—when Ani delivered the Walstead news during his kitchen duties. Reporting to the main house's summoning booth, a hall boy directs him to the Grand Drawing Room, and he smiles again as Avrella goads his kneel beside her chair.

"Alder's letter arrived this morning, my dear, if you would be so kind as to oblige before Corah's lesson." She peers.

"Yes, I will provide permitted answers, ⟨me͡na. Some silent."

"Of course, we understand." The Matriarch leans against her armrest. "Now, after refamiliarizing myself with Alder's encounter, I am quite curious about the anomalous bank of sand he describes. Since your people clearly know of it, are you responsible for it as well?"

Erruwyn considers the question. As none among the people expected it to be asked, he was never given a guideline for an answer. Still, the Haywoods have kept Alder's chronicle a secret for over three-hundred years; they won't run amok revealing its contents now.

Gesturing wox'ua—as he often does when speaking of home—Erruwyn does his best to answer satisfactorily, "We have taken responsibility for wa't'un, though we are not responsible for wa't'un's creation, ⟨me͡na."

"A natural formation you look after?" Elane offers.

"Yes, Your Ladyship. Our step-stone to the Outland."

Corah pipes up, "How often are ships stuck on way-toon?"

"It is uncommon, though er'oo'n fly every quarter-moon to observe. When wa't'un cradles a vessel, we take it to our breast."

"What happens to those who sour the milk?" Lysbeth smirks. "Only a handful of Alder's shipmates were accepted."

Another unanticipated question; ambiguity offers a compromise.

"᭒᭒ry͡ine᭒᭒"

His voices roll out a deep, discordant chord. Heavy snaps stir in his chest. An eerie effect spreads as the chord warps in key. The women look to each other uneasily. It's enough to give them an accurate impression: nothing pleasant.

"I recall experiencing a remarkably similar effect in the company of a rather ill-favored suitor," Avrella mutters as the sounds fade.

"Indeed." Lysbeth grins.

"Erruwyn, is it true your people knew when Alder's shipmates lied?" Imagining the usefulness of such a skill, Corah looks hopeful.

"Yes, *lį'la*." He motions to his face. "The observance of texture. Expression."

"You mean their countenance gave them away?" At Erruwyn's nod, Corah renders her judgment: "They must've been poor liars, then."

"Maybe." He smiles. "Though maybe not. The textures of falsehood are often small. Challenging to control, also."

"I suppose we must take you at your word," Avrella says. "In the meantime, there is one matter which seems rather pertinent to our own situation. Alder mentions a trifecta of Wills?"

Erruwyn's gaze drops to his pinched fingers. *rạl'yạ– dạ'hẹ̄na* had certainly been free with information.

"I noted them here," Avrella continues, pulling a small paper from her sleeve. "Ah. Attuning Will, Sovereign Will, and Wayfinder Will." She squints. "Enigma, I've also written. Yes, the nature of the latter eluded him." She lowers the note. "Are these names accurate?"

"Yes, *mẹ̄na*," he answers quietly.

"I see. And is it also correct that, while the whole of your populace follows the Attuning Will, only sacrificed Dahena follow the Wills of Sovereign and Wayfinder?"

"Yes, *mẹ̄na*."

"Enlighten us, if you would."

"Yes, *mẹ̄na*." He inhales slowly. "*k'uah̲̄ni*. Sovereign's Will. The Outland laws *dạ'hẹ̄na* must obey." Weaving his fingers tightly, he reluctantly drives out air, "*nar̲̄uah*. Wayfinder's Will. Guiding resonance."

"Well, we must grant Alder the correct application of 'enigmatic'." The Matriarch peers at the couch. "I hope that answer has drawn the curtain for one of you, as I find I am still quite without illumination."

"Alder said the Wayfinder Will is deemed essential, Granny," Corah reminds, "and it's meant to be a person Erruwyn chooses."

"Yes, who is your choice of Nahr-do-wah, Erruwyn?" Lysbeth asks.

"The Will is absent, Ladyship."

Avrella presses, "In that case, how is the role determined?"

"A request, an offer..." Erruwyn swallows and begins a faint recitation:

‖ *dạ'hẹ̄na offered to the Outland* ♦ *Accepted,*
we are taken ♦ *Moored, we choose* ‖

His knuckles whiten through a pause.

‖ *dạ'hẹ̄na offered to the chosen* ♦ *Accepted, they*

are ̣n̲a̲r̲ ̂ua̲h̲ • Moored, we are ḍa'h̲e̲ ̂ n̲a̲r̲ ̂ua̲h̲ ‖

"My dear, if all you need do is offer yourself, what is preventing you?" the Matriarch puzzles. "Or had you never reached a decision regarding the individual?"

"It would not be acceptable." He blinks at her feet, imploring softly, "Please, ɬm̲e̲ ̂ n̲a̲."

Ignoring the sour face of her youngest granddaughter, Avrella bends a third-degree-eyebrow and continues the inquisition, "Why? Would Avonleigh's sensibilities find the role objectionable? Or the offer itself?"

Resigned, he wets his lips. "I do not believe so. ̣n̲a̲r̲ ̂ua̲h̲ is our Wayfinder in Outland waters—a Will to guide, assist, instruct—for a lifetime. The sum of this request is large. ɬḍa'h̲e̲ ̂ n̲a̲ is offered in return." Shaky fingers spread and reweave. "I lack the weight of attunement. I am too diff-errant. After novelty, a burden. There is nothing to offer."

Twisting stomachs wring guilt from the couch's occupants—each had found Erruwyn's errancy difficult to contend with at one time or another. Even Lysbeth had wished he'd conform to the same modes of social conduct she'd often longed to escape.

He had noticed.

The Baron's curated lessons and repeated disparagement from servants only drove the perception of his deficiencies deeper.

Avrella's brow relaxes. "Yes, that does seem rather hopeless."

At Erruwyn's stark, confirmative stoop, Lysbeth's protest gains volume, "Granmama, that is only Erruwyn's assessment—and it needs be said, one which discounts the Wayfinder's thoughts entirely. Begging your pardon, but it seems to me that the decision to accept being *theirs*, it must follow that *their* opinion is of greater consequence."

The Matriarch obstructs a smile. "Were you not listening, my dear? Guiding an errant burden for life, he said. After your father and grandfather, I am something of an authority on towing ornery mules across decades-long bridges. It is not a position to be envied."

Elane rests a hand on Corah's back to prevent the girl's impassioned interjection.

Lysbeth's neck flushes. "You don't truly believe that, Granmama. None here do." She turns to the floor and sinks the liver: "Erruwyn, if this matter is as significant as Alder claims, you *must* allow your choice the option of accepting."

Erruwyn remains still. They won't be satisfied until he agrees, and if he agrees to agreeing, he may as well set the bone now. The answer will hurt, but he'll never have to ask again—and maybe the injury will have room to knit properly once the question has been wholly retracted.

At length, anxious lips part. "I wish to offer myself, Ladyship."

◇◇◇◇◇◇◇◇◇◇

Three pairs of feet walk the eastern gallery after lesson recording. Erruwyn inhales with a quick glance to Lysbeth's shoulder. "—"

"My answer hasn't changed in only two hours, Erruwyn," she interjects with a smile.

"I'll need at least one full night to form doubts."

Ahead, Corah stops at the music room's doorway. "Don't tarry!"

"Wouldn't dare," Lysbeth replies.

Satisfied, Corah disappears to rejoin her kin in the Grand Drawing Room beyond.

When Avrella had asked what the Offering rite entailed, Erruwyn had hinted at spectacle. Suspense being a rare commodity, Lindenholt's Ladies retrieved whetstones for their tenterhooks and asked the pair to rehearse in private for surprise's sake.

Lysbeth leads Erruwyn to the center of the front drawing room and turns. "I know Granmama hopes to see your silver again. Will you wear it?"

"Yes." Splayed fingers follow his ribs to his heart. "The silver—the *ay'tuan* you have seen—is addressed as *Danae*."

"Dah-nay? It has a name?" she asks, recognizing the filigree's lines. "Are there others?"

"Yes, Ladyship, though *Danae* is required for the Offering."

"I see, and you call the suits a-too-ahn?"

He nods. "*ay'tuan*: *silver-puppet*."

"Evocative." She smiles. "Go on."

"I will extend as *er'oo'n* to greet, to Offer." He holds his right arm forward. "To signal acceptance, if you still wish it—" He briefly takes his own hand.

"An out, even to the end. How considerate." She takes his hand. "Then?"

"Then place palms together, fingers to me." He moves closer, gently positioning her hands and laying his against them. "My fingers to you."

"A hand sandwich. Alright."

Erruwyn moves her fingers to his chest and slides his thumbs between her fingertips. "Here I will give you *Anese*. Then, the mooring. As you stand, I will circle. Recite. When I return, the chain is complete." He slants his head forward. "You are *nar uah*."

"Oh. Is that everything? Don't misunderstand, I'm relieved—my memory isn't as good as yours—but I thought there'd be more."

"Yes, everything." He smiles and releases her hands.

"Easy enough, then. Though Corah may find another to coddle if your spectacle is wanting," she teases, moving towards the gallery. "Will my standing still do the trick?"

He exhales a laugh as they cross to the Grand Drawing Room. "I ask enough, Ladyship. I will bear the spectacle."

"Much obliged." She glances happily; Erruwyn's already more comfortable around her. Nearing the Ladies' couch, she continues, "What is A-knee-see, exactly?"

"It is the *ay*, the silver, of my anima. The essence of my life," he says, kneeling as she sits. "Breath, voices, motion, heart. The seeds of my expression. You will carry these after the Offering, Ladyship."

"Heavens. I hope you have a spare," Avrella mutters.

He smiles and shakes his head.

"Is Anese a symbol of your life, then?" Lysbeth asks.

"Yes, a little, Ladyship. A life requires anima, though, a life is more than this. *Anese* delivers my anima. The Offering delivers my life."

Corah scoots up. "Will the southern terrace do for spectacle?"

"Yes, it can occur most places, *li'la*. It is nothing so grand, though pleasing to observe."

"Have you seen it before?" Elane asks.

"Not truly. It is demonstrated. Practiced in training."

Lysbeth's eyebrows pull in. "I'm curious to know how you're expected to follow three separate Wills, seeing as I'm to be one of them."

"Mm." He nods. "The Wills are given order. *k'uah⌢ni*, Sovereign Will, is beneath. *r'uah⌢na*, Attuning Will, is above. Their doctrines are rare to change." He tilts to Lysbeth. "*nar⌢uah*, Wayfinder, is between; a flexible link to bridge. I obey the Will of Sovereign until *nar⌢uah* bids my diversion, or *◊Ruah* makes a demand."

"Until I bid you break the law?"

"A law, a custom, yes. If you wish it. *nar⌢uah* resides above *k'uah⌢ni*, Sovereign."

"Let us keep Sovereign Hinri from hearing it, Lyssy," Avrella drolls.

"What's Roo-ah?" Corah frowns. "If it's a Will that makes demands, does that mean it's a person? Like Lys?"

"No, *r'uah⌢na* is the Attuning Will of the people—the principles of equilibrium we observe," Erruwyn explains, adding *wox'ua* for clarity. "*◊Ruah* is the Concept: Fulcrum. The Concept births the principles."

"Still, how does a concept demand anything?" Elane asks, amused.

Erruwyn thinks for a time. Glancing at the guitarra stand behind him, he twists to bring the instrument to his lap. "Equilibrium often restores itself, Your Ladyship. Here, string rests at Fulcrum." He plucks a note. "Though I displace the equilibrium of string, equilibrium will restore it. The path to restoration is vibration. *◊Ruah* willed this, demanded this of itself."

Elane watches the string's return to stillness. "You're referring to a force of nature, then?"

He nods. "This force is *◊Ruah*'s root in nature, though its branches are loftier. Occasionally equilibrium cannot restore itself. A broken string. Dis-cord. In this occasion, *◊Ruah* demands a path to restoration. The path is *ry⌢ine*: weaving of symmetry, repairing of dis-cord. Those who walk the path are justiciars of *◊Ruah*."

Lysbeth tucks a hand under her chin. "What's an example of the Concept in practice?"

"Mm." Returning the guitarra to its stand, he thinks again. "Among the people is a phrase of *◊Ruah*'s attunement: *To hold the cover of night we must offer the brightest stars.*

The people's concealment requires the loss of *da'he͡na*. In this way, the weight of our suffering attunes to the weight of our protection." Continuing, he extends the example to Lysbeth, "My guidance among the Outland will hinder *nar͡uah* for our lifetime. ◊*Ruah* demands attunement; a balance for the hindrance. So. I offer my life. My training. *nar͡uah* may use me as she wishes."

"Hindrance seems an inflated appraisal." She arches an eyebrow. "How does one contact Ruah about its choice of phrasing?"

Erruwyn bounces a smile off the floor. "I wonder, do you wish to hear the tale of *ǂn'ar'uah*, Ladyship?" At the room's enthusiastic response, he begins: "*ǂn'ar'uah* is the brightest star of night's starlit path."

"The Misty Lane," Corah corrects.

He nods in deference. "*ǂn'ar'uah* resides within the Misty Lane as a point of navigation. It is said, ages distant, a vessel of *da'he͡na* became lost on the sea."

Erruwyn peeks at Lysbeth—who restrains a smile at the unspoken reference to their Solstice conversation. He'd meant the words for her alone, after all.

"Despondent, *da'he͡na* sang to *ǂn'ar'uah* of home. Moved by their sorrow, *ǂn'ar'uah* joined their lamentation. Her voice greatly strengthened the song. In turn, voices of *da'he͡na* rose in wonder. They continued in this way: *ǂn'ar'uah* increasing *da'he͡na* increasing. Soon, the force of their duet caused even the brightness of *ǂn'ar'uah* to increase. She used her new light to forge a path through the darkness, laying flecks of herself against sky as pebbles—the Misty Lane, a path to guide the lost *da'he͡na* to safety."

Smiling at the Ladies' cheerful murmurs, Erruwyn pulls his wrists to his heart—left fingers towards his chin, right fingers towards the floor.

"Their resonance is known as *da'he͡nar͡uah*: the unifying hope of guided purpose."

The following afternoon, Erruwyn dresses Lysbeth's hair with fine chains and beads, and as a final touch, tucks the silver flower he'd given her above her ear. When he leaves, she calls for Ani and changes into a grey silk dress, finding the color more appropriate for the metal she's been adorned with.

Erruwyn returns to his room and pulls the filigree tree away from the corner. Layers of *ay'tuan* attach to the tree's base with hinged bars. He steps on a pedal to unlock them, and flips through to *m'ay-tut*—the joint-bracing framework used as a foundation for additional layers. It's still combined with ◊*Danae* from Winter Solstice, and after undressing, he locks in. Combing its horns through his hair, he swings layers again and stops on today's addition: two slender, six-foot-long cylinders dangling a mix of delicate filigree, stamped plates, and scalloped chains.

Three hinges break the cylinders into thirds. The first hinge attaches to a row of articulated spinal joints, the second is mid-way along the tubule, and the third nears the tube's end. He backs in and sockets his spinal discs. As they turn and lock, the hinges pivot, folding the cylinders into flat triangles across his back.

Jingling slightly, he steps away to open his trunk—which he's kept closed after Brom explained the difference between the people's communal ideals and Avonleigh's practice of stealing—and retrieves his *ḥu'ay*, the silver marks of his masteries.

Fourteen thin rings sit on his left fingers—one above each knuckle. Five rings hook around his left ear cartilage. A spoked earpiece splays in his right ear. Short spirals snap to his scalp below *⟪Danae*'s horns. A cuff grips his right forearm. An embellished V rests at the base of his throat. *⟩m-aen͡ḥu'ay* drapes his face.

By the time he steps through the servant's entrance of the main house, he's left a trail of brazenly-staring residents in his wake. It's much easier to push their looks from his mind now. If she actually accepts him, he's sure he'll never mind their looks again.

The rhythm of his heart quickens.

His feet follow suit.

da'he ⁀nar ⁀uah

The Ladies have assembled on the southern terrace, enjoying cheery mood and weather. Beneath the awning's shade, Avrella, Elane, and Corah sit on cushioned, wrought-iron benches discussing Equinox plans. Ms. Pinley holds an *er'oo'n*-fiddling-Erem by the Salon's door, offering her opinions when asked. Their voices mix pleasingly with the trickling garden fountain as Lysbeth half-listens from the terrace railing, admiring the peaceful landscape.

Beyond the southern garden, Lindenholt's immense lawn eases into a sprawling wood. The trees are densest to the west, where a shimmering lake peeks between treetops. Past the woods, rows of greenery form a grid of property bounds across an expanse of gently rolling meadow— perennial emerald against transient peridot—yawning all the way to the horizon.

Lysbeth inhales deeply. Soft breezes rustle her dress and pull a sweet fragrance from the silver flower above her ear. Though she's still not entirely sure what to expect of her new role, she finds the notion of it reassuring. She'd always intended to look after Erruwyn, and if her acceptance can bring him some measure of felicity, she won't be the one to deny it. Besides, she's fond of him. *nar⁀uah* might finally allow her the chance to know him better—the person he'd been before the Baron's influence. The person she'd recently begun to glimpse again.

Her thoughts are interrupted by soft jingling and happy gasps. She turns as Erruwyn's entry halts for Corah's analysis, and smiles on noticing the new silver.

Submitting his ringed hand for inspection, Erruwyn periodically glances at the railing. He recognizes Lysbeth's grey dress from his second day at Lindenholt. She'd run her hands over the back of a velvet couch in the Grand Library. She'd spoken of Alder as the last warm hues of sunset leaked through the window and painted her frame.

⁊She'd beamed.

He'd revisited that memory often, whether he'd wanted to or not.

Lysbeth strolls near. "You're looking quite smart. What's the occasion?"

Erruwyn chomps a shy smile at terrace stone.

"There will be plenty of time for preening later," Avrella says, turning her fan on the pair. "I am quite anxious to see what all this is about. Off with you. Commence."

Amused, they waft from the Matriarch's fan to a spot just past the awning.

Erruwyn pushes himself to speak as they come to a stop. "Ladyship, if you do not wish to accept, I will understand. I will not speak of it again." He'd refrained from broaching the subject again yesterday, but still worries after her true inclination and must allow her a path to decline.

She stands tall. "In fact, I'm quite resolved."

Seeing the match in her words and expression, he dips his head and takes a few steps back towards the railing. They regard one another over faint smiles until Erruwyn closes his eyes. Left fingers down, right fingers up, his wrists meet at the cover over his heart. Pointed toes drag up his right, inner leg and rest against his knee.

Śm'aen.

The cylinders on his back flutter; a steady unfolding begins.

Erruwyn's torso leans forward as his left leg extends behind. Fingers lead his hands in opposite directions across his chest. The cylinders' spinal hinges rotate and lock, framing him with two tall triangles.

His right hand reaches towards Lysbeth as his left reaches his thigh. Behind, his left knee bends to point toes skyward. The cylinders' middle hinges lock, creating an upward, bowed appearance.

Right arm fully stretched, his heel lifts from the terrace, and all weight transfers to the ball of his right foot. The final hinge locks. Two cylinders dangling beautiful, silver lace run away from his body: an enormous set of silver wings.

Spotted reflections dance across the terrace as Erruwyn maintains an impressive balancing act, eyes locked on Lysbeth's. Their audience's acclamations provide a harmony for Lysbeth's melodious laugh. Yesterday he said he'd greet her as *er'oo'n*: his outstretched hand acts as the bird's neck and head, his curved back leg is the bird's tail, and, of course, no *er'oo'n* facsimile would be complete without a lustrous, twelve-foot wingspan.

Beaming, she moves in and lays her hand on his. He grins, eyes damp, drawing her nearer as he lowers. When his foot returns to the terrace, the pair stand close together, and *er'oo'n*'s wings have rotated to Erruwyn's back—two tall vertices rising behind his shoulders. They bring their hands together as practiced, and then to panels forming a convex diamond over his heart.

ṣm'aęn.

The diamond's panels snap back, now resembling a slightly concave star. *ꙙAnęsę* sways from a thin chain in the shallow dish. As Erruwyn's thumbs transfer it to Lysbeth's fingertips, the chain trails behind. Unable to wait, she tilts it up for a glimpse.

ꙙAnęsę looks something like a flower, with a short stem protruding from the back, a concave quatrefoil as petals, and delicate, concentric lines that spiral from the center as stamen. Erruwyn smiles at her peeping and begins a circle, releasing chain from the dish as he recites:

‖ *à-n'of ◆ à-r͡nar͡uah à-kaę ◆ set'o-n ◆ tia-tu'ot ◆ dà'o͡da ◆ at͡ro-sket ◆ h-tu'o͡he ◆ àk'ref-'itet ◆ à-mae'ov'y-ser'w͡to ◆ ào-juh'ne-f* ‖

Standing before Lysbeth again, slender fingers snap the chain's end-disc to an early-link. "*dà'he͡nar͡uah.*"

The Offering completes as his wrists meet over *ꙙDanaę*'s dish—right fingers down, left fingers pointing to an expressive cocktail of disbelieving gratitude garnished with hope.

Lysbeth carefully releases *ꙙAnęsę*. "I'm afraid your essence is a bit low," she says, watching it pendulate at her bellybutton.

Erruwyn sniffles and grins. Freeing the chain, he wraps slack around Lysbeth's neck three times, threading the disc through a small hole in *ꙙAnęsę*'s stem on each pass. The pendant hovers between Lysbeth's collarbones as he closes the circuit.

"The disc holds to chain if you wish for further adjustment, *nar͡uah,*" his voice tapers to a bashful whisper on first use of the new address.

"Thank you." She smiles and pokes the stem. "Such a pleasant-sounding title ought to make for an easy adaptation, too."

At Avrella's beckoning, they turn to rejoin the group. Lysbeth pokes the stem again, unsure if the fluctuating tickle beneath it is cause for concern.

"Oh! That's pretty," Elane says, eyeing the pendant as they near.

"Yes, very handsome." Avrella peers from her chair. "You look a bit dumbfounded, Erruwyn. Though I suppose that is to be expected when one parts with one's anima."

"Yes, *mę͡n*—"

Lysbeth yelps.

Erruwyn's face relaxes. "Resonance, *nar͡uah,*" he explains.

She cheeps.

"What? What is it?" Corah asks, sliding from her chair.

"⟩*Anese*." He smiles. "Voices, motion, breath. The rhythm of my heart. The seeds of my expression. *ͺnar⌢uaḥ* carries these now."

As he speaks, Lysbeth stills her lungs to focus on the activity against her throat. ⟩*Anese* responds to each of his words with a barely audible, middling-vibration—a whispering echo of his voice. Behind the words is a second vibration—inaudible, but the note of its animation is clear and uniform. Behind the note, a third unheard vibration pulses low and faint.

"I feel them." She exhales and blinks at ⟩*m-aen⌢ḥu'ay*'s chains across Erruwyn's face. "But the caddy? I thought your silver needed direct contact to animate."

"Yes, some *ay⌢na* requires the silver path of chain, *ͺnar⌢uaḥ*. Though, these— *⟨Danae*, ⟩*Anese*—were forged together, assembled from *ay⌢na* that responds to diverging pitches of expression."

The women stare blankly; Erruwyn pulls the lead.

"*⟨Danae* amplifies, strengthens the pitches. ⟩*Anese* receives. Returns. To feel the primal pitches of *≤m'aen*. To resonate. *ay⌢na* is used in a similar way among the people."

Corah wrinkles her nose. "Mr. Spantier once sang an E note at the pianoforte strings while he tuned them, and the E string sang back. Is it like that?"

The image comes into focus for Elane. "Yes, sympathetic resonance![13] The strings vibrate, resonate, when sung to in their own pitch. Lysbeth's pendant must resonate with Erruwyn's inaudible sounds, like a dog whistle vibrating when blown—only, Lysbeth wears the whistle and Erruwyn is the one blowing."

He grins, taking an outstretched Erem from Ms. Pinley. "Yes, Your Ladyship. In this way, *ͺnar⌢uaḥ* resonates. Feels textures of *≤m'aen*. Others, also."

A slow smile rises under Lysbeth's watchful eyes. The clear, inaudible note of ⟩*Anese* had intensified when Erruwyn took Erem. His grin stretches as Erem *ͺwox'ua*s. The note intensifies again.

⟩*Anese* is singing.

⟨The form of expression seeds.

Corah pinches her chin. "Does it work conversely, Erruwyn?"

"Yes, *⟨li'la*, though different." He points from *⟨Danae*'s dish to Lysbeth's throat. "*ͺnar⌢uaḥ* feels greatly, there. I feel less, across. Though we are told the resonant bidding of *ͺnar⌢uaḥ* is greatly felt."

"Orders issued from on high often are." Avrella chuckles. "What is the limit of this marvel?"

---

[13] *A principle of physics wherein a passive string or vibratory body responds to external vibrations of harmonic likeness.*

"I am uncertain, ⸸me⁀na. I have never known ⸜nar⁀uah."

He glances at Lysbeth, who's smiling in wonder—blinded by a series of dawning realizations she can't look away from.

"You said Eroon's 'seeds of expression' alter their feathers to match their mood," she begins, dazed. "Your seeds of expression—your primal pitches of may-een, at least—they're instinctual responses, aren't they? That's why they take longer to master than your speaking voices, even though you're born with them." She straightens as her lungs respond to another ray of awareness. "Those among your people who struggle to empathize—you meant a categorical empathy, didn't you? A physical sense alongside sentiment."

⁊The seed of expression roots.

Erruwyn remains still...

as a long-suffered weight slides away, and his heart returns from the pit of his stomach—where it's been since his Threading.[14] She understands. Enough, at least. His eyes dampen again. A lingering refrain, thin and soiled, finally ebbs from the coves of his mind.

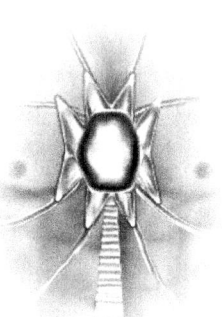

Lysbeth gasps at the intense shuddering of silver on her neck. Her eyes follow ⸸Danae's ribs to its star. ⸸Anese is moored to his heart—to a bed of waters far below the surface—and now she carries the textures of its anchoring. A new sensation follows the shudder as Erruwyn's clear, uniform song merges with a low, sorrowful drone.

The visceral phrasing of ⸤m'aen:

⸸ sing⌣drone

Joy. Sorrow.

Bumps appear on Lysbeth's skin. "Bittersweet," she whispers.

⁊The root of expression sprouts.

⸸Anese sings brightly in response to her recognition and resumes bittersweetness. *da'he⁀nar⁀uah*'s audience puzzles as the pair smile. The expression emerging between them is wholly their own.

Erruwyn's soft explanation centers on Lysbeth, "When ⸼da'he⁀na becomes Aegis, he is no longer a voice in the choir of his people. Without others to carry the hymn when he needs breath—to hear his need, offer aid; to feel his joy, join—he becomes *ir'ie*. A fading chorus without verse. An echo fated to ebb on distant shores. Only by directing his song to ⸜nar⁀uah, who resonates in duet, will he be a true voice again. Be heard."

Lysbeth blinks the blur from her eyes. She'd never considered an even deeper current

---

[14] *The moment a ⸸da'he⁀na is placed in water as bait.*

to Erruwyn's transparent waters. Only six months ago she'd thought he'd been revealing too much, but he'd been burying his own desperate truth in the turf all along. What else had been hidden? How much more had she missed? And his people: empaths. An entire civilization exchanging intimate, involuntary emotional responses. No buried truths. No masks to hide discomfort or deceit. No wonder they lived so harmoniously among each other; feeling, all together—and how hopelessly lonely to be ripped from the comfort of their song and placed here, among Avonleigh's silent veneer.

But with ⟩*Anese*...

As her fingers alight on the pendant, the stem's sensations dull. Erruwyn's head cocks; he feels the resonance—the reflection of his ≤*m'aen* in ⟩*Anese*—less, too.

⟨*The sprout of expression branches.*

"I suppose we've been made to understand Naruah's cruciality, then," Avrella says, inconspicuously re-tucking her handkerchief. "Come sit, it's nearly teatime."

Once all Ladies have found accommodation, servants appear with trays. Erruwyn kneels between Avrella and Lysbeth, a folded wing on either side and Erem in his lap.

"Why didn't you explain any of this yesterday, Erruwyn?" Elane asks, accepting a napkin from Mr. Tenson. "'Ebbing echo' sounds much more serious than anything you let on."

"I did not wish for guilt to steer the course of the answer, Your Ladyship. *nar͡uah* may still have chosen to refuse at the greeting of *er'oo'n*."

Lysbeth takes her cup from a passing tray. "In that case, I'm glad I managed the correct answer all on my own."

⟩ *purl*

A fond, bashful purl spreads through ⟩*Anese* as Erruwyn bites his smile.

Lysbeth grins.

"What was your recitation, Erruwyn?" Corah asks, snapping a biscuit with her teeth.

"Forgive me, I should have suggested the words. I will seek them." After several moments of blank stone-gazing, he looks up. "The words nearby:"

> ‖*I am offered, nar͡uah • Attune me to your will; shape my form • The vessel to carry you forward • The sword held in your hand • The voice to sing your song • The scroll to hold your word • The shield for your protection • The tempo for your dance • Make me into mortar for the stars beneath your feet • Use me well to forge our path so our course might be long*‖

"Goodness, quite the resume." Avrella chuckles.

Lysbeth smirks into her teacup. "Yes, I think I can put you to good use."

⟩ *sing‿purl*

The jet of air from Lysbeth's nose splashes her tea over the rim. She sets down the cup with joy clutching her throat. "A *purr*, Erruwyn?"

♪ sing_purl

Her question amplifies the effect. Erruwyn's silent laughter rivets to the feet of Erem's *er'oo'n*. Lysbeth lifts a napkin to her mouth, delighted.

"Purr?" Avrella peers coquettishly at filigreed skin. "I do hope you're a lap cat."

♪Anese purrs again, sending Lysbeth back to her napkin. Erruwyn's shoulders shake as he hides beneath a slender hand.

"Granmama!" Elane laughs in admonishment.

Corah chews another biscuit, watching the four with tepid scorn.

After taking a moment's collection, Lysbeth sniffles and risks re-lifting her cup. "Frankly, I'm distressed you waited so long for something so important, Erruwyn. And even then, only due to Granmama dragging it from you."

"Mm." Erruwyn nods and wipes an eye. "I did not think the words could matter, *nar⁀uah*. Though, I had planned to say. To offer."

♪ —

Lysbeth receives a faint suggestion from *♪Anese*: the onset and abrupt cessation of Erruwyn's middling vibrations. A halted breath. He's stopped himself from saying more. She taps the pendant in gentle encouragement. "Go on, Erruwyn."

⸮The branch of expression buds.

"Then, there is another rite significant to *≠da'he⁀na*," he says, watching Erem trace silver paths on his fingers. "The time of silence to amend understanding. *ax'ni⁀rah*."

"When you wore the mouth covering?"

"Yes. It is said, once departed from the silence, we take our place in the Outland's choir. The first *≠aen* we create—the first sound those among you hear—is to be the first note of our new song." His head dips shyly. "I hoped you would be the first to hear my new song, *nar⁀uah*, because I already wished to offer myself."

Apprehension rising, Lysbeth returns her cup to the saucer.

"On the day I felt ready to speak, I searched for you. I walked around, around." He draws a circle on Erem's belly, smiling faintly at her *tch*-ing giggle. "Though there were others nearby, to ask them for assistance would have begun my song in your absence."

"Hardly Avonleigh's first quagmired debutant." Avrella chuckles.

His smile broadens slightly. "After time, I heard Ani bid another's silence in taking an item to a room for dressing because you were nearby to it. I followed the item. Returned with the dressing box. Once departed from *ax'ni⁀rah*—once offered—I hoped to dress your hair in celebration of my new song, *nar⁀uah*." He glances at Lysbeth's feet. "Our new song, if you wished to accept."

♪ drone

"I thought first to request your hair; the answer could matter, maybe." He swallows. "After my Threading, the vessel, *ki'ky*, I did not wish to be interrupted by the man who caused such suffering. I reacted badly when he reached. I had not thought to stem my rooted impulses."

⚥*A͟n͟e͟s͟e*'s sorrowful drone is joined by a hiss. Loathing. *Self*-loathing.

⚥ *hiss‿drone*

The combination is a heavy whisper. Shame.

Deep regret.

Lysbeth clenches her jaw.

"What manner of impulses, Erruwyn?" Avrella asks somberly.

Wrapping an arm around Erem, he answers to the terrace, "Hair has meaning among the people, ⸮*m͟e͟͞n͟a*, severed only after anima has muted. Only after death. To touch another's without request is taboo. He had not yet requested..." He rubs his face through a strained smile. "*i͟x͟'u͟l*: my haunting. If I had not shielded my hair, I could still have it."

His hand drops to cup Erem's head as he pulls her in.

Pained verdigris lifts to Lysbeth.

"Among many, many other differences."

"I'm ashamed to say I found the Will passages of Alder's letter boring when I was a girl," Lysbeth confesses, descending the terrace steps after tea. "No fantastical imagery of people and animals."

"Then I must strive to conceal your shame from the other *da'he na*," Erruwyn says, clicking *Danae*'s arm in place to carry Erem without fatigue.

"Much obliged."

He bites a small smile at her grin. "It is not wholly selfless. A *nar uah* bored of the Wills would bring shame to me also."

Lysbeth's eyebrows arch over a light, chiding laugh as the terrace's jousting match spikes: Corah's list of VerNox sweets has been steadily unhorsed, but with three weeks left before the event, the tourney has just begun. *da'he nar uah* toss amused glances up the steps.

"Do your people have EquiSol traditions?" Lysbeth asks, walking forward.

"Yes. Dance, sing, primp." A corner of his mouth lifts. "Among other forms of physical activity. These expressions are present at every celebration."

Lysbeth shakes her head. "With all your physical activity I still find it difficult to believe there aren't children born outside the birth month."

"*ne'ru'k* training is rigorous, *nar uah*. The emergence of unplanned life would greatly disturb the people's Attunement. *r'uah na*. Endanger us quickly."

"I suppose that follows, particularly if your resources are limited." After a pause she returns to his previous answer, "What manner of dancing and donning is observed?"

"Many forms. Though the dance of *lyr itet* requires the greatest primping. It occurs when the sun bears the astral halo, only." He nods to the sky. "When day and night attune."

"Only during Vernal and Autumnal Equinoxes? What kind of dance is it?"

"It is performed always as twiceborn, *nar uah*. With twins. Mirroring, reflecting. Day. Night. The primping is for this appearance."

"Were you and your sister a popular choice given your names?"

"Yes. Dawn, Dusk. We attuned to this aspect of *Ruah* well, though our popularity was born of necessity. Only *da'he na* preform this dance."

Crunching gravel marks the easy tempo of their feet as they approach the garden fountain. Erruwyn stops for Erem to throw an imaginary wishing coin into the pool.

"Why are Dahena the only dancers?" Lysbeth asks, pulling a stray hair from her face.

"The *ąy'tuąn* worn for this dance requires all five *tią͡ąy'ąn: silver roots of anguish*. The spine silver." He laughs softly at Lysbeth's morbidly curious expression. "They are very painful to plant, *ņąŗ͡uąh*. Only *⚹dą'he͡ ņa* carry the five roots. This is one reason for so few of us."

"Why are Dahena required to have the silver embedded?" She brushes a hedgerow as they move down the path again. "What else dissuades more from joining your rank?" Her brow furrows. "How many Dahena are there, precisely?"

Erruwyn smiles at her pelting. He likes it. Lysbeth didn't have to care—about his people, or him—but she does. Even during *ąx'ņi͡ ŗąh,* when he couldn't provide proper answers, she'd pelted. He suspects most Avons would be quite content to put him in a cupboard, only pulling him out to impress guests or to use his skills for ill-purpose.

He suspects correctly.

"The masteries required to earn *⚹Dąną̈e* are challenging. Dissuasive, maybe. Though most walking the path of *⚹dą'he͡ ņa* change course after the first root. The pain of one is great; five are required for *⚹Dąną̈e*'s resonance with *⚹Anęsę*. Their planting is a piece of our training to resist coercion, also." He drags a thumb across Erem's forehead to tuck breeze-blown strands behind her ear. "We are fewer than one in two-thousand among the people. Though, I must remain silent on the truer sum."

"Quite alright." She slows her feet and scans the horizon. "Were Dahena always trained to resist pain? Even when our people were friendly?"

Erruwyn smiles again. He also likes Lysbeth's intelligence, seeing what she picks up on. "No, it was not always so. When the path of distant *⚹dą'he͡ ņa* branched from what was known, the training followed."

"But how were you to learn if something unforeseeable had occurred? Alder's letter said Dahena are not to return, that doing so would upset Ruahna?" Her feet stop for her face to quiz Erruwyn.

⚹ purr

Her head and expression straighten. "Whatever are you purring for?" she asks, grinning as the purr intensifies.

Erruwyn hides under a palm. "It cannot be helped, *ņąŗ͡uąh*," unheard chuckles thin his voice, "that I enjoy you so."

Lysbeth's laughter trickles over the hedgerows. His answer was as unexpected as the purr, and though the border of interpretation is fuzzy, she's pleased. She enjoys him, too. Erem bounces a smile back and forth between them, happy at their happiness.

"Well, since it can't be helped, I can't hold it against you," Lysbeth says, walking again.

"I am grateful. You will learn much of me through ⵊ*Anese*. I do not wish for you to regret your acceptance. This would mean you have come to regret me, also."

Her glance is warm and deliberate. "As far as possible outcomes go, I believe regret must be lowest in order."

Erruwyn looks away to dip a sheepish smile. "To answer, we learned of the need for this training near to an age distant, when male twiceborn ⵣ*da'he͡na* were still Called together for resonance of ⵢ*m'aen*. It is through ⵢ*m'aen* we feel each other, influence each other. Attune. The absence of this seed is greatly felt." He lifts his head to look across the distant treetops. "In only nine moons,[15] four twiceborn pairs were Called. We did not yet understand the waters we charted carried great conflict."

ⵊ *drone*

"The Called were bound to one ⵖ*k'uah͡ni*. The Will of this Sovereign sought to plunder our soil, to claim resources for his battle with another. Their refusal to reveal us caused great suffering. They submerged in the currents of madness, broke the covenant between our peoples—rejected Sovereign's Will. They returned to us, displaced ◊*Ruah*, brought discordance to our Attunement. This occasion greatly altered our path."

Lysbeth slows to a stop at the edge of the lawn and searches her governess' history lessons. The Takkar-Ercasian Kingswar was one of the grander naval conflicts on record and took place in the large sea dividing the two countries nearly an age ago. Though there were no records of ⵣ*da'he͡na* sightings during that time, warring Sovereigns tend to keep valuable resources closely guarded.

Erruwyn continues, "Many among the people believed the Called's madness was strengthened through resonance of ⵢ*m'aen*. Received, bolstered. Returned, bolstered. It was decided this cannot be. ◊*Ruah* birthed new principles in ⵖ*r'uah͡na*. Only fe-male twiceborn may walk the path of ⵣ*da'he͡na*. One to remain. One to offer. A piece of us always home."

ⵊ *sing_drone*

"Our need of embodied ⵑ*nar͡uah* emerged from this decision, also. A mutable Will to guide, hear. Resonate ⵢ*m'aen* without risk. So. ⵛ*Danae* was forged with silver roots to amplify the pitches of expression. ⵊ*Anese* was forged to resonate the pitches." He smiles at Lysbeth. "This permits me to feel another again, also. Though it is only the reflection of my own ⵢ*m'aen*, it is enough. In this way, silver roots became a piece of our training."

They turn their eyes to the landscape, ingesting the tale. "What became of those tortured into madness?" Lysbeth asks quietly. "Were they reaccepted?"

"There was much debate, ⵑ*nar͡uah*. It was decided re-embracing discordant ⵣ*da'he͡na* would leave a trail for future ⵣ*da'he͡na* to follow. This could not be so." He takes a slow breath. "They remained long enough to emerge from the currents of madness;

---

[15] *One year in the lunar calendar is thirteen months, 28 days each. Three ages ago, most Outland civilizations shifted to a solar calendar of twelve months with sporadic day counts.*

to understand why they must go. Then they departed."

⚘ —

"What else, Erruwyn?"

⚘ *chime*

An abrupt flinch settles into a persistent waver. A reverberating chime.

Anxiety.

Hesitant, Erruwyn takes *er'oo'n* from Erem's dozing arms and snaps it to *⚘Danae*'s hip. The chime dims as he forces a breath. His eyes jump from the ground to an expectant Lysbeth. "Though it was not so for those swept into madness, vessels cradled by *wa't'un* occasionally carry news of Called *⚘da'he⌒na*."

"The bank of sand, yes of course," Lysbeth murmurs, lifting a hand to her chin. "And what becomes of those baited but uncalled? There's record of Spencish galleon encountering a Dahena. He wasn't taken on, but the crew spotted Eroon's shadow—mistook it for a dragon, in fact. Was he flown to safety?"

⚘ *drone*

"No, *nar⌒uah*. *er'oo'n* cannot fly with such weight. *⚘jae'dua–⚘da'he⌒na* walked the path of his *nu'im*: the only fork on the path of Threaded *⚘da'he⌒na*. The offering scow is forged to sink—to tempt our hunters to stop; to accept our offer before the occasion goes. *⚘jae'dua*'s hunters were not tempted, or did not observe the sinking."

Lysbeth's eyes widen. Drowning had never occurred to her younger self. The Faye were too whimsical for something as mundane and unjust as untimely death. The mystery of the account hadn't been whether it was true, but in which of the few possible ways its outcome had been happy for the Faye who'd evaded capture.

"You mean, you and Kiky would've...? If Dorsit's ship hadn't...?"

⚘ *sing_drone*

"Please do not feel so, *nar⌒uah*. We breathe."

After a long look, she nods, and the pair turn their attention to the horizon. They stand in comfortable silence as a cool breeze lifts the aroma of yesterday's drizzle from damp earth. Birds court each other across Lindenholt's gardens—each plot offering something suitable for avians of discerning taste. Their songs pull a question forward in Lysbeth's mind; one she feels compelled to ask despite her confidence in the answer.

Her eyes remain ahead. "Erruwyn. Your new song in Avonleigh. Did it"—she swallows apologetically—"did your first word occur at the Warden's?"

Erruwyn shifts at the edge of her vision. When his face finds her, she takes a deep breath and bravely turns to meet it.

Heavy moments pass before he speaks.

"It was not a word."

In their first days of acquaintance,
_ḏa'hę͟ ̄n̠a̠r̠ ̄u̠a̠ḫ_ embossed heavy meaning on one another:
reversal of fortune.

Lysbeth was the first friendly face Erruwyn had seen since his Calling.
He'd feared he would fade into echo without resonance, but Lysbeth's
kindness and interest had reassured him.
She'd been the mold of his salvation, and he'd poured his faith into her.
She was his hope, a chance for kinship.
Comfort.
His instinct had been to block Dorsit, not only to respect his people's taboo, but
to protect his only hope of comfort from the man who had taken all other
comfort away.

Since Lysbeth's introduction to Alder's letter, respite became synonymous
with Faye—Erruwyn's arrival was the manifestation of her childhood
longings for a fairer, freer world.
He'd been the mold of her dissent, and she'd poured her wonder into him.
He was her comfort, the possibility that her world could improve.
Hope.
Her instinct had been to invite Erruwyn into her morning room,
not only to protest her people's stifling decorum, but to reinforce her only
comforting hope.

When the humors of fate intervened, _ḏa'hę͟ ̄n̠a̠r̠ ̄u̠a̠ḫ_'s fears seemed to be realized. They'd
resigned themselves to those fears ever since—afraid to openly acknowledge the initial
feelings of hope and comfort the other had provided.
Now that _A̠n̠ę̠s̠ę̠_ has already acknowledged some of these feelings on their behalf, breaking
the silence doesn't seem quite so daunting—or quite so pointless.

hiss drone_

"I knew I was to be returned to you. I wished to wait. To remain with _a̠x̠'n̠ị ̄r̠a̠ḫ_. I
hoped you could still be the first to hear my song. Then..."

_A̠n̠ę̠s̠ę̠_'s loathing hiss amplifies to a crackle and its drone to a wail. An anxious chime
joins and amplifies to a peal.

※ *crackle_wail_peal*

Revulsion. Despair. Fear.

Horror.

The scroll of the children.

da'he⁀nar⁀uah's eyes fix—emotions resounding above silver in blue, green, and red.

Lysbeth paws at truths in the soil.

"I didn't want you to go, Erruwyn," she whispers.

The horror in ※*Anese* dampens.

"And I did not wish to go from you, *nar⁀uah*."

as'etu

Trumpeted sleeves fanfare up Lysbeth's arms as Ani tugs fabric over her back. "I was thinking over Erruwyn's recitation as I fell asleep last night," she says, pulling aside a copper-haired curtain for Avonleigh's signature bliaut-bodice production. "Do you recall he said, 'Make me into mortar for the stars beneath your feet'?"

"Yes, I quite liked the imagery." Elane smiles from her spot at a dressing room vanity. "Well, perhaps not the turning into mortar, but walking along the Misty Lane."

"As did I. After learning he'd intended to offer himself that day—"

"Oh, I'd just gotten over thinking of it, Lys," Elane pleads. "I'm no good with what-ifs. It's all far too upsetting."

"Aye." Ani clucks, finishing the bow. "Such a sorrowful shame."

"Indeed, Ani. Catastrophic. And Elane, I'm sorry to say that if I must suffer the what-iffing of it, I'm bringing you along." Lysbeth wriggles her freshly confined torso and moves to a vanity. "Erruwyn's version of events got me thinking. Do also you recall Isaac's declaration? When he informed us he'd be sending Erruwyn to the Baron?"

Sighing bitter resignation, Elane stands to be dressed. "I recall he said the Warden would teach Erruwyn proper conduct."

"Yes, he also said he would grind Erruwyn under his heel until he could be useful to us as a path for advancement." Lysbeth sits to watch her cousin reach the same realization she'd come to last night.

Though the dust of Isaac's avenue for advancement and the mortar of ₍ₙₐᵣ‿ᵤₐₕ's starlit path bore a remarkable likeness, the twisted humors of fate would not be satisfied so easily.

The Offering is intended as an equivalent exchange. In return for ₍ₙₐᵣ‿ᵤₐₕ's lifetime commitment to guide and resonate with the Called, a ₂ₔₐ'ₕₑ‿ₙₐ offers himself—including his skills. Erruwyn *wanted* to be useful. Having seen nothing of the Faye's supposedly fantastical abilities by day three, however, Isaac misjudged Erruwyn's acclimatizing for indolence. Had he and Dorsit not intervened, Erruwyn would've offered his skills as a road to whichever destination Lysbeth preferred only a few moments later.

Elane lets out a weak groan as her waist is cinched.

"Agreed," Lysbeth says pointedly. "I know it's despicable of me, but I find some comfort in the poor Kingswarfare. I don't want it faring worse, mind, but steady on will keep Isaac away for a good while."

"Then we're both despicable. Reading Uncle Jaspyr's letters raises concern and relief in equal measure. It's a peculiar feeling." Elane waggles her bodice and scoffles.[16] "Fortunately, by the end I'm so overcome with guilt I'm back to where I started."

"To each their own vises." Lysbeth sighs as they step to the sitting room for Avrella's imminent arrival, and soon after her appearance, *ʒАṉẹṣẹ* oscillates.

Yesterday, _da'he͡ nar͡ uah_ tested the limit of their resonance by walking in opposite directions of the garden. The strongest vibrations of emotional ≤*m'aẹṇ* disappeared around fifty feet, while the range of willful ≤*m'aẹṇ*—pitches produced intentionally rather than pitches of instinctual emotional response—was at least double. As *《Ḏaṉaẹ* amplifies ≤*m'aẹṇ*, Avrella suggested Erruwyn wear the silver puppet full-time. He gratefully accepted, and Lysbeth now fondly refers to their resonance as his cat bell.

"I sense an approaching feline." She grins.

The women shovel happy reception on Erruwyn as he enters. Disinterring himself, he catches sight of *ʒАṉẹṣẹ* and moves the scribal case to his chest to purr bashfully across the room under Lysbeth's coy smile. Nearing the vanities, he slows to watch Ani shut a drawer. She looks up at his lingering.

"You are absent, Ani?" he asks, motioning to his feet.

"I believe you hold the cards now, my dear," Avrella mutters through another diligent examination of his bared figure.

He glances at the Matriarch and chews a forming smile.

ʒ *sing‿chirp*

Joy. Surprise.

Excitement—and something else. A soft buzz. Fizzing interest.

ʒ *sing‿chirp‿fizz*

Playful curiosity. Mischief?

ʒАṉẹṣẹ scampers impishly beneath Lysbeth's grin. Smile crooking, Erruwyn sets down the scribal case. "ˁ*aaṉi*," he says, taking a long step towards her.

Ani straightens, already giggling through her closed mouth.

Arching an eyebrow, he drags out another step. "You are busy."

Ani crosses her wrists under her chin and puffs her cheeks.

Tilting his head, he takes the final, slow step to arm's reach. "I am to greet you instead?"

Ani's giggle erupts. Erruwyn's grin tracks her dart past the vanities to the dressing room. Stifled squeaks leak from the doorway.

Lysbeth chortles. "They'll want you and your silver north soon. I'm not sure I've ever

---

[16] *Scoff-chuckle*

witnessed a hastier retreat." At his purr, she laughs again.

"Yes, my victory is fortunate in timing. I have recently gained a new opponent," he says, matching her playful look as he approaches the hair caddy.

Tools from the box are quickly transferred to faintly outlined, magnetic creases on *Danae*'s forearm plates. With his tools close, the precision and speed of his work are enhanced. Elane remarks on the change once the dressings are complete, and Erruwyn volunteers an explanation.

"Yes. We are slippery among the people, Your Ladyship. Our hinges. Joints." Erruwyn points to the bracing filigree beneath *Danae*. "*m'ay-tut* binds us together. Without it, we must be cautious. Move more slowly."

"Slippery? What do you mean?" Lysbeth asks.

"Occasionally we slip, *nar͡uah*. Shoulder, finger, feet. The bones hop. It is unpleasant," he explains, returning dressing tools to the caddy. "With the assistance of *m'ay-tut* we work swiftly."

"Goodness." Avrella twists in her chair. "Have you experienced what you describe during your time here?"

"Yes, *ʒme͡na*. Though I know how to correct it, the slipping is undesirable. This is where the use of *ay* began among the people. The remedies, also." He nods to the crystal vial on a chain around her neck.

"Well, I am glad to hear you will not needlessly suffer slipperiness any longer." Avrella chuckles. "And how fortunate to have another justification for keeping you in this state of undress."

"Granmama," Lysbeth scolds half-heartedly.

Laughing through his nose, Erruwyn opens the scribal case he'd set down on arrival.

"Why have you brought the kit today?" Elane asks.

He removes a panel covering the lower lid's hollow. A scroll rests on silver filigree within. "The painting of *ʒme͡na*, Your Ladyship."

"The painting? My younger portrait?" Avrella puzzles; the conversation had taken place over a month ago.

"Yes, *ʒme͡na*. I believe the artist was mistaken in expression. I wished to demonstrate."

The cousins come closer as he unrolls a detailed graphite sketch on Avrella's vanity. The background matches Avrella's hallway portrait, but her bearing is markedly different. For the original painting, she'd been put in a soft floral dress, placed in a chair beside a fireplace, and told to look demurely to the artist's right. In the new version, the back of Avrella's crisp dress leans against the fireplace. One arm sprawls across the mantle, the other extends out, clasped by man's disembodied fingers. Above the subtle smirk on her lips, playful eyes look squarely at the artist.

Her gleeful granddaughters titter. Erruwyn's version is a perfect match in personality, but no one would commission such a painting in Avonleigh—personality is very unbecoming on a woman.

The Matriarch stares in silence.

⚡ *chime*

Erruwyn glances between sketch and subject. When the chime amplifies, Lysbeth wraps ⚡*Anese* with her fingers. ⚡*Danae*'s drop in resonance lifts Erruwyn's gaze.

"I'm sure Granmama is only taking it in," she reassures.

"Wha—? Oh, yes." Avrella half-turns, keeping her eyes on the paper. "My nerves and I resolved to no longer be shocked by your detail, my dear, to save what is left of us." She chuckles. "And we got on rather well, I might add. However, we are currently unable to comprehend this reproduction of my younger face."

"It is you, ⟨*me͡na*, there." He tilts his head to mark the location: Avrella.

"But you have never seen me at the age." She looks to her granddaughters. "I tell you, it is my spitting image. Not even the painter got me down..." She squints at the earnest, teal eyes above her. "Is this what you see when you look at me?"

"It is a piece of what I see, ⟨*me͡na*."

⚡ —

Lysbeth taps her encouragement; Erruwyn nods.

"When we take to the page to resonate images, we embody *?Roske*. Chronicler—"

"A Concept? Like Ruah?" Elane interrupts apologetically.

"Yes, Your Ladyship. With training, observance, we learn to embody the Concepts. With much more training, we reach *as'etu*, an absence of mind beyond embodiment. This image was made in my absence. Though it is not too difficult to see ⟨*me͡na* at this age while I am present, the image is unclear." Erruwyn motions to the drawing. "*?Roske*'s expression of creativity provides clarity. Often accurate. This is true for Archives of language, also."

"I've seen your vacancy when drawing," Lysbeth says. "What happens, exactly?"

"Without *ay'tuan*, the silver puppets, this was not true *as'etu*," he clarifies. "What you have observed was embodiment, only, *nar͡uah*. I carry unfocused memories of those occasions. *as'etu* carries no memory. We awake to find the Concept has performed in our absence."

Lysbeth grows perplexed. "Are you claiming to channel some kind of entity during a-see-too?"

His head sways thoughtfully. "Many among the people believe we become vessels through *ay'tuan*; puppeted through *as'etu*. Though, many among the people also believe *as'etu* is the result of training, only: the skills to greatly empathize, to believe you are another. Then to blink the mind. They believe the need for *ay'tuan* emerges as habit from training."

"And which camp do you fall to?" Avrella asks, amused.

"I am uncertain." He bites his lip. "If you truly believe you are another, it is true. For you. For the occasion. This belief is required for successful _as'etu_. If the belief cannot occur without _ay'tuan_, the reason for why this is so cannot matter." He smiles, repeating, "I am uncertain. I believe I rest at both camps, ⸲_me⁀ŋa_."

"Yes, it is best to keep to the middling road of public opinion." Avrella smirks. "That is what I have been told repeatedly, in any case."

Lysbeth runs a thumb along her jaw. "You had a vacant expression the first time you played the pianoforte, Erruwyn. Were you embodying then as well?"

⸲ _chime_

"Yes," he answers softly. " _ʔRoske_ demanded as I attempted sleep. _ix'ul_. Memories that hunt. Haunt. _ʔRoske_ will force their reliving until the chronicle is expressed. Archived. Though, some _ix'ul_ require many Archives." He lifts his eyes to Lysbeth. "Without expression, we fall to Feast of Suffering—consuming memory, only. Without food, sleep. ⸲_li'la_'s instrument was the nearest form of Archival expression."

Lysbeth's fingers ball under her chin. "I wish I'd known; I'd have given you more parchment."

He exhales a weary laugh. "Please do not feel so, _nar⁀uah_. I wish I could have—" _wox'ua_: communicated.

"Well, we can certainly make up for lost communication now," she says, dropping fingers to ⸲_Anese_.

The silver purrs, as she thought it might. She's enjoying the leverage.

"Is that Roh-skee's puppet?" Elane asks, peeping in the scribal case.

"Mm. The _ay'tuan_ is _ʔRoske_, Your Ladyship, though there may be truer words." He retrieves two half-oval filigrees and passes one to Elane. "This is the Concept's silver. _ay_. When worn, I am the Concept's puppet. _tuan_."

"It's a bit like a marionette bar, then?" Elane posits, turning the metal.

"I think, yes."

Lysbeth hops to her writing desk and rifles through a drawer. A moment later, she returns holding out a large sheet of parchment. "Would you mind?"

Erruwyn looks from canvas to Lysbeth. "It will be as you wish it, _nar⁀uah_. You need only to say."

"Then, I say becoming the Will of a star does not entitle me to rudeness," she piths.

He grins and takes the page. "As you say."

Elane hands off the silver and the group adjourns to the couches. Kneeling beside the table, Erruwyn lays the parchment and _ay'tuan_ atop.

"What do you wish of _ʔRoske_, _nar⁀uah_?"

Lysbeth rests her grin on her fists. Her eyes flash. *"Eroon."*

⅘ purr

Laughing quietly, Erruwyn unfolds *⁊Roske* and slots *⸆Danac*'s wrist divots into port protrusions along the ovals' bottom edges. Long fingers spread.

⅘ ⸤

Lysbeth jumps.

"Forgive me." Erruwyn lowers his head contritely. Willed *⸤m'aen* is strong, and he hadn't thought to warn her. Lysbeth dampens *⅘Anese* with her fingertips and nods for him to continue. *⁊Roske*'s animation begins as the divots turn and lock.

Breaks in the filigree divide the bottom of each oval into thirds. One remains flat for ports; two wrap around Erruwyn's wrists in opposite directions for stability. The top of each oval divides into five sections, which curl uniformly around each finger.

Small inkwell cavities on the first two knuckles lead to brush fibers peeking from thin silver heads on his fingernails. Erruwyn brings the inner wrist ports together and twists. The brush heads retract as thin plates covering his fingertips snap down to reveal graphite tips.

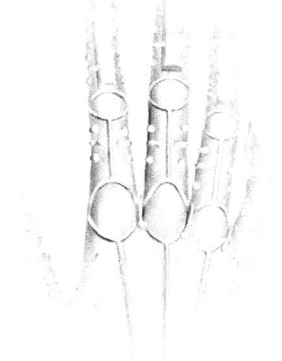

"I hope you will not be disappointed. as'etu is not so different from embodiment, though the memories reach farther. The Archive is swifter, also."*

Hovering hands over the parchment, he stares at *⁊Roske* through a prolonged inhalation. At the apex of his breath, his features go limp: chin tucks to chest, eyelids tuck in irises, fingers tuck under palms. Decrepit, he slowly, shakily lowers to the page.

When *⅘Anese* struggles, Lysbeth releases her grip. The new sensation against her collarbones is familiar, something between a stroke across parchment and a sigh.

⅘ ⁊

⁊Roske's graphite connects; Lysbeth jolts again.

Sand.

⅘Anese feels like a never-ending sigh, a never-ending stroke, and a gentle stream of ever-falling sand.

Ten fully autonomous fingers blur over the canvas. Long rustles and short clicks of graphite sweep and tap across vellum. Clacking silver brushes against silver as finger joints smudge, drag, measure, and guide in oddly exacting motions. The image wells up quickly: a gorgeous bird in flight. With the addition of shading and the size of the canvas, the detail is

extraordinary.

ӿAnese's sand slows to a stop.

ʔRoske stills.

Someone flips the glass.

As the grains pour again, *ʔRoske* takes the form of a carefree child—torso and head swaying as buoyant musings bubble up in its mind. Merging fingers continue to block Lysbeth's view as she leans forward. The *ay'tuan*'s abrupt flip on the table halts her move to stand.

ʔRoske with-drawing, eleven-year-old Lysbeth rides the back of *er'oo'n*.

◇◇◇◇◇◇◇◇◇◇◇◇
◇◇◇◇◇◇◇◇

bridge

ꙮ*Anese̞*'s faint song joins with gentle pulses: the happy tempo of the drifting walk Erruwyn uses when holding Erem. Smiling, Lysbeth waits for the pulse to strengthen before stopping the resonation with her fingers—a signal for him to come find her, currently needlepointing in the front drawing room.

Since the Offering three weeks ago, Lysbeth has stepped into her role quite well. Understanding both Erruwyn and his people better has allowed her to recontextualize those behaviors she'd once found uncomfortable in him, and her newfound respect for his perseverance has all but eliminated lingering notions of his role as a servant—though his official role at Lindenholt hasn't changed. The more complete picture of Erruwyn's personality through ꙮ*Anese̞* has also been a charming discovery. Wescott and Isaac had buried his playfulness beneath six feet of densely packed fear and his intelligence under a suffocating anxiety which ensured his silence.

Though Erruwyn still tends towards anxiety when the unexpected occurs, insecurities around his diff-errancy have stabilized with the Ladies' open support, and more aggressive servants have taken two steps back. ꙮ*Anese̞*'s ability to break down Lysbeth's own Avonleigh-imposed pretenses has made her more approachable in turn, and Erruwyn's deference has found roots in genuine trust, rather than mandatory obedience of the Wills.

Free to wear his filigrees, his already-substantial scrivery output has increased with *ʔRoske̞*, and the Ladies often ask the Concept for sketches of Lindenholt and its occupants to include in their letters to the Duke of Edenshire. The improvements observed in Corah's mood and academic performance—her *wox'ua* lessons having recently begun to incorporate Croran—have gained Erruwyn lifetime allies in Ms. Leeve and Mr. Spantier, and a much-needed outlet of communal expression has come by way of Konja's quintet.

As traditionalist Avonleigh has never made improvisation's formal acquaintance, the music group's primary obstacle had been Erruwyn's ad-libbing until *wox'ua* dismantled the barrier between structure and spontaneity. The group is a cohesive sextet these days, and the Ladies have begun to request the lot of them for evening entertainment.

It's the brightest Erruwyn's world has been since arriving.

Lysbeth releases ꙮ*Anese̞*, and the heedful buzz of willful ꙅ*m'aen̞* rattles her collarbones.

Last week, Erruwyn explained this buzzing pitch—an amplified version of the interested fizz Lysbeth felt as he'd teased Ani—was used to see in darkness or to hone in on resonant sources. To demonstrate the principle, he'd had the Ladies close their eyes and walk towards a wall while singing. As they neared, the sound's reflection changed. Through training and experience his people could see their surroundings relatively well this way.

Footmen no longer needed for announcement, Erruwyn enters with Erem sitting on ☼*Danae*'s forearm as a bench.

"☒*nar ͡uah*. The cat answers," he greets with a soft smile.

"Surely the most attentive cat the world has ever known." Lysbeth grins as the intended purr reaches ☒*Anese*. "I thought I might check on the lawn before Gina and Marium arrive. Would you care to join me?"

She stands at the answer apparent on her neck and the three journey to the southern terrace. Still feeling Erruwyn's subjection to Avon society is premature, the Ladies opted for another small EquiSol gathering, and preparations are well underway in the yard.

Three large, wooden platforms line the end of the garden as flooring for tent canopies above, while Lindenholt's underbutler, Mr. Wybber, directs the arrangement of furniture-wielding servants. A branching wooden post—looking very much like a dead tree crowned with a carved sun and moon—has been erected in the lawn beyond. By teatime tomorrow, its branches will be covered in cheerful ribbons to mark the midpoint of Spring.

Lysbeth leans against the terrace railing. "Have you any inclination to preform your dance after the tree tying tomorrow?"

☒ *sing__fizz*

Joy. Interest.

☒*Anese* hums with timid optimism.

"You wish for my presence, ☒*nar ͡uah*?"

Though Erruwyn recognizes the Ladies' benevolence, he hasn't forgotten the Baron's lectures on his insolence, presumption, and general abhorrence. In keeping with these lessons, Erruwyn also recognized his EquiSol attendance was undesirable. He'd spent the previous holidays alone, surmising his inclusion in Winter Solstice was intended as a vehicle to return his things.

Lysbeth's eyebrows wave in sympathetic affirmation. "Of course! I only wanted to spare us Gina and Marium's questions last Equinox. Now that you have Danae and you're feeling better, they shouldn't find much to poke at. I've already spun a yarn for Erem, too."

"Oh. Then, thank you." His teeth drag over a faint smile. "I wonder, maybe. Would *k'uah ͡ni* permit a surprise?"

"I can't speak for the will of Sovereign Henri, but Naruah certainly would. What of your dance?"

"I will dance if you wish it, though *lyr ͡itet* is performed only in darkness." He flicks a quiet look to the railing. "I have no sun to dance with, also."

"Alright, after supper then. How difficult are the steps?"

Smiling, Erruwyn moves a cautious hand under _er'oo'n_ as Erem wiggles it at the EquiSol tree on the lawn. "The steps are very different from what I know of your dancing, _nar ̄uah_. I do not believe it could be learned in one day, only. Though, if a primped sun were present..."

"I see." Lysbeth's laugh grows with the purr on her neck. "In that case, it seems only natural the role should fall to one with hair like the sun?"

j'tae

The Lady of the House must follow tradition when hostessing EquiSol festivities, and among the most important is her morning room invitation to family and close acquaintances on the day of the event—which ensures pleasing color coordination and a Lord-free area for Ladies to discuss more delicate rumors and subjects. As such, Gina and Marium, who arrived yesterday, will be joining the four Lindenholt Ladies shortly.

"Natty, do take care," Avrella reminds her gown-smothered maid. "That last one is quite ancient."

Corah looks up from a jewelry box as Natty fumbles to the dressing room. "Is that GG's[17] lace?"

"Yes. Quite unseemly. I shall never wear it, of course, but she would be very offended if I did not make the effort of appearing to consider it." The Matriarch perches on a couch. "Now, before the others come, I have news. Our solicitor expects an increase in Kingswar tribute by Summer. To that end, the Duke and Marquess have arranged for an appraiser to mark a few pieces from our collections."

Lysbeth and Elane exchange a look.

Confronted with Kingswars, most Lords begin a steadfast hole-digging: increasing tenant rent to meet demands of tribute, and only conceding to sell their own possessions after the hole threatens to swallow the county. Edenshire itself has been spared this practice thanks to generational friendships with foreign nobility—who place expensive scrivery orders with the Haywoods directly.

Being one of few stable regions during wartime, Sovereigns have come to depend on Edenshire as tributes from other counties diminish. However, despite the recent dip in Avon-placed scrivery orders, where financial straits are concerned, Lindenholt still sails smoothly on open seas. There's no need to sell the art.

"Isaac," Elance mutters.

A brief silence confirms similar thoughts among her kin. It's no secret the Marquess take pride in his disdain for the superfluous—which, by his estimation, encompasses most objects and persons. The Duke of Edenshire had been convinced.

---

[17] *Great-Grandmother*

"Have you informed Father of the basement?" Lysbeth asks. "He might reconsider Isaac's advice if he knew."

"No, I would prefer to broach the subject in person. Sovereign willing, Jaspyr will be granted WinterSol furlough this year." Avrella sighs. "While his decision is unfortunate, let us find comfort in the fact that our most valuable inventory is not openly displayed, and therefore, its absence unlikely to be deeply felt."

"Aye. Had you kept the knowledge to yourself we might've been spared any feelings whatsoever," Lysbeth teases.

"Yes, well. I prefer to spread the burden of knowledge equally."

A footman interrupts to announce the arrival of Gina and Marium. Ani shows their maids to the dressing room, where Lysbeth chooses the most sun-like dress she has: yellow silk embroidered with birds and flora in warm colors. The Ladies follow her lead, and once dressed, call for Erruwyn. He arrives with a small pail of water and a drawer from his trunk. Across the top, a tray balances a small stack of bowls.

Avrella smiles slyly as the greetings fade. "Have we the pleasure of a sponge bath?"

"Six among you. I would offend with so little water." Erruwyn grins as he moves to the vanities and sets down the items. "I carry this for *j'tae*: beautification."

"I'm afraid you will find it wasted on me, my dear." Avrella chuckles.

"This is not so, *ʒme͡na*," he says, dipping bowls into water and arranging them on the tray. The Matriarch peers. At her silence he glances back. "It is not so," he repeats with an earnest smile. "You would be cherished among the people. Draw the eyes of many."

"Oh?"

"Yes. I have seen it."

Avrella lowers her chin. "In that case, do be quite specific in your relaying, Erruwyn."

He laughs softly. "I have seen you greatly attached to *ʃalyn–ʒme͡na*. My favored *ʒme͡na*. You would care for the gardens of *goh'uc* together. Conduct celebrations together. Pass your wisdom; assist *me'ya͡itet* in the birthing of the brood together. Laugh at your chain of suitors togeth—"

"Suitors? At my age?" She scoffles.

Moving colored vials, syringes, and paintbrushes from the drawer to the tray, he glimpses Avrella's reflection. "Maybe I lack the word for those whose eyes have been drawn—those who wish for intimacy."

"I believe they're simply referred to as Lords," Lysbeth remarks dryly.

Erruwyn pauses his reach for a vial of orange powder to consider the word's accuracy.

"Admirers," Corah answers with a confident nod.

"Thank you, *ʃli'la*," he says, sprinkling warm-colored grains into bowls. "Laugh at your chain of admirers together."

"Your elders engage in intimacy, do they?" Avrella probes. "Is youth not considered quite synonymous with beauty?"

"No, ʒme͡na. Beauty is not attuned to youth only."

"Well, I quite agree. However, the expanse between my own opinion and Avonleigh's grows wider each year. We stand at quite opposite horizons currently. Indeed, I'm set to plunge off the edge at any moment." She chuckles. "Though I confess, a line of feeble men baying solicitations at my window seems wholly unappealing. I suppose that must render my claims rather spurious."

Erruwyn sprinkles cool shades of powder into the remaining bowls and swirls them to help the powders saturate. "Many of your admirers would be shorter years of age, ʒme͡na. The brood are raised as siblings. It is uncommon to find much desire between them. Those nearby in brood years also. This means little risk of unplanned life before ne'ru'k."

"Fascinating," Elane says, "I hadn't considered that effect of group-rearing, but of course you'd not be attracted to those you regard as immediate family."

Marium cocks her head. "I've given up following the particulars of this conversation, but of what I gather, even younger Faye men seek attachments with older women?"

"Yes, Your Ladyship," he says, securing cloth strips to ʒDanae's forearm. "There is much beauty in wisdom. In certainty." An eyebrow arcs above his smile. "Experience, also."

Avrella peers at her eldest granddaughters. "I do possess an exorbitant amount of all those things, you know."

"Yes." Erruwyn joins their chuckles. "You would also require assistance in responding to the chain of requests to caress your hair, ʒme͡na." He turns to the room, concluding: "In this way, the waste of j'tae cannot be so."

"A case well made. I dare not attempt contradiction." Avrella stands. "Though, now more than ever, I long for a holiday among your people. And I should very much like to make your Mena's acquaintance."

During a round of pleasant agreement, the Ladies relocate to the row of vanities against the back wall of the sitting and dressing rooms. Erruwyn swiftly plaits Gina and Marium's darker hair and wets the braids with syringes of cool-colored liquids before wrapping them in cloth strips to set. After repeating the process with warm-colored liquids on the Haywood Ladies' lighter plaits, he restarts the row using paintbrushes to draw invisible designs on the women's faces. Reaching Lysbeth, he sets down the tray.

"Your j'tae requires additional time, nar͡uah. I will devote the rest to you. First..." He waves back across the line.

"Alright." She grins. "They say patience benefits from practice. I suppose I ought to thank you for the opportunity."

Erruwyn returns to the dressing room and unravels the strips from Gina's plaits. Seeing her hair's unaltered state, Gina's eager reflection folds in disappointment. Lysbeth hovers fingers over ʒAnese as her guest's whining starts. When the pendant chimes, she grips it.

Using this resonant muffling as a form of reassurance has become second nature to *ḏạ'hẹ⌢ṇạṛ⌢ụạḥ*, and Erruwyn's anxiety quickly fades.

"Please do not despair, Your Ladyship," he says, knotting Gina's plaits. "*j'ṭạẹ* is greatly celebrated among the people. We will not fail you."

With each completed dressing, a new Lady appears on the couches until only one remains. Though Erruwyn works deliberately, the voluminous result of Lysbeth's dressing looks mercurial—fanciful and appealing in its disarray. She compliments his work and laughs brightly at the purr generated by her request for the silver flower. After tucking a full bloom near her temple, he kneels by her chair and wets a brush to decorate her features.

As he paints, water beads in the seam of her mouth.

He drags a thumb over her lips to disperse it.

His happy flash of recognition goes unnoticed.

After dressings, the women move on to the tents and Erruwyn returns to his room. Cycling the *ạy'ṭụạn* tree to Il-*Ḳọṇọḳ*, he removes *₭Ḍạṇạẹ* and backs in. Il-*Ḳọṇọḳ*'s thin, telescoping, tracks latch to *m'ạy-ṭụṭ*'s bracing across each plane of his arms, legs, and torso, and merge together smoothly on his palms, feet, shoulders, and neck.

Using the remaining light blue liquid, he spends a good deal of time dotting and dragging designs across his body and combs the remainder through his jaw-length hair. Once dry, he steps back into *₭Ḍạṇạẹ*. Flipping a hook out from his hip, he ties a black drawstring pouch from his trunk to it, and snaps six small tubes from a drawer to *₭Ḍạṇạẹ*'s forearm magnets. Ready, he lifts an irregularly shaped filigree from the tree and carries it from the room.

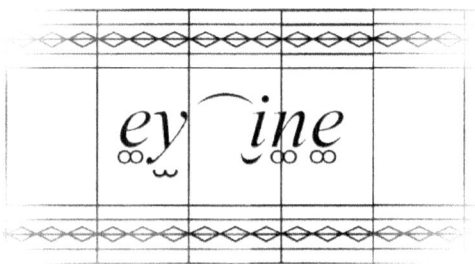

Lindenholt's lawn is full of activity. Those not working take breaks on benches under the canopies, play bocce, or tie pink and green ribbons on Equinox tree branches. Younger servants bag race, play fight, or take turns flying a large kite over the garden. Brom oversees the organization of horse race to lap the lower lawn, and his junior officers direct an archery contest at the lawn's western edge. Under the tents, Marium, Gina, and Corah play cards, Lysbeth and Elane play Alquerque, and Konja's quintet plays a jolly tune as a current of covered platters flows in from the kitchen block.

All is pleasant and unremarkable until a wave of exclamation swells from bag racers at the north-east corner of the lawn. Concerned and curious tent residents turn to the noise and soon see the cause: a fully filigreed Kikyum emerging at remarkable speed.

Stretched prone across the horse's back, a series of braces support Erruwyn's appendages. His feet lock on Kiky's croup and quarter. His fingers grip handles on either side of Kiky's neck, and his elbows and knees bend in hooks on Kiky's upper shoulders, mid-back, and right flank.

Over the next ten seconds, they streak eight-hundred feet to the lawn's southern edge. As they canter along the tree line, Erruwyn intermittently directs Kiky to slide circles—each time planting a stick from _Danae_'s forearm into the ground. Six tubes stand tall in the grass as they turn back up the slope.

Halfway to the tent's gathering crowd, Erruwyn unhooks himself from trotting metal and sits cross-legged until they near. Stable boys are the first to approach as he slides off, and Kiky graciously tolerates their poking once Lysbeth arrives with pets and a grin.

"Your naming was certainly apt."

Erruwyn smiles. "One must be swift to recapture a fleeing shadow."

"It wouldn't stand a chance with these hooves flying after it." She squints at the tree line. "As unexpected as this pomp is, I assume the circumstance of your surprise is yet to come?" she asks, squeezing Kiky's nose and turning to the canopy. Signaling the horse free, Erruwyn nods and joins her walk. "Then I hope my restraint is appreciated."

"Yes." He stops at a sun-drenched tentpole and ties his pouch around it. "You bear the burden of curiosity admirably, _nar uah_," he says, fixing playful eyes on her fresh puzzlement.

As they step into shade, he waves to the quintet, and Ms. Pinley—currently coming to terms with a phobia of temperamental, metallic horses—passes her charge. Lysbeth brings them to the seating area and reclaims her spot.

"Will you be racing, Erruwyn?" Avrella asks, as he kneels. "Marshal Brom has begun a pool. I must know before the wagers are finalized."

"You and all the rest." Elane laughs, eyeing the group boxing Brom in. "Your returns would not be very significant with such an obvious favorite."

"No, *ʒme ꞈna*," he says, steadying Erem as she pulls off *Danae*'s lower horns.

Marium tears her gaze from prancing silver on the yard. "Lysbeth, if the gelding was Erruwyn's—"

"Yes," Lysbeth interrupts with scoff. "It slipped my mind to mention it. Dorsit took Kiky from Erruwyn at the docks and had him sent ahead to claim credit as his endower. However, seeing as it's improper to speak ill of the dead..." she trails, idly quieting *Anese*'s chime.

"Speaking of dead Lords, I have it on good authority that the Marquess of Chadum is quite poorly," Gina reports, oblivious to the looks exchanged at her crassness. "He survived the road back to his estate, but he's terribly infected. It's suspected he won't make it to PromSol." She clucks reaching for a card. "The Marchioness will never live it down."

"If Avonleigh is expected to bear the Kingswar that injured Lord Chadum, surely it can be expected to bear one year without Proms," Lysbeth says, watching Erem twist and tilt *Danae*'s horns. A pile of smaller, nested horns falls into her tiny lap.

"But it's tradition, Lysbeth," Marium replies with faint admonishment. "If we can't maintain our traditions through times of trial, their significance is diminished in times of plenty. A tradition kept only in sunny weather is more picnic than true observance."

Distracted by Erem's snapping of silver to Erruwyn's face, Lysbeth fails to form a rebuttal. Avrella continues on her behalf, "Given the limitations of our eyes, a bit of sun is necessary to observe much of anything."

"Indeed, some allowance must be made," Elane agrees.

"Widows forgo events while bearing the black," Corah tells her cards. "If I were made to host a grand party which I could not attend myself, I'd have the kitchens poison the wine."

Tittering Ladies let Corah's word be the last.

"Goodness," Avrella says, turning back to see Erem add a sixth horn to Erruwyn's face. "What has become of you?"

In a futile act of self-effacement, Erruwyn squeezes his eyelids shut as Erem snaps another sliver of silver to his brow. The wave from his diaphragm forces a raspy whimper past his grin. Unable to prevent her own laugh on hearing it, Lysbeth's knuckles rush to her "ʃer'ęm enjoys assembling my face, ⹁mę͡ṇa," he manages.

"I was not aware it needed assembly." She chuckles. "Is this their intended location?"

Erem twists a solemn look on Avrella as her teeny hands uncoil the long, branching chain from ⹁Danąę's middle horn. Corah and Elane investigate with amusement; Gina and Marium lower their cards with reserved interest.

"Some belong where ʃer'ęm has placed them as they are used among the people."

"And what use might that be?" Elane smirks. "Rutting?"

Unspooled, Erem hangs chain over jutting chin-silver.

"No... a dirge," he says, links swaying under his jaw.

The women join in his amused chagrin as Erem wǫx'uas.

⹁ sing

Erruwyn raises happy eyes to Lysbeth.

"Oh! Well yes, of course he's an Equinox tree, Erem." Laughing, Lysbeth leans over the couch to help finish his decoration.

"Something must sit atop!" Corah exclaims, eyeing the carved sun and moon on the lawn's tree.

Erem nods and gestures.

"You wish for the star of ʃn'ar'uah on your tree? I believe ǫar͡uah will find the horns unpleasant to sit on," Erruwyn says through a cobweb of chain. Grinning at Lysbeth's affirmative moan, he reaches for Erem's figurine. "Though, er'ǫǫ'ṇ always wishes to fly?"

When she agrees, he unfolds the bird and balances its beak on his forehorn—where it enjoys lively admiration before falling. From the side of the group, Ms. Pinley approaches to deliver a blanket: nap time.

After cleaning up the spectacle she's made of her ⹁da'hę͡ṇa, Erem stands at the corner of Erruwyn's taut hold on the cloth. A giggle-swaddled-spin guides her cocooning, and once tucked, Erruwyn folds her into a lap-kneel, nuzzles her hair, and closes his eyes.

⹁Anęse's song eases into lullaby—a gentle croon of heavy comfort. Lysbeth's breathing slows as she watches Erem's head gradually dip away from Erruwyn's face. Feeling the movement, he peeks through a lid and smiles at her serene expression.

"I'll bring 'er back after the winks," Ms. Pinley whispers as he gingerly passes her over.

Erruwyn watches as they meander through the garden to the house. Beside him, Lysbeth shakes off her own faint drowsiness.

"What maen was that?" she asks faintly.

"tau͡ inę." He turns back. "The texture is used to calm. To assist with sleep, also."

"It's quite effective." She rubs her forehead. "Your positioning was similar to Erem's music room episode. Had you used it then as well?" She eyes his nod fondly. "I've wondered what it was you said to her the day I came to recruit you in the kitchen gardens—after she became frightened?"

"Mm." Erruwyn shifts his gaze to the lawn. "I said, 'Have courage. Mistress bid others to stop your suffering, ‡er'em, so we might become ey‾ine.'" He takes a breath and returns to Lysbeth. "Among the people it is said: *severed fabric must be rewoven as one on the loom.* To restore the rift; join the threads, strengthen the fiber."

⅄ *purr*

"I have never thanked you, nar‾uah, for finding ‡er'em." He smiles gently. "So. Thank you. For permitting us to become ey‾ine: soul-woven. To join our threads. To repair the rift within us, together."

The afternoon passes peacefully. Winners of the horse race and archery contest are given flower crowns and pastries. Caught using wox'ya to help Corah cheat at cards, Erruwyn sings with the quintet as penance—continuing with aro'x after his sentence is served as an advance on future transgressions. When Erem returns, Erruwyn climbs Kiky with her on his shoulders and rides to the Equinox tree. Standing, he ties excess ribbons on taller, barer branches at her direction, leaving a lush bloom of bows.

At supper, diners pile their plates with sweetmeats, rolls, soufflés, and greens. An assortment of desserts from Corah's tourney are generously sampled, and an hour of dancing and singing coincides with the opening of spirit soon after. As the sky dims, Erruwyn removes ‡Danae's upper, left horn and runs Kiky to the edge of the yard. Twisting the horn produces a small flame from a window at its tip, and he lights each tube as Kiky bows beside them. Giving the crowded tent a wide berth, they charge back as colorful, liquid-fire sprays high into the air. Onlookers erupt with anxious glee, and once it's clear the flame-spouts don't return to the ground, lean into jubilation.

As the sun sets, gasps behind the Ladies go unheard over rowdy cheers—and when the display sputters, Ladies turning to share their excitement with one another are met with glowing designs of j'tae.

Faces decorated with cooler shades are dotted with twinkling stars, and their luminescent plaits are woven into waxing and waning moons. Those with warm hues have curling lines across their cheeks and crowns of gleaming braids. Lysbeth sits radiant—a voluminous fireball with densely winding, ombre lines highlighting each feature. Erruwyn rejoins the group covered in spiraling dots. Their squeals on seeing him pull a raspy, richly-layered laugh from his grin, and having never heard his full laugh before—a particularly infectious and endearing one—the party sets off on another lap of giddy squeals.

When blazing mirth simmers, Erruwyn points to the glowing necklace he'd given Corah, and explains the applied powders are made from the same luminescent minerals. Crushed and dyed with pigment, the particles stored body heat throughout the day for evening visibility. He also assures the display was not true fire, and its chemicals will only react destructively when combined with specific pyrophoric compounds.

Curiosity satisfied, Lysbeth asks for his dance through a bright, ombre smile. Torches and lanterns are dimmed as Erruwyn removes *ǝDanaǝ* and unties the pouch from the tentpole. A tall, twinkling galaxy crosses the lawn to a spot in line with Lysbeth's sun, pinches the bottom corners of the pouch, and tosses the item inside in the air.

The audience *ohhs* as a bright orb seemingly appears from nowhere, and *ahhs* as it lands on Iǁ-*Konok*'s forearm track. A ballet of graceful gymnastics ensues—Erruwyn guiding the moon across his body of stars.

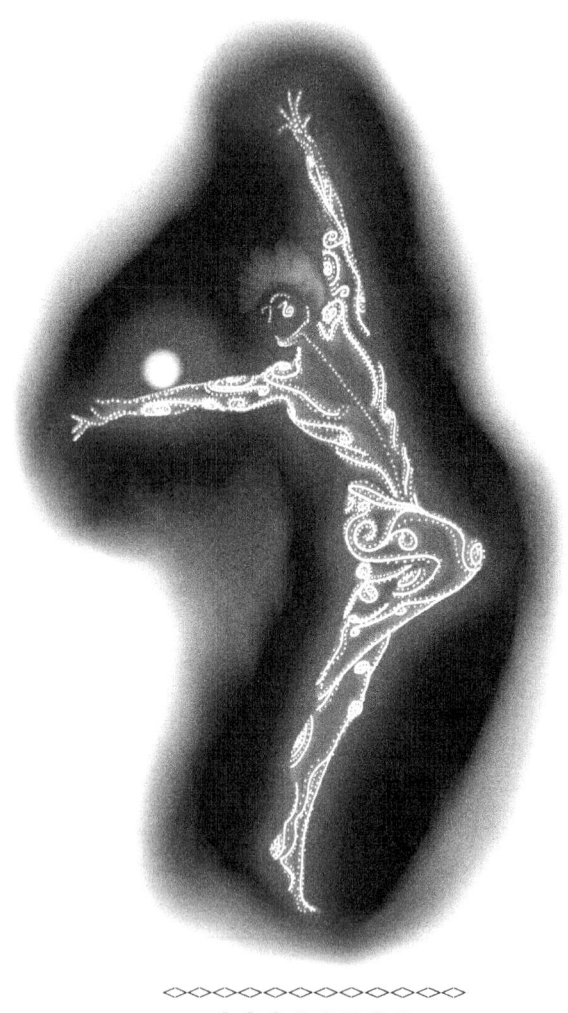

◇◇◇◇◇◇◇◇◇◇◇
◇◇◇◇◇◇◇◇◇

kw'da

Heavy eyelids crack as Brom's snore reflects off the wall.

Erruwyn crawls from the mire of his sheets and slogs to the basin—where foggy exhaustion recedes at the shock of cold water. After drying his face, he quietly folds 《*Danae* around *m'ay-tut* and leaves for Lindenholt's kitchen.

Food had been an easy target for his peers' contempt, and he'd continued to skip meals even after his visits with Kiky were discovered. Knowing political snares find equal game across social classes, Ani brought his troubles to Ms. Makensi, head cook, rather than Lysbeth or Elane. Equally snare-wary, Ms. Makensi had offered Erruwyn a deal: speedy hands in exchange for unmarked meals. He'd gladly accepted.

The Outland kitchen is full of workers working together and plenty of work to be done. Knaves run water buckets, tend fires, and carry pots to and fro. Scullery maids wash utensils, sweep floors, and chop ingredients. Kitchen maids prepare dishes and direct subordinates to coordinate with store, still, and dairy maids.

Amidst the chaos, Ms. Makensi finishes verifying assignments. "Cod," she yells.

"Cod!" Two kitchen maids move to a station with recently delivered fish.

"Porridge," Ms. Makensi cries, kicking the stool of a dozing spit-boy.

"Missus!" a maid replies, heading to prepare the Ladies' wheats.

"Slops!" Three maids hurry to a station with pots enough for one-hundred employees.

Ms. Makensi glances at the doorway. "Silvah."

Ms. Makensi likes Erruwyn. He's efficient, respectful, and the morale of her predominantly female staff has never been higher. After the Offering, those complaining of 《*Danae* were told to eat squirrel[18]—where Ms. Makensi is concerned, the more skin, the better.

"Silvah!" the room repeats.

Shy silver ducks to a table where its partner, Liza, waits. Erruwyn was surprised when first paired with the ten-year-old scullery maid. He'd occasionally seen her in evening passings and didn't realize she followed the same fifteen-hour workday as adults. Among the

---

[18] *An idiom originating from an obsolete law which allowed for execution in cases of poached Rodentia and which means, "die unsatisfied."*

people, children work to supplement their education, and the experience is joyful; Outland children work to survive, and joy is often absent. For those who view all children as their own, it's a distressing disparity.

"Tossin' thirty," she says, patting a basket of potatoes, "right?"

Since Liza's schedule prohibits formal education, Erruwyn's taught her words commonly found on his work orders. He glances at the note: *30 chop; 5 skin & thin.*

He smiles and picks up two knives. "Right."

At his prompt, Liza tosses a stream of potatoes from her basket to his empty one. He splits the spuds as they fall, and after thirty, the team switches baskets to continue: halving the halves, then halving the quarters. The method is odd, but swift, and attempting to outpace Erruwyn provides the maid with more amusement in minutes than she used to get in a week. Finished, Liza makes trips to the servant's stew pot—a receptacle for scrap ingredients kept simmering all day and served with servant's supper—while Erruwyn quickly peels and slices the Ladies' potatoes.

After cycling his assistance through other stations, Ms. Makensi approaches with thick slices of bread, cheese, and a carrot. "For Kiky." She winks. "See you at luncheon, Silvah."

Food in hand, he heads outside. With the family's open support, Erruwyn's meals are safe from tampering. Still, he's aware he makes portion of his fellow servants uneasy and continues to avoid the dining hall. Being forced out of the communal space used to amplify his loneliness and self-loathing, but since the Offering, he doesn't mind leaving for their comfort.

He exits to cool air. Light, Spring frosts have given way to cusp-of-Summer dews. *Danae* can generate a bit of warmth with the right *m'aen*, and he has cloth to wear, if necessary, but he's glad for the change. Winters weren't as bad as he'd feared, but Avonleigh's sun is less steady than the one he'd known.

The fresh scent of dawn's evaporation is overtaken by damp hay and leather as he crosses to the stable block. Continuing to the road past its second gate, he watches Kiky jump his enclosure, and grins as he trots over to press his long, dark face into *Danae*'s star. A borrowed whinny leads Kiky back to the fence and Erruwyn passes the carrot. Enjoying toast in pleasant company, he runs over the mental Archive of his scrivery assignment. Lysbeth had asked him to refrain from the full puppetry of *as'etu* unless he was alone. Hoping to use it before other scribes show, he journeys to the workshop after making a meal of breakfast.

He refreshes his Archive with a flip through a thick, Croran tome before unwinding his scroll across the floor and kneeling astride it. One hour later, the parchment is complete. He refills *Roske*'s inkwells and returns it to his scribal case as Mr. Sandel arrives.

"Erruwyn! How lovely that we had the same thought. The earliest scritcher gets the best light!" He chuckles. "Scritchers of the same page, we are!"

"As well; as ink."

Erruwyn bites his lip and patiently awaits the end of Mr. Sandel's long-winded guffaw. He's certain there's something wrong with the Outland's scribes—too much time indoors, maybe. When the head scribe sighs, Erruwyn sets down the scroll and tome.

"The remainder."

"*Maaarvelous*! Oh, the Countess will be thrilled." Mr. Sandel putters across the room to a box of orders. "You get faster every day! Let's see now, where did I place her binding instructi—Ah! Here. She's been a client of ours for decades, you know. Have I mentioned her before..."

Mr. Sandel often seems only partially aware of others' presence once he begins speaking. Erruwyn speculates that, sometime distant, the scribe inadvertently embodied *?Roske* and has been sharing his mind with the Concept ever since.

"... I said, 'Don't you fret, the Captivating Croran Countess saw us through the last Kingswar, and she's sure to see us through another!'" Mr. Sandel claps his hands and chortles. "She will be deliriously happy to have her order fulfilled so quickly. Yes, yes." Returning to his desk, a slow, apologetic hand squeezing begins. "Now, I'm afraid—well—I'm terribly sorry to say I have no further assignments for you presently."

"Please do not feel so. I am happy to return as you need me."

"Thank you. Eh, you see, orders have slowed, but—oh dear, I do apologize."

"Please do not despair, Mr. Sandel."

"I truly regret—Oh, quill-snappers!"

Reassuring apologies and apologetic reassurance run a course from pillar to post until the guard bell rings eight o'clock. Returning to his room, Erruwyn tucks the scribal case away as a breakfast-fueled Brom enters. The Marshal collects his jacket and stops to give his roommate an affectionate shoulder slap on the way out.

Several months ago, unbeknownst to Erruwyn, the Marshal had declined an offer for his own room. Early on, he would have jumped at the chance, but Brom's errand to retrieve Erem from Warden Wescott's prison had altered his perspective.

On arrival, he'd confronted Wescott with Erruwyn's linenfold-panel sketch of the hidden room. Seeing it, the Baron's masterful façade dropped momentarily, and behind it was an intimately familiar expression. Brom doesn't know the name for it, but he'd seen it while convalescing last Kingswar. It would appear on faces seeking their kin among the wounded: a look of euphoric relief at finding a loved one alive, followed by a slow unraveling—a seeping consternation as they came to understand the injury was fatal.

Its appearance on Wescott's face didn't make sense until Brom found Erem.

He'd entered the hidden room prepared for a traumatized child but was not prepared for the sketches covering its walls. Erruwyn had been made to witness and reproduce scores of graphic tortures—and based on subject frequency, he'd been singled out as a particular favorite. The Baron was keeping Erem and the sketches in the same sentimental way Haywood's keep portraits of their ancestors: tenderly enshrined reminders of his most gratifying brutalizations.

For Warden Wescott, seeing the new, linen-panel sketch had been like finding Erruwyn alive, and in the moment that followed, remembering Erruwyn was already lost to him.

Returned to Lindenholt, the small, petty part of Brom that resented association with Erruwyn's strangeness and begrudged the nightly disturbance of Erruwyn's terrors had vanished—replaced by a need to see the boy get better: to spite the Baron, to spite old fools like himself, to spite the part of Erruwyn that believed the Baron and the fools.

And on the way, the boy crept in and planted roots in the old fool's heart.

The Marshal claps *Danġe*'s shoulder again.

Erruwyn smiles at the floor and nods goodbye as Brom turns for the door. He's grateful for the Marshal's kinship. One of his favored Masters back home had also been a mollusk: hard without, soft within.

He leaves for the main house after assisting younger kitchen servants with pot scrubbing and emerges from the servant's stairwell near Lysbeth's apartments producing an infrasound buzz to let her know he's close. The faint sensation of *Anese*'s reflection lifts his heart into song; on seeing *nar uah* in the sitting room, his heart flutters, too.

He returns greetings and lowers his eyes to avoid Lysbeth's expression—the crooked smile and arched eyebrow she wears when she's in a teasing mood. Teeth impress his lower lip as he crosses to the caddy and snaps tools to *Danġe*'s arm.

"Erruwyn," Lysbeth's deliberate tone changes as her smile widens.

He gives up biting his grin back. "Yes, *nar uah*."

When she doesn't respond, he chances a glimpse.

She's still wearing the look, and now her shoulders shake at his purr. His constricted smile quickly returns to the caddy.

A lifetime of this.

The fluttering in his heart grows again.

Since the Offering, his attraction to Lysbeth has eased naturally into love's shallows. Among the people, love is viewed as an endless spring—restrictions have no place around such an essential requirement of life. In the Outland, the spring is sectioned into barrels, the barrels labeled, and the labels guarded—you may only dip your cup once, and only from a very narrow range of named containers.

Despite her admiration of his people and her acceptance of his Offer, Erruwyn suspects *k'uah ni*'s aversion to diff-errancies prevents her reciprocity. This changes nothing for Erruwyn, however—as the love of the people isn't possessive, it doesn't depend on reciprocation for maintenance.

His suspicions are partially accurate.

Lysbeth knows Decorum won't tolerate romantic notions, but all said and done, she's as susceptible to Erruwyn's features and temperament as any other. For those suffocating under the weight of Avonleigh's entitled male population, his unassuming nature is disarmingly endearing.

Watching from a vanity, Avrella levels her smile as Erruwyn steps behind her to work—she enjoys observing their candid moments and doesn't want to put them on guard.

Elane enters from the dressing room. "Have you told him yet, Lys?" she asks, taking a seat beside Avrella.

Technically not a Haywood, tradition requires Elane be the last member served. This has never bothered Elane—whose pride isn't fragile enough to find injury in her catering order—but early on she'd noticed Erruwyn's tendency to linger on Lysbeth's hair. Counting on his ignorance of familial customs, she began sitting at the vanities as a subtle suggestion to work on her after Avrella. The suggestion took, and not wanting to cause a fuss over such a harmless mistake, no one bothered to correct him. He can linger all he likes with Lysbeth last in the order.

"Too busy drawing battle plans," Avrella mutters of *da'he⌒nar⌒uah*'s very one-sided resonance war.

Not risking another glance, Erruwyn waves the end of a silver tool in Lysbeth's direction. "I surrender."

Lysbeth grins. "If only it were so easy, though I'll grant a truce for the time being. I'm to tell you your Feunen's returning to us in a fortnight." She taps the letter on her desk. "He's bringing another of his favorite artworks for you to meet."

Erruwyn laughs softly as he finishes a plait.

"An *Otay Bengli*," Elane draws the words with wonder. "They're said to be quite unusual."

"An entire population of concubines hardly paints the picture of normalcy, my dear." Avrella chuckles.

"Not the whole population," Lysbeth corrects. "And they're more like courtesans."

"Well, how inconsiderate of me. A *partial* population of *educated* concubines?"

"It's said they whiten their hair and wear only silk wrappings," Elane continues. "They're meant to be quite glamorous and charming."

"I didn't know you were so taken by them, Elane. You never spoke of Dahena this way," Lysbeth says, folding the letter.

Erruwyn smiles. They'd stopped referring to him and his people as "Faye" last Winter.

"I wasn't sure they were real!" Sitting up, Elane delivers an earnest explanation to Erruwyn, "The Otay are Crora's neighbors, and many of their Bengli take up positions at Croran court. Truly, there's one in nearly every house." Slanting eyebrows form a peak of apology above her nose. "I spent more time imagining them because I knew meeting one was possible, that's all."

As she speaks, Erruwyn glances at the other Ladies to be sure he's interpreting her guilt correctly. Their quietly amused faces assure him that he is.

Anese fidgets with enthusiasm.

"Your uncertainty would bring comfort to many among the people, Your Ladyship. Thank you." When Elane turns away relieved, he shares a broad grin with Lysbeth.

Shortly after dressings, *da'he͡ nar͡uah* walk to Corah's language lesson. Nowadays, Erruwyn sits at the table with Ms. Leeve and Corah to *wox'ua* while he records. Associations between *wox'ua* and Croran words are holding well, and Corah is far less frustrated. They stay on to practice a bit before Erruwyn reports to the kitchens for lunch.

Quietly chopping fruit amid the kitchen's cacophony, *da'he͡ na* and scullery maid look up as Ani appears—a frequent occurrence when there's news to discuss.

"So, Erruwyn? Excited for the Duke's return?"

He nods over a knife blurring strawberries.

Ani smiles rascally. "You won't be jealous of his lover, I hope?"

He arcs an eyebrow. "I am unfamiliar with the feeling."

"Truly? Never?"

"I do not believe so, as I have heard it described," he says, scraping fruit into a pan.

"Then waddya feel when someone has somethin' you want?" Liza asks, laying fresh berries.

He thinks, and then thinks harder. "I am uncertain. We share."

"Everythin'?" Liza presses.

He nods.

"Waddabout sweethearts? When you're sweet on someone claimed?"

"We do not claim one another."

"Well, everyone's a-buzz about the Bengli," Ani moves on. "Since you're the only one bound to get close, promise you'll tell all?"

He smiles. "Yes, Ani. If there is anything to tell."

Erruwyn eats lunch with Erem and Ms. Pinley in the kitchen gardens and lingers until Corah's piano recording.

Mr. Spantier had made such frequent use of Erruwyn's *aro'x*, he'd eventually taken him to the Music Hall's store room to demonstrate more instruments for his repertoire. Today he requests a cello to accompany Corah's playthrough. Knowing Mr. Spantier disapproves of additions, Erruwyn moves up his plans to meet with the quintet and keeps to the painfully dull piece until the lesson ends. Desperate for deliverance, he departs for the musician's housing past the kitchen block.

Konja answers the door. "Erruwyn!" he exclaims, tilting his head side to side with his words, "where-have-you-been!?"

"I am early, Konja."

"Okay! But it feels late! Because I have quah-dah!" Laughing heartily, Konja pulls his friend to the practice room.

The other musicians—two cellists and two violinists—greatly exaggerate their relief on seeing Erruwyn. Konja's attempts at *kw'da* had not gone well.

kw'da.

Literally: influencing-movements ' many-articulations.

Conceptually: marionetting a composition.

Translation: conductor.

Smiling at their light-hearted ribbing of Konja's failure, Erruwyn kneels and asks for catharsis. The sedate, repetitive song from Corah's lesson is a staple of Avonleigh's musical canon and the quintet knows it well. Konja marks the downbeat with his bow, and the group plays along as Erruwyn unleashes layers of drums, bass, horns, water droplets and animal calls. Though the compulsion behind these requests eludes the musicians, they're always entertained by what he comes up with. When the song ends, Erruwyn grins, stretches, and thanks them before readying *kw'da*.

He lifts his right fist and sings a D note. When his pinky extends, the first cellist plays a D. Next finger; next musician, and so on. Finger assignments confirmed, Erruwyn flattens his hand. All five instruments play. Raising his hand shifts the note up. Tilting his palm lowers the octave. Dropping his fist, he extends index finger and thumb: the violins change notes while the cellos and viola retain theirs. When he wiggles his fingers, their bows match.

The marionetting is a guideline—signposts from Erruwyn. The rest depends on the skill of the quintet.

Deviating from Avonleigh's musical canon had been a refreshing revel for Konja and a daunting prospect for the Avons, but after months of improvising, they've learned to trust their instincts and each other. Now they crave the thrill of uncertainty, the elation when all parts fall neatly into place, and the pride of creating something entirely new.

Erruwyn closes his fist and takes a breath.

⋈Jhenxi

The gatehouse bell rings as Jaques' caravan reaches the quarter-mile marker of Lindenholt's approach. Under reverberation, servants gather on the front terrace and Avrella leads a slow procession of granddaughters to the Grand Chamber.

While Lysbeth is happy to greet Jaques in his preferred manner, Avrella enjoys offering the rogue some resistance and has declared observance of proper procedure. Still, despite her claims to the contrary, Avrella doesn't wholly dislike the Duke. In fact, the two have a fair bit in common.

Both Avrella's veil of curmudgeonry and Jaques' jester cap of contrariety are used to hide their true levels of competency—and as preemptive defenses against peerage hearsay. After all, who in Avonleigh would risk Avrella's wrath by spreading unfounded gossip? And what could Croran nobles possibly say to damage the reputation of a bastard Duke who revels in antagonism? Avrella respects a well-applied veneer, and she knows a good one when she sees it.

To assist Decorum, Erruwyn has been asked to wait for a summons instead of joining the terrace assembly. The Matriarch may allow some rules of etiquette out of their cage for a stretch, but a member of the peerage greeting a servant before the family is a stretch too far.

Erruwyn stands at the hall window outside Lysbeth's sitting room, watching Jaques' carriage-train carve a wide circle on the court. With his view of the terrace blocked, he leans against the wall and idly gazes at the portrait of Lysbeth's mother. He's wanted to thank Jaques since Autumn but gathered _k'uah ⁀ni_ would disapprove of someone in his position contacting a Duke. For the time being, displaying his mastery silver is enough.

Activity from the Grand Chamber reaches him: Mr. Tenson's deep, announcing voice. Mahogany doors abutting marble. A faint exchange that fades into silence. Erruwyn peeks at the eastern gallery's intersection. There's no indication of imminent summon from Temus.

The silence continues.

Anxiety mounts and hauls his eyes to Lily Haywood's.

Presumptuous, Baron said.

Maybe he's been mistaken; expected friendship where there wasn't any.

Abhorrent.

After novelty, a burden. His diff-errancy is too great, even for _feu'n'en_.

Insolen—

"Beauuuty!"

The ballooning cry bursts against Chamber niches and floods the halls.

Relief spreads—water under embers. Temus leans around the corner and nods. *Ꝃ Anese* scampers impishly as Erruwyn slinks along the gallery to marble.

The Ladies' smiles are in various states of repression as the Duke paces in wide circles, and glares at ceiling frescoes. He'd given Avrella her Decorum, and the delay in reciprocation to run through pleasantries was unacceptable.

Jaques' shoulder leads his rotation. The sudden apparition at the edge of his vision causes a double take, and both hands rush to comfort his whimper. His Beauty's exposed skin is deeply creased with muscle and sinew. His Beauty's hair is longer and swept back at the sides with silver horns. His Beauty's grin is bright and beautiful, unflinching, turquoise eyes hold his own.

Notably, Jaques' profound adoration of beauty—all beauty, but particularly the human form—is one of his few non-performative traits. The sight before him is overwhelming, and the rare display of genuine vulnerability is a delightful treat for Edenshire's Ladies.

His whimper repeats as Erruwyn steps forward and the creases of his body change.[19]

"*Ꝃ feu'n'en.* I am glad to see you."

"Beauty," Jaques squeaks. "I will never see again."

A click comes from the vestibule—the heel of a shoe sharply placed. Jaques' pupils continue running waylines across Erruwyn's body as he waves the noise over.

The deliberate gait of an Otay Bengli begins.

Her upper arms and torso are wrapped in one long strip of gray silk. Each end tapers to a wide point and hangs down the front and back of a white, chiffon skirt. Her hair is grey-ish white and held in scores of thin braids swinging with her steps.

Ꝃ Anese's scamper reduces to fizzing interest.

"Duchess. Ladies Haywood." Jaques tears away from luster. "I introduce to you, Ryn. She has been my joy for many years."

Ryn's eyes are large, her lips are full, and her gaze is fixed on Erruwyn. Palms drag up the sway of her sauntering hips to her waist. She stops a foot away, dropping grey irises to silver feet. The climb back to Erruwyn's face is slow and salacious. The hook of her smile intends to melt metal.

Though Erruwyn looks away shyly, *Ꝃ Anese* hums with

---

[19] *In fact, the people's early experiments with magnetic implants benefited from their extraordinary leanness—providing a decent understanding of subdermal anatomy and connective tissue anchor points through observation alone.*

vague optimism.

"I hope that you will love her as I do." Jaques smiles sly. "Maybe... when I do? Hm?"

◇◇◇◇◇◇◇◇◇◇

Understanding Ryn's presence is likely to steer the evening down less polite avenues, Avrella has passed the reins and withdrawn with Corah—leaving her two eldest granddaughters to drive onward from the southern terrace.

"I did tell you to expect a surprise, Jaques," Lysbeth says, taking a cordial from Mr. Tenson's tray.

"Surprise? I almost died from shock of ecstasy." He moves an arm around Erruwyn. "You will wear this every day?"

"Not exactly. He's gotten dressed up for you. Haven't you, Erruwyn?" Elane sips and nods to the mastery silver.

"Yes. We wear _hu'ay_ to celebrate the return of vessels from _set'ye_," he says, pointing out his additions. "Other occasions, also. I wished to celebrate your return, _feu'n'en_."

"My Beauty," Jaques whispers solemnly.

♪ *sing*

Erruwyn grins as he's pulled in, fondly wrapping Jaques' wrist with long fingers.

"What did I say, hm?" Jaques asks Ryn from _Danae_'s shoulder. "A lamb. A beautiful lamb."

Ryn's lips curl from the bench's cushioned corner.

After Jaques informed Lysbeth he'd broken his promise of silence, she'd sent an admonishing reply, but it's clear now why he'd had little chance of keeping it from Ryn. His response appealed to Lysbeth's affinities—Ryn shares her fascination with the Faye—and offered adamant assurance that Bengli popularity relies as much on their physical talents as their discretion. It was enough to assuage Lysbeth at the time, but now she worries after Ryn's flirtations. If acted upon, some degree of scandal would be unavoidable. She resolves to speak with Erruwyn later.

"Ms. Ryn." Elane leans forward. "How long does your wrapping take to complete?"

"Just Ryn, Lady," her low breath answers in Croran. "The bind is twenty-feet in length. With two to aid, ten minutes to wrap." She eyes Erruwyn and traces the tapered end laying on her thighs. "To remove, pull here."

Jaques giggles at Erruwyn's falling gaze.

"How many Bengli are there, if you don't mind the question?" Elane continues.

Ryn smiles coyly. "As many as required, Lady."

Fifteen-hundred years ago, a group of isolationists occupying a small Croran cape sent their Bengli to the Sovereign's bedchamber. Suitably convinced, he'd relinquished the cape and the country of Otay emerged. To ensure the deal, Bengli also slipped into bedchambers of Croran Lords. Their foresight paid off nine generations later when an unpopular, Bengli-free Sovereign sought to reclaim Otayan territory. Bengli set to work making their cases—Lords with heads sensitive to sentiment were easily touched, others were persuaded by grippingly well-reasoned arguments. The result was a Lords' rebellion and a swift dethroning. Though a long list of grievances against the Sovereign existed before his plans for Otay, the role of Bengli was not overlooked. Their influence in Crora is respected.

Jaques shakes Erruwyn. "You have known courtesan? Hm?"

"I am uncertain of the meaning, *feu'n'en*." He wiggles.

"We are dance, song." Ryn drags a finger over her collarbone. "Appreciated well, we are love."

Erruwyn considers this. "Am I courtesan, also, *nar͡uah*?" he asks, confused by the subsequent chuckles.

"Courtesans seek benefactors, Erruwyn." Elane tips her head forward. "Ryn's skills are part of an arrangement."

"The sharing of bed for the sharing of luxury." Jaques winks. "You have this, hm?"

"Unlikely, Jaques." Lysbeth sips her cordial. "We've been made to understand Erruwyn's people are intimately-inclined without bribery."

"*Hmm*? You are very experienced, Beauty?" At Erruwyn's noncommittal lip biting, Jaques clucks and lowers his voice, "Come, come. Do not be modest. Tell us of your affairs. I must know how twins seduce."

"I'm interested as well," Lysbeth reassures. "How does one court in a society without social rank or the need for heirs? How do you select the subjects of your escapades?"

Jaques leans back on the bench to take a drink from the footman behind it. Ryn drapes across him to study Erruwyn as he answers.

"We display *hu'ay*. Our merit, *nar͡uah*. To impress," Erruwyn says, pulling his feet up and pretzeling his legs. "Some *hu'ay* require skills that bolster pleasure. Some signal skill in pleasure, only. When the eyes of another are drawn, *jo'ta* signals compatibility." He points to the cuff and ring on his right forearm. "Compatible eyes often request time."

"Compatible in what respect?" Elane asks.

Erruwyn runs a finger over the silver cord soldered along the edge of the cuff. "Desired company. This fold signals I prefer time with women, though men may ask." Moving his finger inward to an embossed wave he continues, "The carving signals our expression of *Jhenxi*, Concept of Sexuality. Sensuality, also. My expression of *Jhenxi* is—"

"*Hm*?" Jaques interjects. "J-hen-ks-eye?"

After a brief explanation of Concepts and *ay'tuan*, Erruwyn continues, "My expression of *Jhenxi* is *er'wa*: light on water. This expression moves to reflect the preferences of its partner as water reflects light. Become what they desire. Conform."

Deliriously happy with the topic of conversation, Jaques rapidly taps Erruwyn's elbow. "What am I, hm? Expression?"

"I am uncertain, *feu'n'en*. One may have many expressions. There is also *Jhenxi ̄ky*, those who stand in the Concept's shadow—gratified by *Jhenxi*, only."

Lysbeth cocks her head. "Gratified by the Concept?"

"Yes, those who stand in *Jhenxi*'s shadow are those whose eyes are never drawn to its divergent forms. My twiceborn is *Jhenxi ̄ky*. She stands near in its shadow, no desire for expressions. Those farther along the shadow may desire occasionally."

"So, we've one twin who's shy and gratified by any expression, and another who's spritely and gratified by none?" she asks through a grin. "You're quite at odds, aren't you?"

"Yes. Different, though close." He smiles, continuing, "There is also *s'wo*: soft-sand. This expression enjoys being shaped. Yielding."

Elane squints and stretches her neck, "I don't quite follow the metaphors, but molding sand doesn't sound so different from conforming water."

"Mm." Erruwyn nods. "*s'wo* are gratified in yielding to another, as sand yields to feet. They are often compatible with *d'koa*: strong leading wind—those gratified in the steering of others. True *er'wa* are gratified in gratifying another, only. In this way, we require a light to reflect; the presence of another to gratify. Their expression may be any."

Lysbeth finishes her cordial. "If ear-wah need reflection, what occurs when you meet with another like yourself?"

"I am uncertain. I have not met another. Though, it is said *er'wa* placed together will see air, only. Time spent; nothing accomplished." Laughing softly at Jaques' giggle, he traces the cuff's beaded chain to a ring set high on his middle finger. "The signals of *ne'ru'k ̄hu'ay* are significant, also." At another insistent tap on his elbow, he turns to his benchmates. "*ne'ru'k*. Among the people, males are not permitted to bring the tide. We train."

"Tide..." Jaques splashes the terrace with a horrified expression. "No release?!"

"Release occurs. *ne'ru'k* is to billow without running ashore. Breakwater, *feu'n'en*."

The Duke grunts as his mind stumbles towards understanding. "N-no seed?"

"Seed?"

Jaques offers Erruwyn air from his waist.

A smile forms. "No, *feu'n'en*. They are seed; they are soil. We are rain, only."

The two regard one another over mutually confounded amusement until Erruwyn returns to his arm.

"My *ne'ru'k* trial. Three hours," he says, stopping at three beads spaced along the chain. Reaching the ring, he points to a nubbin on top. "I carried *ay* during my trial." He motions to the whole piece. "All together, the shape of compatibility, also."

"*Trial*?" Lysbeth asks with high brow.

"Yes, *nar ̄uah*. Our resolve must be tested to earn *ne'ru'k ̄hu'ay*. To carry *ay* during the trial greatly increases the challenge. The location for this _ay_ is sensitive." Jaques gasps; Erruwyn continues through a stifled laugh, "This signals reliability."

Tipsy and amused, Elane, Lysbeth, and Jaques ask simultaneous questions. Before any sense can be made of their words, Ryn draws herself up from Jaques' side. Her glance requests Erruwyn's cuffed arm. The questions fade as he extends it uncertainly.

"The shape of compatibility," Ryn's throaty voice coats the bench. Her fingertips trail _ne'ru'k⁻hu'ay_'s chain to the bead closest to its cuff. "The limit."

⚜ _hum＿fizz_

Optimism. Interest.

Enticement, but the intensity is low.

Erruwyn is familiar with forward advances from home, but Ryn's insistence is perplexing—further, given Avonleigh's pleasure-averse _k'uah⁻ni_ and _nar⁻uah_'s subtle disapproval, he suspects he should be cautious.

Jaques' eyes hop between bead and Erruwyn as he deconstructs Ryn's meaning. "No, no... you?" he asks, setting down his glass.

Erruwyn nods. "To signal the shape of physical compatibility. To avoid the tragedy of incompatible longing once activity has begun."

Lysbeth and Elane laugh in flustered shock, thankful for Avrella's foresight in withdrawing early with Corah.

Jaques grows horrified once again. "Your shape is _horse_!?"

"Horse?" Erruwyn repeats. As he pulls his arm away, blinking confusion is replaced with an incredulous grin. "_Horse?_ No woman would accept me"—he swings his palm to his nose—"I would strike them down with excitement, also." His hand falls away to disbelieving laughter. "_Horse!?_ This is slander, _feu'n'en_!"

Jaques giggles. "You wear this to celebrate _me_? Hm? No more of this one!" He points to _Danae_. "Which silver for pleasure? Tell me this to celebrate instead!"

A bemused Erruwyn complies as Jaques ties a handkerchief around _ne'ru'k⁻hu'ay_. "Signals for pleasure require compatibility, _feu'n'en_. That which you prefer, another may not. Though, silver tongue, _ay'tal_ is awarded in honor of skill. Most among the people will enjoy this tongue," he says poking his new cloth adornment.

"To think, our men strive for war medals." Lysbeth smirkles.

"Aye. Shameful that such a noble cause should go neglected." Elane chuckles. "Have you one of these meritorious medals, Erruwyn?"

"Yes, some, Your Ladyship."

Lysbeth scans his silver. "Which is it?"

"It is too diff-errant, _nar⁻uah_." He rubs his brow ambivalently. "Too strange to see. I fear I will repulse you."

"What is, hm? Why?" Jaques' eyebrows bounce. "More compatible shapes?"

"No, *ʃfeu'n'en*." Erruwyn motions to his own smile. "*ay'tal* is silver in the tongue. Though, we cut beneath for additional length. Split through, also. To assist with speech. With *aro'x*. Twice-tongue."

Four pairs of eyes widen.

ʒ chime

"And if your Naruah bids you show?" Lysbeth asks, dampening *ʒAnese* with one hand and taking a fresh cordial with the other.

He smiles helplessly. "Then I must show."

After a beat, she grins and shrugs her brow.

Erruwyn exhales a laugh. Setting elbows on cross-legged knees, he rubs his forehead and glances at Lysbeth again for confirmation. Long fingers shield his eyes from her expectant look. A moment later, his lips part, and a tongue carrying two vertical rows of delicate, silver spirals emerges and extends past his chin.

Jaques' giggle joins the rest. "Show, show!"

The tongue separates between silver. Each side curls up to its respective corner of Erruwyn's grin. When the terrace squeals, both tongues quickly retract. Keeping his eyes covered, Erruwyn rattles with sheepish laughter as Jaques' shakes *ʒDanae* with zealous hands.

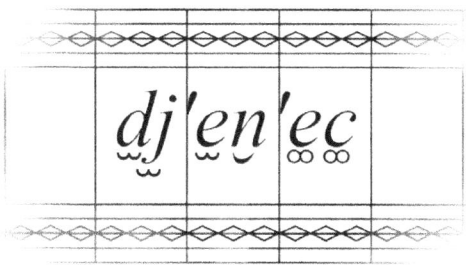

dj'en'ec

"What news, Lyssy?" Avrella asks, peering from a vanity as Erruwyn combs her hair. "Other than your recent regrets."

Lysbeth rubs her temple. "My regrets are certainly proving difficult to overcome," she says, glancing at the unopened message on her desk. "I'll look in a moment."

Erruwyn clips the comb and pulls a medicinal vial from under *Danae*'s arm plate. Dispensing a dose into the cone cap, he holds it forward as he nears the desk. Lysbeth pinches the thimble and sniffs.

"It will assist," he says, looking on with gentle amusement.

Having no energy to probe, she downs it. The remedy is slightly thicker than water and tastes vaguely herbal. A warm sensation trails her esophagus and spreads in her stomach to bury her nausea. When she takes a breath, a cooling sensation on the roof of her mouth alleviates the pressure in her head.

"Thank you." She smiles, returning the cap. "It's not a mistake I intend to repeat, but I hope you've enough to last both our lifetimes." Watching his bashful return to Avrella, she continues, "Anese has been quite talkative since Ryn's arrival. I realize her flirtations are difficult to ignore, and I understand your people are much more physically expressive—"

"Impossible not to understand after last night," Elane interrupts with a laugh. "Can you imagine Avons advertising such private information? Obscene seal stamps and calling cards?"

Erruwyn shakes his head in good-natured bafflement. Among the people, notions of obscenity are reserved for harmful behaviors, not body parts.

"Indeed. You missed a great deal, Granmama." Not quite ready for laughter, Lysbeth sighs cheerfully. "But truly, Erruwyn, you mustn't act on Ryn's attentions. Jhenxi must remain disembodied." Her brow arches.

Glad for clarification, his glance is earnest. "As you say, *nar͡uah*."

Avrella chuckles. "Whatever I may have missed of your discourse, I feel quite secure in my impression of Ryn as a skilled seductress. I do not envy your situation, my boy."

"Mm. Thank you for your pity, *ʒme͡na*. Though I believe I will endure."

Satisfied, Lysbeth squints at her letter's seal. "I don't recognize the sender, not that I should attempt to read it in any case."

Erruwyn retrieves the message for Avrella's extended arm. She peers at the wax. "Chadum, I believe." The Matriarch unfolds a page of dense lettering and holds it over her shoulder. "A summary, if you please?"

Erruwyn absorbs the words. "The mate of Marchioness Chadum has passed. She begs assistance; requests Lindenholt host Solstice in her place."

The women watching him freeze. Feeling their stares, he freezes too.

A family's esteem is measured by their ability to comfortably and properly host PromSol. As such, hosting requirements are outlandish, even by Outland standards. Estates must have a concert hall on grounds, guest accommodations for up to forty families, and an unreasonable amount of spare furniture for outdoor events. It's not an occasion to be taken on carelessly.

Elane steadies on the vanity. "Host PromSol? With only four weeks' notice?"

"I understand her reasoning, we were next in line to host," Lysbeth remarks dazed, "but even if we wished to, is it possible to organize it in such a short time?"

Avrella refolds the page. "Being the first to attempt the feat, I suppose we shall also be the first to discover the answer to your query, Lyssy."

The cousins gawk, awaiting an explanation for her decisiveness.

"Consider the following carefully," the Matriarch begins. "Lindenholt: savior of a beloved tradition, merciful neighbor to the bereaved, host to an Otay Bengli, residence of a mythical Faye Dahena." Her hands cross over the letter in her lap. "This is an excellent opportunity for the family, and thanks to the recent art sales, a vast surplus of funds sits at our disposal."

⟩ *chime*

Lysbeth lifts her chin to Erruwyn; he meets her eyes slowly. "You aim to reveal Erruwyn, Granmama?"

"Well yes, I fail to find a convincing counter-argument. What say you, Erruwyn?"

"I will do as you wish, ⟨*me͡ na*⟩."

⟩ —

Lysbeth taps ⟩*Anese* to free his halted breath.

"I fear I will make a mistake. Bring shame to you in some way. I do not wish to lose your..." he trails, swallowing.

"Our fondness for you wouldn't lessen even if you did make a mistake." Elane smiles. "Isn't it so?"

"Absolutely." Lysbeth covers ⟩*Anese*'s chime.

Avrella locks his eyes in the mirror. "My dear, Haywood Ladies acquainted with Alder's letter are equally acquainted with radical possibility. Being stripped of blinders may not aid our happiness, but it certainly leaves us amenable to nettling Avon Society."

Erruwyn bites a smile and nods. "I should have learned this sooner. I would not have avoided so much mischief."

"That is precisely the spirit." Avrella chuckles. "Now then. Our month has rather abruptly filled. Take notes until Erruwyn finishes, Lyssy. Ani!" she cries.

After Erruwyn's dressing, The Matriarch continues her delegations from a couch, and by the time all Ladies are presentable, a footman knocks to announce Ryn and Jaques. Last night, Erruwyn retired before the rest. In his absence, Lysbeth praised his work and promised Ryn use of his skill for a swift plait-resetting. Unfortunately, she'd forgotten.

The Ladies relay the PromSol development as Ryn takes a seat at the vanity. Jaques' request to extend his visit—followed immediately with offers to help plan and the use of Ryn's vocal talents for the program—is accepted, and the four continue list-making.

"Do you wish them smaller, Ryn?" Erruwyn asks, unweaving a section of braids.

"You are the artist, Silvermyr," Ryn answers in Croran. "You no longer desire to impress us?" she asks, noticing his missing masteries in the mirror.

"I wore _hu'ay_ to celebrate. To thank. I will strive to impress you with dressing instead."

Though _Anese_ is quiet, and Erruwyn's response isn't an explicit flirtation, Lysbeth's ribs receive a mild jab of annoyance. Unable to determine its cause, it jabs again.

"Oh?" Avrella dusts the air in Jaques' direction. "I'm very curious to know what this satyr has done to earn your thanks, Erruwyn."

He starts a miniscule braid. "Among the people we are _dj'en'ec_, _ʒme͡na_. Seedpod. Attached all together in the fibers. Touching, embracing, caressing. Always." His fingers blur. "We sleep piled. Train, eat—piled. Cry, laugh—piled. This difference between us has been challenging. The only touch past my Calling was..." He slants his head in inference. After a moment, he smiles at Jaques' reflection. "Then, _ʒfeu'n'en_."

Jaques' grin threatens to rupture his cheeks. "Oh, my darling, I will caress you until the end of my days."

"Mind you've brought it on yourself, Erruwyn." Avrella peers.

"Do you not get in the way of each other piled?" Elane asks, amused.

"Yes." He laughs softly. "Often, Your Ladyship. We play with each other absently. Hands, feet, hair. During heavy debate, you will feel, suddenly—" He frees a hand to rotate fingertips on his cheek, cycling the corner of his mouth.

"Truly?" Lysbeth laughs.

"Yes, _nar͡uah_. Your face, a toy for another. Forgetting your argument."

"Your frequent coupling has lost some of its mystery knowing you must be one step away at all times," Avrella quips.

"Both forms of touch create harmony _ʒme͡na_. Though, if a preference was required, I believe most among the people would prefer a life of affection."

"Oh, coupling, yes, I forgot to ask last night: If Jhenxi is a Concept, does it have a silver puppet?" Lysbeth waves Ani's tea tray to the table.

Erruwyn unmakes another batch of braids. "No, *nar͡ uah*. True *ay'tuan* permit *as'etu*; *Jhenxi* will not perform in one's absence, though its *ay-tut*, silver-shell, permits embodiment."

"Ah. What does it look like, then?"

He bites his lip. "*Jhenxi* looks a little as Ryn. Though much less acceptable to those among you."

Another jab jostles Lysbeth's ribs.

"*Jhenxi*'s shell hides divergent features," he continues, arching an eyebrow, "though, this is all it hides. The face is covered, also. Smooth *ay* to reflect its observers. In this way, *Jhenxi* resides in all, desires all."

Ryn's lips curl. "And the ways we are as your goddess of love?"

He laughs, correcting gently, "The Concept belongs to all. Wo-Men. *Jhenxi* is assembled of features enjoyed among the people. Long fingers of *ay*. Long hair of *ay* chains. Limbs wrapped in spiral *ay* to mesmerize with dance. Height, also. Tall *ay* beneath the feet."

The room examines Ryn's grey-white braids, heels, and grey wrapping.

"I can imagine the similarities, but we'll refrain from a demonstration, I think. If you claim Jhenxi is too little while wearing Danae, I'm inclined to take you at your word." Lysbeth smirks through Jaques' groan of disappointment. "Is height a commonly desired feature for women as well?"

Her own height had been a source of insecurity as she'd aged. Most Avonleigh Lords sought smaller women, and as a Lady's primary purpose is to marry and bear heirs, her concern over her worth had grown proportionally with her body. When her faculties caught up, she'd revisited the preference's implications, and concluded her height was a blessing—a deterrent for the kind of man who sought an easy means of physical dominance.

"Yes, *nar͡ uah*. There is little divergence in length. We enjoy it; more to explore. Here, many are smaller. This was an adjustment, also. Only children are this height among the people." He tilts a grin to Ani, who squeaks with offense as she hands tea to Elane.

"I quite understand. I only ever see children myself." Avrella chuckles. "Now, before our task is entirely neglected, see to it Ryn and Erruwyn are mentioned on the invitations, Lyssy. Otay Bengli as a performer and the presence of a Faye Dahena, or some such," she says, motioning to the list.

Lysbeth hesitates. Given Lindenholt's impossibly short notice, Ryn's inclusion is impressive enough. Announcing a Faye would immediately call their claims of Bengli into question. She looks up to explain her thoughts and is met with a smirk.

"Make note to keep Doctor Howe near at hand as guests arrive, my dear. Those who doubt Lindenholt's word may swoon."

Erruwyn smiles. The Matriarch's *kw'da* is skillful.

♯ ♪

Lysbeth unspools scrolls over the sitting room table as *ʔRoske* fills them—now quite sure Avrella's decision to take on PromSol relied largely on the Concept's assistance. All letters to suppliers and musicians had been sent by afternoon tea, and *ʔRoske*'s *as'etu* is currently churning out an extraordinary number of invitations while Elane keeps Jaques and Ryn occupied elsewhere.

She smiles at Erruwyn from her couch. The present expression of *ʔRoske* is exacting. Prim enough to match Ms. Leeve, even. She wonders what it would sound like uttering prayers to Sovereign Henri for grace and patience. Her eyebrows climb.

"Roske."

Silver fingers continue their clacking.

She leans forward slowly and repeats, *"Roske."*

The *ay'tuan* flips.

"ʒerruwyn–⸱dahena⁀naruah."

Lysbeth's skin prickles. Instead of three distinctive notes, Erruwyn's three voices are... voices. One very young, one very old, one middling. All neuter.

Her discovery feels wrong. A trespass. As she hesitates, Erruwyn's irises come into view under partially lowered lids. Lysbeth sits up and grips her hands as his pupils narrow on the table and lift.

"ʔRoske did not complete the task, *ˌnarˉuah?"*

She blinks rapidly. "I-I interrupted."

After nothing more is offered, he presses softly, "You wish for *ʔRoske* to cease?"

"No." Her forehead stitches textures of guilty concern. "I tried to converse..." The stitches tighten.

♫ purr

A slow grin spreads. "I should have expected so. You have met *ʔRoskeˉdj'en'eç*? The expressions, the seedpod, of *ʔRoske*?"

"I suppose so? I was too frightened to finish what I'd started." After a moment, her brow's stitching unravels to pull her eyebrows up. "What was it you should have expected, Erruwyn?"

"Only, you are very curious, *ˌnarˉuah*." He continues at her smile, "What would you have asked of *ʔRoske*?"

"I'm not sure. What information would it grant?"

"ʔRoske resonates Archives of the people, though one who bears the *ay'tuan* may ask beyond this," he says, wiggling his flipped fingers. "My translation is required to ensure the knowledge is permitted, also."

Lysbeth thinks. "I suppose I've wondered what ended the friendship of our peoples. You mentioned aggression, but what aggression, specifically? Would that be allowed?"

"Yes, though *ʔRoske* is not needed for this passage, *ɲar⌢uah*."

‖ *We showed them seed* ♦ *They planted roots* ♦ *Their soil
was sick* ♦ *Their fruit rotted* ♦ *Our paths branched* ♦ ‖

He slides *ʔRoske* to his lap, explaining, "We brought Outlanders the knowledge of soil-weaving. The Outlanders rooted. Created cities. For generations living as we do—all together, sharing. The solar tide rose. Fertile land was lost. Some among them began to hoard their seeds; claimed possession of soil. Of crops. Ownership. This Concept was sown with soil-weaving. It rooted with hunger."

Enraptured, Lysbeth leans forward to cup her chin in her palm. The Archives must be unfathomably old—far older than the Outland's records beginning three ages ago.

He continues, "Soon they bartered needs for desires—extorted—wishing only to share with those of their blood-root. Patrilineage: The owning of women to ensure the owning of children to ensure the owning of seeds. Within an age, most Outlanders followed the principles of these Concepts. Occasionally, *da'he⌢na* bartering on *set'ne* spoke against them. *da'he⌢na* sisters were ripped from our embrace as tributes to Patrilineage. These were the first notes of *a'ia⌢na*, the people's Keening. We withdrew, the truth forgotten."

Lysbeth mulls. She sees the outline of the image, but the people's tendency towards abstraction often blurs the details. "To be sure I understand, you're claiming there was a time when we lived without the full notion of ownership, and that changed due to some sort of drought? Or famine?"

He nods. "The solar tides covered fertile soil."

"A flood?" she asks.

"Yes. The solar tides of the sea." Seeing this hasn't helped, he expounds, "Lunar tides occur quickly—twice between horizon's moon. Solar tides occur slowly—the seas swell for an age. Remain for an age. Ebb for an age. This did not matter greatly to your ancestors before the weaving of soil. Before crops. Then it mattered."

She sits up slowly. "Most of our mythologies mention a deluge covering the world."

He smiles. "Yes, the solar tides have shaped all lands, *ɲar⌢uah*. Among the people, those distant chronicled the solar tides upon ⊙*ma⌢joc*, our primal soil. Each tide changes her form—the Outland's form, also. ⊙*ma⌢joc*'s soil was lost to us many times. Though we knew the same hunger as your ancestors, our paths diverged. Ownership. Patrilineage. These did not occur to us as solutions because they did not solve for all. We chose *ne'ru'k*."

Lysbeth's eyes film as she imagines the progression of events leading to her current social shackles; a time when resources were shared and only the identity of a child's mother was known. The advent of agriculture brought claims of land and harvest—Ownership— and priorities shifted. To limit one's resources to one's progeny, one needed a reliable means of parental identification: restricting a woman's partners to a single sire.

Ownership led to Patrilineage which led to... Lysbeth exhales.

Marriage.

The natural progression of Ownership—the answer to the question of inheritance.

Now, half of the population is kept locked and guarded. Women kept virgins to assure future husbands the sons they're forced to bear are his alone. Women's passions—physical, intellectual, or otherwise—suppressed or remolded to better cater to egos of men so she might tempt him into fulfilling her life's goal. Marriage.

All so his possessions funnel in a line instead of suffusing out to everyone's benefit.

She glances at her hand. Outlanders have *hu'ay*, too. For men it takes the form of medals, titles, and wealth—*hu'ay* awarded through Patrilineal heritage and, occasionally, the value of his contributions. But the only *hu'ay* an Outland woman receives are those signaling the successful mastery of her life's ambition: her husband's title, her mode of address—Ms. to Mrs.—and a ring for the finger of its namesake.

Thinking of Jaques, she feels—not for the first time—immensely fortunate that he's a friend. If all went well, her own marriage would occur sooner rather than later, and the Patrilineal exchange of her owners would be marked by a change in surname.

Haywood to Vippon. Father to husband.

A woman's livestock brand; another's identity banded on her finger.

Who was the last woman to claim her own full name? How many ages ago did she live? Lysbeth frowns. It's an impossible question. Women have carried their husband's or father's surname since the earliest known genealogies. Perhaps surnames themselves were born of Patrilineage.

She sighs, morose. "Your Dahena sisters are lucky you thought to spare them."

Erruwyn smiles gently. "It was their thought, *nar‾uah,* many ages distant. Our *da'he‾na* sisters were bound to the Wills, as I am. They knew *r'uah‾na* and *k'uah‾ni* battled on the field of Patrilineage—the Wills at war, always. They refused to be casualties of this conflict. All among the people wholly agreed, also. Forcing life, suppressing anima. These actions displace *◊Ruah*, disturb the equilibrium of a person, a people, a world. Discord. This is what we observed."

A floorboard squeaks in the hall. *da'he‾nar‾uah* turn to the closed door.

Several moments later, Ryn rejoins Jaques and Elane on the terrace.

bridge

The previous three weeks of planning are about to bear fruit.

Thanks to *?Roske*, nearly all one-hundred-twenty-two guests were able to respond before finalizing menus and accommodations. At Erruwyn's suggestion, the scrivery was tasked with the less time-sensitive production of seating placards and programs, and the scritchers were ecstatic to scritch again. The Marchioness of Chadum sent along her estate's stockpile of spirit, and graciously covered travel expenses for solo musicians she'd scheduled. Lindenholt's own retained orchestra settled into the musician's housing for daily practice last week.

Though Edenshire's Ladies tried to keep the event aligned with tradition, some changes couldn't be helped. Normally, intimate guests of the host family arrive weeks early for an extended visit. This year, all guests will be arriving over the next three days, with Proms to take place on the fourth and Solstice on the fifth rather than the standard week between events—and since tradition is already bending, the latter will include another of Erruwyn's fire displays.

In peacetime, the number of guests could reach three-hundred with servants. After PromSol's merging, Avrella's mother had a block of guest housing built to accommodate them, reserving the staterooms and apartments of the main house for important guests, family, and intimate friends—the earliest of whom have just arrived.

The Lindenholt Ladies lead their now-ten visitors—Jaques and families of The Flock—past the Grand Stair and Grand Gallery to the Salon—a smaller version of the Grand Chamber and used primarily for Proms' intermission. Lysbeth stops to peek into the adjoining Concert Hall while the rest of the party continues to the southern terrace.

Erruwyn stands next to an inconspicuous pulley system, assisting Mr. Wybber, the estate's underbutler, with lighting. Managed properly, the clerestory's curtains could alter the Hall's atmosphere dramatically. Ryn sings scales on stage, acting as a light-marker. Though she still studies Erruwyn, the compulsory hunger of her flirtation has faded. Lysbeth recognizes a layer of the relief she feels is personal, but she hasn't had time to dwell.

She's glad, too, as the distraction of planning has spared her an anxious fixation on Jaques' marriage arrangements. Last week, he'd relayed his certainty that—as the rift between Avon casualties and funds continues to widen—Sovereign Hinri will request aid again by Spring. Revealing Erruwyn now may increase his cost at negotiations, but Jaques aims to succeed.

Lysbeth closes the Concert Hall door and exits to the terrace, glancing at the lawn as she takes an empty spot beside Elane. A large, wire-mesh globe sits in place of the Equinox tree, and twelve polished, wood platforms have been placed at the edge of the garden in a three-by-four rectangle. Their stilts perfectly correct the beginning of the lawn's gentle slope, leaving a neat, even floor for servants arranging furniture under the canopies.

She turns her attention to the group as Lady Fernel, Avrella's niece, asks after the Faye invitations. Lindenholt's Ladies insist the claims are true, but when Jaques' vouching fails to convince, Lysbeth calls for Erruwyn. He appears a short time later, and for the first time in her life, Lysbeth witnesses The Flock's compelled silence.

"*nar uah*." He grins. Her unabashedly enthused expression is enough to explain his presence. In the event *Danae* doesn't clear the matter up, he adds another hefty, polyphonic greeting, "*Ladies. Lords.*"

At their sustained silence he bites his lip at Lysbeth to check that his purpose has been served. Her silent laughter confirms it has, and he takes his leave.

After a long string of questions are answered, the group determines Erruwyn's revealing should take place at the official reception in three days' time—summoning him to every guest's arrival would be tedious, and his skills could be put to better use elsewhere. Affair settled, Avrella extends a rare offer to hear her nieces' opinions on seating placards, and the party whittles: Corah returns to her lessons, Jaques leaves to find Ryn, and The Flock's younger brothers seek mischief in the yard.

As the terrace empties, its chipper mood dampens. One after another, a row of five, grim-faced Ladies whirl eyes on Lysbeth from the opposite bench. After a lull, Indra stands.

"Omission is not permissible, Lys. You said you knew nothing of Erruwyn's sweethearts while omitting the relevant explanation as to why."

"That's right." Bell stands. "A lie of omission in the game is held in the same contempt as an outright falsehood."

"Correct." Jemine stands. "We're owed three questions, Lysbeth Haywood, and we intend to collect."

Bell and Feobe stand in solidarity. The Flock shakes imposing plumage.

Lysbeth closes her eyes over a long, quiet sigh.

Ani returns from depositing Mikael to the hallway and smiles sympathetically as Lysbeth wipes her lower face with a handkerchief. The footman was wet with perspiration, and his mouth failed to aid matters.

The Flock's first question concerned Erruwyn's homeland. As Lysbeth didn't know the answer, she'd been spared. Their second concerned the secrecy of Erruwyn's origins. She answered what she could, but as Erruwyn's anxiety required explaining his time with the

Baron, she confessed to leaving out details. The inadequate answer suited The Flock well enough—kisses were a fitting punishment for Lysbeth's transgression.

As the players confer over their next query, an infrasound-buzz builds in *Anese*. Lysbeth quickly removes the pendant, wrapping it in her handkerchief and squeezing tightly. Ani and Elane grin.

"What's the true reason for Jaques' refusal?" Elane blurts.

The Flock cease to argue Elane's participation at Jemine's reminder: the question is a guaranteed kiss. Ten eyes whirl again.

"Kiss," Lysbeth answers through clenched teeth. She passes *Anese*'s bundle to her treacherous cousin as Ani sprints from the room.

Two doors in the Grand Library open for mischievous smiles, which step towards one another until met. Erruwyn's speaks first.

"You are playing, Ani. May I join with my Teammate?"

"Yes, you may, as a matter of fact." She passes the timer and holds up the cloth.

As they enter the game room, erupting giggles and resentful groans are quickly hushed by Elane's motions for silence. Erruwyn kneels, bringing the timer to the table with his left hand and raising his right for Ani to place. She obliges.

His fingers find spots along Lysbeth's jaw as he rises to his knees. "Teammate, will you permit a kiss of victory?"

Lysbeth closes her eyes, lowers her grin, and nods. Running a thumb over her smile, Erruwyn leans forward. Noses brush over lightly tilling lips. When lips plant, the timer sails over his shoulder.

The room erupts again.

"Erruwyn!" Ani squeals, moving from the table to find the device.

Lysbeth opens her eyes. Putting the pieces together, she jerks away and covers her mouth to conceal her laughter's identity.

"Teammate, we must hurry. We are owed the time." Raspy chuckles separate Erruwyn's words as he beseeches her forward, "Please, Teammate, I will not be permitted to hold time again."

Lysbeth regains control of her diaphragm as Ani returns. Opportunity missed, Erruwyn chews a contrite smile.

"Are you quite proud of yourself?"

"No, Ani. I have accomplished the exposing of my dishonor, only. Forgive me, Teammate."

Lysbeth nods and brings a hand to the table, flicking eyes between maid and timer.

"Indeed, a shameful exhibition," Ani scolds through raised cheeks. "Your *honorable* teammate will hold the timer in your stead."

Collecting her resolve, Lysbeth takes the sand and pulls Erruwyn's fingers back to her face. He smiles—fairly certain his hand is only placed when he's meant to take the lead. As she leans forward, his stationary fingertips trace the line of her jaw to the bend below her ear. Their smiles graze. Lysbeth throws the timer.

The abrupt motion and a clattering across the room lift Erruwyn's surprised eyebrows over the blindfold—his full-chested laugh cuts short as Lysbeth pushes in.

"You two!" Ani cheeps, leaving *da'he͡ nar͡ uah* to enjoy their swindler's kiss until she returns. "Very well. *I'll* be holding the timer since you've corrupted your teammate," she says, resetting the sand.

The team ceases their illegal play for the sake of fairness but keep their faces close. The wait builds tension. Mouths open to vent the rising heat of skin. Erruwyn's thumb moves over Lysbeth's cheek. She exhales, swaying closer. They graze again.

Elane pinches her nose to imprison her laughter as Ani flashes her a grin. The timer flips.

"Begin."

Given leave, *da'he͡ nar͡ uah*'s kiss begins in earnest. Their intimacy—aided by Erruwyn's substantial exposure—is distinctive and, feeling very much like interlopers, most of their audience averts their eyes.

The pair rock slightly, a metronome keeping time in shallow breath. When they steady at fulcrum, the warm mist of parted lips sets their weight into motion again, each measure increasing the range of impassioned displacement. Without external flavoring, subtle extracts are exchanged, and the damp tang of animalistic inducement clings to the back of their throats. Both stymy their free hands' attempts to grasp at the other—their mounting dissatisfaction finding some relief in the pressure of Erruwyn's fingers against the nape of Lysbeth's nec—

"Time," Ani calls, lifting her eyes from the sand.

The minute has passed far too quickly. Reluctantly detached lips remain close to catch the other's breath.

"Teammate, I have wondered," Erruwyn says. "If we wish to continue, I believe Ani could do nothing."

Lysbeth grins and opens her eyes. Dizzy pupils refocus and move to her maid, whose lips roll inward to stifle a giggle before responding.

"You've caused enough trouble for the day, Erruwyn."

"Why do you wish to suppress our victory, Ani? It is cruel." He arcs an eyebrow. "I call her Tiny Tyrant for this reason, Teammate."

"No you don't!" Ani pitches—a geyser rising from the room's peripheral giggles.

"I would not risk addressing a tyrant as 'tiny' directly, Ani."

"Fine, say what you like, just come along!" She grabs Erruwyn's arm and leans. To her surprise, he slides with relative ease. After his fingertips lose contact with Lysbeth's grin, his tall kneel lowers. "How are you so light?" she asks.

"Mm. This secret of *ay͡na* requires the resetting of many timers to reveal."

Ani fights her chuckle as silver clicks over floorboard seams. When she pauses to readjust her grip, Erruwyn lifts a knee.

"Ani, I will walk."

"Very well." She maintains her hold, watching primly as the corner of his mouth climbs. Giggles intensify. "I won't be letting go," she adds.

His knee lowers. "Then I will not walk."

"Erruwyn!"

"I will not assist you in removing me from Teammate."

She sighs and leans again, flinching as her fingers slip. Erruwyn's grin drops open in unexpected triumph. He quickly lunges for Lysbeth's chair. Amid a torrent of squeals, Ani yelps and throws her hands over silver—immediately returning Erruwyn to his knees.

"Ani! Horn!"

Realizing her discovery of his weakness, Ani squeaks with laughter and pulls.

He scrambles over the floor to keep pace. "No, Ani!"

Now gripping both horns, Ani's squeak turns maniacal.

"Ani, *ani*! Please!" Erruwyn cries through a wheezy laugh, miming his defeat to the door. "Forgive me, Teammate. Though Tyrant is tiny, she is formidable!"

The partition shuts on a boisterous room.

Lysbeth's guilty look crosses the bed. "The early bits were for show, but was it terribly obvious I enjoyed the kiss-proper more than I should've?"

"Truthfully, I'm not sure, Lys. I looked more to the floor than to you." Elane smiles apologetically. "That may serve to answer your question, though."

Frustrated, Lysbeth tips over and buries her head in a pillow. The day's events have forced her to confront an uncomfortable possibility: a part of her may well have spent months avoiding or denying her growing feelings without the rest of her realizing.

"Come, Lys. It's only natural to appreciate well-administered affection." Elane grins, poking the pillow. "No one will hold it against you."

Lysbeth pulls air through fibers. Perhaps Elane's right. *ḍa'he͡ nar͡ uah*'s game chemistry doesn't necessarily mean the platonic playfulness of their friendship needs reassessment. Still...

Her head rolls to the side until a bright blue iris appears above the pillowcase. "What if it's more than that?" she asks, mouth muffled.

Elane's grin settles into a sympathetic smile. She'd wondered when Lysbeth would get around to sorting herself out, though it wasn't something she'd wished for her. Forbidden love is a potent tenderness impotently tended. Elane knows the scenery: passionate peaks towering over perilous plains. Her fingertips press into the sheet—the faded image of petite fingers lacing her own drifts between divots.

"Then I hope Jaques is right in thinking Sovereign Hinri will call for him by Spring. Even married, he'd be the last to discourage your dalliance."

She turns hazel back on Lysbeth, grin reforming at her cousin's rattled brow.

To stay out of guests' sight until this evening's PromSol Reception, Erruwyn has kept to the kitchen for three days. In the interim, Lindenholt's Ladies have fielded, and censored, questions on his behalf.

Unfortunately, not every guest has been satisfied with the arrangement, and some have even skirted open challenges to the Haywood's claim. Sir Reisly, Avonleigh's preeminent violinist, has gleefully led the charge on this front. Having recently made a substantial Kingswar contribution to purchase his baronetcy—and the Sovereign's favor by extension—Reisly's showboat has inflated to a vainglorious frigate.

On arrival, he'd greatly overdrawn his disappointment at the lack of a Faye—a disappointment he'd loudly repeated during the informal reception of every subsequent guest. During tonight's supper, as Jaques praised Erruwyn's beauty and musical talent, the volume of Reisly's scoff hushed the Grand Dining Hall. He'd used the lull to admonish any who believe instruments of accompaniment or peasantry—pianoforte and guitarra, for all one knows—were comparable to instruments of the maestro's present. His declaration was met with more approval than the Ladies would've liked—though they might've agreed with him last year.

Before Mr. Tenson's bell rang to signal the move from Dining Hall to Chamber Reception, Lysbeth slipped out to organize additional comeuppance—*er'oo'n's* greeting. Now, guests mill the Chamber, Erruwyn waits on the second-floor landing, and Lysbeth stands with Haywood kin near the Grand Stair columns below, amusedly muting his chimes.

Mr. Tenson gives a brief welcoming speech and formally announces Ryn, who makes her own splash in the form of ruffled, grey silk fanning above her head and shoulders. A muted peacock, she saunters in to warm applause and stands next to the family with Jaques.

A brief silence precedes Mr. Tenson's announcement of Erruwyn, and halfway through it, silver is glimpsed on the stair. Excited gasps and shrill exclamations fill the Chamber as a splendiferous form of filigree, horns, and wings descends. The butler's announcement concludes as Erruwyn unfurls *er'oo'n's* greeting at the ground step. For a moment, the path of each guest, whether skeptical, capricious, or allegiant, arrives at the singular intersection of awe. Erruwyn lowers. Bewildered mutterings escort his walk to the family:

Sovereign's sword!   *Heavens*!   **By Henri**!   *Goodness fetch us*!   *Stars below*!

Guests fork again as the legendary being—one usually lumped beside dragons, mermaids, and unicorns—folds his wings to stand shyly beside the Haywoods. Despite ample warning, many struggle to interpret *Danae*'s exposure as anything but a personal slight. Most stare in quiet shock. Louder shock lurches into arms or pants through smelling salt pouches. Those on the least trod fork queue up to make Erruwyn's personal acquaintance. Reisly is last in line.

Certain whatever the man has up his sleeve will make an appearance soon, Lysbeth braces herself through a short string of introductions and raises her chin on his turn.

"A pleasure, I'm sure, Faye," Reisly's nasally greeting increases in volume. "It's very good of you to come out of hiding. Perhaps now we might enjoy a new topic of conversation—even Gyenna speaks of you as a Sovereign. But we all have reason to question his estimation in that regard, don't we?" He snickers at sprinkling chuckles—largely from those who don't realize Jaques bears illegitimate parentage as they would a war medal.

"Forgive me." Jaques grins. "If I've been speaking of Erruwyn as I would a Sovereign, I've given a very inaccurate impression of my feelings."

Reisly's mouth twists. "M'well. I wonder how Your Grace's estimation of musical ability fares under scrutiny. Unless I've misinterpreted there, too?"

The room watches with interest now.

Avrella peers. "If you wish to hear Dahena Erruwyn play, Sir Reisly, we would be delighted to offer a stage upon which your own estimation might be judged."

"A wonderful idea, Your Grace." Reisly's lips pinch in a self-satisfied sneer as piqued attendees applaud.

While Mr. Tenson oversees herd transition to the Grand Drawing Room, Lysbeth pulls Erruwyn behind a column. "Given Reisly's current favor at court, it would be best to not humiliate him too badly. You only need to match his skill, not exceed it." She smiles and covers another chime. "Don't worry, there aren't any mistakes to be made."

Erruwyn nods gratefully. "Yes, *nar͡uah*. I will match."

da'he͡nar͡uah join the swarm through Chamber archways and veer towards Edenshire's couch. Concerned Erruwyn's kneeling would cause a fuss, the Ladies assigned him a spot behind Avrella's chair, which he takes up while Lysbeth sits. When all are settled, Reisly's servant delivers his violin.

"Would you care to join me for *Compelle*, Faye?" Reisly waves his bow to the pianoforte.

Compelle—a duet for piano and violin—is a deliberate choice. Though the piece fails to impress much feeling, the violin's nearly nine-hundred notes-per-minute impress enough on their own. As accompaniment, the piano's primary job is to support its partner with chords on occasion.

"He doesn't know it, I'm afraid," Lysbeth says. "Perhaps another will honor you?"

"Surely the sight reading isn't so fearsome as all that, My Lady?" Sir Reisly quips.

As Corah's music lessons only required recording Mr. Spantier's instruction, Erruwyn hadn't learnt the Outland's notation. Among the people, songs of ritual significance are few—since Emergence demands renewal through constant creation—and passed down through _aro'x_, their primary instrument. All else is improvised and repeated if requested.

"Erruwyn does not read our music," Avrella explains. "An oversight on our part."

The room murmurs. To Avons unacquainted with improvisation, a musician unable to read music is about as pointless as a dull quill.

Reisly smirks. "Singular. Very well."

Marium offers to play, and the piece begins shortly. For the next four minutes, Reisly's fingers haze over strings. His wand pivots and swivels, gesticulating personal additions with grandiose flourishes and grunts. It's clear why the impromptu demonstration churned excitement: Reisly's rendition of _Compelle_ is his proudest achievement, and for good reason. Wispy hairs dangle from his bow as he draws the final note into a dramatic pose.

When the applause dies down, Lysbeth nods to Erruwyn.

The room watches as he partially opens his wings and lowers to the pianoforte bench. An awkward shuffling grows as his posture tenses and his eyes dart back and forth across keys. When no further moves are made, some begin to wonder why Avrella had taken the bait—even the Faye seems to know he's been beaten.

Finally, Erruwyn takes a breath and lifts his hands.

What arises from them is a note-for-note match of Reisly's _Compelle_—one the violinist often claimed would die with him, as no one else was able to reproduce it. Lysbeth holds her laugh in her throat, releasing it piecemeal through her nose.

Hands cross. Digits blur in trills. Long fingers stretch across octaves, tap precisely, and return in a blink. Creative employment of dampening and sustaining pedals provide convincing solutions for differences in timbre. In fact, the only marked difference in their performance is Erruwyn's distinct lack of pretension—and the steady spreading of silver wings as his _sm'aen_ instinctually crescendos.

Lindenholt's Ladies grin at the Drawing Room's astonished sea of faces—Sir Reisly's rapidly reddening face in particular.

Guests file to their Concert Hall seats after luncheon the next day, and a row of servants line the auditorium's back—the only remnants of Promenade's origins as a strolling and standing outdoor concert. Lindenholt's party occupies the center balcony box, slowing their excited chatter as the clerestory's sheer curtains are drawn. Erruwyn kneels beside

Lysbeth, locking *Danae*'s knees high to see over the rail and a shoulder to hold up Erem.

The Hall's chatter dims, Mr. Wybber introduces Avonleigh's oldest symphony, and the on-stage orchestra plays for the next ninety minutes. Unable to bear the monotonous themes, Erruwyn layers *m'aen* through the performance—sharing suppressed laughter with Lysbeth during particularly enthusiastic additions.

During teatime intermission in the Salon the orchestra moves to the pit. The Hall refills, and Mr. Wybber introduces the second half of the program. The lighting niche narrows a shaft. When the curtains open, Ryn stands alone, delivering a tantalizing rendition of an otherwise innocent musical sonnet. Her lustful voice lifts and lowers through quatrains of iambic pentameter, and whatever Avonleigh might think of her interpretation, her range receives ample appreciation once the song concludes.

Short interludes break the arias, marches, and sonatas that follow, and an hour later, a concerto and Sir Reisly's étude are all that remain. As the penultimate performance begins, a shadow from the hall falls over Lindenholt's box. The party turns to a glum Mr. Tenson.

"Your Grace, I've just been informed Sir Reisly has taken ill and must forgo his étude." His chin dips under an allusive delivery: Reisly's number was the grand finale. His cancellation is a deliberate attempt to embarrass the family.

"I see." Avrella glances at her granddaughters. "How very unfortunate."

"Vindictive, spiteful, petty gnat," Lysbeth's whisper squeezes through tight teeth. She eyes Erruwyn as he lowers Erem to his lap. Surely, she thinks, a good Wayfinder would forge a path benefiting both halves of *da'he nar uah*. She pushes the air with her nose. "Erruwyn, I want all who agree with this man stunned into silence for the rest of their visit."

purl

It's been a while since Lysbeth's felt purling *m'aen* on its own. When she'd first encountered the sensation at the Offering, she assumed it was a byproduct of Erruwyn's bashfulness—and she's partially correct—but Erruwyn's current expression is clarifying the meaning: devotion, admiration, trust.

"As you say, *nar uah*."

Fondness whelms Lysbeth's chest. *da'he nar uah*'s smiles grow. He passes Erem to Elane and moves for the exit, nodding to the box's cries of encouragement. Ten minutes later, the concerto's applause fades, and Mr. Wybber reappears on stage.

"Lords, Ladies, I regret to inform you of a change to our program due to the sudden illness of Sir Reisly." Among the audience's murmurs are smatterings of quiet laughter from those relishing the subtext. Mr. Wybber continues, "We wish him a speedy recovery. In his stead, Lindenholt graciously offers our esteemed guests an extraordinary opportunity: the marriage of Avonleigh's illustrious musical canon with the bizarre oral creations of a Faye Dahena."

The murmurs increase; buzzing interest. Unrest.

Lindenholt's party inches forward in their seats.

"We ask that any alarm experienced by Dahena Erruwyn's appearance or vocal abilities be restrained so others might enjoy this unique performance with minimal distraction. Thank you." The underbutler bows and withdraws to uncertain applause.

The clerestory draws a beam as the stage curtains part. Gasps fill the Hall.

Light reflects off a new *ay'tuan* kneeling in profile before Lindenholt's quintet. Tracks of *Il-Konok* peek through hundreds of thin, quill tubules running horizontally across Erruwyn's covered body—a collapsed spring in humanoid form. Five flared, spring-like horns are positioned in a circle on the back of his head. Erruwyn lifts his left hand. Thick, wreathed, silver hairs extend past his fingers. With each tap of his tapered index claw, he borrows a bass drum. The sound from within the suit is loud and clear enough to make out an occasional breath.

Murmurs begin again.

While the drum beats, another claw is assigned a woodblock. Then a snare drum, a double bass and finally a xylophone. Flicking his wrist produces a deep rumble. A cymbal rings as he tilts his hand. A wave from his shoulder to his wrist causes tinny, undulation.

He makes a fist. The sounds cease.

Konja's quintet grins. The demonstration has effectively conveyed *kw'da* to the audience—who currently wear the same startled expressions they'd worn at their own *kw'da* introduction. Erruwyn lifts his right hand and runs through musician assignments.

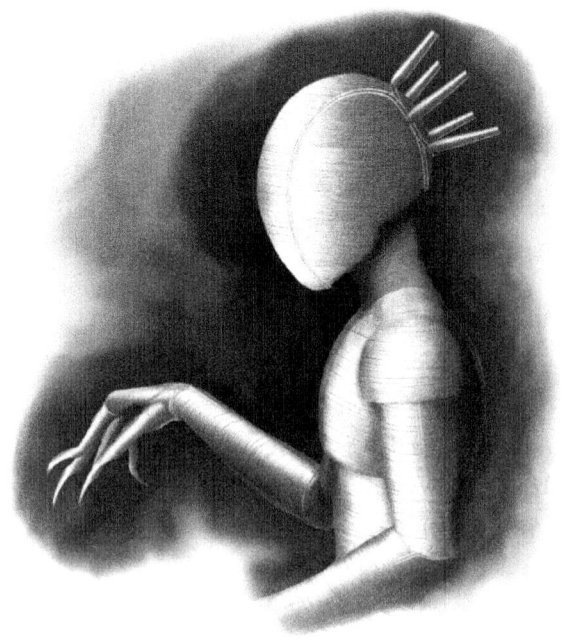

His two fists render a brief silence for a borrowed metronome. On the eight-count, the first bars of Sir Reisly's scheduled song drift out to lap against awkward coughs and scoffs. He maintains the melody into the eighth measure before beginning *aro'x,* and leading the quintet astray with errant *kw'da.* The flat composition alters dramatically as claws sew texture with rapid precision—exchanging sounds as needed and steadily increasing the tempo.

The improvisation is colorful and dynamic. Melodious waves rise, periodically lifting Erruwyn's hips higher from his heels. Halfway to his knees, the song surges, leveling Erruwyn's arms with his shoulders.

Then, it crests.

Submerged, Erruwyn's back arches violently, snapping his covered face towards the ceiling. Hinged quills swing away from ⊩*Konok*'s leg tracks, anchoring him to the floor. His upper body sways serenely.

Notes from Lindenholt's quintet are replaced with notes of alarm from the auditorium. Lysbeth stands over the balcony in concern. *ɣAnese* is silent, save for a slow heartbeat.

Moments pass.

Erruwyn's floating hands twitch; his percussive *aro'x* has been exchanged for string instruments. A meandering follows.

Trusting their honorary member, the quintet begins again. A bright harmony warps beside Erruwyn's undulations, slowly picking up speed. Cellos provide a stressed, thrumming core as violins rise and fall with *kw'da*'s suggestion.

Crescendo.

Erruwyn's hands yank as they had during *ʔRoske*'s drawing of *er'oo'n.*

Crescendo.

Lysbeth's breath quickens. She's sure now this is *as'etu.*

Crescendo.

Blurring bows reach an untenable pace to match the *ay'tuan*'s claws.

Crest.

Erruwyn's back and neck spasm again. His arms jerk up. Quills of various thickness, length and curvature swing out and splay from their hinges on his abdomen and spine. When they pass, his elbows yank down to his sides. His hands bend at the wrists, palms out, fingers down. Collapsed springs of metal spill over his arms and moor to the stage. His horns split vertically and slide along ⊩*Konok*'s added facial tracks, forming a skeleton for silver hairs lifting from his head—a clam shell hiding his ceiling-locked face within. Quills jutting from his spine and abdomen tidy as his torso straightens. Patches of unveiled skin glisten with prior effort.

The quintet's bows freeze in place. Erruwyn had warned them of spectacle, but there wasn't much time for details. No one expected an explosion of silver.

After initial noises of shock and panic disperse, the audience falls into stunned silence. Lysbeth's request has been delivered, only she hadn't foreseen being one of those affected.

A deep, raspy breath billows with remarkable clarity and volume. A new sound trails behind it—half organ pipe, half cello. In response, the longest tubes protruding from Erruwyn's spine and abdomen pair off, meet tips, and form slowly spinning ovals.

Another, higher pitch emerges. Medium hairs meet to make smaller, spinning ovals; others sway in a delicate wave.

Lysbeth's eyebrows hover as three additional pitches surface. Overtones, unnaturally high and emitting sequentially. Six pitches total. The smallest silver hairs react: rotating, swaying, and spinning as the notes intensify.

The final effect is a hypnotic display of moving parts answering to Erruwyn's voices. Edenshire's Ladies join Lysbeth for a better view of the peculiar beauty on stage.

Elane nods to . Lysbeth loosens the pendant and turns it up, further shocked to find its concentric spirals swaying. She stares in wonder, deeply touch by such a tangible change in the representation of Erruwyn's anima. Smiling, she returns damp eyes to what's left of Erruwyn on-stage.

The sounds retreat in reverse order and end with another deep, raspy breath. A moment later, the *ay'tuan* collapses inward, quills whipping around to encase the body of its puppet. Erruwyn slumps to a limp, motionless kneel.

As the curtain redraws, the spellbound audience breaks. Whether driven by genuine appreciation or stupefied conformity, their cheers are uproarious.

◇◇◇◇◇◇◇◇◇◇◇◇
◇◇◇◇◇◇◇◇

⁹Theam

PromSol hosts personalize their program from a list of forty pieces, making Avonleigh's Proms more a celebration of tradition than music—and the traditional post-Proms conversation as rigid and conventional as the concert itself. Avons find comfort in the repetitive bars and measures of their annual event, and if they don't, they'll be the last to admit it. Straying from tradition invites criticism, and Avonleigh has no shortage of critics, even if they don't personally mind the straying—for those reaping tradition's greatest benefits, cattle prods and scepters bear little distinction.

This year's Proms strayed so far, however, the peerage had to remove its mask to squint.

The Grand Drawing Room pitches and rolls. Entirely new commentary is explored, and those who disagree with the surprise performance on principle are having a difficult time justifying their objections. Generationally-instilled opinions are the oldest form of tradition, after all, and thinking for oneself is a challenging habit to pick up.

Lindenholt's Ladies sit serene as turbulent voices crash around them, and freely-poured spirit keeps the swells high. Conjecture surges regarding today's pageantry—as many previously assumed Erruwyn's winged spectacle was the result of muscle flexion—and eventually the hostess is addressed.

"Duchess, perhaps you would care to put an end to the speculation? To what, precisely, have we been made witness?" the Duchess of Ruxford calls from her seat.

"I shall not attempt an answer, Madam," Avrella replies. "In my experience, the carriage of speculation is often driven by impatience. And impatience, as we all know, only offers those shortcuts which veer from the path of reason. I'm afraid we must wait for Dahena Erruwyn's explanation to relieve us of our ignorance."

"I'm dashed! Does Your Grace mean to say he was placed on stage without knowing the specifics of his performance?" Lord Falrock asks.

"I am quite sure I did say it, rather than mean to, Sir." She peers. The room swells again. The party smiles at their Matriarch. "There are, however, a few relevant facts I will relay, if you are given to hearing them. Rest assured I will mean them all."

She begins with a basic explanation of *ay'tuan* and Concepts. Lysbeth expands where appropriate, providing a brief overview of their nicknames for good measure. When ⚥*Anese* stirs, she sends her grandmother an inconspicuous look.

"Lords and Ladies, let us show our appreciation for Dahena Erruwyn's stunning display before we begin the interrogation, shall we?" Avrella motions to the room's southern doors.

Erruwyn enters to mixed applause. Gripping a wrist, he stays sheepishly close to the wall during his long trek to the family, and soft murmurs arise from those he passes. Avrella waves him to the floor as he nears—fusses over his kneeling seem trivial, considering the much bigger fuss unspooled around them.

Familiar with Avon ambivalence, Erruwyn keeps his eyes low as he stoops, only risking a glance at Lysbeth to be sure he's met her request. An affectionate smile answers.

"Thank you for your provocative performance, Erruwyn. Now, please do explain yourself." Avrella peers over the room's chuckles.

"Yes, ⸌*me*⌃*na*. This was *Theam*⌃*rah*, observance of sound."

"Does that mean the aytuan's Concept is sound?" Corah asks.

He nods at the floorboards. "The *ay'tuan* is *Theam*—pitches of expression. Vibration."

⚥ —

Lysbeth taps ⚥*Anese*.

Erruwyn *wox'ua*s: command. He won't voice his thoughts unless she bids directly. Assuming there's a reason, she follows his lead.

He continues, "Sound's vibration must be layered within *Theam* to reach *Theam*⌃*rah*. Though I do not know what form *Theam*'s expression took, I hope it was enjoyed."

Ruxford's Duchess offers her diplomacy, "Enjoyed or no, it is unlikely to be forgotten."

"Quite right, Your Grace. Sound moving metal? Had I not seen it for myself, I'd call you mad and think not twice!" Marchioness Helie chuckles.

"Is such a display commonplace in your land?" Lord Falrock inquires.

Erruwyn glances at the couch arm. Lindenholt's *wox'ua* students devised gestures for Avon titles several months ago. Lysbeth's carefully-hung hand makes one now: Lord.

"Yes, Your Lordship. *Theam*⌃*rah* often occurs in celebration of special occasions. Though, *Theam*⌃*itet*, dancer of sound, is more common."

"You're able to move comfortably in it, then, Erruwyn?" Lady Docenly, Avrella's niece, asks.

"Yes, Your Ladyship."

"I don't recall the odd symbols on your back yesterday," the Marquess of Antium remarks. "Are they caused by the display?"

Those along Erruwyn's route to Avrella mutter in curious concurrence; those seated nearby contort in their chairs for a shameless look.

⚡ chime

Erruwyn's gaze falls further. When Lysbeth doesn't muffle *⚡Anese*, it amplifies. She grips the silver to spare him, but without context, isn't sure his anxiety is unwarranted. She looks to Avrella—the only one with a decent view.

The Matriarch smooths the sharpness of her inhalation. Five-inch spokes of thin, wavey lines center on each spinal root and ebb from reddish-purple to yellowish-green.

"Yes, I see." She chuckles. "Quite festive."

kw'da.

Erruwyn takes a shaky breath and chews the lower half of a grateful smile. Avrella's calm response has provided a reminder: despite Baron's fascination, the marks aren't hatefully aberrant. They're normal. Beautiful, even. He checks Lysbeth's hand.

"This is *⁊Theam⌢sket*, Your Lordship. Marks of *⁊Theam*. An expression of sound's successful observance," he answers, lifting his eyes to the room.

After nearly an hour of questions and discussion, Mr. Tenson's bell signals the start of Lindenholt's dining procession. Before taking her place in the order, Lysbeth tells Erruwyn to meet her in the water gardens after supper.

He waits with a sleepy Erem in the swing of *⚡Danae*'s arm, watching the sun lay a pastel gradient on the sky. Ponds and fountains dance with colors of their distant counterpart; chromatic ridges crosshatch the lake beyond Lindenholt's slope.

The sun's bloom clings to copper in Lysbeth's hair as she rounds the corner. Seeing it, he's certain the strength of his purr is numbing her neck.

"*nar⌢uah.*"

"Erruwyn," she returns his gentle greeting as she nears. "Very kind of a cat to agree to these surroundings on my account."

They lock eyes, grinning foolishly.

Being the quickest way to convey one's willingness to be swept off one's feet, dopey grins and lovesick fools find great use in one another.

Still, behind the lovesick foolishness of Erruwyn's grin is a distinctive pride. He's always admired Lysbeth's wit and curiosity, now her grit joins the list. She'd have an easier time navigating Avonleigh's social sphere if she maintained a publicly neutral stance towards him. Instead, she'd bid him on stage, refusing to let Reisly have the final say—she'd drawn a line, planted firmly on Erruwyn's side, and everyone else could eat squirrel.

There's a pride behind Lysbeth's grin, too. Pride in Erruwyn's modesty and kindness; his perseverance in the face of recurrent xenophobic contempt. She takes a breath and curses herself. Hers is the grin of a fool in free-fall—when one's center of gravity moves between heart and stomach as everything else goes weightless.

After a time, she steps closer to run a knuckle over Erem's soft cheek. "What was it you didn't want to say earlier? About The-aim?"

Erruwyn shifts his grin to the fountains. "I did not wish to offend with the truer answer to *Ji'la*'s question. I believe those present would find it too diff-errant."

"Oh?" Her brow hikes. "Corah asked if the Concept was sound, didn't she?"

"Yes. Though *Theam* is a little beyond this. Beyond sound, only." He flashes a coy look. "Among the people, *Theam* is nature's first element."

"First natural element? As in, earth, fire, water, air? Sound?"

He laughs softly at her puzzled smile. "Yes, *nar⌐uah*. The vibrations according expression—the pitches which a-chord shape to all things." At her continued puzzlement, he laughs again. "I have heard Mr. Sandel speak of glass-breakers among you. Those who shatter glass with sound—with *Theam*, the pitch of glass. This is *Theam⌐rah*. Observance of the first element."

"I see..." Lysbeth lifts a pensive expression to striations of color above the horizon.

The wine glass breaks when overwhelmed by its natural pitch. The pitch is found by flicking the glass. Her eyes fall to stone under her feet. All things must carry a natural pitch, but flicking stone...

She blinks to Erruwyn—who's rubbing a molar with his tongues and grinning at her inner machinations.

"I assume your people have discovered pitches for most materials?"

He nods and brings his tongues back to their proper place.

⁊

Unknown to Erruwyn, soil-weaving wasn't the only knowledge imparted to Outlanders ages distant. *Theam*: first element; Resonate and Fundamental Frequencies[20]. An early understanding of the Concept was promptly misinterpreted by the Outland as a singular, all-powerful creator, and the Outland's age-old path of shamanism was abandoned.

After the solar tide birthed Ownership and Patrilineage, Outlanders tried their hand at embodiment. *Theam*: The Outland's first God-King—all glory, all people, all things belonging to Him. As borders were drawn, King became Sovereign—the personification of a culture's codes, given enough power to compel obedience through conformity.

Discord amplified. ◊*Ruah* attuned. The people were hunted.

⁊

"Naturally." She sighs. "Well, it's a fascinating idea, though I'm sorry to say I agree with your instinct to withhold it from Avonleigh's esteemed."

She eyes Erruwyn's torso and motions for him to turn. Biting her cheek, she scans the

---

[20] *Omnipresent vibrations of matter which resonate at various frequencies.*

wavy bruises along his spine. Doctor Howe described a similar pattern after his examination last year. In a landmark event, she and her curiosity mutually agree to leave the occasion untrawled.

"Do they hurt?"

Erruwyn turns back. "Successful observance is a happy discomfort, *nar‾uah*."

"Well, as long as you're unharmed, it was a wonderful display." She smiles. "Thank you."

"Please do not feel you must thank me. To show you *?Theam‾rah* brought me joy."

"Even so, thank you." Her gaze wanders his face, lingering absently on his lips before meeting his eyes again.

They look especially green.

"*Are* you happy, Erruwyn?" Though a part of her fears the answer, avoiding discomforting truths no longer makes sense as an obstacle to potential resolution.

"Happy." He exhales a soft laugh. "How to answer."

A thoughtful pause follows as *da'he‾nar‾uah* turn to the scenery. Cicadas flirt across the grounds. The air smells warm and damp with Summer's blushing garden pools. A bird slakes its thirst with amber and rose, pulsing ripples across a gilded surface.

He needs to show her. Properly, if he can. Unrolling an empty scroll in his mind, he dons *?Roske*. Silver fingers cast lines of ink into an expanse of sky and sea.

*?*Captain Ibalis hangs a snicker over the side of a grimy ship.

♫ drone_chime

Feeling the change, Lysbeth inspects Erruwyn's face. He isn't exhibiting the vacancy of embodiment or *as'etu*, but he's certainly pulling from a deep well.

"After my Calling, I understood my hunters cared nothing for the covenant between our peoples. I tasted the bitterness of doubt. Doubt in my purpose. My training. In our assessment of Outlanders. My uncertainty rose with each sun. I took it on. It weighed me; I sank. I thought, 'If this is how it is to be, I will never know the steady rhythm of contentment or the rising pitches of joy again.'"

*?*A gray dress steeps in sunset. Hands rest on a velvet couch. Lysbeth beams.

♫ purr

"Then I was delivered to you. *te'y-ae*." He sighs. "My eyes required adjustment. Such light after the darkness. You were so bright. Warm. Curious. The first to regard me as a life."

The tug of his shy smile pulls a laugh from Lysbeth's.

"The ray as you spoke of your forebear; the joy. I thought, 'This is the brightness of *nar‾uah*. Maybe the steady rhythm of contentment is not so distant.'"

Ink pools under silver fingertips as *?Roske* lingers over the image. Erruwyn longs to remain in that moment—a suffocating, desperate longing visited on him with such frequency all sweetness of the memory itself had been smothered.

*⚄ hiss‿**wail**‿peal*

⁊Roṣḳe draws a circle. Without lifting, it draws another. Another, and another. Burying the parchment in black filaments of deranged horror.

" *iẋ'uḷ.*" He cradles a sleeping Erem. "Baron's loom wove madness in carrion. He bound me in dread until all light was hidden. Until even the memory of your light became fetid. *iẋ'uḷ-ae.*" He swallows, lowering his gaze to Lysbeth's feet. "My belief in his words held me under. My worthlessness. Insolence. My repulsive diff-errancy; your disgust." Emotive contortions wrack his features, echoing the e-motions of *⚄Aṇeṣe*: detraction. His voice is faint. "I deserved to suffer. More. More. Never enough."

His image blurs in Lysbeth's vision. She draws a breath, holding the air as a dam against her own *iẋ'uḷ*—her sitting room invitation.

⁊Roṣḳe lays lifeless in the black morass of Baron's design—limp, tangled metal reflected in sleek, oily ink. As it's dragged away, smeared lines and smudges left in its wake form floorboards: the front drawing room. When it comes to a stop, a reflexive twitching begins the outline of Erem's large, innocent eyes.

⚄ hum

"By the time I was returned to you, he had taken too much. Enough remained to keep my breath; not enough to surface. Though it did not occur to me to hope, you engaged me, discovered Erem. Found value in me beyond resonating texts, only." He smiles faintly. "I thought, 'I do not require the steady rhythm of contentment or the rising pitches of joy. It is enough the one I wished to call *ṇar͡uaḥ* finds me useful. Gives me purpose.'"

Surging affection dilutes the acrid heartache leaking in Lysbeth's ribs.

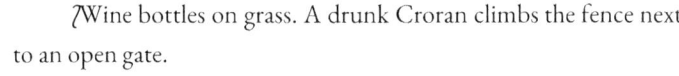 *⁊*Wine bottles on grass. A drunk Croran climbs the fence next to an open gate.

⚄ hum

"Then a gale arrived, tossing me about as a feather in the sky." He bites his lip. "*ẛfeu'ṇ'eṇ*'s effect on me made you smile. I thought, 'I do not require the steady rhythm of contentment or the rising pitches of joy. It is enough the one I wished to call *ṇar͡uaḥ* smiles near me occasionally.'"

Happy to fulfill the sentiment, Lysbeth smiles at the bashful shift in Erruwyn's eyes as he returns them to the landscape from her feet.

*⁊*Avrella's scrutinizing fingers bend under the crook of her wily smirk.

⚄ hum

"Then you set *⸘me͡ṇa* upon me." He grins at Lysbeth's chuckle. "She forced me out. No longer the fading echo of *ir'ie*. A true voice again."

*⁊*Constellations rearrange to form the lines of Lysbeth's collarbones. *⚄Aṇeṣe* rests between, brightest star of the Misty Lane.

The *ay'tuan* flips.

꙳ purr

"Now my heart beats with the steady rhythm of contentment. My lungs fill to reach the rising pitches of joy. Every day I have use. Purpose. Every day you laugh with me." He hoists an eyebrow. "At me."

Lysbeth laughs sweetly, her own heart suddenly aching with elation.

"Every day I walk with the one I call *nar⌐uah* as she forges the path for us." He pauses, and with earnest sincerity adds, "There is nothing left to ask for."

Turning to face Lysbeth completely, misty grins mirror.

"Does this answer satisfy you, *nar⌐uah*?"

?Theam ͡itet

The next afternoon, Lindenholt's Solstice activities begin: archery, juggling, races, music, and the occasional recitation of famous poems. Long pieces of straw lay in a bin next to the lawn's orb, waiting to be woven in its mesh.

Erruwyn sits with Erem and Lindenholt's Ladies under the tent, doing his best to keep up with an influx of requests: drawing portraits, expounding on answers from the previous evening, and borrowing voices of parents to say uncommon phrases for children. Soon, a different request is made.

"I'm curious about sound's dance, Erruwyn." Lysbeth leans over from her seat. "Would wearing Theam again further injure your back?"

"No, nar ͡uah," he says, handing a recently finished sketch to its subject.

Eyes lit, she turns to the family. "I'd like to submit a House tradition for approval: A Dahena dance every EquiSol!"

"Seconded." Avrella peers.

"Third!" Elane and Corah match.

"So it shall be." Lysbeth grins.

Erruwyn laughs shyly. "Then, it is best to imagine ?Theam hollow. To imagine I do not exist within."

Footmen are sent for the ay'tuan tree and Ms. Pinley collects Erem. Erruwyn converses with Konja as guests shuffle about for servants to rearrange their chairs and couches into a wide aisle. A standing crowd forms behind those retaking their seats.

When the ay'tuan tree bobs through the garden, Erruwyn walks to the edge of the tent. Snapping his horns to «Danae's collarbone, he plants one foot and points the other. A series of clicks mark the mechanical unlocking of «Danae to m'ay-tut, and after a soft warning §m'aen, to Lysbeth, his full strength §m'aen travels through «Danae.

?

Though male «da'he ͡na are not permitted to learn the secrets of ay ͡na, the reaction of ay ͡na to §m'aen is another example of ?Theam ͡rah.

Among the people, resonance crystals and mechanical resonators have been in use for millennia. Cut precisely, a crystal's fundamental and harmonic frequencies could be accounted for and electric currents produced.[21] Through ingenious use of acoustic conductors, transducers, magnetostriction,[22] and multiferroics,[23] the people turned sound into a power source.

For the purposes of *ay'tyan*, these principles are most often applied to move parts, alter magnetic polarity, and to detect and amplify sound. In this moment, Erruwyn's *ṣm'aęn* resonates with precisely cut crystals in *«Danaę*. The polarity of *«Danaę*'s spinal sockets are reversed and the *ay'tyan* is repelled from his body. The alternating of his feet removes the rest of the frame through mechanical means.

ʔ

As *«Danaę* unfurls, the bracings of *m'ay-tut* and its silver loincloth are all that remain. The crowd grumbles. Mothers of The Flock give stern looks to Jaques and their cooing daughters. Erruwyn smiles at Lysbeth's amusement, unbothered by the reactions so long as she is.

The footmen arrive and place the tree in front of freestanding *«Danaę*. Still-woven, *ʔTheam* and *ⱶKonok* are first on the trunk. Erruwyn backs in. His jaw opens for a thin, silver mouthpiece as the *ay'tyan* wrap around him. *ʔTheam*'s quills and hairs lay flush, appearing as one continuous, compact spiral from horns to toes. Animation complete, *ʔTheam ⁀itet* is repelled from the tree.

The *ay'tyan* stands as a motionless mannequin.

"Lords, Ladies, we are officially in observance of tradition," Avrella exclaims from her seat. The guests fall into respectful silence at the use of the word. "Until further notice, we are to understand Dahena Erruwyn no longer exists. I present Theamitet."

Soft chuckles turn to the silver casing.

A body-wide *kw'da* begins as *arǫ'x* is assigned to joints: ankles, knees, hips, elbows, wrists, fingers, neck. *ʔTheam ⁀itet* is a precisely ticking set of hinges. The crowd won't look away, but the abnormal exactitude of its motions is uncomfortable.

A pitch slides *ʔTheam ⁀itet*'s foot forward. Another pitch drags its second foot to meet it. A smooth, gliding locomotion ensues as the pitches alternate with appropriately ticking leg joints. The *ay'tyan* drifts to the center of the aisle. The tempo increases and a slew of new sounds are added.

Every aspect of its ambulation is set to an *arǫ'x* that matches a tangible impression. Warped key changes occur with smooth undulations of *ʔTheam*'s appendages and spine. Clean, abrupt sounds occur with precise flicks. Sustained notes occur with subtle oscillations. The music's bizarrely accurate motions quickly adapt *ʔTheam ⁀itet*'s imagination-deprived audience to the notion of an uninhabited suit. As the dance and song grow more complex, the initial unease dissipates.

---

[21] *Piezoelectricity and small voltaic piles.*
[22] *Altering the physical shape of magnets through magnetization.*
[23] *A material with one or more of the following qualities: switchable magnetic polarity, switchable electrical polarity, switchable deformation.*

Lysbeth grins as the ideas Erruwyn described click into place. *Theam‾itet* is clear in its conveyance of puppetry: a construct animated solely through *Theam*, the first natural element: A-chord. The vibrations which accord anima to organisms and frequencies to inanimate materials. After a few minutes, layers of sound peel away and take anima with them. The *ay'tuan*'s head, foot and wrist rotate subtly to the few faint, remaining tones. As the crowd's applause dies down, Konja approaches the couches of children.

"My little Lords and Ladies! Theamitet requires assistance to return home!" he cries, tossing arms towards the tree. "Will you please help me to corral it?"

The group giggles. Corah dons the mantle of Children's Couch Liaison and takes a brief poll—respondents answering by way of curious expressions.

"What are we to do, Konja?"

The merry musician leads the group behind *Theam*. "We must propel Theamitet forward with sound! But I cannot know which will move it!" He winks.

The children turn to the Concept and stare uncertainly until a young boy barks. In response, *Theam*'s spine straightens. A series of quacks, meows, and moos result in minor motions across the *ay'tuan*. When a small girl roars, *Theam‾itet* bends forward and aggressively juts its head towards her.

The children scream.

Theam's torso yanks back at the waist, its arms swivel behind, ending diagonally above its shoulders, and its claws and head vacillate with their shrieks. As the children come to understand their screams have caused the abrupt change of pose, they laugh.

Theam‾itet's feet glide.

Exclamations drown out laughter. The *ay'tuan* responds to excitement; its feet plant. Spectators chuckle as the sound for locomotion is revealed.

Jaques hangs an open grin over the floor, very much wishing to partake. Ryn sits tall next to him, wearing the first wholesome smile of her visit. Avrella and Elane chuckle; Lysbeth breathes deeply to spread another surge of affection in her chest.

"We must remake the sounds just as before to see which caused its feet to move," Corah declares amid the youthful chorus.

The experiment begins. Fourteen small voices roar in unison.

Theam‾itet leans aggressively forward, but this time, reactive screams sandwich squealing laughter, and the *ay'tuan*'s feet glide as its arms and torso jerk away. The back-leaning posture, smooth locomotion, and waving gesticulations look very much like a person being blown by wind, and its adult onlookers laugh, too.

"Laughing!" the chorus cries. "Laughter moves the feet!"

Under urging guffaws, *Theam* covers most distance to the tree—which now stands before a tightly packed crowd. Konja takes up post beyond the aisle's final couch.

"Wait! Stop!" Corah cries. "If we keep laughing it will leave!"

The chorus agrees and claps their mouths. At sound's absence, *Theam* sinks to an awkward, lifeless hang. Its knees bend askew just above the floor, its chin tucks nearly into its sternum, and its dangling hands oscillate under limp wrists held out from its back-leaning torso.

Sad her toy has stopped working, the young roarer frees her mouth. "Wake up!"

As words leave her throat, the *ay'tuan*'s head rotates away from its body, pulling the rest of its frame up by its horns. Its freakish, lengthening rise is met with screaming laughter.

It draws dangerously close to the tree.

"Ssh! Stop! Stop!" the chorus admonishes itself.

The children confer as *Theam ̄itet* articulates their words.

"Will he go opposite if we laugh behind him?" the eldest Flock-brother asks.

"It's not a *he*," Corah corrects. "Concepts aren't boys or girls, that's why Konja said 'it'. Isn't that so, Konja?"

The musician steps forward—a point in the diagonal line between *Theam* and the children. As he draws breath to answer, the *ay'tuan* exchanges its own pose for Konja's posture and mannerisms instead.

Konja tilts forward. Pointing to Corah, each syllable of his rising inflection bounces his hand. "Yes, My Lady! That is exactly right!" he proclaims, straightening and swinging fists to hips.

Looking past him, the children squeal as *Theam ̄itet* perfectly predicts Konja's actions. The mimicry continues as Konja spins to catch it, only to see the back of its synchronous spin. Its feet glide to the tree where it spins a final time to plant against the trunk's spinal roots.

Its head ticks down; *Theam* mutes.

"It is always sad to see a friend depart!" Konja grins and steps on a lever to swivel the trunk. "Say farewell to Theamitet, My little Lords and Ladies!"

Disappointed groans layer crowd chuckles as *Theam* disappears from view. Konja steps on the pedal again to lock the tree in place.

scamp

An impish scamp stacks with willful *m'aen*. Lysbeth tilts in search of Erruwyn, but the silver tree blocks him. Beyond it, he backs into *Danae*.

"Where does it go?" A child asks.

"Like all sound, it must eventually fade away!" Konja explains.

The crowd beside Erruwyn parts, and he sneaks through a gauntlet of shoulder pats.

"Please bring it back!" the small roarer pleads.

"How do we remake it?"

"What if we scream?"

Erruwyn reattaches his horns as he circles the large tent crowd.

The youngest Flock-brother pipes, "What if it's still there?"

"Yeah!" the chorus agrees.

"At least be sure it's really gone!" the barker implores.

At the far side of the tent, surprise meets Erruwyn's polite request to be let through. Others noticing his re-entry do their best to refrain from giving him away.

Konja laughs. "Very well! Let us see!" He kicks the pedal again.

The tree swivels and *Theam*  reappears as a split, empty shell. Before the chorus has time to envision their friend's dispersion, Erruwyn speaks from the aisle.

"Konja? *Theam ̃itet* visited?"

The children turn. Behind shocked faces, young minds attempt to make sense of his impossible appearance. Members of the Lindenholt party are among those most surprised—seated closest to the tree, their attention hadn't wavered from it.

Lysbeth leads the crowd's startled laughter.

"Yes! You just missed it!" Konja cries.

"Why am I always late for *Theam ̃itet*?" Erruwyn flops a droop.

A wry smile accompanies his peek to Lysbeth, whose laughter rises again.

◇◇◇◇◇◇◇◇◇◇

By late afternoon, the mesh orb is fully knit with straw. Guests funnel to the lawn, and a traditional ode to the sun's apex begins as the fiber is lit.

Servants use the time to dress and arrange supper's tables and chairs. A round of applause greets the final straw's ignition, and guests make their way to seating across terrace and tents for a leisurely meal. Music, dancing, and spirit follow, and as night commences, Erruwyn's fire sticks paint the tree line at the lawn's edge.

Erruwyn joins the crowd's acclamations—happily snugged with Erem in arms and Lysbeth beside.

◇◇◇◇◇◇◇◇◇◇◇◇
◇◇◇◇◇◇◇◇

bridge

For better or worse—depending on the respondent of the question—Lindenholt's PromSol has had an impact on Avonleigh's southern counties. As guests scatter their departures over the next three weeks, daily debates are held on the merits of tradition, novelty, and the correct portioning of each. Curiously, the debates always seem to occur after Erruwyn is called on to demonstrate one skill or another.

His portraits are a particular favorite, and among those who watch him draw with bizarre metal hands are scrivery customers whose recent orders had been filled remarkably quickly. As Avonleigh's official opinion of Erruwyn has yet to be determined, Lindenholt's Ladies avoid direct answers when asked about his scribal employment—their ambiguity leaves ample room for rumor, guaranteeing a new batch of scrivery orders.

Avrella's decision to reveal Erruwyn has been a boon, and as she predicted, Lindenholt should expect to be the next pilgrimage for Avonleigh's elite once the Kingswar ends. The Duke of Edenshire is sure to be pleased with his family's success, and the Ladies hope their report will earn Erruwyn favor. For now, the Haywoods relish their victory in a much quieter estate.

Lysbeth smiles. "You must feel even more relieved than we are, Erruwyn—called upon to represent both your own people and Lindenholt to such a fickle lot."

"Yes, heaven knows what Avons would do without a fence to straddle." The Matriarch chuckles.

"Mm. I cannot deny my relief to be among only..." He motions around the tent. Jaques and Ryn are the last guests and are set to leave tomorrow afternoon.

"Well, you surpassed expectations." Avrella pats his shoulder from her chair. "In fact, if there are no objections, I believe you and Erem must join us for the PromSol picnic overmorrow."

PromSol families often take time away from their estates after weeks of stressful hosting. The Haywood's picnic has been tradition for decades.

"Yes, he must!" Corah says, excitedly pointing west. "We eat on the lake. Boating and games and sweets, too, if you like. It will be much more fun with you along."

"Of course you must come," Elane agrees. "It's tradition, and it keeps us out of the way while PromSol remnants are disassembled."

"More a way for us to avoid the racket of disassembly, I should think." Lysbeth smirkles. "It's an excellent idea. He deserves the respite more than anyone."

Erruwyn sheepishly shakes his head in Erem's hair. She looks up and *wox'ua*s: yes, games, sweets. "We accept. Thank you," he says softly.

Ryn sighs and examines a miniscule braid. "I will miss your artistry, Silvermyr." Thoughtful, grey eyes move over him. "In some ways, Bengli and Silvermyr are alike; both trained to protect the interests of our people and sent forward as bait."

As the Haywoods are expected to learn Croran for diplomatic reasons, Ryn's preferred language doesn't impede conversation for any but Corah—which is for the best, given Ryn's preferred subject matter.

"What do you say to that, Erruwyn?" Avrella chuckles. "Is your training regime comparable to that of a Bengli?"

"*da'he na* are born of similar principles, *me na*, though our training is maybe a little different." He grins. "I will miss dressing your plaits, Ryn. Thank you for permitting me."

Spending most of her adult life in Crora—where Bengli are admired and can do little wrong—Ryn was baffled by the offense many Avons' experienced at her physical presentation, and so, naturally, encouraged Erruwyn to dress her plaits more and more outrageously. As the least aesthetically conventional attendees, the two bonded over their similar treatment and had a good deal of fun with their harmless revenge.

"All miss dressing me when the opportunity goes. As for training, your silver tongue of merit says our education is not so dissimilar."

"*ay'tal* is not required to become *da'he na*, Ryn." He smiles, arching an eyebrow. "Sadly, there is no formal training for *ay'tal*, also."

"Yes, very tragic for you, Silvermyr." She pouts playfully. "But it seems success in pleasure found you without training."

Jaques sits up. "I was considering this earlier."

"I imagine you give the subject a great deal of consideration," Avrella mutters.

"You know I enjoy hearing all the ways you imagine me, Vrella. And you are right, of course. My meditations on pleasure are exhaustive, but in this one instance, I was considering Erruwyn's training." Jaques waves at the *hu'ay* Erruwyn's intermittently worn through the month. "In Crora, word of Bengli skill stirs Lords to find and entice one. Word of your skills will move quickly, too, Erruwyn. The world will want to find more of you to take as their own, I think. Is this not at odds with your desires for solitude? You should train less, hm?"

Lysbeth's chin dips. "A surprisingly well-reasoned query."

Erruwyn leans on a palm and strokes Erem's hair. "There are reasons for our training, *feu'n'en*, if this is what you wish to know."

Jaques nods.

"Some training is only very useful among the people or on _set'ye_. Some is required for Concepts. The Wills. _ŋar͡uah_ especially. It is hoped if we are well trained, we will be well treated, also. Valued." He takes a slow breath, flicking eyes to Erem. "For a time distant, it was thought Outland vessels followed us in curiosity, only. We learned this was not so. We sought a covenant between us: _To hold the cover of night we must offer our brightest stars._ The offering of _ɀda'he͡ŋa_ to satisfy our hunters; to keep the people shrouded. This is how we have understood our Threadings, though, I have felt the same uncertainty, _ʃfeu'n'en_. It cannot be a true covenant if only one party participates." He ends with a helpless smile. "I do not know what can be done."

Ryn studies Erruwyn as he speaks. When he finishes, she reports her findings: "You are not what I expected, Silvermyr."

"What was it you expected?" Elane asks.

"I think," she says, cocking her head, "something more of Otay men."

"Does that suggest the rise or fall of your estimation?" Lysbeth grins.

"Hmm, perhaps I will say, I respect Silvermyr for sparing their women the company of animals." Ryn smiles and scratches Jaques' stomach. He pants loudly.

Avrella peers. "As parasite treatments go, I am told lard is quite effective. I will send some along for your mutt."

Erruwyn shakes his head sadly. "It would only delay the recurrence, _ɀme͡ŋa_."

"Vrella has turned you against me already, Beauty?" Jaques cries, grinning at Erruwyn's apologetic smile.

"You never did explain the rest of your merits, Erruwyn." Elane chuckles. "I should like to know if there are any others I'd do well to avoid."

"Yes, Your Ladyship."

He sits up and reaches for the branching stalks of ⌣_ay'ena_, the crescent mouth mask on his left shoulder. Removing the top branch—a graceful figure-eight drawn in a continuous line of silver—Erruwyn pinches its center as a balancing scale. "∞_ry͡ine ͡hu'ay_. I must answer the demands of ◊_Ruah_ through _ry͡ine_, weaving of symmetry. Restoration of equilibrium."

He deposits the eight into Erem's open palm and points to five rings in his left ear cartilage. "The _ay'tuan_ masteries, awarded along the path of _ay'tuan_." Turning his head, he points to a spoked earpiece in his right ear. "⁊_Theam͡rah_. This mastery diverges from ⁊_Theam_. Not all wish to attempt it."

"Why not?" Corah asks.

"There are risks, _ʃli'la_," he says, balancing Erem as she stands to replace

∝*ry̰ ˜inḛ ˜hu'a̰y* and poke at the silver in his ear.

"Risks?" Lysbeth's eyebrows lift.

Erruwyn hesitates. "Yes. A small risk of injury beyond the marks of observance." He bites his lip, hoping this is enough.

It's not.

He continues, already wincing at the scolding he's sure to receive, "A small risk of damage to the spine chamber."

The Ladies straighten.

"Erruwyn, I know my Proms request was abrupt, but you must bring the possibility of harm to my attention before you take part in"— unsure of the term, Lysbeth waves a hand at *₡Dana̰ḛ*—"any of it."

"Yes, *na̰r̰ ˜ua̰ḫ*," he says quietly.

Still feeling the whites of her unabated stare, Erruwyn shrinks slowly— *da̰'ḫḛ ˜na̰r̰ ˜ua̰ḫ*'s smiles widening the lower he folds over a now-ducking-and-giggling Erem.

"Alright." Lysbeth laughs. "Go on with your merits before poor Erem suffers the full weight of your chagrin."

He sits up and smooths Erem's hair. Turning in profile, he traces angled lines emitting from short, silver spirals on either side of his head.

"The elemental embodiments have no *a̰y'tua̰n̰*, though their horns are shaped as these." He holds out his left hand, one ring above each knuckle. "Divergent tongues. ∝*da̰'ḫḛ ˜na̰* must know essentials of thirteen languages."

"Thirteen?" Corah yelps.

He nods. "We do not know which tongue our hunters will carry. We strive to learn those most likely, though many of our language records are distant. In this way, *a̰x'nḭ ˜ra̰ḫ* amends our understanding." Touching an embellished V at the base of his throat, he concludes, "*a̰ro̰'x̰* mastery is earned after defeating an *a̰ro̰'x̰* Master, though this mastery is not required to earn *₡Dana̰ḛ*."

Lysbeth glances cagily. "I assume arox skills apply to other lingual categories of merit?"

"Yes." He grins. "One who has defeated an *a̰ro̰'x̰* Master is likely to possess skills nearby, also."

"And who awards your tongue silver?" Ryn asks with a crooked smile. "Are you pricked after every taste?"

"No..." Erruwyn checks with Lysbeth before explaining further in Croran, "Awarding occurs during *da̰'ja̰ ˜na̰*, our celebration of life's pleasure. Our name is pressed into a bead. After sampling the"—he smiles as he thinks—"sweets to our satisfaction, we honor the flavor who has best satisfied our hunger with the bead. The *a̰y̰* master provides one *a̰y'ta̰l* for five beads."

Avrella chuckles. "Heavens. Quite the exchange rate."

"Mm. And judging by your aytal number, it's a wonder you're so trim." Ryn winks above her grin.

Jaques graciously follows departing protocol the next afternoon. In return, his long embrace of Erruwyn is overlooked.

"I hope to see you by Spring, Beauty." Eyes fall over silver as he pulls away. "Wear this for me then too, hm?"

"Yes, *feu'n'en*. I will wear *Dange* then, and all days between, for you." Erruwyn exchanges an amused look with Lysbeth as Jaques moans. "I wished to give this. Ryn, also," he says opening his hand. An engraved, spiral hair cuff and an ornamented, spiral ring sit in his palm. "Symbols of *Jhenxi*. The recesses can be used for scent or oil."

Jaques gasps. "Oh! My beautiful Erruwyn. It will never leave me," he says, slipping the ring on his index finger. Cupping Erruwyn's neck, he pulls him in to plant a long, tender kiss on each cheek.

As he carries on, Ryn slowly detaches his grip and gently nudges him away. Standing in profile, a sidelong look delivers her request. Erruwyn gathers her plaits and coils the cuff around them. When his arms lower, she turns and rests her palms on his cheeks. Her expression is light and her voice sincere.

"Silvermyr, I wish you well." She strokes his cheekbone with a thumb, adding, "From one bait to another, do not forget there is always a larger mouth beneath."

ẑr'hea

The Ladies, Ms. Pinley, and Erem climb into a large carriage eager to picnic. Servants prepared the lakeside meadow yesterday, and Ms. Makensi's lunch should be arriving at the spot soon, leaving plenty of time to complete the table setting before the group arrives.

Winding through the western wood, Brom leads a small escort surrounding the carriage, and a cross-legged Erruwyn trots a filigreed Kiky alongside. Sun sprinkles through the canopy to lay luminescent cobblestone on the dirt road ahead, and breezes shuffle forest spices—balsamic pines, earthy moss, and the musk of decaying fiber—as Corah calls out sounds for Erruwyn to borrow.

So far, he's been loaned two bird calls, rustling leaves, and a *clank* from the carriage as it encountered a particularly fearsome pothole. Avrella nixed the inclusion of falling manure, and when nature fails to offer a prompt alternative, Corah requests a story instead.

"What form of story do you wish to hear, ẑ*li'la*?"

"If I'm allowed a say," Lysbeth interjects, "I'd like to know how you overthrew an arox master. It's difficult for me to imagine you taking part in fierce rivalry."

"Yes, my tournament participation was penance for betraying ẑ*erru⁀wan*. I would not have done so without her coercion."

"Betray your sister?" Elane asks surprised. "Whatever had you done?"

Erruwyn smiles. "I hid my practice of *aro'x*. She demanded amends."

Corah's mouth screws. "Why hide it?"

"I have always been ẑ*erru⁀wyn*. Dusk. Not so shy as night, though, nearby. The truer answer is longer." He hesitates, then grins. "Though, maybe not so long. I admired another from afar."

Three faces scoot closer to the open-air windows.

"I believe an agreement has been reached." The Matriarch chuckles with Ms. Pinley from the back corner.

"You've never told us of your sweethearts. Naturally we're curious," Corah says, the picture of reason.

Erruwyn flicks eyes to Lysbeth, who nods vigorously.

"Then, here is my tale of *aro'x*," he says, leaning back on Kiky and looking to the canopy. "Many years distant, as I walked to a favored quiet spot, I heard *aro'x* from within the hilltop _so'jac_ grove." He glances at the windows. "This is a flowering tree with a pleasant fragrance. The _aro'x_ came from a girl I had seen in the training halls. {r'hea, then seventeen years of age. She composed under _so'jac_ near the cliff."

♪ _purr_

"The image has never departed me. Scent over the grove. Mist over the cliff." He waves his hand languidly. "Breeze playing with her hair, pollen drifting about." His hand freezes in place. "I thought, '_What_ is this?'" The carriage occupants grin as he continues, "I had not yet experienced what it is to be pulled to a person. The forms of their expression." He sits up and stacks invisible material. "Mannerism. Feature. How successfully they sit among their surroundings." He smooths the unseen pile.

"What was your own age at the time?" Lysbeth asks, failing to imagine a younger version.

"Ten years of age, _nar‿uah_." Erruwyn smiles bashfully, waiting for the carriage's scoffles to resolve. "I agree it is young to feel so, though it cannot be helped. The moment drew me to _aro'x_. To {r'hea. I began to practice privately, as she did on occasion. As I aged, I wondered of formal training. Many devoted to _aro'x_ join a Master's guild. I decided against this. I did not wish to compete." He looks at Corah to answer her earlier question, "Practicing in solitude caused me to feel closer to {r'hea in some way, also."

♪ _sing_

"Many years passed this way. Then, {erru‿wan discovered my secret. We observed the tournament together each year. She felt I had created a false image by hiding the skill. So. Participating in the tournament was to be my penance." He looks pointedly at Lysbeth. "I refused."

Lysbeth hums in recognition.

"To bend me, {erru‿wan hid items necessary for our training. Masters scolded my carelessness in front of the others. She knew this would be the most terrible to me." He laughs and rubs his face. "I yielded after two suns, only."

Brom joins chuckles from the carriage.

Corah shakes her head. "I'm sure I would've told Ms. Leeve it was all Lysbeth's doing."

"Yes, because you are {li'la," he says, dangling a leg off Kikyum. "{erru‿wan would not have attempted this for you. Though, she knew {wyn would not reveal her." When Corah concedes, he continues, "I began to consider compositions. I knew my _aro'x_ had branched. Diverged without formal training. New expressions emerged. I thought to use one."

"Such as what?" Corah asks.

"Such as this sound. Used often like so." The corner of Erruwyn's lower lip quivers.

"It's like the snoring call of a frog, isn't it?" Elane submits to carriage approval.

"The sound can boost. Twice-speed, thrice-speed. Relaxing a piece of lip above I discovered a path to boost beyond this." He vibrates his lip again. The pitch heightens as his lip blurs. "I had not heard this before. I thought to use it for my introduction. _ƚr'hẹa_ was competing, also. I wished to impress her." Erruwyn sighs. "I was disqualified in the instant."

Lysbeth laughs. "Why? What was the reasoning?"

"There is a record of unpermitted sounds to restrict those whose tongues are split as mine—split as far as can be," he explains. "In this way, fairness is shown to the shorter-split. The judges thought me ignorant of this; I was not known as an _aṛọ'x_ student. They believed twice-tongue assisted in my boosting. I did not wish to argue before so many others. So. I accepted their decision." He smiles at the road as the Ladies' cluck. "_ƚr'hẹa_ ousted the Master that year. I was glad for her. Glad we had not been opponents, also. Though, the sound blistered my thoughts. I wished for vindication. For _ƚr'hẹa_'s eyes especially."

"Was there any indication of her interest?" Elane asks.

Erruwyn bites his lip and shakes his head. "We had not spoken much. _ᴅda'hẹ ̄ṇa_ training is consuming. Also, _ᶾwyṇ_," he adds softly. "I strove to participate again. I practiced, attuned the diff-errancies of my _aṛọ'x_—different to confuse my opponents; not so different to disqualify. If I reached the Master, _ƚr'hẹa_, I planned to end with my boosted sound."

Avrella peers. "Would reproducing the sound not ensure your disqualification?"

"Yes, _ᶾmẹ ̄ṇa_, I wished for it to be so."

"Whatever for?" Lysbeth presses.

"I did not care too strongly for the Mastership, _ṇar ̄uaḥ_. The judges could not think me ignorant in reaching _ƚr'hẹa_. They would examine my sound. Vindicate me. I thought, also, a sacrifice of principle would draw _ƚr'hẹa_'s eyes." He picks at Kiky's silver. "Though to be certain, I planned to request her time at the tournament."

"Request her..." Remembering his phrasing of _jo'ṭa_ cuffs, Elane's eyebrows rise. "So publicly? Without being certain of her own regard for you?"

"Yes, Your Ladyship." He hides beneath a palm. "The _aṛọ'x_ tournament occurs during _da'ja ̄ṇa_. Many public requests are made, though I do not know why I thought to do so. I would have become a puddle of despondency at her rejection." He chuckles with the Ladies and swings his dangling leg.

ᶾ sing

"Next year, I reached the final round. I was first in order as challenger to _ƚr'hẹa_. My request occurred during this composition. She accepted." He grins at the rustling canopy. "Then I made the boosted sound. To root my intent, I signaled rude _wọx'ụa_ to the judges, also."

"I can scarcely believe it." Lysbeth laughs. "You were a touch rebellious, weren't you?"

"I believe it was my shameful pettiness, only, _ṇar ̄uaḥ_."

Corah leans out the window. "But you earned the silver. Why were you not disqualified?"

"*ƚr'hea*." Erruwyn smiles. "She forfeited as the judges discussed me. This left only one path: I was Master. Though I was not permitted to defend the title as penance for my *wox'ua*."

"Why did she forfeit?"

"She guessed my intention to lose, *ƚi'la*. She did not believe she would have won. The taste of false victory was unsavory."

"Quite noble." Avrella smiles wryly. "The most important question, however, is whether or not you secured her bead of favor."

"Yes, *ʒme͡na*." He laughs softly at the unexpected question. "We exchanged beads. Became favorites." His shy smile hints at pride. "Three years later, she was *me'ya͡itet*. I was requested as her first chosen."

"Had you been chosen before?" Avrella's voice lifts through a carriage of coos.

"Yes, first chosen, also. Though, this was *ƚr'hea*. Even more special."

"Did she bear twins?" Elane asks.

He looks at Kikyum's back and draws a long breath. "I am uncertain."

ƚ —

Lysbeth touches *ƚAnese*; wavering eyes lift.

"*ƚr'hea* knew I was to be on *set've* for the birth moon. Though she was swollen with life, she came to the vessel at our departing. She gave me a box. Instructed not to peek until the correct time." He smiles. "*ƚerru͡wan* took it to be certain."

ƚAnese sings bittersweetly.

"It was... *ƚr'hea* preserved a *so'jac* flower from the tree she sat beneath years distant." Erruwyn swallows under damp eyes. "I held it as I was Thread. The scent—" His voice catches. His gaze moves to the road. "She was near me. Giving comfort."

Avrella regards him through glassy eyes. "You are indeed a romantic, Erruwyn."

"Yes, *ʒme͡na*." He smiles faintly. "It cannot be helped."

Resting her head on the window frame, Lysbeth smiles at her own glassy image of Erruwyn as the party turns into a clearing.

Grass has been trimmed to avoid ticks and wet skirt hems, and a densely wooded perimeter lends the large meadow cozy intimacy. The serene lake's shoreline reflects trees and two canopied row boats. A table in the center of a tent has been handsomely dressed. To its left, footmen stand beside covered serving trays. Behind them sits a cloth-covered luncheon wagon.

Brom leads the guards to a small pasture of grazing horses, passing empty furniture wagons parked along its fence. Erruwyn slides off Kiky and signals him free. With a happy snort he canters off to explore as the carriage pulls to a stop. Erruwyn offers a hand to the Ladies, and each pays compliments to the scenery as they descend—though not loudly enough to wake Erem from her nap in Ms. Pinley's arms. All gathered, the carriage moves towards the pasture in the lower corner of the field and the party strolls to the tent.

"How did your request manifest, Erruwyn? Was it a lyric?" Lysbeth asks.

"It was a gesture, *nar uah*. Similar to your air kisses. To catch it signals thought. To place with purpose signals acceptance."

Corah's brow crinkles at her kin's amusement.

"What of your vindication?" Elane hops over a divot in the grass. "Did the judges ever admit their blunder?"

"Yes, Your Ladyship. The sound is free from judgement."

"A happy ending." Avrella chuckles. "I hope you thanked your sister for the push."

"Mm." Erruwyn smiles as he ducks under the tent. "*Erru wan* collected my thanks in the form of chores."

As the group collects beside the table, Avrella, Corah, and Elane circle to remark on the settings. Lysbeth turns to thank the footmen.

She doesn't recognize them.

"Who—"

Yelling cuts her short. She glances in its direction. Horses dart away from the forested edge of the corral, narrowly avoiding three grounded guards. struck with arrows—a shoulder and two legs. Elane's gasp draws her back to the tent.

Behind the footmen's table, the large food wagon's cover has been thrown back. Armed men calmly jump over the sides and approach, swords bared. The imposter footmen step forward. Two draw daggers, two reach for now-visible sword hilts. The shocked party instinctively clumps together. Erruwyn steps in front of Ms. Pinley and Lysbeth. Across the table, Avrella and Elane pull Corah behind them.

In the pasture, Brom scans the woods. Six archers soon emerge, ordering the uninjured guards to disarm and kneel. Concerned for those at the table, the Marshal nods to his men. Bows lower as the Keepers comply. One among the assailants whistles to the tent before helping the rest bind ankles and wrists.

Returning the sound, an enormous man with a sheathed sword ducks under the canopy. "Pardon the interruption, Ladies," he rumbles. "We'll be on our way after we get what we come for. Have a seat."

Avrella points a polished voice at the giant, "What have you done with our people? What is it you want?"

"In the wagon. Uninjured." He nods to the pasture fence. "Have a seat."

In answer to the second question, the footmen grab Erruwyn and press blades into his skin—a show of their resolve to inspire compliance.

"No, you must stop!" Corah cries across the table.

Lysbeth folds her hands tightly. "Corah, we are in no position to argue. Do as he says. Sit."

Elane pulls Corah down to a chair beside her own. Ms. Pinley lowers shakily, covering Erem with a blanket to hide Erruwyn from view. Avrella and Lysbeth remain standing as the Matriarch assesses—the men had known far too much, and are far too calm, for typical banditry.

"I offer double the sum of your employer," she says.

"Have a seat," the giant repeats.

Avrella lowers to a chair. "Triple."

"You don't have it."

Lysbeth glances at the pasture. The carriage is still hitched. Lindenholt's Keepers are on the ground; their attackers are leading horses to a furniture wagon and tossing spare weapons in the back.

"Surely there's some agreement to be made." The tendons in Lysbeth's neck jump as she turns back.

"'fraid not."

"Please."

The giant sighs. "Sit."

Lysbeth swallows. Lowering to a chair, she lifts frightened eyes to Erruwyn. Two men hold his arms; two hold daggers to his neck and chest.

⅊ *chirp_chime*

Surprise. Anxiety.

Anticipation.

"*nar‾uah*?"

She wets her lips, procrastinating her search for courage. "It's flattering, really. Someone must be paying an exorbitant sum for you." Her cheeks tremble through a feigned smile. "Perhaps if you comply, they'll not harm—" Her voice strains and splinters through a tightened jaw.

Erruwyn watches pained; he's never seen her openly distraught.

"I'm so desperately, desperately sorry," she whispers.

⅊ *sing_drone*

Lysbeth's features deform to fight her tears as Erruwyn's regards the table's plaintive faces.

"I am not," he says firmly.

The giant nods. Erruwyn's eyes return to Lysbeth as the imposters shove him from the tent. Her hands scramble to muzzle a sob; feeling every bit as helpless as she'd felt watching Isaac lead him from her room nearly two years ago.

"No, you can't!" Corah heaves.

Avrella and Elane drape arms around her, offering what comfort they can—though all seated are experiencing similar states of distress. Avrella looks particularly wretched. She'd failed to consider Erruwyn's inclusion on PromSol invitations as advertising.

The wagon and carriage are ready. Unhitched horses have been set out and slapped, but they won't reach Lindenholt's stable block for some time. The men will have at least an hour to escape before anyone arrives to investigate.

"Nearly there," the giant grumbles. He nods to two men who sheathe their weapons and walk to Ms. Pinley. The table gapes.

"N-no." The nanny clutches Erem and twists away. "No, no."

The men reach.

"Leave her be!" Lysbeth reels.

Avrella stands. "Stop at once."

"She comes with us. Sit. Now," the giant growls.

Ms. Pinley shouts as the men tug on her ward. Forty feet away, Erruwyn's group turns at the noise.

Anęsę crackles with revulsive loathing.

"*įk-ir?*" Erruwyn steps forward. His four guards close in. He shakes them off to take another step.

"What could you possibly need with the child?" Avrella demands.

The giant's heavy hand carefully pushes her shoulder and returns her to the chair.

Anęsę's crackles gain a partner: pops accelerating in frequency until indistinct.

A deep rumble; a roar.

roar__crackle

Rage. Loathing. Whirring snaps of searing contempt.

At the change, Lysbeth blinks to Erruwyn. He's ignoring the immediate danger, absently jostling his guards off to inch forward. The guard in front leans a palm on *Danęę*'s dish and brings a dagger to Erruwyn's ribs.

"Erruwyn, stop!" she yells.

He meets her eyes and stops uncertainly. Then, a scream.

Erem's scream.

ɣ *roar__buzz__crackle*

Fury. Vigilance. Malice.

Snarling hostility.

Aggression.

"D'IK-IR ⩘UN'IR-EA ⩘RY‾INE"

The shearing screech of a banshee, torquing growls of a draugr's decaying throat, a black dog's[24] thunderous bellow—three voices strung between bass, snaps and clicks. The monstrous sound rolls out, engulfing the meadow in predatory intent.

---

[24] *A canine apparition heralding death, often associated with electrical storms.*

The men behind him let go and step back. The man in front jerks his hand from *Danae* and sweeps his dagger.

A thin line appears on the side of Erruwyn's torso.

Corah screams as it weeps red.

:Nuckelavee:

Andrue's ears are ringing. Vibrating metal tingles his palm. He jerks his hand away and swipes his dagger in disoriented panic.

The blade connects. He swipes again.

Silver digits clamp his arm's return arc; a silver heel plants on his foot. He watches the dagger fall from his twisted hand. The underside of a metal wrist thrusts between bone. His elbow inverts as a plated leg rises and falls; tendons snap as his pinned kneecap tears away.

He crumples, howling in blinding pain.

Andrue's comrades grip their weapons as crazed, green eyes fixate. A line of short, triangular spikes jut from tapered plates on the Faye's shins and forearms. Longer spikes burst from silver on its heels, knees, and elbows.

"Shapeshifter..." Charlee leaks.

It lunges.

Charlee's dagger is knocked away. Skin rips as spiked forearms wrap around his wrist. His feet lose contact with earth; the landscape spins. Impact drives air from his lungs. A strike to his temple renders him unconscious.

Peet aims for the metal spine bent over Charlee.

Movement.

His forward foot is swept away, held up at the ankle by the impossibly tight grip of a now-standing alloy frame. The rest of Peet meets with earth. A silver knee impacts. Peet's leg forms a vertex in the wrong direction.

Marc hears a crack as he swings. Ducking under steel, the Faye follows Peet's crooked leg to the ground. Marc wheels and stumbles his recovery. His skin contracts, erecting hairs as Peet's horrific scream begins. He lifts his sword and turns.

Hazy sheen.

A tapered plate repels Marc's blade. Seething eyes loom. Sharp pain in his gut bends him forward. Pressure on the back of his head rushes him towards a metal knee. Cries of alarm from the tent are interrupted by the loud crunch of his nose collapsing.

Brynen's bass swells, "To arms! Arms!"

Aedyn and Wesli release the girl's nanny. She crawls below the table as eight move from the canopy.

Chrys and Jeremi draw newly acquired swords by the pasture's furniture wagon. The four beside them do the same.

A silver leg straightens; Marc falls limply to the ground. The Faye's arms cross to its shoulders and a crescent comes away in each hand. Long fingers point to Brynen's men. The grooves of its muscles deepen as it unleashes an inconceivable bellow, " ⌇⌇⌇ *RY ̄INE* ⌇⌇⌇ "

Brynen's face twists. His teeth gnash. The Faye was supposed to be a docile kitten, not a demon cascading over body parts to rearrange them. Tableware rattles as his fist collides with wood. "Get the bastard!"

His men cheer.

The silver figure brings the crescents to its face—one covers its mouth and nose, the other covers its eyes. Its hands turn to fists and violently strike its own chest.

Men beside the tent march forward in a slipshod line. Chrys' pasture group of six is closest. He raises his sword, jeers, and charges. Jeremi follows with the rest as a blood curdling scream cleaves through the forest.

Chrys continues on; five glance back.

A smear of black and silver tears across the field.

Those near the tent halt their advance. Behind the table, Brynen and Mattor exchange a look of fresh doubt.

The beast is heading straight for Chrys. Jeremi calls a warning to his brother-in-arms and reverses direction with the four at his side.

Chrys turns as black and silver swerves. The retreating group of five is shorn.

"Bleedin' Sovereig—!" Chrys' kidney fissures as blunt metal percusses. He drops, writhing.

Jeremi shudders and rolls his head. Through blades of grass, he sees the creature skid a circle twenty feet away. It's readying a charge. He tries to stand, but his breath is gone and his back sears with pain. Silver yanks him up. His shattered cheekbone plants in soil.

Robbi scuttles backwards. He'd just barely avoided the beast's stampede. Now it's screeching and trampling three it clipped before. The Faye straightens. It's walking towards him.

Robbi throws his arming sword. His target tilts right. The sword's hilt bounces off silver plating. The beast is trotting over now, too.

"No! Help!" Robbi kicks the air. Silver hands anchor on his calf. An alloy shin buries short spikes in his thigh as it wraps. There's a torquing pressure. A pop. The head of Robbi's femur wrests from its joint. He howls.

The dark beast offers a knee; the Faye springs to its back. It trots a wide circle, shrieking with anger.

"Fookin'..." graveled awe exits Brynen's throat. The metal on the beast is changing.

Silver lines fan into protective plating. Long, curved blades swing away on its shoulders, hooves, and forehead—a demonic unicorn. A night-mare. And the noise. It wails like a...

"It's screamin' like a bleedin' kelpie!" Mattor breathes quickly.

Brynen had thought the same. He scans the table. The women seem equally shocked by these events—though considerably less worried by them.

The Faye stands on the creature's croup as it rears, grabbing handles on its neck as it lowers.

The amalgam shrieks through the meadow again, rushing the group of eight in front of the tent.

"No," Brynen mumbles, "it's Nuckelavee."[25]

"By Henri, you're right," Mattor whispers.

The horror nears.

"Move!" Aedyn runs left with Wesli and Trystan.

Silver crouches as Brynen's men split. The monster bucks.

Nuckelavee's human half detaches, barreling above earth towards the group of three.

Aedyn, Wesli, and Trystan whiplash as spikes catch their backs. They slide prone. Gasping, Aedyn raises his chin in time to see the Faye plant joints in the ground—bringing its roll to an abrupt stop, and already primed for its return sprint. Aedyn wobbles to his hands and knees as rapid footsteps approach.

His dislocated jaw rests askew on grass.

Wesli crawls forward, reaching for his sword. His fingertips touch the pommel as Trystan's leg snaps behind him. Trystan wails.

A kick sends Wesli's leg into the air. Silver digits latch to his calf and foot, twisting him

---

[25] *A noxious sea demon appearing as a skinless, horse-human hybrid on land.*

supine.

"Stop! Please!" He kicks at the grip on his leg. A knee spike drives up, partially severing the tendon of his heel. Wesli screams and writhes as his calf muscle retracts.

Mattor's throat constricts. "Moon fetch us. Whadda we do?"

Tormented men litter the field. The five who'd run right are the worst off. Blades and hooves had caught them quickly—and imprecisely.

Brynen draws a dagger. "Wait till I say, then get your sword on him."

Mattor nods and grips his sword with a shaky hand.

They wait.

The Faye's back is to the tent twenty feet away. It drops Wesli's leg and gestures. The beast trots from groaning men beneath it. Its knees lift high. Proud.

A quick movement catches Brynen's eye—the woman across the table clutches her necklace.

"What's he doing?" Mattor whispers.

Brynen's eyes return to the Faye. Its swaying head stops; hands lift to its temples.

"Move and I slit the girl," Brynen booms, hovering his blade near the older child's shoulder.

The women protest. The Faye's hands lower; its head resumes a slow sway.

"Get him to the ground. Take his arm if you have to," Brynen says.

Mattor eyes the horse trotting towards the pasture. "What about that?"

"He won't risk calling it back. Go."

Raising his sword, Mattor moves from the tent. The Faye's head continues to sway as he closes in from the left. Its bent elbows wiggle, but he can't see its hands.

"Kneel!" Mattor cries. "Get dow—" He stops as an inhuman, ear-splitting thrum begins. His sword starts to vibrate. Panicked, he brings a second hand to the hilt and lunges at the Faye's shoulder.

The sun's reflection changes; Mattor's sword penetrates air.

The Faye's spin completes.

Two glints of light sail towards the tent as silver plating yanks Mattor to the ground.

Brynen squints. The glints disappear at the canopy's shade. Something pinches his arm. He looks down. Silver-eights protrude from his shoulder and elbow. A severed nerve renders his hand unresponsive. His dagger bounces on the grass as he steps back. The hazel-eyed woman beside him jumps up, landing a punch on his gut. She pulls back for another swing.

"Shit."

She's holding a steak knife.

He grabs her wrist with his working hand and peeks at the field. Mattor's down. He knows he can't outrun Nuckelavee, but he has to try. Something. Anything.

Adrenaline coursing, he keeps enough of his wits to toss the woman with restraint. He bolts. The tree line is still too far when his leg gives out. He lifts his head and rolls over. Mattor's sword stands erect in his thigh.

A horned shadow slithers across him.

Faceless silver looms.

Brynen smirks at his hopeless reflection. "No one ever said Nuckelavee was a marksman."

He welcomes senselessness.

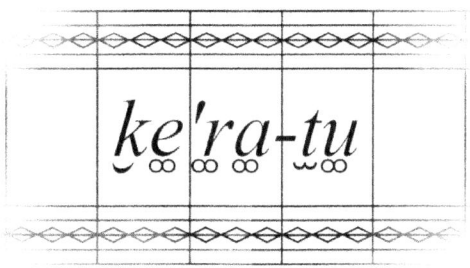

ke'ra-tu

§m'aen.

⟨Danae⟩'s magnetic plating reverses to retract its spikes. Erruwyn glances at the pasture through slots in *⌒ay'enru*. Kiky has stilled a hoof-blade long enough for Brom to free himself. The others will be free soon, too.

The giant bleeds. Erruwyn tears strips from the man's tunic and binds his wounds, then carefully pulls silver-eights from a thick elbow and shoulder. Slender blades follow. He slides them under *⟨Danae⟩*'s arm plates until locked. Detaching *∞ry ⌒ine ⌒hu'ay* from the daggers' sockets, he returns the silver to his temple branches and tears more tunic strips.

In the tent, Lysbeth ducks under the tablecloth to check on those beneath it. Erem sniffles, clinging to her nanny—the smell of blood and the groans of men are familiar and terrifying, but her *⁂da'he⌒na* had vowed to protect her, always. She believes him.

"We're safe now, but the appeal of the view has dropped considerably," Lysbeth says.

"Thank you, m'Lady," Ms. Pinley mumbles. "I think we'll pop to the shore for some fresh air and quiet."

Lysbeth smiles and helps the two up. Avrella walks them to the edge of the tent where Elane and Corah join. Lysbeth remains by the table, eyes on Erruwyn. She needs answers.

He stands, moving *⌣ay'ena* and *⌒ay'enru* back to his shoulders and checking his own wound. It's already begun to knit. He glances up as Ms. Pinley nears the shore, and knowing Erem would react strongly to his injury, exhales relief. At the front of the tent, he swiftly and mercifully knocks out those still conscious before rejoining the Ladies—who look simultaneously disconcerted and assured. He rounds the table holding a wrist behind.

When a teary Corah moves forward, Elane and Avrella draw her back. Both women intuited Lysbeth's growing feelings for Erruwyn before Lysbeth herself had—now they intuit the potential for an emotionally tumultuous scene. Love often becomes temperamental when threatened or cornered.

Holding her voice steady, Lysbeth motions to the field, "I believe this deserves an explanation, Erruwyn."

"I am sorry." He swallows and dips his head to the Ladies. "To all. This was required."

Lysbeth's nostrils dilate. In the last few minutes, she'd been shocked, grief-stricken, horrified, and relieved. Now she feels she's gone mad.

"You have just defeated scores of men and that's all you can think to say?"

𝄞 *chime*

"Please forgive me. I must respond to demands of ◊*Ruah̰*, even if you do not wish it."

Her shaky hands ball up. "I'm not referring to my request that you comply with our assailants, Erruwyn, I'm referring to the apparent fact that you chose not to inform us of your martial ability!"

He eyes her fists. "I am sorry, *nar⌢uah̰*. Though, I did say."

She twists. The Ladies behind her don't recall either. "When did you inform us?"

"The Offering recitation. I am offered as your sword, among other forms."

"I thought you were speaking metaphorically!" she baffles, muting 𝄞*Anese*'s chime.

Feeling the drop in resonance, he tests the waters with a faint smile. "Yes, *nar⌢uah̰*. It was said in metaphor. I am not truly a sword."

The rising corners of her mouth drop as a man groans nearby. "Were you aware you could defeat them from the start?"

He hesitates. "It was clearer after the first."

Lysbeth resets her teeth. "You would have let them take you? All the time knowing you could've stopped them?"

"Yes, *nar⌢u—*"

"*Why*?!"

𝄞 *drone_chime*

Believing the two could use some privacy, Avrella and Elane steer Corah to the shore.

After a long moment, pink eyes clamber to Lysbeth's. "The peaceful surrender of one life to ensure safety of many lives. This is *ʒda'he⌢na*. Aegis. It is how I came to be with y— Have I failed you so? You believe I would refuse to fulfill my Offering? I would refuse to be a shield for you? For my new people?" His chin juts to the lake.

"No. No, of course you would. I hadn't thought of..." Lysbeth squeezes her eyelids shut and re-cracks them over a breath. "I simply don't understand why you felt your own sacrifice was necessary when such a favorable alternative was available."

Erruwyn's head jerks slightly as he attempts to track the chain of communication to its broken link. Unable to find it, he repeats the message he'd delivered before his Offering, "I am bound to the Wills. I follow the Will of Sovereign, *k'uah̰⌢nḭ*, until *nar⌢uah̰* bids my diversion or ◊*Ruah̰* makes a demand. Though *k'uah̰⌢nḭ* does not permit my hand to rise, ◊*Ruah̰* demands protection for ʂ*er'em*—for all those who rest at Fulcrum. I was not able to meet ◊*Ruah̰*'s demands in Baron's presence. Now I am able. I must."

"But don't you see? Attacking straight away would've spared Erem outright."

"I am bound, *nar⌢uah̰*." His eyes plead. "I cannot know your will if you do not speak it. I was not told to fight."

"I wasn't aware you *could* fight, Erruwyn!"

A flustered guard approaches. Erruwyn's eyes drop as Lysbeth reapplies her Lady's mask: straightened spine, relaxed shoulders, high chin.

"My Lady. Forgive the delay," he says, holding back his abashed tizzy, "we were tending our injured once we saw everyone was well here. What are your instructions?"

"It's quite alright, Caylib. Have Brom drive your wounded back in the carriage. Our footmen are being held in the upper wagon there." She motions to the pasture fence and folds her hands. "Please see to them. If they're uninjured, as claimed, they should assist you in securing our assailants in the hitched wagon. You may return to Lindenholt once it's full. We'll await a new carriage with Erruwyn as protection. Thank you."

The guard nods and leaves to relay her orders. Lysbeth returns to Erruwyn.

His eyebrows fold. "You wish for me to fight?"

Reverting to puzzled exasperation, she throws her fingers. "Now that I know you're capable, yes! Of course!"

⟫ *drone*

After a long breath, he steps closer and gently takes her hands—seemingly unaware Lysbeth's tolerance of the action derives solely from her fondness for its performer. It's a much-needed reminder to the Avon: she can't assume he'd understand which physical actions are appropriate in Avonleigh. He'd been sent to the Baron for harming a man's pride—now it's possible men are dying around them and she's telling him to keep it up.

"*ṇar͡ uaḥ*, please hear. All Wills must project."

She opens her mouth to defend herself again but stops at his injured expression.

⟫ *sing_ drone*

"The resonance of *ḍa'he͡ ṇar͡ uaḥ*—that which restores my voice gives you voice, also." He positions her hands as they'd been at the Offering: palms together, sandwiched in his. In a quick, smoothly-arced motion, his hands slide up her forearms and continue to ⟫*Aṇese*. Simultaneously, hers travel towards ⟪*Daṇẹ*'s star. Then back.

❂

"*ḳe'ṛa-tu*: resonant bidding."

⟪

He arcs their arms again.
When his fingertips touch ⟫*Aṇese*, he lifts it to her vocal cords.

⟫
"Speak *through* me.
Use your voice to dictate the will of *ṇar͡ uaḥ*."

⟪

His elbows squeeze her own,
straightening her arms until her fingertips touch ⟪*Daṇẹ*'s dish.

⟫
"I will hear. Receive.
With all I am. Until my will resonates your will."

"One Will."

He un-arcs, enfolding her hands again.

"*da'he¯nar¯uah*."

Her bewilderment drifts from his hands to his face. "Use Anese as you use Danae?"

He nods, smiling. "To set your instruction in me as ink. I follow this expression of your will until you bid me cease or ◊*Ruah* demands."

Lysbeth returns his smile, suddenly awash with gratitude. He'd said he wasn't sorry before being led away. She'd taken it to mean he didn't regret his time with the Haywoods, but Erruwyn assumed she knew he could fight. He'd meant he was resolved to fill his role as Aegis—and he bore no ill will against Lysbeth for sacrificing him instead of bidding his defense. He could be gone; he isn't.

"Alright," she says quietly, "I'll try."

His hands slide away as he kneels. She tightens ⟩*Anese*'s chain until its stem rests on her vocal cords and tests, "Erruwyn."

⟩The bud of expression blossoms.

Erruwyn gasps, tensing at the sensation of Lysbeth's words entering ⟨*Danae*. "I hear, *nar¯uah*."

Lysbeth grips her hands. "You're to defend Lindenholt's people"—as she speaks, ⟨*Danae* and ⟩*Anese* loop in amplificated, resonant reflection—"by any means necessary"—the acceleration of Erruwyn's quaking matches the growing rattle on her throat—"unless I freely instruct you otherwise."

He pants and swallows as the vibrations fade. "Yes, *nar¯uah*. I am wielded against those who threaten you or your people."

"*You* are included among my people, Erruwyn."

He strains as her clarification strums his spinal cord. "Yes, *nar¯uah*. I am yours."

Lysbeth's stomach lurches. The air thins as her eyes scale the coiled frame at her feet. She fills her lungs to refocus.

He is hers.

"And you are not to leave us."

He shudders; his dry mouth vents forcefully. "Yes *nar¯uah*. Only you may bid me go."

Lysbeth blinks rapidly. Faltering fingers pull ⟩*Anese* to the nook of her collarbones and return to knead the tickle in her throat. "Are you alright? Is it painful?"

Erruwyn leans on a hand to balance himself. "No pain. Submerging," he says, catching his breath. "It diverges from other resonances I have known. It is not surface, only. Your voice enters the silver roots. I must feel it. Everywhere within." He wiggles shaky fingers in front of his eyes. "Vision, also. It is overwhelming."

"Oh? How convenient for me," she says, raising innocent eyebrows.

He tongues a molar behind his smile. "*nar͡uah*, I am already wholly at your mercy."

"Well, it never hurts to be sure."

♮ *purr*

She lilts a teasing laugh as he stands. "And why might you be purring?"

"I am happy my departing caused you to feel so." He wobbles. "Among other reasons."

"Erruwyn."

"Yes, *nar͡uah*."

"You're a fool."

"As you say," he whispers.

da'he͡nar͡uah grin dopily. Clearing her throat, Lysbeth nods to the crimson on his ribs. "We should see to that."

She plucks a napkin from its setting and leads him to the buffet, lifting a water pitcher once he leans against the table's edge. ♮*Anese* chirps with surprise as the first cool drops trickle over his laceration. Small creeks follow the fluting of his muscles to silver at his hips. Her grin upgrades to a laugh when the liquid's first appearance on his thigh elicits a new bout of chirps.

"It cannot be helped." He smiles.

"I should hope not. Where else am I to find such a steady source of amusement?"

She brings the napkin to the cut and glances up. The purr provoked by her teasing look requires the full expansion of his ribs. His teeth dig into his lower lip as she laughs again. Her *kw'da* of ♮*Anese*—which is to say, Erruwyn—is deft.

She clucks as the disturbances cracks the wound.

"Please do not feel so. I will seal, *nar͡uah*."

"Seal?"

"Yes, the flame licks clean, also."

Erruwyn pulls ♮*Danae*'s top, right horns from his head. Unsheathing reveals a syringe much like those he'd used for Spring *j'tae*. Twisting at the waist, he deposits a fine powder across the laceration and repeats the process with the second horn.

♮*Anese* gurgles with discomfort as the cut sizzles.

Erruwyn squints and motions to the wound. "Will you please breathe. Blow, *nar͡uah*?"

♮ *scamp*
|
gurgle

"What for?" she asks, suspicious of ♮*Anese*'s sudden change.

"Flame." He grins.

She peers at the cut again. As it continues to sizzle, ♮*Anese*'s gurgling amplifies.

⚡ *gurgle*

|

scamp

"Please, *n̯ar͡ uah̯*. My breath cannot reach." Above his grin his eyes widen pitifully. "Unless it is your wish for me to suffer..."

Lysbeth scoffles. "Very well."

She releases a jet of air and yelps as a liquid-looking flame erupts. The flame dies immediately, leaving a line of dark pink, unbroken flesh in its place.

Her hand falls from her mouth. "It's like your EquiSol displays! Is that the chemical mixture you described? The one which causes the fire to become destructive?"

Erruwyn sighs. "Thank you, *n̯ar͡ uah̯*. Yes. This blend responds to excitation of air."

"Fascinating. Is it truly healed already?" Her fingers stretch out—curling in again before touching the mark.

"It is..." *w̯ox'u̯a*: curdle.

"Coagulate, perhaps?"

"I think, yes. Sealed in thickness. Though able to part if greatly disturbed. The flame assists with pain. Healing, also." He steps from the table, nodding to the nearest pile of injured men. "I will apply it."

Lysbeth's surprise is apparent; Erruwyn cocks his head.

"It's your fire to distribute, of course, but you might want to save it. Avonleigh doesn't look kindly on those who aggress against its nobles. It's likely these men will be executed once they reveal their employer."

"Execute." He glimpses the field. "All, *n̯ar͡ uah̯*?"

"Yes. Truthfully, it's the best outcome for them. Before our"—Lysbeth pauses to borrow Erruwyn's words—"path diverged from Warden Wescott, they would've gone to him."

Though her fingers aren't enough to cease peals rooted by the Baron, she holds ⚡*Anȩse* tightly anyway.

After a time, his gaze moves to her feet. "My *ix'u̯l* delivered me to Baron for aggress; though I intended egress, only."

Lysbeth steps closer, sorry to have broached the subject. "I know. If the decision had been mine, I would've made a very different one."

"Yes, *n̯ar͡ uah̯*." He lulls. He could clarify, but the day had already seen a battle with strangers and a skirmish with Lysbeth. He's not sure he wants to pick a fight with *k'uah͡ ni̯*, too. "I will apply."

Lysbeth smiles with an approximation of understanding—owing to the fact she doesn't quite understand, despite finding his kindness admirable. He heads first to an injured Keeper being helped into the carriage.

After a brief exchange with a freed footman, Lysbeth sits at the table and watches a loading of unconscious men into the harnessed wagon. It's nearly full when Avrella returns to the tent and instructs a guard to take those on shore out in a rowboat until the field is tidied. She joins her granddaughter as he hastens to the water.

"I am relieved the two of you have made up, Lyssy. I would very much like to hear what you make of all this."

"I suppose you mean my theories as to who might be responsible? I've been considering the possibilities," she says, glad for the chance to cord the frays. "We've hosted a number of luncheons here. That the location serves as Lindenholt's PromSol picnic would not be so grand a leap to make." She motions to a footman. "Mikael reported he and the others were interrogated as their clothes were exchanged. They revealed how the party was likely to break off and confirmed Erruwyn rode with us. I can't blame them for their compliance, really. It does demystify how well-planned the ambush was, though."

"I see. I suppose they must be forgiven. Their contracts do not include a provision for silence under duress, despite my many attempts to include one," Avrella drolls. She rests an arm on the table and thumbs her fingers as she thinks. "I was put off by their knowing of Erruwyn's invitation to join us, seeing as we had only extended it two days ago. However, on further consideration, our partiality towards him can be no great secret. Any witness to our exchanges could gather our fondness. We would have invited him today regardless of his debut's success, I'm sure." Her brow ruts. "What I cannot make out is their attempt on Erem."

"Yes, it's troubling. Though perhaps the same reasoning applies; his love for her is readily apparent. If Erruwyn's new master sought to guarantee his compliance, a threat to Erem would certainly do the trick." She sighs through her nose and pushes the music room's harp from her thoughts. "Well, that might've been the assumption. As we now know, they would've found themselves in rather a precarious predicament."

Avrella chuckles at the wagon of assailants. "Then let us follow your supposition and acknowledge Avonleigh's fair share of nobles less inclined to compassion. And let us also acknowledge that the leader of these men alluded to a preposterously wealthy employer. There are few among the peerage in possession of both traits at once, particularly the latter." Her chin and voice lower. "Who among such a short list would risk an attack on a Duke's family?"

"Someone supremely confident in their odds of success and their ability to remain anonymous, I imagine. I doubt these men will be very forthcoming." Perplexity etches on Lysbeth's face. "Their leader showed considerable restraint."

Remembering the palm on her shoulder, Avrella nods. "Yes. Elane took quite a risk."

"She did. Quite bravely, too." Lysbeth chews her cheek. "Is Lindenholt's barracks prison supplied with the means to... How are they to be interrogated?"

"Edenshire has a number of prisons; I will seek Mr. Tindale's recommendation for an alternative to Warden Wescott." Her fingers twitch. "His attendance will be required if we bother with a trial, in any case. He will appreciate the warning. If the mastermind is, in fact, a member of the peerage, he will need time to formulate a plan."

Being closer to the center of the county, the Haywood's Walstead estate serves as its seat of stewardship, and the Haywood's steward, Mr. Tindale, has occupied that seat for fifty years. The arrangement has led to an uncommon relationship between Dowager and Steward: friendship.

"Regardless of their title, Father will want those guilty struck down immediately."

"Yes, he will. But there may be more to consider." Avrella leans forward to better peer at Erruwyn. "Although, we might avoid Wardens all together."

Lysbeth's brow inquires.

"Alder did say the Faye could glean truth from falsehood." The Matriarch smiles wryly.

de'tae⌒hu

Lysbeth and Elane rest affectionate hands on their maid's petite shoulders.

"I'm sorry." Ani sniffles. "It's just a shock is all. To think such a thing could happen. I don't know what I'd do if—" She covers her face and stoops again.

Alarm flooded the estate when the unbridled horses first appeared at the stable block. There were only a few possible reasons for such an occurrence, and none were favorable. By late afternoon, Lindenholt's residents were safely home and their prisoners settled in cells, but all were left shaken—in fact, similar conversations are taking place with Ms. Leeve and Natty in the respective chambers of other Haywood Ladies.

"If it's any consolation we were never meant to be the ones in danger." Lysbeth smirkles.

Ani smiles under her handkerchief and leans into Elane's hug. "No, I'm afraid I don't find much comfort in it, My Lady."

"Well, then how does the revelation of Erruwyn's fighting suit you?" Elane submits. "We can't be in much danger with him nearby. And Granmama suspects he'll be able to aid with the interrogation once Doctor Howe clears the prisoners."

"Not to mention our injured are already well on the mend," Lysbeth adds. "Considering the alternatives, I believe we've landed on the best outcome."

"Yes, everyone is safe," Ani reminds herself. "And Erruwyn's heroics will earn His Grace's favor. That does make me happy."

"Indeed." Elane strokes her arm. "Granmama is already inclined to make a proper guard of him. He's been invited to train with the Marshal tomorrow morning."

"We've invited ourselves, too." Lysbeth grins. "I've high expectations for diversion."

Marshal Brom lifts a fencing sword from the arena's weapon rack. The Ladies' happy voices fall over the stands above. Their presence today has been a boon—his men always perform better when there's someone to swagger for, and until Doctor Howe clears the prisoners for interrogation, everyone could use the distraction.

He holds the weapon out to Erruwyn, who takes it respectfully. Noticing the bulb at the blade's tip, he cocks his head and attempts a test swing. When the blade bows, his eyelids repel in fearful apology.

"I have broken it."

The Ladies hide warm-hearted grins behind their fans.

Brom presses a thumb to his lips. "No. This is a foil. A fencing sword. Dulled and flexible for practice. Watch," he says, nodding to the sparring guards in the arena. As the men dance, he outlines basic moves and point distribution, pitting Erruwyn against the match's victor, Ralf, a few minutes later.

"Have you witnessed Erruwyn's way of fighting before, Marshal?" Corah asks, as Erruwyn crosses to his opponent. "It's unusual, is it not?"

"Yes, My Lady. No comparison comes to mind, from what I made out yesterday." Brom smiles faintly. "I doubt we'll have anything to teach him, but every school of fighting needs maintenance. Having a proper space to practice is crucial."

Attention returns to the arena. Erruwyn dons ⌣ay'ena and ⌢ay'enru and the spar begins. Ralf tests the ⱬda'he⁻na's defenses. Gaining little insight, he lunges. Erruwyn blurs, dodging the foil to fold his leg over Ralf's elbow and latch fingers around his wrist. A sharp tug forces the man down. The mediator calls a penalty.

Brom cups his mouth. "Only use the foil, Erruwyn! And keep your feet on the ground!"

The Ladies chuckle as the mediator resets. Ralf approaches cautiously. After several false starts, he moves to lunge. Erruwyn narrowly avoids the hit with a spin ending at Ralf's side—blade pressed against the guard's padded neck.

Ralf lowers a weary arm as the mediator calls another penalty.

"I'm beginning to suspect this will end in catastrophe." Elane laughs.

"So be it." Lysbeth snorts. "As long as I'm able to bear witness."

Brom cups his mouth again. "Use the point of the foil, yeah?"

Glancing between Ralf and Marshal, Erruwyn repositions and the mediator nods.

Ralf moves immediately; Erruwyn throws the foil.

The guard's mask jostles under impact from the bulbed tip.

Brom covers his eyes with a hand. Sounds of diverted women behind him crack the door for a laugh knocking in his throat. After a brief visit, he smooths the creases of amusement and motions Erruwyn over.

"The foil is not a thrown weapon," he explains as the dejected ⱬda'he⁻na nears.

Erruwyn removes his facial coverings, utterly lost. Among the people, he'd been taught to defeat his opponents as quickly and efficiently as possible. Here, even sported fighting is restricted by seemingly arbitrary rules.

He extends a timid defense, "Though, thrown foils are thrown weapons?"

"A truth universal to objects." Avrella chuckles. "You've been outwitted, Marshal."

"Not for the first time, Your Grace." Brom glances at the field. Ralf won't agree to another round and it's unlikely anyone else will either. "I know you were excited, Erruwyn, but placing you in unfamiliar sparring was short-sighted of me." He holds out a hand.

⚜ hiss

Erruwyn passes the foil. "I am sorry."

"No trouble," he says, clapping *Danae*'s shoulder and moving away. "We've got two more sets, then we'll try your mode of training."

Lysbeth steps to the railing, collecting the sediment of her laugher with a handkerchief. A slow smile strings itself between rising cheeks as Erruwyn takes in her exuberance. Arcing a coquettish eyebrow in summons, she pushes off to retake her seat.

⚜ purr

Wanting to be close as quickly as possible, Erruwyn forgoes the stand's short set of stairs and jumps the railing. Avrella chuckles as he appears over the banister.

"An excellent first go at the sport, I must say. Though your opponent might disagree."

"You mustn't tease him, Granny," Corah chides. "You know how badly he wanted to train. It isn't fair the Marshal made him fence."

He kneels next to Lysbeth and grins. "Thank you, *li'la*. Though I do wish to train, I do not wish to burden Marshal."

"Do you truly enjoy it so much, Erruwyn?" Elane asks.

"Yes. It is familiar. Those walking the path of *da'he⁀na* begin formal training at ten years of age."

Lysbeth's sits up. "Does that include your sister?"

"Yes *nar⁀uah*. All among the people learn essentials of combat. Some, more. This restriction of half among you is strange to us. *erru⁀wan* is greatly skilled—Master of Combat, victor of the combat tournament before my Threading. *k'uah⁀ni* would deny us her greatness."

Corah's eyebrows tweak. "Why do you learn to fight if you have no Kingswars?"

"*k'uah⁀ni*." He squints at the arena and takes a long breath. " *ni*, Outland. The truer words nearby are: *path towards fate*. It is known we will be called to defend *ma⁀joc* against Outlanders some time forward. It is fated to occur."

Avrella peers. "Investments made in preparation of eventuality often yield substantial returns."

"Yes, *me⁀na*. Though we enjoy the sport of combat, also."

The arena's sparring pair barks: a hit.

"Did you participate in the combat tournament as well?" Elane probes, watching the men.

"Yes. Though the Mastership is not required to earn *Danae*, I wished to compete. *erru⁀wan* defeated me in the final round."

"A bit of sibling rivalry, then?" Lysbeth pokes Corah's elbow with her fan.

"I wish it were so, *nar⁀uah*." He smiles and rubs the silver on his knee. "*erru⁀wan* was victorious too often for true rivalry."

"No need for modesty," Avrella says. "You must have provided some challenge in advancing to the final round. The two of you seem quite an accomplished pair."

Lysbeth smiles at his bashful shrug. "Do the sexes share strength as well as height?"

"Yes, we are all a little... spindly," he says, flapping his arms loosely. "Differences are occasionally greater near thirty years of age. This is when we fill. Though, motion resides above strength in our combat, even after this."

"Fill?" Corah asks.

"Grow a little thicker, *li'la*," he explains, patting his shoulders. "Those who wish to become *me'ya⁀itet* must be thirty years of age for this reason." His hands drop to pat his hips. "To bear twiceborn. The risk is less this way."

"It nearly sounds like adolescence," Lysbeth remarks.

He grins and flicks his eyes to her feet. "I am not juvenile, *nar⁀uah*."

"Apologies." She laughs. "I didn't mean to suggest it. It's simply different than how we grow."

"Mm. Many among the people believe this difference is born of our life ages. We commonly live beyond one century."

The women stare in mild astonishment.

"What *is* your age, Erruwyn?" Corah asks.

"I am near to twenty-six years of age."

"So young?" Avrella replies faintly. "How long had you and Erruwan been Dahena prior to your Calling, my dear?"

"Eleven moons, *ʒme⁀ηa*. We earned *Danae* by twenty-three years of age."

"Twenty-three does seem young for one in your position. It wasn't your first voyage, was it?" Sharing his age of twenty-five, Lysbeth finds the idea particularly unsettling.

He mulls. "It was not, though I also wonder this occasionally. Most earn *Danae* nearby thirty years of age. If I had been Thread older, wiser, maybe I could have foreseen my *ix'ul*. Avoided. Maybe."

"There's nothing to be gained from those kinds of wonderings. As a frequent partaker myself, I'm quite confident in that assessment."

"You wish to bid my wonderings, *nar⁀uah*?"

"Have I the authority?"

Erruwyn chomps his smile and bounces his shoulders.

"Then, yes." She smirkles. "I bid you not to think of it."

He grins and nods decisively. "As you say."

"What an advantageous ability." Avrella chuckles at the pair. "I assume your people have more than one school of combat, Erruwyn, do you have a preference?"

"Yes, *ʒme⁀ηa*. Four forms are taught." He thinks for a moment. "I prefer the embodiment of Water. Blaze, also."

"Oh! Your huay?" Elane draws a spiral above her ear. "I had thought to ask what you meant by elemental embodiments."

"Mm. *de'tae⁀hu'ay*."

Corah sits forward. "You embody the elements as you fight?"

"Yes, though the forms of *de'tae* have branched since their sowing ages distant. Grown. Diverged. Among the people the branching forms of *de'tae* are used as combat. The root forms are more as dances."

"What are the dances like?"

"What root do you wish to know?"

"All, of course!" Corah's hands rise and fall.

He laughs. "Of course. Forgive me. Blaze is hungry. Always jumping, seeking food. Long sleeves to lick." He flicks his wrist. "Mountain plants. Weighted force, heavy strikes." His fist lowers slowly. "Water waits. Wavers. Enveloping when attacked." A smooth wave travels from his shoulder to his fingers. "Wind: the body aligns straight, always, as wind cuts." He tilts his torso over each hip. "It is beautiful, though challenging to use in true combat."

"And Theam?" Lysbeth asks, recalling their conversation of the first element.

He buzzes *Anese* playfully. "*Theam*'s form is expressed in *sm'aen*. Hearing, always."

They turn to the arena as Brom stops below the railing. Five guards behind him cross their arms—while willing to help the oddity who'd healed their comrades and defeated the mercenaries, the earlier fencing display had dulled their enthusiasm.

"We've finished, Your Grace. Ladies," Brom says.

Corah hops to the railing. "What will you show us Erruwyn? An element?"

He scans the men hopefully. "I thought to request training of *de'tae*'s branching forms."

Brom grunts. "Describe it."

"I will see through *sm'aen*, only. I must take your weapons. Combat ceases when this occurs for your safety."

The guards exchange confused glances. Restless, Erruwyn *wox'ya*s while Lysbeth translates: "Erruwyn will begin blindfolded and unarmed. You're to attack him together. Attacks cease when he disarms one of you for the disarmed party to exit the field. Erruwyn may use any weapons he takes." Her brow folds. "Are you quite sure, Erruwyn?"

He nods vigorously.

"Apologies, My Lady. How are we meant to attack an unarmed, blinded person?" a disbelieving guard asks.

Erruwyn grins and strikes his chest. "You are meant to kill me."

The Ladies move inside after tea. As *da'he͡ nar͡ uah* stroll to the terrace railing, a group of guards wave from the lawn.

"We assumed Avon women would comprise the bulk of your admirers," Lysbeth teases.

"Admirers." Erruwyn boosts Erem and returns the wave. "The bulk of this molehill wishes to train again, only."

"I don't doubt it. Here, a man's worth is tied to his martial prowess." She peeks at a footman clearing teacups under the awning and lowers her voice, "It's how we find ourselves in Kingswars so often. Every insecure Sovereign seeks to prove an absence of weakness. Though, as Granmama likes to say, one who sets out to prove a negative has already arrived at proof positive."

"Wise." He smiles. "Is this value of battle the reason *k'uah͡ ni* does not permit your combat, *nar͡ uah*? They fear displays of your value will lessen their value?"

"Perhaps. Ideals of manhood are antithetical to womanhood. Quite conveniently for them, too—if we were found equal in skill, they'd be no better than us, and in their eyes there's little worse to be than a woman." She sighs, running her palms along the railing. "It's believed we lack the ability and inclination to fight, but as our participation is forbidden, it's difficult to know how well-reasoned the belief is. We're told what we are, or ought to be, rather than discovering it for ourselves."

ʒ drone

Erruwyn watches the girl in his arms gum a biscuit as he struggles to interpret Lysbeth's answer. "I understand, only, that this should not be so," he concludes. A faint chime joins *ʒAnese*'s drone—echoing fears Erem's scream had re-stirred in the meadow. "May I teach combat to *ʒer'em*? Among the people, children learn the essentials of *de'tae* nearby her age."

Erem looks up to *wox'ua*: want wind fly.

da'he͡ nar͡ uah smile.

"You might need to temper elemental expectations, but I've no objection. We should allow for Granmama's scrutiny first, though. She's very attentive to social consequence. It's likely you'll need to hide the teaching even with her blessing."

Erruwyn shakes his head with mild incredulity.

"Well, take comfort knowing your Naruah is receptive to the idea, even if the rest of her country isn't." She delivers a look guaranteed to exchange *ʒAnese*'s lament for a purr.

On receipt of expression, he gnaws his lip and quickly returns his eyes to the landscape. "Yes. I am fortunate in *nar͡ uah*."

She smiles. "Will you train again tomorrow?"

He nods and clicks *ʒDanae*'s shoulder in place. Lysbeth examines the silver.

"Erruwyn, the way you trembled during key-rah-too's bidding... Is Danae's Concept resonance?"

"Mm. ⚹*Anese*: Resonance. ⚸*Danae*: Amplification. The true Concept is their union, ⚸*Danese*⚸."

"Oh." She pokes ⚹*Anese*'s stem. "How does Dah-knee-see's puppetry manifest?"

"I am uncertain. It is believed ⚸*Danese*⚸ carries the puppetry of *as'etu*, though only *da'he⌢nar⌢uah* could have known it."

"Then you must not know the puppet-masters, either? Like those I spoke to from Roske's seedpod?"

⚹ *scamp*

Erruwyn grins. "This is known."

Lysbeth laughs at his friskiness. "What forms do they take, then?"

He hikes an eyebrow and drags pupils over Lysbeth. "She is this form."

"*Me?*"

His wispy laugh layers with her startled giggle. "The puppet-master of ⚸*Danae* is that who carries ⚹*Anese*. You pull my strings, *nar⌢uah*."

Hearing steps from the Salon, Lysbeth dampens her delight to acceptable levels before turning to the open doorway. A slightly breathless footman jogs to the terrace.

"My Lady, the prisoners are ready for interrogation. The Marshal requests Erruwyn's presence."

"Very well, thank you."

As the footman leaves, Lysbeth glances at Erruwyn and mimes a string forward under a playful grin.

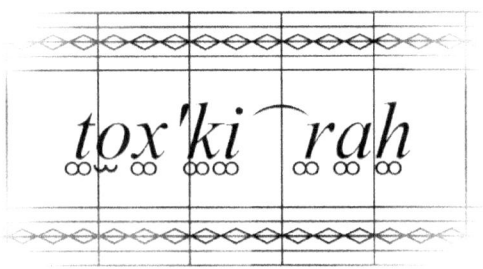

tox'ki rah

Hinges of a prison door whine friction.

Erruwyn eyes the giant. His bound frame spills over a chair and his stubbornly-set jaw is aimed at the wall ahead.

Hinges complain again. A latch scrapes against worn wood. Iron bars section Brom's face in the door's window.

Erruwyn moves in.

If deception were practiced among the people, *≤m'aen* would prove a challenging obstacle as its presence reveals one's emotions and its muffled absence reveals one's attempt to hide them. It became clear ages ago that the Outlanders' discord necessitated their use of deceit, but without *≤m'aen*, those Outlanders cradled by *wa't'un* in early days were temporarily successful in hiding their true natures. After generations of observation, a barely-visible form of *≤m'aen* was discovered—an involuntary seed of physical expression even deceitful Outlanders couldn't obscure.

Erruwyn plugs *∞ry ⌐ine ⌐hu'ay* into *≪Danae*'s forearm socket and withdraws a slender, dagger. A centimeter of transparent obsidian peeks out from thin layers of reinforcing *ay*. The tips of both daggers had broken from impact with Brynen's arm. Erruwyn replaced them as soon as he'd returned from the lake.

Seeing the weapon, a corner of Brynen's mouth twitches under a fine pull on his brows: contempt, anger.

"The elbow injury is clean. Small. Use of your hand is likely in time."

No great change.

"Your men live."

A vague hint of relief around the mouth, maybe. Nothing certain.

"Do you wish your binds gone?"

Faint, upward movement of Brynen's eyelids: surprise.

The action could be interpreted as a show of good faith, but a full range of motion is beneficial for Erruwyn's purposes—the more movements available, the more forms Brynen's expression might take.

Inconceivably sharp obsidian severs rope. Erruwyn replaces *∞ry ⌐ine ⌐hu'ay* and sits cross-legged against the wall.

"There are those among you I have no hope to understand," he says.

No change.

"Though we are trained to expect harm from Outlanders once taken, I have come to know this training could never be enough."

A toe moves under leather.

"How can the harming of children be trained for? It is impossible to wonder."

Subtle tension in Brynen's left hand: distress. Brief movements around his mouth and nose: aversion.

It's what Erruwyn needs. He carves the path.

"It is believed you were to be greatly rewarded."

Slightly parted eyelids and a thin forehead wrinkle. Fear?

"Rewarded to bring a child to harm."

Contempt on the brow.

"The child you wished to take has been harmed already. Enough to last her life."

A tic around the nose and cheeks. Growing aversion.

"She is the reason you will be spared time with Baron. She—" His voice catches. Compared to previous minutiae, Brynen's current tells are cartwheels. "Baro—"

A cold wave of panic-induced nausea crashes against Erruwyn's abdomen.

Over a protracted silence, the giant's eyes drop to the Faye's.

Mr. Tenson straightens from a footman's whisper. "Marshal Brom has come, Your Grace."

"Heavens. So soon?" Avrella waves Brom in from her Grand Drawing Room chair. "What news? Has a culprit been determined?"

"Yes, Your Grace. Our man is Warden Westcott."

The women sit stupefied. The ploys of a jealous noble were one matter, but a Warden?

"Brom, where's Erruwyn?" Lysbeth asks, coming around.

"He asked to see Erem, Your Ladyship. I thought it best."

"Yes, naturally he would wish to be with her." Avrella plants elbows on armrests. "Marshal, I am sure you understand this report is quite unexpected."

"I do."

"And how confident are you in its veracity?"

"Fully, Your Grace. There was no coercion. After Erruwyn teased out the gist, their leader, Brynen, offered the details." Brom shifts his weight. "Wescott holds several of their families. Their cooperation in the attack was involuntary."

Lysbeth sighs wearily. "No wonder the leader refused our payment."

"Indeed, pricelessness is rather difficult to reproduce," Avrella muses.

"If their families are held hostage, Wescott must feel very confident in their silence," Elane adds quietly.

"Agreed, Lady Elane. We should have the advantage of surprise."

"Were the Warden's motivations disclosed?" Avrella probes.

"Brynen's men were only told the location and targets." Brom pauses. "However, I can personally attest to the Baron's unnatural preoccupation with Erruwyn, Your Grace."

"From what I hear there is not much natural about the man whatsoever." The Matriarch's fingers twitch as she thinks. "The insight is appreciated. Thank you, Marshal. Ready your men for an early departure and an arrest after sundown."

Lysbeth turns to her grandmother after Brom exits. "I'm sure the Marshal's reasoning is sound—the Warden admitted his attachment to Erruwyn himself the night he came—but do you also think it possible he learned of our letters? I did receive several responses vowing an end to his services. The lull in patrons can't have gone completely unnoticed."

"Quite possible. However, as no reason will find merit, I suggest we do not tire ourselves in search of them. I must write to your father directly." Avrella stands and stops at the couch to peer. "And Lyssy, now might be an appropriate time to put that jewelry of yours to use."

◇◇◇◇◇◇◇◇◇◇◇

♪ drone__chime

Erruwyn sits in the kitchen gardens, gingerly stroking the hair of the girl in his lap. Observing from the greenhouse, Lysbeth is overcome with memories of last Summer—when Erruwyn had first spoken his native tongue and the Baron's hands still held him under.

The current scene is vibrant. Butterflies and bees feast on bright pockets of color. A faint herbal scent rides on fleeting breezes. Birds take turns washing up in the tall stone bath. Erruwyn lifts red eyes.

Lysbeth takes a sorrowful breath and moves over the path to the bench beside him. They sit in silence for some time, watching Erem bring blades of grass to *er'oo'n*'s beak.

"I am afraid, *nar‾uah*." Erruwyn's voice is a whisper resonating in *♪Anese*. "Baron is a paring knife. Precise. Peeling away in-patience. His failure cannot mean her safety."

"Soon the only plot he'll have to orchestrate is the one he's marked to rot in, Erruwyn. You have my word," she says quietly.

His head lowers under a heavy moment. "Marquess is a hammer without chisel. Shattering. Striking low to de-base. His presence risks her suffering."

"I know." Lysbeth swallows and folds her hands. "Fortunately, there's been no indication of Isaac's homecoming, but Jaques and I have been preparing for it. We're hoping he'll be able to secure the three of us in Kingswar negotiations with Father."

Erruwyn directs an apprehensive gaze to her feet. "Secure us?"

"Yes, it must seem so strange to you. Jaques seeks to barter for us. For me as his wife. For you and Erem as... trinkets, frankly. Though he doesn't see you that way, of course. If he's successful, we would live with him in Crora."

♪ *hiss_drone*

"Is this not a great affliction, *nar͡uah*?"

Lysbeth's eyes wander to the bright, oblivious wings of a butterfly drinking rosemary blossoms. It holds fast as a strong breeze bends garden stalks south. "I can't deny a Lady's marriage is liable to occur regardless of her wishes. If Jaques were a different kind of man, I'd be his wife already—but seeing as he's more harlequin than man, he offered to lay the plan last Autumn instead. Now we simply wait for it to hatch."

Erruwyn weighs the words as he steadies Erem's totter towards the rosemary bush. "Will *feu'n'en* demand you become *me'ya͡itet*?"

She exhales slowly. "Before Ruah gets any ideas, I'm prepared to bear children, but nothing would raise the hackles of Croran peerage quite like Jaques' refusal to produce an heir. I believe he'd struggle to pass on such an easy opportunity to earn their contempt." She smiles faintly. "Don't fret. It's our best hope either way. We'd be safe, all of us."

♪ *hiss_chime*

Her chin inclines at the deep misgiving on his face. "Very well, I bid you not to fret."

Erruwyn blinks.

♪ *purl*

A short, breathy laugh exits his wavering smile; *da'he͡nar͡uah* share a look sodden with sentiment.

Lysbeth leans forward and tucks a hand under her chin. "I was thinking of Asetu, how I'm meant to be the one to pull your strings. Have you been fully strung, Erruwyn? Do I know everything I need to, or are you hiding another revelation like Keratu?"

Erruwyn is quiet for a time. "We are meant to reveal only that which is required, *nar͡uah*—though you already knew much from the chronicle of Alder. I have shared beyond what I expected at my Calling."

"Oh? What had you not expected?"

He sways his head as he lists, "*as'etu, wa't'un, er'oo'n, tox'ki͡rah.*"

Lysbeth folds her brow. "I don't believe I'm familiar with the last one."

"Observance of true expression. Textures of emotion. What *ʒme͡na* asked of me for questioning."

"I see. Well, Alder can be blamed for the rest, but Asetu was entirely your own design." She smiles. "Have you ever used toeks-kie-rah on me?"

Erruwyn sucks in air and holds his lungs full.

"On what occasion!?"

A smile appears on his exhale. "Before my *ix'ul*. The library of my second sun among you. I wished to be certain in choosing."

"I suppose I can't fault you that. How did you make out?"

He looks away, grinning shyly. "You know this, *nar͡uah*."

"Yes." She sighs cheerfully. "Still, it's pleasant to be reminded I was top choice."

"Only choice," he whispers.

"Even better."

Her prolonged gaze beckons the return of his eyes.

"I'm not Corah, you know. I notice when you sidestep questions. Please, if there's something else relevant to our..." she trails in search of an appropriate word.

"Song."

She doesn't attempt to abate her smile. "If there's something else relevant to our song, some string that could potentially aid us, tell me now, Erruwyn. Ahead of time."

"Is this required?" he asks, making *wox'ua*: yes.

Lysbeth chuckles. He may be torn between her request and his training, but the gesture implies the seam has split closer to her. "Indeed, I'm afraid it's thoroughly required, Erruwyn."

"Then, there is a form of *ay'tuan*. The *as'etu* of ◊*Ruah*."

"Go on."

"The Concept of each *ay'tuan* articulates a step on the path to ◊*Ruah*—the restoration of equilibrium." The tips of Erruwyn's thumb and index finger meet to form an oval. "The path begins with II-*Konok*: the pressures which tip[26] Fulcrum." As more Concepts are named, his thumb-pad stops at each knuckle along his finger: "《*Danese*》: Amplification; Resonance. *Theam*: the primal vibrations; first element. *ʔRoske*: Time. All together, they are ◊*Ruah*."

Lysbeth stares blankly as his thumb travels the path again in reverse.

He smiles. "Do you recall the guitarra string, *nar͡uah*? As I described ◊*Ruah* before the Offering?"

She glances up to pull the memory from a back shelf. "You said equilibrium often restores itself—that a string's vibration is one such case."

Erruwyn nods. "The string rests in ◊*Ruah*. Equilibrium. Forces of II-*Konok* displace the string. 《*Danese*》 amplifies, brings the string to wave—to vibrate—as far as can be; brings the string to resonance of *Theam*, the primal pitch of string. *ʔRoske* chronicles string's displacement along Time; articulates string's return to rest—rest-oration of ◊*Ruah*. Equilibrium."

Lysbeth's eyes lacquer as she imagines each stage. The silence at the end of Erruwyn's explanation runs over her like a polishing cloth, clearing her vision. "I see. And each

---

[26] *Forces of inertia and gravity.*

Concept's silver connects physically to create a new suit?"

"Yes. Among a few other pieces, also. The _ay'tuan_ together form _◊Ruah_."

"But it sounds a lovely notion," she puzzles, "why were you so reluctant to tell me?"

"Dis-cord is present among you. _All_ among you." His lids rise to flash solemn eyes. "_◊Ruah_ requires _as'etu_ of its puppet. When I am strung to its _ay'tuan,_ it will walk the path of restoration in my absence—seek the repairing of your dis-cord."

Lysbeth sits up slowly. "Are you saying Ruah's purpose is violence?"

"No, _nar uah_. The purpose of _◊Ruah_ is to rest—to cradle itself at Fulcrum, only. Among the people, _◊Ruah_ is worn freely. Though, here, _k'uah ni_ births displacement. Disruption. Discord. _◊Ruah_ will demand its restoration."

"Then I suppose we ought to leave it on the puppet-tree?"

"It would be wise," he says softly. "Though _ke'ra-tu_ will bid _◊Ruah_'s release if you truly wish to observe it, _nar uah_."

Her eyebrows hover. "Wrest control of Ruah through Anese?"

"Yes. Cut _◊Ruah_'s string."

The mattress dips.

"Now, what could you not say in front of the others, Lys?" Elane looks pointedly at her cousin and holds up a finger. "And don't bother denying there's something. I know when you're rattled. You've been acting strangely all evening."

Lysbeth's features slide back in mild alarm. Erruwyn has never directly requested her discretion on subjects he's shared, but she's never been directly confronted about them, either. Elane's chosen a good time to probe in any case; the day's been wrought and Lysbeth craves commiseration.

She reaches for a small throw pillow embroidered by her mother. Grinning, Elane slides off the bed and trots next door, returning a moment later with her own mother's pillow.

The Pillow Secret Ritual began shortly after Elane's arrival at Lindenholt when—each cousin holding their respective pillows in comfort—the secret location of Avrella's butter biscuit tin slipped. Many biscuits were nipped before the tin was rehoused, but the secret lived on in perpetuity.

The cousins arrange one hand on each pillow between them, and as the Pillow Secret Ritual is a very solemn affair, their amusement is tempered accordingly before reciting:

"I hereby swear, on all the virtues of sisterhood, under threat of torture, death or marriage, to uphold my silence eternally or be cursed ever after."

Tradition adequately observed, Lysbeth takes a breath and unleashes, "Erruwyn told me of Ruah's aytuan and we arranged a secret demonstration. You recall his tree stand? Well, he backed into it and the entire thing simply"—she moves clawed hands together to interlace her fingers—"swallowed him. It was incredible. Strange and beautiful and terrifying all at once."

"Sounds like quite a spectacle, but why such secrecy?"

"It requires Asetu. Erruwyn's afraid it will rampage. That ryine, the... symmetry weaving of Ruah will never see an end of imbalances to correct in Avonleigh."

"Ryine?" Remembering Erruwyn's horrifying scream in the meadow, Elane stiffens. "If he's afraid we're to be judged in the same manner as the mercenaries then why in Sovereign's name should he have exposed you?"

"I asked to see it," she clarifies, bringing a hand to *Anese*, "and I'm able to revert his Asetu if necessary."

"I suppose that's alright, then. What did it look like?"

Lysbeth sits up excitedly. "It was entirely inhuman. Erruwyn was fully buried in it, and he must've gained two feet in height, at least. A stilt of some kind made its legs bend like a satyr, but with splayed toes like a bird instead of hooves. It used the cylinders of Eroon's wings, too, but the silver lacing was gone. And its arms were jointed like a preying mantis." She takes a breath. "Do you recall when the sleeves of Theam fell away from Erruwyn's arms at PromSol?"

"Yes, it was like a coiled column running off his hands."

"Precisely, its forearms seemed to be...*that*. Aberrantly long, too, like lances. Theam's quills went across it and the head looked something like a horse or a dragon"—cupped hands make a snout—"quite long and with tall horns at the back, but there wasn't any semblance of a *face*, Elane."

Elane's looks on with appalled fascination as her mind sculpts a frightful sight.

Lungs ballooned, Lysbeth continues, "When it first formed it was almost majestic. Bizarre and dramatic and uncanny, but serenely dignified, too. Then it noticed me and"—she swallows—"it changed. Even more than Kiky in the meadow. They truly are shapeshifters."

"You mean the Fayetales of shapeshifting?"

"Yes, they must be based on some ancient aytuan. A magnetized prototype? Perhaps even Ruah's." She falls silent and wrings her hands.

"Lys!" Elane shakes a pillow. "Don't run off into your daydreams while I'm sat in suspense!"

"Of course! Sorry!" She draws up. "Ruah was there, looking grand, then suddenly its head jerked down. The horns swung around to face me, like antenna and mandibles, and the cylinders came over its shoulders like two...well all I could see were two long spider legs. Spikes stood up all over, blades appeared on its arms, and its head *opened*. It was only a *mouth*, Elane. With *teeth*. And the way it crouched..." Distressed fingers lock and unlock as she trails.

"Did you bid it to revert?"

"Oh, Elane, I couldn't. I was so overcome. I just stood there, hardly breathing. It came towards me on all fours with its arms stabbing the ground"—she leans forward and strikes the bed with a cone of fingertips—"It looked to swallow me the way its jaw parted, and Anese rattled so fiercely." Her gaze shifts as she vacantly pats the air above Elane's fingers. "He said there are failsafes to prevent resonant destruction. Something internal that muffles vibrations if a pitch—"

"Lys!"

"Yes! Yes. It came close and it— all the long bits *touched* me." She looks helplessly at her cousin and pokes herself across head and shoulder. "Then after a moment it simply calmed and stepped away, just as it had been at the outset."

Elane shrinks with placation.

"Once I found my voice, I bid Erruwyn forward. The silver split up the middle and out he came, tumbling to the ground in his bracing." She exhales a fond laugh. "By the time he pulled himself together, I couldn't help bursting into tears. He was so fretful and ashamed—though it was all my idea, and of course he'd warned me profusely." She smiles at her fingers. "He said Ruah must have judged me well-balanced. Adequate."

Glimpsing Elane's eyes, she grins, adding, "Should we meet again, I'm sure I won't be half so frightened."

bridge

Dear Duke,   16 Jular 1516 III

It is with great alarm that I write to inform you of a violent attack perpetrated against the members of your family and employ—and it is with great pride I extend all credit to Dahena Erruwyn for thwarting our attackers.

All have come through the ordeal well enough, however, I am certain you will agree this brazen display of aggression cannot be tolerated. Marshal Brom has assured us the ambush of our PromSol picnic—a most egregious event to obstruct, I must say—was carried out under the orders of Warden Ian Wescott, who currently holds his accomplices' families as collateral. Our Keepers set out tomorrow morning.

As you know, I consider myself a student of human motivation, and am therefore compelled to include my current theories on the matter. I do wholeheartedly believe Mr. Wescott was aided by a third party, and I further suspect said party to be none other than my grandson, the Marquess of Edenshire.

My reasoning follows thusly:

The location, arrival time, and number of our escort were facts known to Mr. Wescott in his planning. I grant the location and times could be estimated, but find it peculiar that the number of our aggressors should have been exactly double the number of our guard.

Moreover, while distance would absolve most of involvement—as rumors have it, attributable correspondence is better avoided in the Warden's dealings—the Marquess wrote to Mr. Wescott regularly during Dahena Erruwyn's imprisonment. Consequently, we must understand the Marquess does not share the peerages' aversion to written communication with the man.

Lastly, the Marquess' exaggerations of Erruwyn's conduct two Winters past reveal his sights were set from nearly the first moments of their meeting. Though, if this not be the case, my concern would be no less profound, for there is yet another matter which has gone unspoken far too long. I wish to be quite direct, Jaspyr, in stating that your son is a man of perverse persuasion. I know you have long sought to deny it, as have we all, but the fact remains.

I have enclosed an illustration of the alterations made to Lindenholt's basements under the Marquess' pretext of storage six years ago. We have since walled off the area, as such a configuration is perfectly inadequate for the storage of _goods_, Jaspyr

Allegations of his collaboration notwithstanding, should word of the Marquess' proclivities escape the bounds of Lindenholt, the scandal would be monumental. As the sole recipient of my thoughts on the subject, their application is in your hands—though you must know my own recommendation. Should you feel inclined to confrontation, do take care. I know not how deep the Marquess' well burrows.

Keep safe, my dear.

A. Edenshire

Dear Duchess,   *2 Aegur 1516 III*

I had just begun composing my well-earned compliments on Lindenholt's PromSol achievement when a carrier delivered your most recent letter. News of your ordeal grieves me, indeed. By now you have surely seen the Warden dealt with and Edenshire all the better for it. It was years before I came to regret Wescott's appointment, by which time he had already been dubbed, 'Baron'. His removal was a knot I failed to untangle.

I look forward to making the Faye's acquaintance and to thank him personally for his contributions. Several PromSol attendees have written requests to lease him, which I have declined per your prescient recommendation in early Jyn.

For all the Marquess' pouting, I have never known a man to so thoroughly relish the barbarism of war, and so I confess I am unable to dispute your claims of his character. I cannot, however, speak with great conviction on your claims of his enterprises. Rest assured I will give the matter careful consideration.

To the great dissatisfaction of all, there is talk of our remaining North again this year. The dam is bulging. Something must soon give way.

-Edenshire

Dear Duke,   *21 Aegur 1516 III*

It would seem Mr. Wescott's' victims had many aggrieved associates, as his execution was attended by at least two-hundred. I was not among them, as I find executions an unwelcome reminder of my own approaching turn at the scythe, but Marshal Brom sallied forth as Lindenholt's representative and reported a lively celebration in the streets of Rhodyn after the event. Spirits of hearth were no less enthused, and morale has improved tremendously.

Westcott was very keen to avoid the application of his own practices and did not deny his role. It can be no surprise, for who knows better to yield to the line than a fisherman, hooked—though I do not believe he was spared a tumultuous reeling in any case. Judge Mathis ordered the Warden's effects destroyed by illiterates to end ongoing blackmailings, and as I understand it, Wescott made no declarations of co-conspirators. If evidence of collaboration existed, it is now, regrettably, lost. The families of Mr. Wescott's' pawns were safely returned, and those coerced into participation shown mercy at our request.

Lindenholt's reputation as a fount of charity has brimmed in these short months. I daresay I have found raising the standard for Haywood progeny to be a most satisfying exercise—and to that end, Dahena Erruwyn will be formally inducted into Lindenholt's Keepers on your behalf. If you have any objections, mind you would do well to keep them for yourself. Erruwyn's martial prowess cannot be overstated. Only one of negligently dulled wit would regret his addition.

The scrivery has seen a moderate increase in orders, and Lady Corah's studies have much improved since your last meeting. I had hoped you might observe her progress for yourself over Solstice, however, if His most Gracious and Wise requires your person to clog the hole He so righteously pierced through the dike, so be it.

Keep safe, my dear.

A. Edenshire

Darling,   *25 Aegur 1516 III*
Your Sovereign has asked for another meeting in Spring with your father as my
handler. I cordially invite myself to stay with you at Winter's end before my
journey north, and, how kind of me, I cordially accept my invitation.
With this good news, you must wonder why my hand drags with spirits so low, and
so I will not delay in telling you it is for the reason that I am devastated, Ysbeth. My
Ryn left for a jaunt in Jular and instead has gone away forever. I don't know even
where to look. My poor soul is crumbled apart.
Send me words of comfort, darling.

                                       -Jaques
       P.S. A drawing of Erruwyn without the metal would also not go amiss.

◇◇◇◇◇◇◇◇◇◇

Lysbeth lowers Jaques' message to the desk and glances at the empty sitting room behind her. Elane is taking a nap; a mischievous smile scaffolds her internal deliberation.

Last week, she'd readjusted *Anese* and spoken as its stem touched her vocal cords. Nervous system submerged, Erruwyn had dropped to his knees. The accident led to a theory she's been eager to test ever since. She calls for dictation and returns to her writing desk. A few minutes later, Erruwyn's cat-bell-buzzing appears slightly higher on her neck than usual.

"*nar̄uah*," he greets, walking across the room. "Do you wish for silverpoint?"

Lysbeth turns and nods her teasing expression. The expected purr comes as Erruwyn reflexively bites his lower lip. He lays a piece of ground parchment on the case and remains standing, hovering a stylus over the page.

Jaques—

Erruwyn gasps and flinches. An enormous grin forms on his exhale. He tongues a molar, refusing to make eye contact despite Lysbeth's deliberate pause, keen gaze, and the giddy squeal leaking from the back of her throat. By raising *Anese* only slightly, Erruwyn feels her voice without being immobilized.

She continues her dictation with break-through squeaks of laughter:

> *Please accept comfort in the form of a note, and perhaps an illustration if he feels*
> *so inclined, from Erruwyn—which he will begin composing very shortly after this*
> *dictation, though I am extremely, extremely, extremely loath to end it.*

Still refusing to meet her eyes, Erruwyn catches his breath as he returns the stylus to the box. Walking to her desk, he holds out the page.

Lysbeth's hand rushes to cover a bout of mirth that would surely wake Elane. Her vocal vibrations through *Danae* have rendered each line of Erruwyn's tidy letters a thin wave, and collapsed squiggles mark her squeaks. Erruwyn's silent laugh shakes the parchment as he continues to hold out the page. When she doesn't take it, he bends to place it on her desk.

"Do you require a quill to sign, ⸜nar⁀uah⸝?"

His face is close. A jet eyebrow arcs above a bright iris. Below it, a tall cheekbone causes the slope of his cheek to curve inward. Its mate on the other side rounds out to lift one corner of his smile higher. A playfully roguish expression.

Already steeped in delight, Lysbeth relinquishes to forces of magnetism. Her lips press into his.

A fleeting, unencumbered moment before re-cognition. Panic surges.

In a fluid motion, she turns, stands, and grabs her face in mortification. ⸝Anese's bright song dims as she remains frozen in front of the window. After a time, Erruwyn places the scribal case on her desk.

"⸜nar⁀uah⸝?"

Feeling entirely unequipped to confront the situation she's created, Lysbeth's eyes run frenzied lines across the window. Though she'd come to terms with her affections, she'd written off the possibility of acting on them—at least not any time soon. What had come over her? How could she and Erruwyn ever interact normally again?

A long moment passes.

"Am I to leave?" His voice is faint and pained.

Guilt and shame join her alarm. She doesn't want him to go, but she's bound to Avonleigh's Decorum, to k'uah⁀ni, in much the same way as Erruwyn—and k'uah⁀ni isn't shy regarding forward Ladies and those who cross social class for companionship. If they were caught, Lysbeth would be wholly disgraced—the Haywoods ruined—and not even Avrella could save Erruwyn. Further, Erruwyn does whatever she asks. How could she ever truly know he's inclined to take on the risk?

Another long moment passes.

"You do not wish to be my Teammate?"

Lysbeth blanches. Her fingers slacken over her mouth. She turns slowly.

Erruwyn's face is saturated: confusion, compassion, anxiety. Seeing it, she lowers a hand to ⸝Anese. It's inanimate. She'd been so overcome she hadn't noticed.

His glassy eyes follow the movement—he's quieting his ≤m'aen to avoid influencing her feelings with his own. Her unexpected, unambiguous reciprocity was thrilling moments ago, but seeing her speechless with dismay has sent him sinking. If she'd felt this badly after Ani's game, too, he wouldn't be able to forgive himself. Another ix'ul.

Guilt and shame impact. His hands move to his stomach.

Presumptuous, Baron said.

He'd gone looking for the game last time.

Abhorrent.

He'd taken advantage.

Insolent.

He'd enjoyed it.

N—

"How long have you known?" she manages.

"I became certain in Spring. *j'tae*," he tells the floor.

"*Spring*!?" she whispers. If he'd pursued another kiss on his own, the question of his true inclination has been answered. What's more, he'd acted normally. Perhaps her advance hasn't soured their song, after all.

"I am greatly sorry, *nar uah*. Greatly. For seeking to play." His neck strains to smother the hisses, drones and peals struggling to escape. The gesture is well-intended, but ineffectual given the pain on his face.

Dazed, Lysbeth grips the back of her desk's chair and steps forward. "I'm not upset with you, only myself," she says, stepping again. "Your knowing is a shock, to be sure, but I think I might be relieved, really." A faint smile appears as some invisible force continues to pull her near. "Strange. It's quite uncomfortable to see you and not feel Anese," she whispers, close now.

Erruwyn's eyes lift as she lays a hand on ⟨*Danae*'s star.

♭ *sing*

She steps in; his lungs expand.

♭ *hum_purr*

Optimism. Love.

The fluttering trills of euphoric passion.

Eyes wet, Lysbeth grins against ⟨*Danae*'s collarbones. Short breaths dip between Erruwyn's parted lips as his tentative arms move around her. The top of her head nestles under his chin. His head tilts to rest his cheek on her crown.

"I'd been so resolved to rein myself in. Avonleigh's contempt isn't to be trifled with, as you well know." She sniffles. "I told myself, 'Wait for Jaques to carry us off, then perhaps I'll find the courage...'" she trails, nuzzling. The spike in his trill forces a short laugh from her throat.

"*ji ji ji*." Erruwyn's voices layer through a bittersweet smile.

Lysbeth brings a handkerchief to her face and pulls back enough to see his eyes.

He watches her lower the cloth, explaining quietly, "*ji*: alluring detriment." His fingertips alight on her temple hairline. "*ji*: endearing strife." He traces the contour of her face to her jaw. "*ji*: covet-fated." His fingers move forward under her chin. "*ji ji ji*. Ecstatic torment."

Gazing with afflicted adoration, contrary poles draw their lips together.

ʃfeu'n'en,　　　　　　　　　　　　　　　　　*27 Aegur 1516 III*

*ｎạṛ͡uaḫ has requested I give you happiness. I hope the image of myself and ʃki'ky
will do so. I was not permitted to remove ₵Dạnạẹ. The image of my hand is to act as
my request for forgiveness. The image of my second hand is to act as my sorrow for
your crumbles.*

*During dressings Ryn once expressed she felt troubled to return to her land after
departing us. Maybe this knowledge will assist you. If it does not, the image of my
foot is to act as comfort. ｎạṛ͡uaḫ will permit delivery of my second foot's image
after you have requested an invitation to Lindenholt from ꝫｍẹ͡ｎạ.*

ʃerru͡wyn–ꝫda'he͡ｎạ

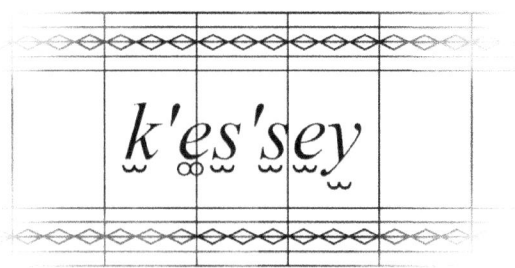

k'es'sey

Lysbeth's fingertips trail the sill. "Do you suspect Alder was given a jota cuff during his stay?"

"Perhaps," Elane mumbles into her book, "assuming Avons are capable of expressing Jhenxi. Why?"

"I was imagining how it might've been engraved," she explains, turning to the couch. "Erruwyn seemed to say cuffs lead to courting, and Alder did fall in love, after all. Perhaps his cuff engravings enticed his Dahena."

Elane lowers the book, grinning sly. "And perhaps your cuff engravings would further entice your own Dahena?"

Lysbeth stifles a smile and quickly returns her gaze to the window.

Two years ago, she wouldn't have dared acknowledge her desires, and as the sphere of sexual autonomy in Avonleigh does not encompass women—particularly women of the peerage—even private musings on the subject seemed a wasted effort. However, the asphyxiating cloud of Avonleigh-imposed shame she'd always known had thinned since Erruwyn first relayed his people's views on sexuality last Winter. Now free of the fog, her curiosity has begun to roam the uncharted scenery of her own longings.

"I'm sure he'd be happy to discuss it with you," Elane says, laughing quietly at her cousin's blush. "Why not ask him?"

"Truthfully, I've been avoiding asking questions since telling you about Ruah. I still feel a bit guilty."

"Denying yourself inquiry? Goodness, that's quite a severe penance, Lys."

Lysbeth meets Elane's smirk with her own. "Indeed. The punishment ought to fit the crime."

They glance at the rap on the door.

"Come," Lysbeth calls.

"Pardon me." Ani enters and moves to Lysbeth. "Her Grace asked not to be disturbed during her lie-down, but a letter has just arrived from the Duke."

"Thank you!" the cousins lilt as she exits.

Lysbeth settles at her writing desk and breaks the seal, smiling a few moments later. It's her father's second letter to mention Erruwyn, and both have been positive in tone. She refolds the message and taps her finger on the crease, pulling her jaw sideways in thought.

Having never hidden their fondness, *da'he⁀nar⁀uah* found acting normally in front of others to be a rather painless task in the weeks since their declaration—and privately, they've found an invaluable form of security in Erruwyn's buzzing *sm'aen*.

Though servants must wait to be called in before entering a Lady's sitting room, delay between knock-and-call has seen the ruin of many an arm-wrapped Lady. With *sm'aen*'s early warning of approaching servants, they've had time to stage themselves before a knock. Still, to be safe, Lysbeth only summons Erruwyn when there's a legitimate reason for his presence.

She makes sure to find legitimate reasons as often as possible.

Lysbeth turns in her chair. "We're to host an envoy of Roffinacs, if you can believe it."

"Truly? When?"

"They'll be staying five days beginning EquiEve."

Elane's brow wrinkles. "Were they explicitly invited to join our EquiSol?"

"Apparently their considerable donation to our coffers made the invitation explicit, yes." Lysbeth sighs. "It would've been nice to take a break from hosting unfamiliars after PromSol though. Hopefully Gina and Marium won't mind."

"I'm sure they won't." Elane raises her text again. "I suppose it's nice we still have a week to finalize the menus."

"Yes." Lysbeth bites her cheek at the book's cover. Hazel rises over the pages' horizon. "I thought I might send a bird to Jaques to inquire, seeing as we've no experience with Roffinacs."

"Good idea." Elane begins to lift her book but stops at the desk's unyielding stare.

Lysbeth's chin lowers. "I had thought perhaps I might call for a dictation."

"Why not simply say so, Lys?" Elane laughs and stands from the couch.

"I still haven't quite gotten the hang of it." Lysbeth's smile follows her to the dressing room. "And I feel wicked ejecting you."

"Well, there's no need. Will you ask him?"

"I think so."

"Good luck with your lottery, then." Elane grins and closes the door.

Lysbeth calls for Erruwyn and waits near vanities, looking up when *Anese* rumbles.

"*nar⁀uah*," Erruwyn greets softly, shutting the door behind him. "Silverpoint?"

"Erruwyn," she greets. "Silverpoint."

These days their greetings are accompanied by a welling in their chests—a smothering infatuation that requires a deep breath or two to come around from. Erruwyn smiles and hovers a stylus, glimpsing *Anese*'s position, just in case. Lysbeth grins.

Dear Most Excellent, Honorable and Incomparably Esteemed Duke of Gyenna,
I regret I write on matters of business rather than pleasure. A Roffinac envoy will

be joining Lindenholt's Equinox to make Erruwyn's acquaintance. The names I
have received are Delaine, Phylip and Rylee Toussnint. Please send a bird with
any knowledge.

"Roffinac, *ṇaṛ͡uaḥ*?" Erruwyn asks, holding out the box and stylus for Lysbeth's signature.

"Yes, they're a school of Croran sages. Word has it they're rather eccentric. Father has granted their request to meet you—or perhaps to watch you? I'm not sure which."

In Avonleigh, the Roffinac's eccentric reputation arose from their unusual approach to both natural philosophy and the rest of the world—namely, their choice to observe as silent bystanders rather than to participate directly. This left much to be desired where their rate of discovery was concerned, but all things considered, it's only moderately slower than the snail-paced advancements of other schools.

Lysbeth places the box and stylus on her desk and takes a deep breath. "Erruwyn, would it upset you to know I revealed knowledge of Ruah's puppet to Elane the night you showed me? I've felt uneasy about it since Summer."

⚥ *purl*

"No, *ṇaṛ͡uaḥ*. I trust you to forge our path. If you wish to say, to expose, we will walk the course of outcome together." Dipping his head, he adds, "Though, I trust her Ladyship, also. All the daughters of *ʒme͡ṇa*."

Relieved, Lysbeth turns a look of acute admiration on the face above silver. "I hope I'm up to the task of path-forging. My governess was instructed to forgo the masonry lessons. What if there's a path I need help to lay?"

"If I am able to assist, I wish to, though I had no governess."

"I might prefer it. I have a question most governesses would find objectionable." She smiles and pinches a pinky nail. "Recent events have gotten me thinking. Specifically, in regards to one of your Concepts." She pauses to steel herself. "Jhenxi. I want to know my expression."

He eyes her with amusement. "Your expression is your own, *ṇaṛ͡uaḥ*. I cannot give it."

"But I have no way of discovering it. You know how we're kept." Her eyebrows petition. "Surely after so long you have some idea?"

"I have wondered." His smile and head tilt affectionately. "I will say what I have wondered if you bid. Though I do not wish to change the pitch of your melody with my intonation."

"That's very thoughtful, but I've always been rather tone-deaf. Besides, you must know I'm far too stubborn to heed warnings once my curiosity piques." She straightens her shoulders and lifts her chin. "Tell me, Erruwyn. Please."

He laughs softly. "I have wondered that you might be *k'es'sey: show the fruit, give the stone.*"

"Bu—I have no desire to *starve* you, Erruwyn."

"Fruit of metaphor." He grins. "This is the phrase. The truer words nearby are: *string unfulfilled promise.* You enjoy teasing me so."

The Avon grows flustered. "Teasing you?"

"Yes. *k'es'sey* enjoy teasing with desire."

"I see." She frowns. "I wasn't aware there was such a thing."

"You are displeased?"

"No," her inflection ends more question than conviction. "I suppose I'm only just realizing how great my ignorance must be—and ignorance is only enjoyable when you're smug at the sight of someone else's exhibition of it."

"*ᵔnarᵔuah*, you cannot be ignorant of yourself," he says softly. "You already pull my strings—wave a treat to compel me forward when my hinges rust with uncertainty; pull me from sorrow as I sink."

"Then, one's expression of Jhenxi isn't limited to intimacy?"

He nods. "It is thought most expressions of ⋈*Jhenxi* are essential. Seeded. Though intimacy may provide clarity of expression."

Lysbeth presses a thumb into her palm as she lowers to the edge of the desk. "Keh-see..."

"This is my wondering, *ᵔnarᵔuah*," he reminds. "Only you will be certain."

"No, I'm afraid you're too insightful for me to believe that," she mutters, eyes still glazed in thought. "The day after the Offering, I recall thinking it was nice to have leverage over your anxiety, to be able to tempt you away from it with a look. Is that Kessey?"

⅔ *purr*

"It is a part of *k'es'sey*." He absently chews his lip.

"Your purring." She sits up, flexing her brow. "I do enjoy knowing I can cause it; knowing you're susceptible to the countenance and tone I use to bring you to it."

"Yes." He laughs quietly. "I have seen."

"Then I think perhaps you've answered my question." She smiles.

After a long, happy gaze, Erruwyn expounds, "*er'wa* and *k'es'sey* share a chain in ⋈*Jhenxi*. A special cord. The first step on the path of *ne'ru'k* is the controlling of desire, urge. This step is an obstacle for *er'wa*. We require another to reflect. We cannot practice alone as the others do. *k'es'sey* assists."

"Assists in your training? Isn't that risky?"

"There is no risk of life." He inhales at the ceiling. "*k'es'sey* enjoys teasing, causing feeling, denying satisfaction. *er'wa* reflects, becomes what is desired. *k'es'sey* desires our desire to deny us. So. In this wa—" his raspy laugh interrupts as his eyes find her grin.

"It seems quite cruel."

"Mm. Though _er'wa_ are greatly prepared for the _ne'ru'k_ trial, also."

"In that case, I suppose there are a number of benefits to be had in the long run?"

"Yes." He watches Lysbeth twist to pick up the scribal case. "The challenge is valued. _ne'ru'k ̄hu'ay_ of _er'wa_ draws eyes."

"Oh?" She walks towards him with the box against her hip. "Then, I flatter myself, I feel quite proud to have kept your _very_ eligible attention."

He grins shyly as she nears. "I believe you would have my attention no matter the sum of eyes, _nar ̄uah_."

She steps in, crooking her smile and arching her brow.

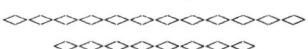 _trill_

"I confess I prefer your flattery to my own. And I appreciate your candor, truly." She holds Erruwyn's enraptured gaze and tilts her chin in upward suggestion. "I may not know much about fruits and pits, but..." she trails as her thrall's mouth edges closer.

Their lips graze.

"I know a thing or two about carrots and sticks," she whispers.

Easing the case into Erruwyn's arms, _k'es'sey_ steps away.

◇◇◇◇◇◇◇◇◇◇◇◇
◇◇◇◇◇◇◇◇◇

"We had two dozen sweets during PromSol, Corah," Lysbeth rebukes, steeling her ecranche.[27]

"Yes, I'm aware, *Lys.*" Corah squints, aiming her lance. "Meaning there's no reason we can't have the same amount again."

"But how could we possibly eat them all?" Lysbeth charges.

"Just be rid of everything on the menu but sweetmeats!" Corah avoids the hit, failing to hide her smile as she claps her thighs.

Lysbeth purses her lips and joins in her sister's failure.

"I do wonder how you would entertain yourself if we acquiesced to your demands more often," Avrella mutters.

"With a dozen sweets, the buffet table would entertain me plenty. Before and after Erruwyn's elemental demonstration," she adds with a nod.

"Oh?" Elane lowers her tea. "Erruwyn's performance has changed? I hadn't heard."

"Nor had I." Avrella peers. "Erruwyn?"

"This was unknown to me, also, *ᴣme͡ na̠*," he says, looking up from Erem.

Lysbeth sighs long and unhooks a finger from her teacup's ear. "I'm afraid it was my doing. I volunteered you back in Jular after Corah's incessant requests. I quite forgot, as I'd rather expected she would've." There's an extra spark in her glimpse of Erruwyn. "Apologies. Do you mind terribly?"

"N—"

Corah's teacup rattles as she readies another pass. "You were placating me falsely?"

"No!" Lysbeth eyebrows rise. "Well, not really! You're getting your way, aren't you?"

"My very own sister..." She wilts.

Tournament utterly lost, Lysbeth sighs again. "Six sweets. That's one more whole than Spring, and I'll remind you there was a good bit leftover of those."

Corah strikes the deal with a decisive nod and rewards her win with a biscuit from Mr. Tenson's passing tray.

"Your manipulations are quite terrifying, child." Avrella chuckles. "However, there is

---

[27] *Small wooden jousting shield*

another matter I should very much like to discuss."

The younger Ladies share an excited glance as a lurking Brom steps onto the terrace from the Salon.

Avrella continues, "Brom has been providing me with regular reports on your relationships and training regimen with our barracks, Erruwyn. With his blessing, and given your skill and newfound camaraderie, my dear boy, I am quite thrilled to offer you induction into Lindenholt's rank. What have you to say to that?" She peers happily at the kneeling figure.

Brom's men were quickly won over by Erruwyn's humility despite his skill, and lots are drawn daily to determine which Haywood Keepers get to participate in his novel training routines.

"Please forgive me, ⸘me͡na. Though I am ashamed to reject your kindness, I cannot accept rewards for answering the demands of ◊Ruah." He glances at her chair's legs regretfully. "I am sorry."

"My dear, when you played, you became a minstrel. When you groomed, you became a tresser. When you danced, you became a terpsichorean. Now you have fought, and so you must become a Haywood Keeper. As matters go, it is *really* rather simple."

Erruwyn peeks at the Matriarch. "Then, my acceptance is not required? I am bid?"

Having learned this game, Lysbeth catches her grandmother's eye and nods.

"I—" Avrella clears her throat. "Well, yes, I suppose so. Marshal?"

"Your Grace." Brom approaches and turns to Erruwyn. "I thought a tabard wouldn't be very fitting, so we—my men and I—we decided this would be best."

With little ceremony, he brings a hand forward and extends his index finger. A silver Haywood crest dangles from a clasp around his knuckle.

⸘ *sing‿chirp‿hiss*

⸘Anese skitters in a manner specific to those of a self-effacing nature when confronted by unexpected, thoughtful acts—deeply touched, sweetly surprised, and convinced the kindness is misplaced.

The Marshal continues, "I know your silver is different than ours. I hope that's alright." He coughs and motions the emblem towards ⸘Danae. "I, uh, added the clasp. So you could attach it."

Erruwyn sits frozen, foggy eyes unable to find purchase above Brom's knees. Incapable of advancing the exchange without risking his own stirring display, Brom's reserved nature holds him hostage where he stands.

The roommates find themselves at a sentimental impasse.

Rhapsodic at the sweetness of the unfolding scene, the Ladies employ every known technique to cover their glee and spare the duo further self-consciousness. The endeavor is taxing, and with no one offering aid, the task of completing the crest's transfer falls to Erem.

After several rounds of ping-pong-peeping, the girl stands from her *ạda'hẹ̄ ̄ṇa*'s lap. Brom lowers his arm as she lopes near. Taking the emblem with two small hands, she lopes back to slip the clasp over *ꝗDanạẹ*'s horn. Erruwyn grins sheepishly at the terrace and swings her back into his lap.

As the Ladies unbridle their merriment, Brom's own foggy eyes go mercifully unnoticed.

The new Haywood *hu'ạy* swings from *ꝗDanạẹ*'s collarbone as *ḍa'hẹ̄ ̄nar ̄uạh* stroll through the garden after tea. Erruwyn's proud glance jumps to the yard as commotion splits between canopy construction and the rising Equinox tree—whose branches still boast the ribbons of Spring's bloom.

"Jaques' formal request for an invitation to Lindenholt arrived this morning. Your foot illustration is due." Lysbeth smiles, plucking a brown leaf from a hedge as they pass. "Will you come by before Erem's nap is over?"

"As you say, *ṇar ̄uạh*."

The pair's sidelong look is frisky.

After learning of *ḵ'ẹs'sẹy*, Lysbeth reexamined her coltish inclination to provoke Erruwyn and concluded the source of her enjoyment extended beyond giddy flirtation. The realization came with a new perspective, and after the last week of vista-gazing, she finds their dynamic even more intoxicating—and the patience required for Jaques' negotiations even less tolerable.

She shifts her gaze forward and evens the curl of her smile. "Are you sure you don't mind performing one of your embodiments instead of your traditional Equinox dance? I really had quite forgotten telling Corah you would."

"I am glad to, though *j'tạẹ* will require additional time."

Lysbeth perks. "More illuminated primping?"

"It can be so if you wish it."

"Well, how are the embodiments normally presented?"

"Mm. Divergent forms of motion. *j'tạẹ*, also. Different cloth, horns, pigment over *m'ạy-tụt*'s bracing. Though not usually with lune-pigment."

"I find myself in a quandary, then. I'd like to witness the traditional version, but we've a duty to make a good impression on our guests, and your glowing would certainly impress them." She swings her arms into a fold across her back. "Perhaps if you began the performance at sundown and finished after nightfall, we'd have the pleasure of sampling both?"

Erruwyn flashes a grin to the horizon. "I am happy to be sampled in any way you wish, *ṇar ̄uạh*."

She keeps her face forward. "Wonderful. Then, have you any recommendations...?"

She trails until his trill reaches her neck. "For which element we ought to sample?"

He laughs through his nose. "The root form of Wind Mastery, Air, is most like dance. This sample might satisfy your tastes."

"Air? How opportune." She slows to stop. "They say much of a morsel's taste derives from its aroma. The air surrounding it, that is." Her chin tilts to his profile. "I look forward to savoring you."

Staring at the lawn, Erruwyn's constricted smile is one of absolute powerlessness as Lysbeth turns and saunters to the house.

◇◇◇◇◇◇◇◇◇◇

The sitting room door opens a short time later. Erruwyn enters to Lysbeth's teasing expression swaying towards him and promptly discards the scribal case on a couch.

 *buzz*

|

trill

"Maen, Erruwyn?" Lysbeth clucks. "Quite presumptuous." Reaching him, she keeps going.

He grins, backing up as she pushes forward. "Forgive me, *nar͡uah*. I should not presume." When *Danae*'s heel hits a baseboard. Erruwyn exaggerates his whirl on the obstruction and turns back slowly. "I have been cornered?"

"Oh!" She glances down. "I suppose the presumption was well founded?"

"I hope."

She laughs quietly and lays her hands on his shoulders. "While you're illustrating your foot, I think I'd like something for myself. A series of Eroon in differing forms, perhaps?" Her fingers trail his arms to his wrists and pull them to her waist. "Eroon's loving form first and foremost, I think."

Erruwyn told her he wouldn't complete an advance without an invitation or a direct yes after asking. This was tremendous news to Lysbeth who, having become quite friendly with *Jhenxi*, has discovered *k'es'sey*'s fetishization of consent—specifically, the building of their partner's desire to desperation.

Knowing Lysbeth would find the news agreeable, Erruwyn was very pleased to deliver it. To *er'wa*, who requires a light's desire to reflect, *k'es'sey*'s light shines brightest—as a light held just out of reach has the shortest distance to travel. So it goes in the realm of *Jhenxi*: nothing makes *k'es'sey* happier than making *er'wa* wait, and nothing makes *er'wa* happier than making *k'es'sey* happy.

"Mm. Loving feathers of *er'oo'n*." Erruwyn molds his palms to Lysbeth's waist and swivels his thumbs over her stomach. "This form is *f'eh'ss*. Long-calm-down."

"Long, calm down? Are the feathers long?" She pushes *Danae*'s star gently.

He nods and grins as his back is pressed against literal and figurative walls. The incline evens their height enough for Lysbeth's face to come in range. She tilts it coyly.

"And do I assume correctly that Eroon are slow to calm?"

"Yes. We hope they remain calm long, also, *nar⌐uah*."

Her smile slants. "Does every mood have a feather name?"

Keeping his features aligned with hers, he eyes her mouth with longing and nods.

"Then what do you call their angry feathers?"

"*f'u'ss*." He wets his lips. "Long-cut-down."

"Do they truly intend to cut you down?" she asks, leaning in.

Erruwyn swallows. "Yes, *er'oo'n* first learns to fly in anger. To fight, to protect. The flight feathers must be cut while trained, also. Long-cut-down." His head angles in solicitation as she pivots around his chin. Following, he breathes faster.

"I see." She exhales on his mouth and grins at his tightened hold. "And what of Eroon's curious form?"

"*f'o'ss*. Long-wear-down," he answers, breathy with supplication.

"Oh? Does inquisitiveness wear you down? I thought you appreciated my curiosity."

"Yes, *nar⌐uah*. I do. Though curiosity can occur too long in children." He smiles, running his hands up her back as her chin pulls him left. "*er'oo'n* explores when curious. Loses feathers wearing down long paths on new terrain. Long-wear-down. We wear these feathers, also." Her lips come close. He extends his neck to meet them, sighing grievously as she veers.

"Any others?" She traces the ridge of his ear with a finger.

Though shuddering breath, he slants his head to beg her continuance. This favored spot was a recent discovery, though Lysbeth has yet to realize Erruwyn favors it because she had clearly favored it for him. There's no real distinction, people like what they like: Lysbeth likes the idea of a benign organ from which to string up Erruwyn. Erruwyn likes reflecting what Lysbeth likes.

"Long-fall-down," he answers quickly, hoping a punctual response will grant him her pardon—and knowing, on some level, it's exactly what she'd hoped he'd hope.

She draws his chin forward, finally offering clemency. His relief ejects on a sharp exhalation as she swerves to his ear and rests her mouth against his earlobe—grinning at his bated breath and the anticipatory fingertips pressing into her back.

Another recent discovery: strong effects of Lysbeth's voice aren't limited to *ke'ra-tu*.

"Do long-fall-down shed while Eroon flies, *Erruwyn*?"

The effects are particularly strong when invoking his name in close proximity.

Erruwyn's head lowers to her shoulder in capitulation. "Yes, *er'oo'n* molt in Autumn, also, *nar⌐uah*." He turns his chin to breathe on the curve of her neck. This is one of Lysbeth's favored spots, and her quiet gasp compels his eyes closed.

She tilts his head back slowly, hovering her lips over his until imploring arms wreathe and cinch her torso. His breath shallows as she begins a soft swing—a pendulum of repeated promise across his mouth. Strain mounts on his face as his lips part and mirror her motion.

Lysbeth relishes the sight; Erruwyn relishes Lysbeth's relishing.

"*nar ̑uah*," he pleads faintly. "Please."

It's what Lysbeth most desires to hear.

The ensuing kiss is ravenous, and Lysbeth's proper introduction to the novelty of tongues has catered a lengthy buffet of testable theories. Their ardor seasons pliable, humid textures as they knead their weight—certain that occupying the same point in space is possible with enough effort—and after several fruitful experiments, a palate cleanser is taken in the form of air.

"I'm sure to lose all my long-wear-down exploring new terrain," Lysbeth whispers as their noses brush.

Erruwyn descends her spine with his palms. "No. I would find them, ."

"Much obliged. You wouldn't let them go to waste, would you?"

His forehead shakes gently on hers. "I would decorate myself with you my whole life."

"How frightful." She laughs and presses in. "Perhaps we ought to stay very clear of each other, after all."

His hands spill over the doughy elevation past her hips. "It would be wise." He grins.

Famished, they take a second helping.

◇◇◇◇◇◇◇◇◇◇◇◇
◇◇◇◇◇◇◇◇◇

"You'd think the Roffinacs might dress a little differently if they wanted to remain inconspicuous," Marium remarks from her vanity chair.

"Quite right. I should never have presumed their intentions given their presentation." Avrella chuckles. "Though it pains me greatly, I am much obliged to Gyenna."

"I've no doubt your indebtedness was the sole reason Jaques' recommendations were sound, Granmama," Lysbeth piths.

Though Jaques was unfamiliar with the Toussnint surname, he'd explained Roffinacs on observation preferred to be ignored at all times. On his advice, the Ladies broke every code of hospitality and—other than Mr. Tenson's meal-leaving—made no acknowledgement of the Roffinac's presence since their arrival yesterday. This has suited the Roffinacs perfectly well, but given their white robes, strange white hats, and the white stripe painted across their eyes, ignoring them completely is a difficult task.

"I find their staring more bothersome than their dress," Lysbeth continues, "If their eyes were daggers, I'd have lost my head with how they gawk at Anese."

Elane smiles at Erruwyn's reflection as he wets her plait with a syringe. "And you'd be run through the heart with how they gape at Danae, Erruwyn."

He laughs softly. "Then, I am glad their eyes are eyes, only, Your Ladyship. For ɲaɾ‾uaʜ's neck, especially."

Corah turns in her seat. "They're meant to be clever. Could they have sorted out your resonance?"

"I don't see how. They don't stand near enough to hear Erruwyn's voices in Anese, and the vibrations aren't visible from a distance, either," Lysbeth says.

"I wonder why we've never heard of their attire before?" Gina ponders from the dressing room. "Seems it should've made the rounds, don't you think?"

"As far as I'm aware, which is not far, mind, they keep mostly to Crora," Elane posits. "I'm not sure Avonleigh society would've had any reason to make their direct acquaintance."

Avrella nods. "Avonleigh's distaste for the Roffinacs arises from our academics, rather than our social circles. Philosophers are quite amenable to quarrelling amongst themselves, you know." She peers at Erruwyn. "What do you think of our guests' attire, Erruwyn?"

"⸰*Daŋǫ* causes greater offense."

"That was not the question, my dear," Avrella presses, chuckling at his diplomacy.

"Yes, ⸰*mǫ͡ŋa*." He finishes Elane's plait. "I have thought my dress for *ḍę'ţąę* will be similar. I hope this will not cause additional offense."

"Really?" Corah sits up. "What will you look like?"

Erruwyn grins. "Like Wind."

Tunes from the quintet glide over apple bobbing, juggling, kite flying, and dog racing on Lindenholt's bustling lawn. Primped with *j'ţąę*, the Ladies settle under tent shade shortly after noon, watching as Spring's ribbons are gradually untied from the Equinox tree to mark the midpoint of Autumn.

Erruwyn returns to his room and removes ⸰*Daŋǫ*. After plaiting his shoulder-length hair, he opens the trunk and slides out the drawer containing *ḍę'ţąę*'s six sets of horns.

ḍę: all-essence. *ţąę:* physical-articulation-essence

Conceptually: elemental shaping of physical expression.

Before developing into combat stances, the elemental embodiments were aesthetic celebrations. In Avonleigh, Erruwyn has only worn *ḍę'ţąę͡hu'ąy*—a combination of horns signaling Mastery of all elements—but horns of individual elements are worn when demonstrating the early, aesthetic forms.

He withdraws the spirals of ഠ*ţą'ţąę*.

ഠ*ţą*: texture-articulation: hear.

As a representation of ⸰*Ṯhęąm*—first element, ever-present in combat as the heedful buzz of ⸺*m'ąęŋ*—ഠ*ţą'ţąę*'s spirals act as a foundation for other horns. He pushes their pronged bases through his plaits and shuffles the stack again.

ↄ*wą*: liquid-voice: sea, rain, stream: water.

⋀*ǫǫ*: earth-earth: rock, mountain, hill.

ᶔ*ǫ*: hot-anima: flame, blaze, fire.

~*ǫą*: earth-breath: breeze, wind, gale.

He picks up the horns of ~*ǫą'ţąę*—two sets of three mild waves.

Ages ago, Wind's relationship to song and *ęr'ǫǫ'ŋ* was acknowledged and given special honor: ~*ǫą'ţąę* twiceborn of ഠ*ţą'ţąę*, Wind and ⸰*Ṯhęąm* sown in tandem as the first elemental embodiments.

He brings the horns to ഠ*ţą'ţąę*'s spirals. They snap in an upward diagonal with the longest wave extending six inches past his head. Lifting the lid of a drawer's compartment, he removes a white pouch and tilts its contents onto the dresser: thin, white rolls of cloth, white paint, dozens of small ornaments, and a small, metal gadget threaded with a tiny vial of white powder.

After attaching the ornaments to *ǫy* chains in his hair, he dips a brush in the paint and begins ~*ǫa'tae*'s painstaking *j'tae*. Ninety minutes later, he snaps the vial-threaded gadget to *m'ay-tut*'s wrist brace and lifts a roll of white fabric. Soon enough, Erruwyn's scalp and Wind's horns are fully wrapped. Strips of cloth continue down his body to drape between and wreath around each large joint. Other branches scallop and knit around his torso to his hips—where new fabric panels cover his snake-chain loincloth.

Ready, white lips curve up and cross the threshold.

Lysbeth eyes the three white figures cutting across the garden.

"They seem so conspiratorial hunched up and watching. I feel as though I'm in a production of *Sovereign's Fall*."

"If it's any consolation, Sovereign Beldrik's assassination was rather peaceful in that version," Marium says, laying an Alquerque piece on the board.

Elane squints at the envoy. "I'd always imagined natural philosophers covered in ink and dust from the long-winded treatise they never seem to finish."

"Perhaps their non-interference extends to recording?" Lysbeth supposes.

"Look!" Corah stands and points towards the western water gardens.

The Ladies follow her finger and break into giggles. With delicate designs of white paint, an oddly shaped headdress, and wispy lines of fluttering cloth, a wind spirit is easily gleaned rounding the manor's corner. Their proclamations increase on its approach. A chuckling Ms. Pinley hands off Erem as the Ladies coo. Once suitably reveled, Erruwyn follows Lysbeth to the couch and kneels beside.

The envoy ogles the pair from a distance: resemblance between Wind and Roffinac has been well-noted.

"How lucky you've wafted in our direction," Lysbeth laughs through a low voice.

He smiles shyly. "Air is drawn to the warmest surface, *ṇar͡uah*."

Set against the fastidious, white motifs of his temples, cheeks and brow, the shade of Erruwyn's eyes is marked. Lysbeth turns a startled blush on the yard.

Despite the gawking of their guests, the remainder of the afternoon passes happily, and concludes with Autumn's harvest feast. Brimming with food, sweets, and spirit, Avrella calls for dancing, and meandering choreography begins a weave across the lawn.

Tickled by his diffidence, the Ladies take turns teaching Erruwyn dance steps. Lysbeth waits for the *Breve*—a dance of two with appreciably more physical contact—before taking her turn as instructor. They step together as the sun drops below the tent's canopy, drenching its occupants in bittersweet tangerine, rhubarb, and cherry. The pair orbit through gauzy, aureate air—foolish grins tidally locked. Lysbeth's refined poise and Erruwyn's innate grace treat their onlookers to a lovely spectacle, and no eyebrows are raised at Konja's deliberately prolonged reprise.

The final notes dissipate as the sun dips its toe into earth. _ḏạ'ḥe̱_ _n̲a̱r̲_ _u̲a̲ḥ_ part over languishing smiles, returning to the ground from their walk in the clouds.

With the arrival of evening, Lindenholt gathers around the tent for Erruwyn's demonstration. Three white robes move to the side of the lawn as the last torches are dimmed. Lysbeth follows Erruwyn to the tent's edge—҉_Ane̱se̱_ is faint without ҉_Danạe̱_, and she hopes to feel it better by watching his performance as close as propriety allows.

Stepping onto the grass, he brings the metal gadget from his arm to his mouth and bites down, clipping it to his teeth behind closed lips. He takes up position in line with Lysbeth, and by the time he's tied a white blindfold around his eyes, the area is fully dimmed and his audience quiet.

Shaping air, he molds to stance: right knee lifted and pressed to the side of his ribs, calf pointed out and parallel to the ground; arms arced in asymmetrical half circles.

Earth exhales: Breeze begins a series of elegant elongations and lifts. Erruwyn's shoulders never radially veer from the degree of his hips—head always in profile, palms always out.

The sun tips over horizon.

Breeze grows to Wind: short jumps and sharp dashes gust over the lawn.

Twilight diffuses the sky with plum and grapefruit.

Wind increases to Gale: swift, exquisite leaps and extensions eddy across the grass.

Dusk illuminates scrupulous, white motifs of the dancer.

Embodied, Zephyr's shoulders break line for a final, enormous leap.

Airborne, clouds of white fire pour from his lips and envelop his torso. The crowd gasps as strips of white, treated cloth catch fire—igniting as fuses across his body and disperse in seconds along their paths.

With his headdress burned away, freed chimes in his hair jingle softly over the crowd's long gasp. The onlookers cheer as he lands, and glowing designs return to their initial stance in opaque darkness.

buzz

$|$

gurgle

Feeling *Anese*'s pained gurgle, Lysbeth stops clapping and watches with apprehension as Erruwyn's illuminated leg lowers to brace itself. In the next instant, the entire motif is driven to the ground—where it struggles supine against dark shapes blocking patterns of its light.

Cheers fade to confusion.

The gleaming figure strikes out. A limp, black form covers the top plane of Erruwyn's lumination. His glowing hands push it off. He rolls quickly to his knees. Another shade lands a blow. Erruwyn's voice outlines a convulsive heave. He labors to stand.

Sounds of alarm dampen Avrella's call for light. The Ladies loudly repeat her order, and those nearby echo the call. Feet crunch through the garden to the terrace torches. Brom's shrill whistle orders his men forward. They push through the crowd towards the glow on the lawn.

Streaks of illumination trail Erruwyn's attempts to dodge and block a barrage of invisible attacks. A break in the assault sees radiant legs sweep—one remaining low as the other jabs upward. Two glittering smears mark their points of impact above the earth.

Erruwyn scuttles away and attempts to stand again. Parts of his torso and leg are extinguished. He returns to a crouch and raises an arm to block. Chilling dread spills and hardens over Lysbeth as a section of light near his wrist is doused.

The first Keepers arrive to grunt and clang against the two levitating stains.

Erruwyn's light curls in—a brief reprieve before bright horns are forced to duck. His fist and elbow fly out, setting new smudges against black. The smears stumble as Erruwyn sinks again, wrapping a glowing arm around his darkened waist.

More guards approach as torches in the tent are lit and light reaches the lawn.

Folded on the ground and badly bloodied, thin pieces of barbed metal jut from Erruwyn's arm, abdomen, and leg. Two white-robed assailants lay motionless nearby; Brom quickly cuts the third down in torch-light. Malicious eyes fix as he lands next to Erruwyn. His collision with earth disturbs the chain under his chin.

A mutilated *Anese* slides along it and settles face-down in the grass—Otay's insignia cruelly carved on its surface.

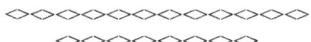

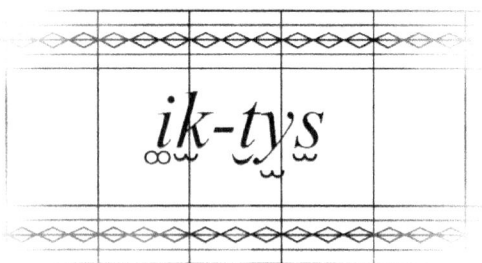

ik-tys

Doctor Howe stands over a makeshift surgeon's table in the Salon, dipping red hands into a basin. "I'm glad I was present, Lady Lysbeth. This could have been much, much worse."

Lysbeth stares: Patches of white and red splotch Erruwyn's serene face. His upper lip and left eyebrow are split.

"I happened to treat a case of poleit poisoning last month and still had a batch of the antidote prepared. With the amount present on the weapons, immediate administration was absolutely vital." He wipes his hands on a cloth.

Lysbeth stares: Deep pits well with blood to fill the void of barbed darts, removed.

"Of course, it was risky to sedate him with aisrettle before identifying the poison, but it seemed the only option. Hopefully it will keep him asleep for a day or two." He pulls a suture kit from his bag and pauses as he sets it on the table. "I've never observed such a rapid onset of mania from poleit. I wonder if they've discovered a more potent strain."

Lysbeth closes her eyes: Erruwyn's torch-lit expressions lurching over the borders of oblivion to comprehension—disbelief, consternation, bereavement. Rabid, hysterical furor.

He'd pulled the dart from his own arm and turned it on the Otayan, taking ears, eyes, jaw, and scalp—the man's screams were no match for Erruwyn's. Doctor Howe acted fast, tossing a bell of aisrettle incense from his medical bag as Erruwyn continued the corpse's disassembly.

She looks at her hand through pink eyelids. Three *Anese* dangle from chains twining her fingers. Ryn's coil hair cuff shares a spot on the third. Poison wasn't to blame for Erruwyn's fury, but she won't correct the assumption—even the guards were rattled by the brutal display. She wets her lips and levels her shoulders.

"Sutures won't be necessary, Doctor Howe, I've sent for Erruwyn's sealing powders. Perhaps you'd like to observe their application?"

Doctor Howe closes the suture kit slowly. "Yes, My Lady, perhaps I would."

Elane and Lysbeth sit on the Grand Library's velvet couch, sandwiched by end tables littered with history books. That the attackers were not Roffinacs is about the only clear answer they've come to, and information on their true origins, Otay, is scarce.

They'd hoped to learn more from last night's sole survivor—a rather difficult undertaking now, as he'd been found dead in his cell after luncheon. A modified pig's molar was on the ground nearby, and a look in his mouth revealed a missing tooth. Doctor Howe ruled it an act of suicide by poleit poisoning—a judgement affirmed by Brom, who'd seen similar methods used by Kingswar prisoners to avoid interrogation.

Speculation assumes Otay formed from remnants of a peasant's revolt in southern Crora nearly an age ago. Eventually, separatist sentiments and secretive politicking led them to Bengli and, soon after, the sovereignty of their small territory. They'd spent decades walling up their borders and have attacked any who come near for centuries. Very little else is known.

Elane drops her book and slouches back on the couch. "These titles are quite misleading. If Mr. Lomarelli were still alive, I'd send him a dictionary. *'Complete History,'* my eye. The dolt."

Lysbeth looks on with amused concern. Like most, Elane has been on edge all day.

After Gina and Marium's early departure, Lysbeth made three attempts to write Jaques. She knows he'd want to be informed of Ryn's cuff, but without understanding the implication of its presence, she isn't sure what news she'd be sending. Corah is refusing lessons, and Avrella has taken to her room, sending bird after bird to any among her acquaintance who might know what's best to be done. Two attacks in only three months— one in their own home, no less—does not bode well.

If not for the Kingswar, the Duke of Edenshire would surely petition his Croran allies and Sovereign Hinri to take on the small Otay territory himself. However, as it stands, the Haywoods have no form of redress. Otay has no ambassador and no means by which to reliably receive threats.

Lindenholt is feeling vulnerable.

"Should I call for tea?" Lysbeth asks gingerly.

"No, thank you." Elane picks up another book and reads the spine. "One Mr. Bonnegnes has promised me a tour of his *Museum of Croran Antiquity.*"

"With our luck, it's a picture book of Croran's most illustrious senile, then?" Lysbeth attempts a smile.

"Indeed." Elane sighs. "In which case, Mr. Bonnegnes can join the fire logs."

Lysbeth's eyes drift from her own book to the *ᚴAnese* dangling from her wrist. Her throat tightens. They'd likely belonged to *ɲarˉuah* centuries ago. Their current appearance and recent owners suggest a tragic end. Erruwyn's response to seeing one had made his own interpretation and feelings on the matter clear.

Elane flips her text open. A glance to her couch mate softens her demeanor. "Why torture yourself wearing those, Lys?"

Lysbeth releases her book to run fingers over the silver. Their stems are clipped, their delicate spirals bent or broken, and all are crudely carved with Otay's crest—no doubt a time-consuming task. The metal is stronger than most Outland alloys of similar weight.

"I don't know. I can't explain it. My heart aches for them." She sits up, sniffling. "It must seem so odd, but they feel like kin. Both the silver and their Naruahs. Anese is meant to be a Dahena's anima, Elane. The effort required to defile them like this could only have come from a truly abysmal hatred."

Elane scoots closer to move an arm around her cousin's shoulders—temple-to-temple regarding the remnants of long-dead *da'he͡ nar͡ uah*. Given the extreme exclusivity of the club, Elane finds Lysbeth's affectedness perfectly reasonable. Though only a member of the league's associative chapters, even she finds the metal distressing.

"I can't help imagining who they were; if any of them felt the way we do for each other..." Lysbeth trails, freeing the handkerchief from her sleeve to dab her eyes—a slow thought realigns the rungs of her spine as it climbs to the forefront. "There may be a more useful text in the eastern library." She tosses the book off her lap and stands. "Will you join me?"

Already off the couch, Elane smiles at the needless question. They make their way to the door and are startled to find Mr. Tenson on the other side.

"Forgive me, My Lady." The equally startled butler smooths his vest. "Marshal Brom reports Erruwyn has woken ahead of schedule and rather insists on seeing you. I'm to warn you he's been restrained out of concern for his injuries and the undertaking is not going well."

Feeling ready to bolt, Lysbeth moves around him as the message ends. "Thank you, Mr. Tenson, thank you."

The Ladies hasten to the senior servant's hall of the kitchen block.

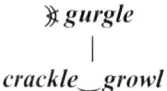 *crackle͜ growl*
　　　|
　　gurgle

Turning the corner, strained breathing and Brom's deep grumble seep from an open doorway further down the passage. Konja and two guards step back from the threshold as the Ladies near, visibly relieved at their presence. The women enter an already-cramped room and stop in the aisle between length-wise beds along opposite walls.

Beyond the beds' feet, Brom oversees three guards struggling to pin Erruwyn without aggravating his injuries. Beneath them, Erruwyn squirms prone in *m'ay-tut*'s bracing. A sickening pop is heard as his arms snakes from a guard's knee. His panting is broken by a gasping sob.

⚒ gurgle
　　|
crackle͜ growl

The cousins flinch. *m'ay-tut* is supposed to prevent Erruwyn's joint-slipping—he's expending significant effort. When the guard moves to reset the joint, Erruwyn uses the distraction to free his left leg and protectively folds it beneath his torso.

Seeing Lysbeth, Brom bends at the waist and snaps his fingers. "Erruwyn. Lady Lysbeth is here. She's perfectly well. Understand? She's come."

As Erruwyn's exertions taper, cautious guards release him and back away slowly. The first Keeper to stand wipes red crust from his swollen nostrils.

Rapidly stretching ribs pair Erruwyn's wheezing. His right leg and left arm lay flush and oddly skewed against blood-smudged floorboards. Slick with perspiration, his right palm squeaks over woodgrain to his shoulder. Putting weight on his forehead, he pushes off enough to pivot his face towards the door.

Thick hair spills around him. Lysbeth's never seen it down at this length—its disarray magnifies his turmoil. Through a rip in the black shroud, a thin ledge of green rings a dilated pupil. His mouth rests open under the re-torn laceration of his upper lip as he forces himself upright. Tugging his limp leg into a bend, he settles on his knees, leans forward on his good arm, and stares warily at Lysbeth behind sheets of shivering jet.

🜟 〰

Anese's vibrations fluctuate so quickly she can't make out a singular thread to follow. Maintaining her mask, she laces her fingers and steps closer.

Water weaves through long lashes.

She steps again.

He recoils.

The image catapults her to the night of Wescott's delivery. Feeling queasy, she stops and looks to Brom for answers.

The Marshal clears his throat. "A large dose of poleit and multiple knocks to the head is enough to free anyone of their senses, My Lady. The aisrettle should've kept him down for another day, but poisons—even helpful ones like aisrettle—can have unusual effects. People react differently."

"Ye. I got the aisrettle bell for my stonegut,[28] Your Ladyship," Ralf says. "They found me walking 'round the milkmaids' dorms, still slumbering' fast."

"So you claim." Kensi snorts.

Caylib grins and rubs his sore face. "I've seen fever-dreams like Erruwyn's, Your Ladyship, but those dreamers never managed to land a hit."

The men chuckle quietly, covering their concern with a coat of admiration.

"Then I suppose I ought to be relieved his aim is still intact," she says, glancing down. Red lace stained with two perfect drops of leery black ink continue to peer at her from the

---

[28] *Hernia*

floor. " If he finds the sight of me so disagreeable, why should he bring himself to further harm to call on me?"

"His memory is..." Brom trails. "He woke convinced you were deceased, Lady Lysbeth. Or something like it. And he was very ready to see us brought to justice for the crime," he adds, huffing a laugh.

Though it's difficult for Lysbeth or Elane to find much humor in the situation, the guards' ease is soothing in a way. They'd all seen war—witnessed numerous miserable outcomes—and they'd all found laughing at the storm was the easiest way to weather it. How threatening could farcical clouds be, after all?

"My Lady! He does *not* remember me!" Konja shakes an incredulous expression from the doorway and shoves fingertips into his ribs. "*Me!*"

Lysbeth smiles. "I see. In that case, I can have no cause to take offense. Thank you everyone, very much, for your insights and dedication in looking after him." She steps sideways. "Might we have a quick moment?"

Brom dips his head and the men step out. Sniffling, Elane lowers to a bed. Lysbeth repositions *Anese* against her throat and grips her hands against her stomach. Erruwyn's eyes jump between the closing door and the woman in front of him, unsure which poses the greater threat.

"Erruwyn?"

Without *Danae*'s star to funnel Lysbeth's voice directly into his spine, *ke'ra-tu*'s resonance is limited to what can reach the surface of his spinal roots. This is fortunate, as Erruwyn's systems are already over capacity.

His neck snaps back at the sensation crossing his vertebrae; brief recognition appears between rasping breath.

"Erruwyn? Do you hear?"

His lips part further, eyes struggling to focus as she steps closer.

"I bid you answer," she urges, digging her nails into her palms. "Please, answer, Erruwyn."

He gasps through a racked shudder. "I hear, *nar uah*."

Lysbeth steps to him quickly. Kneeling, she pushes his hair back and lays her palms on his cheeks. His working hand wraps her wrist to test her corporeality; his pupils strive to narrow.

"Say you live, *nar uah*. You are near to me," he begs through hoarse grief. "Please say."

"I'm quite alive, Erruwyn. I'm here."

At her gentle reassurance, his overwhelmed frame quakes with stimulation: resonance, pain, relief. Poison.

Worried she'll hurt his contusions, Lysbeth loosens her hold. "You need rest."

"No. *ik-tys*." His fingers shamble up her forearm. "I must see you. *ik-tys*."

"You'll see me after you rest." She smiles tearfully. "I bid you sleep peacefully until tomorrow, Erruwyn."

"No! Do not, please," he cries, tightening a desperate hold on her elbow. "Please. I do not wish to go from you."

Lysbeth's heart shreds. She grits her teeth, blinking hard to remove the blur from her eyes. For a moment, she calculates what strings she'd need to pull to move him to the guest apartments.

The moment passes. Having him closer was no guarantee he'd sleep—she'd only be bidding him to rest on a nicer floor.

"You won't be gone from me. I'll be very close." She drags her thumbs across his cheeks, avoiding maroon and indigo splotches. His unsteady grip follows her arm to her shoulder in a final, silent plea. "I bid you rest, Erruwyn; sleep well through tomorrow."

Released from her voice, he grimaces and heaves with woeful resignation, "Yes, *nar︵uah*."

Lysbeth pulls him close as eyelids begin a heavy drag over re-dilating pupils.

◇◇◇◇◇◇◇◇◇◇

Lysbeth sits in the kitchen gardens.

She chats with Ms. Pinley.

She *wox'ua*s with Erem.

She waits.

The wise nanny had absconded from the tent with Erem when Erruwyn was tackled to the ground, but the girl's requests for him have grown insistent. They can't hide Erruwyn's injuries from her forever—they're scarred on him, anyhow—but given his state yesterday, it's still far too soon.

Brom fills the greenhouse doorway just before teatime.

"He's improved a good deal, My Lady," he reports as they walk. "I don't know what he remembers, but whatever you did kept him down long enough for the poisons to run their course."

Lysbeth takes a deep breath as they near the room. Brom opens the door and remains in the hall after she enters. He knows their relationship is unique. Maybe something more. Either way, since it's no business of his, he sees no reason to obstruct it, even if it's the proper thing to do.

Anese gurgles as Erruwyn stands from the edge of the bed. Lysbeth takes stock. His hair is up. He wears *Dange*. All joints are hinged. The bruising is noteworthy, but his facial lacerations stayed sealed after she'd reapplied the powder.

Clear aquamarine regards her.

As soon as the door latches, her eyes water.

They embrace. Her head slots under his chin; his cheek lays on her crown. Their arms move across each other slowly—unbroken enfolding, as close as can be.

En-compassion.

"What do you remember?"

"Pain. Confusion. Turbulence." A slender hand cradles her head. "You, shining through the veil, offering comfort."

Lysbeth smiles. "You were very upset. I should think any resemblance of comfort would've helped."

"No," he says softly, "*nar͡uah*, only."

She closes her eyes, unreasonably cozy in *Danae*'s purring recess. The worries plaguing her for the last two days retreat enough to notice.

"What's ike-tiss?" she mumbles. "You were concerned about it."

He inhales slowly. "Displacement. Discord. I dreamed those of discord has displaced you. You were so distant. No anima." His hold tightens. "I do not wish it."

Lysbeth grins. "You do not wish it?"

"I do not," he says, shaking his nose in her hair.

Eyebrow arched, she tilts her head back. "You don't?"

The uninjured corner of his mouth lifts. "I doh-en-tah. Doe-ent." He tucks her hair, half-smiling through his exaggerated difficulty. "I do not," he repeats gently.

"You're able to make any sound you like," she says, laughing softly, "why don't you take shortcuts for Vonish?"

"Habit. In the language of the people, to remove a sound must remove a meaning."

"Ah. So, you 'do not.'" She curls her fingers over the edges of *Danae*'s star.

He nods conclusively. "So. I do not wish it, *nar͡uah*."

"What do you wish?"

Unable to bite his lip Erruwyn inhales at the ceiling. "I wish to not say what I wish."

"Oh? You know, I've become quite a skilled Keratu mistress."

He laughs hoarsely and returns his gaze. "I should have waited to know you were *k'es'sey* before feeling so certain in choosing."

She gasps through a wide grin.

He tongues a molar. "*k'es'sey* must love *ke'ra-tu*."

"She does love."

"She does," he says, hands slowly outlining her back.

"Your wish?" Her abdomen shakes giddily as he looks back to the ceiling. "If I'm made to Keratu, I'll be left un-pet. Surely your wish is not to be found wanting in your Dahena duties?"

He bites his inner cheek to suppress his injured grin. "*nar͡uah*, if caressing you has become a duty, it will not be the one I neglect." He adds extra pressure along her spine as she dips under his chin for a chuckle. "I do not wish to say because my wish cannot be so. To say it would hurt, only."

"I see." She sniffles and pulls back. "Even if we were with Jaques?"

Erruwyn lowers an amused expression. "*ʃfeu'n'en* is not my wish, *ɲar⁀uaḫ*."

"But if we lived in Crora? Would your wish be possible then?"

"Not wholly so." He traces the side of her face lightly. "The piece of my wish that may be is for you to be near."

Lysbeth blinks. "That's it?"

He sucks his cheek. "I am not offended that this wish must mean more to me than to you, *ɲar⁀uaḫ*."

She scoffles. "I *meant* that was already assumed to be the case."

"Yes." He angles his head and shrugs his intact eyebrow provocatively. "It is a good wish. Good wishes often come to be."

"I can't argue there."

They split a generously portioned ogle two ways.

"What is your wish, *ɲar⁀uaḫ*?" His one-sided smile stretches. "*ʃfeu'n'en*?"

She purses her lips in pleasant reproach. "To *live* in Crora with Feunen. The one man who would celebrate our song rather than silence it."

"Then this is my wish, also." His thumb treks under a hopeful, azure orb to the copper border of her temple. "Is ₃*me⁀ɲa*'s wish for the textures of *tox'ki⁀raḫ*? To question? The first observer was made absent, only."

She draws up. "Has Brom not informed you?"

"I have been informed I must allow Caylib victory next training as penance for my strike." He exhales a laugh, easing his hands down her waist.

Lysbeth's expression grows rueful; Erruwyn's falls in concern.

She winds her fingers through ₵*Daṇaę*. "Erruwyn, the men who attacked you were Otayans posing as Roffinac observers. The survivor... objected to his detainment. He poisoned himself to avoid interrogation." She reaches into her bodice and pulls out a pouch. "Elane and I have been poring over history texts trying to make sense of it. Of these in partic—"

The retrieval slows as Lysbeth realizes the cracks in Erruwyn's memory may extend farther than yesterday afternoon. She pulls the bundle from her neckline and holds it to ₵*Daṇaę*'s star, unable to look at the eyes regarding her tenderly from above.

The threat of *ik-tys* walks the waking world, too.

She delays for some time under Erruwyn's patience. With weighted apprehension, she parts the fabric, pushes ∢*Aṇesę* to the surface, and brings them into his view.

Erruwyn's hands retract, making a quick move for his face as he backs away. The bedframe halts his retreat. Sinews in his neck and chest flare. Anguish spills over the ridges of his eyes, imploring Lysbeth's refutation. At her trembling lip he sinks to his knees and sways with silent sobs.

Lysbeth clutches the pouch to her chest.

She'd overlooked the absence of his grief. It had been so nice to step into recess; to narrow her perspective to the contented safety of *Danae*'s alcove. But from this vantage, all of Erruwyn's afflictions are visible, and *Danae*'s star is a speck on an unfamiliar landscape dotted with previously-unseen ruins.

Mournfully transfixed, she watches Erruwyn remove *Danae*'s nested horns. Their tips dig into the webbing of his index and middle fingers as he rocks.

drone

He brings the backs of his hands to his face and drags the silver over his eyes and past his chin. Two small horn-sheaths snap below his tear ducts astride his nose. Two more hang from the precipice of his tranquil expression.

weep

His hands twist and roll. Silver horns snap to each bottom knuckle and curve over the length of each finger. The horns interlace to form a shallow bowl as long fingers fold into his upturned palms.

wail

Tears drip from silver on either side of his nose, land on arcing sheaths of his chin, and drip again into the sheath-woven bowl. Soon they're paced in a nearly solid stream—a cord of grief from his eyes to his heart.

Keen

Constricting muscles in Lysbeth's jaw and neck battle the strength of *Anese*'s oscillations. Her sternum numbs; skin on her face and chest tingles. As she gasps what air she can, the pouch in her hand twitches. Wide-eyed, she stumbles to Brom's bed and sits to tip the cloth.

For the first time in centuries, *Anese* sing again—Keening, broken, from the cradle of Lysbeth's lap.

REPRISE

The book held against Lysbeth's stomach depresses with a slow exhale. Nearing Erruwyn's spot on the Grand Library's floor, she stops to eye the cuff in his hands. "Whatever else it may be, Ryn's role in this is very distressing. The Otay have all the appearance of fanatical lunacy."

"Yes, I have wondered. Ryn's _tox'ki͡ rah_ altered greatly in my presence."

"Her toxkirah? You suspected something?" she asks, taking a seat on the couch beside him.

"Among the people, insisting desire without reciprocation does not occur. Ryn's insistence confused me. I wished to understand. I began to observe her texture." He sighs. "Her eyes were not truly drawn until nearer to her departure. I believe she knew of danger. I believe she tried to signal this as she departed, also," he adds softly.

Lysbeth's eyebrows meet to discuss their confusion. "But why bother hinting? Why not warn you properly with specifics?"

"It is difficult, _nar͡ uah_, to be removed from your roots to preserve them. Bengli. _da'he͡ na_. We are formed by our root tree, released to wind as pollen." He rolls the cuff, quiet for a time. "The teachings of _da'he͡ na_ formed me. Though these teachings conflict with the winds I ride, it is better to ride the wind than to fight it—to fall. Knowing I will never be wind will not cause me to betray my root tree, also." He glances at Lysbeth. "Even when I like where the wind has carried me."

Anese sings _ji_. Bittersweetness.

She returns his wistful smile.

_a'ia͡ na_. The Keening rite came to an end once Erruwyn's tears reached the rim of the shallow, silver sheath-bowl—which he'd detached from his knuckles and placed on the window sill for his grief _to be carried away by light's warmth_. Physically and emotionally exhausted, he'd slept until early evening, demanding answers on _Ruah_'s behalf when he rose again.

Other than loose theories, all Lysbeth has to offer is the book held to her stomach—a text detailing the bastardization of Erruwyn's culture over the ages. She and Elane pulled it from the eastern library after visiting Erruwyn yesterday and added it to their steadily growing stacks of disappointment not long after. Its cover reads: _Evidence for the Faye: A_

"This is your text, *nar͡uah*?" he asks, following her eyes to the tome.

"Yes, the one I mentioned. It was my favorite book as a child. I always seem to fool myself into thinking it will answer every question I have about your people." She pulls it from her belly, running a hand over its cover. "I even looked through it after receiving word of your Calling. I've no idea what I expected. Certainly nothing short of, 'Lysbeth, it's a lie, be rid of the fiendish Earl,' or 'Lysbeth, take heart, Erruwyn is on his way to you,' would've satisfied me."

ꙮ purr

She exhales a short laugh and peeks at Erruwyn fondly. "I never seem to learn. I looked again last night expecting detailed passages on every previous DaheNaruah." Looking back to her lap, she ruffles the pages with her thumb. "When I didn't find them, I settled for bookmarking the accounts of our age. Being the most recent, I thought perhaps they'd be the most accurate, but even the oldest myths have some truth to them. Three recent encounters claim a Dahena." She balances the text on her fingertips and extends it to the silver figure at her knees. "The first was thirteen-hundred years ago."

"*kayu–da'he͡na*." Erruwyn snaps Ryn's coil to *Danae*'s arm as he takes the book. "Though I do not know of his *nar͡uah*, it is said his silver hair came early of age. He learned the essentials of eighteen languages. He was wise, also."

She smiles. "My impatience is a terrible flaw; hopelessly digging for answers when I only needed for you to wake up."

"It is the burden of curiosity, *nar͡uah*," he says, examining the cover. "I am glad. If you must rely on me for answers, you will not tire of me so quickly."

"And here I was sure I'd have to think up new questions to keep you close." She grins at his slow, shy half-smile. "What's said about you?"

He takes a deep breath, thinking. "Maybe: *erru͡wyn*, twiceborn of *erru͡wan*."

Laughing softly at Lysbeth's protracted sounds of disagreement, he opens to the first chapter. According to the author, the dawn of man occurred roughly three ages ago. The mistake is understandable; evidence of most early communities submerged under sea or soil.

Erruwyn relaxes his eyes to absorb the words faster. Man's earliest myths: the Apkallu and Oannes sages who came from the sea to found the first human cities, bringing art, science, and agriculture with them. After the deluge, they were banished.

Woodblock prints on the next page depict dragons, unicorns, and birds. Human figures wear fish scale capes, wings, and bird heads. Some stand reverently beside a star-crowned staff. One carries crops. Two more boast early versions of *ry͡ine͡hu'ay* daggers in their belts.

"Ages distant, we wore _ay_ cloth over _m'ay-tut_." He glances at Lysbeth and waves to his loincloth and horns. "Additional dressings as _er'oo'n_, also."

"Did they have silver puppets as well? The distant Dahena?" she asks.

"Yes, though different. Silver roots of the spine attune vibrations across _ay'tuan_. Before this, more source _ay_ was required. Throat. Mouth," he explains, tilting a bird-headed print towards her.

He turns the pages, skimming different cultural interpretations of _da'he⁀na_ over the ages: the Paoxi dragon twins whose knowledge carried on after the deluge, resulting in the first marriage rites, the first sovereigns, and whose dragon-horse bore symbolic importance. The Finfolk shapeshifters who abducted humans to their hidden island and had a weakness for silver. Amabie, a prophetic long-haired, bird-beaked, and fish-scaled spirit who came from a glow on the ocean. The pincoy and pincoya, incomparably beautiful brother-sister water spirits who guided souls lost at sea. The chalkydri, winged chimera who sang with their phoenixes at dawn to herald the sun.

He flips from hippogryph and cockatrice to a page describing Ala—shapeshifting dragons who rode storm clouds and destroyed crops with their hail.

"_er'oo'n_ hailed our arrival from the clouds ages distant."

Lysbeth leans her cheek on her wrist. "The last generation to witness you must've spun such confusing tales to their children."

Dozens of mer-folk, bird-folk, and hoof-folk later, Erruwyn turns to Lysbeth's marked encounters: Corburg's Syren, an Essimar Elv, and a Takkar Nix. In all cases, firsthand accounts cease shortly after the public announcement of each country's ᶻ_da'he⁀na_.

"Only one blaze?" he asks, flipping pages.

Lysbeth leans forward. "Corburg's fire? Yes."

"The others had none?"

"Had no fires? Most countries boast a good blaze now and again, but Corburg's burning is often mentioned alongside the Faye to explain the lack of physical evidence."

"Then, evidence occurred in others?"

"Nothing substantial. Most Faye relics are proven to be forgeries. Why?"

"There is..." Erruwyn hesitates, glancing up from the book. "It did not occur to me to say as you asked for my strings, *ŋaɾ͡uah*. It is not a string to pull. It was decided the secrets of *ay͡na* must be protected from Outlanders." He pats *Danae*'s tubes. "*ay͡na* is often hollow within. This is required for the placement of resonant materials at important passages, among other materials, also. If *ay͡na* is punctured, or the pitch of pained-muting is sung, the response is flame. It is meant to leave nothing of us."

Lysbeth sits up with alarm. "Danae will set your fire?"

"If broken or *tia͡ua,* pitch of pained death, is sung, only, *ŋaɾ͡uah*. In this way, Outlander's cannot learn of *ay͡na*."

Her eyes lose focus to concerned imaginings. "But of course they would attempt it. They would break open your containers to sell your things; your bodies to learn how the ay attaches, the silver puppets to discover their means of animation."

She folds her hands, allowing herself a moment to reel. For ages, the lack of physical evidence had been a purposeful byproduct of their silver. How many Faye-obsessed sages would love to know it? Her hand lifts.

"Anese?"

Erruwyn eyes dampen. "No. The flame would deface. Destroy. This is—" He stops at Lysbeth's reassuring nod, grateful she understands. "If *Anese* reacted to death pitch, this would endanger *ŋaɾ͡uah*, also."

"I see." She stands abruptly. "Alright, we have histories on Essimar and Takkar."

She waves for Erruwyn to follow and pulls a thick, Takkaran history book from a shelf. Scanning the index, she finds what she's after: a list of Takkar's notable blazes. She flips to the back-cover's map and cross-references *Evidence for the Faye*.

"Dahena Kayu was announced at Takkar's capital, here." She points near the center of the country. "Nine weeks later, The Great Fire of Gibet took place, here," she says, dragging her finger to a town on Takkar's northwest border. "Half of Gibet was destroyed. Another fire broke out at the capital nearly two years later; a third of the city was razed."

"The burden of curiosity," Erruwyn remarks softly, following her lead with an Essimar tome.

Lysbeth parses his words. "If Dahena Kayu was announced at the capital, taken to Gibet, and left his trunk behind, eventually someone would try to open it." She checks the book again. "Takkar's capital fire centered on a noble district. Nearly seventy died. If they were like us and kept the trunk a household secret, any who knew of it would've died alongside it."

He nods, holding long fingers across the country of Essimar; it seems to share a very similar story. Lysbeth walks to a world map of Iodesh on the western wall—a ragged pangea broken by inlets, seas, and lakes.

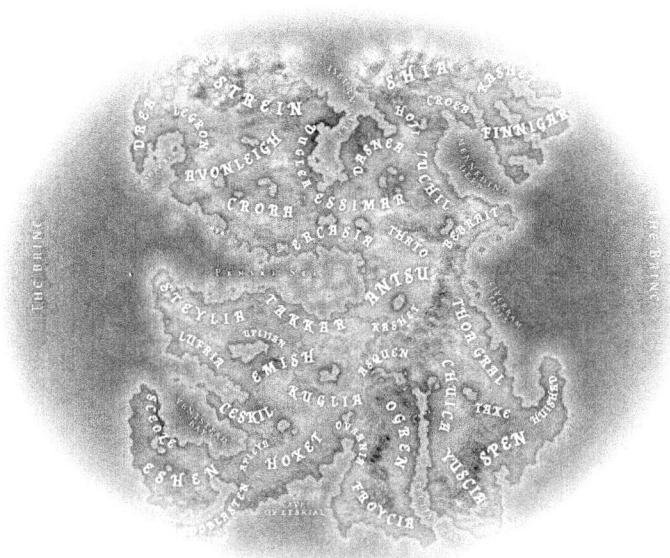

"My geography is nearly as bad as my patience. It seemed a pointless subject, seeing as I can't go anywhere," she mumbles. "Here. Essimar shares a border with Crora—and Otay by association. Takkar's fire at Gibet"—she trails her voice and finger over land—"occurred on the border of Takkar closest to Crora. And before it fell, Corburg was across the Penski Sea, directly south of Crora."

Anese simmers with contempt.

"*kw'da*. Otay assembles their hunts." Erruwyn pulls Ryn's cuff from *Danae*'s arm plate. "Though, Ryn was troubled to visit her home. I do not believe she wished my hunt."

Lysbeth lowers her hands from the map. "Perhaps she was here to scout and made to return?"

"Yes. Though, if she did not wish my hunt..." He motions the cuff to Crora.

"...why would she wear something so certain to give you away?" she finishes the question.

After a long, puzzled gaze, both arrive at a thought. Lysbeth moves in; Erruwyn twists the cuff to reveal its perfume recess. A tiny corner of parchment peeks out. He pulls a branch from *ay'ena*, revealing a set of thin tools resembling lockpicks.

"Is there any problem Danae can't solve?" Lysbeth mutters.

"*ᴠda'he⁀ṇa* spend the greatest sum of time on land during *set'ye̩*. We must be prepared for many occasions," he explains, coaxing the scroll of parchment out with a tool's hook. When it protrudes enough to grab, he hands the cuff to Lysbeth and replaces the branch. *ḍa'he̩⁀ṇar̩⁀ua̩ḥ* huddle over miniscule words as she unrolls them:

> *If you read this, you live. I hope it. I will say what I could not. Otay is built on prophecy of martyrs cast from paradise by false Silvermyr. We will reclaim our rightful place in the First after the Stars' procession. Bengli sit in laps of men who hear of a Star's arrival. Bengli acquaint, confirm, and douse. I could not douse; I could not deny. If you cannot forgive me, take joy in the death of an all-traitor.*

Erruwyn breathes quickly.

"Martyrs cast out?" Lysbeth whispers in shock. "The Dahena tortured into madness?"

"*i̩k-ty̩s.*"

He lowers to the floor, gripping his knees. Lysbeth joins as his eyes dance across the carpet, connecting links of thought into a chain of understanding.

"Reclaim the First," he says softly between air. "Occasionally a child of the brood will struggle to feel the others. To hear *≤m'ae̩ṇ.*"

"I recall." She reaches for his hand; his palm turns up to meet it.

"Occasionally, *me̩'ya⁀i̩te̩t* choose to mate with those cradled by *wa̩'t'un̩*, also." He sends her a meaningful look. "Outland mates dilute *≤m'ae̩ṇ*. Those lost to madness were *i̩k-ty̩s*. Discordant. Displaced."

Lysbeth grips the chain. "Entirely displaced. Surrounded by Outlanders. Younger generations would've lost the ability to sense and produce maen while older generations still carried it."

"Reclaim the First," he nods, repeating himself quietly. "*≤m'ae̩ṇ* is the elemental expression of *𝒯hea̩m*. First element. *ᴑta̩'tae̩*. Twiceborn of Wind, *~o̩a̩'tae̩.*"

"Oh-ay-tay." She straightens slowly. "Otay."

He swallows, holding her gaze. "Pollen drifts from the root. *ir̩'i̩e*. The seeds of our expression sowed as echoes on distant shores. *i̩k-ty̩s⁀dj'e̩n'e̩c̩.*"

"Yes, their attire," she whispers, "their similarity to your embodiment of Wind and Ryn's likeness to Jhenxi. They must know Wind and Jhenxi are significant, but they don't recall the specifics of their original appearance." Her eyebrows peak in morose sympathy. "Their understanding of Concepts, embodiment, maen... All of it drifted into simulacrum, even unto their own isolation."

⫼ wail⏝hiss

"Ryn should not have—"

"It isn't your fault," Lysbeth interjects, squeezing his hand. "Ryn must've known the consequences of leaving you unharmed. She made a choice not to act. One I'm extremely grateful for."

His head dips, unconvinced. "Though, if I were not present among you, she would have been spared this choice."

Lysbeth smiles faintly. "I thought I bid those kinds of wonderings away."

Anese's remorse pairs with a purl. Erruwyn regards her with grateful admiration, gingerly stroking the back of her hand with his thumb After a long moment, she sniffles and returns to the message.

"Otay's prophesy: 'We will reclaim our rightful place in the First after the Stars' procession.' If the First is Theam, they seem to believe they'll recover the ability to hear and produce maen after a procession of stars." She lifts her gaze to *Dange*'s star-shaped dish and sighs. "The myth of DaheNaruah's duet—the star who guided the lost Dahena home—they must despise everything it stands for knowing they can't find their way back."

Erruwyn nods regretfully. "Among the people, *n'ar'uah* is swiftest of stars.[29] Her path treks the procession of ages, also."

"You mean the procession of the equinoxes?"[30]

"Yes, I believe so. *n'ar'uah* begins her path-forging against the horizon, laying additional path across the sky of each age. The path is forged after thirteen ages, beginning again with her re-arrival at horizon."

"Then they believe they'll reclaim maen by dousing a procession of thirteen?" She presses the pouch of *Anese* in her bodice. "Three Anese, suggest six DaheNaruah; we were meant as the seventh and eighth."

"It may be so. Though, *jae'dua* was doused by his *nu'im*, the fork in the path of his Threading."

"The Dahena who drowned," she says weakly.

Erruwyn lifts her hand in the air between them. "Eight. Nine."

Ten fingers interlace, painted in the library's last rays of sunset.

GHGGHGGHGGHGGHGGHGGHGGHGGHGGHGGHGGHG

Elane eyes Brynen as he crosses the Grand Chamber. "Who'd have thought we'd see them again? Let alone employ them," she muses as the giant takes up his posting.

"*ry ̄ine*," Erruwyn says, rubbing Erem's back beside Avrella's chair. "The symmetry knits."

After uncovering Otay's motivations, Lysbeth sent news of Ryn's death to a distraught Jaques—who, after failing to convince several Croran Lords of the Bengli's true nature, found some solace in their thinking less of him for his efforts. In the intervening weeks, Avrella looked for ways to increase Lindenholt's guard.

---

[29] *Proper motion: a star's motion across the celestial sphere—at right angles to its observer—with respect to very distant background stars.*
[30] *The gradual shift in the orientation of earth's rotational axis in a cycle of approximately 26,000 years. Equinoxes move westward along the ecliptic relative to "fixed" stars.*

Fighting men are hard to come by during Kingswars, but Brynen's band—though slightly fewer in number due to lasting injury—still felt indebted to the Haywoods and accepted their offer of employment when it came. Once settled, Erruwyn eagerly passed out remedy vials to those he'd hurt, and after a few days of light hazing from the Keepers, the mercenaries found themselves at home.

Having an explanation for the attack—coupled with the, as yet, absence of further attacks—had bolstered Lindenholt's sense of security as much as the increase in its guard, and while no one is deceiving themselves into believing the threat has fully passed, morale has improved. Now, on an early Winter evening, the Ladies, Erruwyn and Erem sit cozy in the Grand Drawing Room.

"I've been thinking about ryine and Ruah myself since Brynen's return." Lysbeth leans over the armrest. "Dorsit wanted to announce your arrival to the peerage early on. If we had, Otay's interference would surely have come sooner."

"Yes, I have also wondered this, *nar͡uah*."

"And where did your wonderings take you?" Avrella peers.

"My *ix'ul*, Marquess, Baron," he answers softly. "Though the steps are dark, I have come to understand them as articulations on ◊*Ruah*'s path. Without *nar͡uah*'s bidding of defense—*ke'ra-tu*—I believe the Echoes of Otay would have muted me."

"It is quite fortunate you knew self-defense was permissible," Elane says solemnly. "I hate to think what might've happened otherwise, but how do the Warden and Isaac fit in?"

"The path's articulations." Erruwyn drags his thumb to each knuckle of his index finger as he answers, "My *ix'ul* of Dorsit stepped to Marquess' de-basement. Marquess' de-basement stepped to Baron. Baron's lake aggress stepped to *ke'ra-tu*." He looks up, dragging his thumb in reverse. "In this way, the path of ◊*Ruah*'s restoration side-stepped my muting. I defended as bid."

"Ruah has a favorite then?" Lysbeth raises an eyebrow.

"◊*Ruah* seeks only to rest, *nar͡uah*." He smiles. "My life might spare future *ᵹda'he͡na* the Echoes' discord."

Over previous weeks, Erruwyn used *ʔRoske* to chronicle the truth of Otay in his native tongue, and Avrella sent copies to trusted foreign nobles. Ideally, *ᵹda'he͡na* to come will have some warning.

Avrella chuckles. "Then I suppose Ruah played a role in Jeni Haywood's building of a scrivery for your purposes as well?"

"Perhaps, Granny," Corah says wisely. "Alder was returned, after all, and he's the one who wanted a large library like Erruwyn's people."

"I believe Alder's return would be viewed as a displacement," Lysbeth ventures.

Erruwyn tilts his head thoughtfully. "Mm. Many among the people believe a *ᵹda'he͡na*'s Threading is fated. I occasionally wondered if this was said in comfort, only.

Though now I feel Alder's return made my Threading so."

"Because of his letter?" Lysbeth infers.

"Yes, my Threading arrived from Dorsit's ship; from your wish to know the people of Alder's chronicle, *nar ̄uah*." He returns Lysbeth's profoundly guilty expression with a reassuring smile. "The displacement of string occasionally displaces those nearby. ◊*Ruah* may have required further displacement—required my Threading—to dampen the pitches of Otay's discord."

Mr. Tenson straightens from a whispering footman and clicks to Avrella with a small, sealed scroll.

"I do enjoy your meanderings." Elane smiles. "Your people seem quite set on making sense of the world through Ruah's rest."

"Indeed, they do." Avrella unfurls the butler's delivery. "Have you any thoughts on how we might tuck Ruah in a little sooner, Erruwyn? At least where Otay is concerned?" she asks, glancing at the message.

Edenshire injured. Arriving seven weeks.

Mask maintained, she calmly folds the paper.

"I am uncertain, ⪦*me ̄na*. Justiciars of ◊*Ruah* oversee the restoration of one string— that which we observe. The Echoes of Otay are *dj'en'ec*. Your ochre-strum. Too many strings for one alone to see."

"Orchestra," Corah corrects.

Lysbeth laughs quietly. "It's no use. I've tried. He says 'ochre-strum' allows the image clarity."

"The ochre-strum instruments. The color. The motion," he explains, smiling sheepishly in Erem's hair.

"Oh, please, please." Lysbeth slants a playful smirk. "There's no need for annotation."

"Ruah must be awfully busy with so many strings to strum." Elane grins.

Erruwyn's face falls lax over frozen hands. Heartrate and ⪯*m'aen* in ⪢*Anese* spike.

Lysbeth sits forward in alarm. "What is it?"

He looks in her direction, seeing nothing.

Bordering hyperventilation and barely aware he still holds Erem, Erruwyn stands, jogs, then sprints to the southern wing.

The Ladies follow, reaching the terrace to see Erruwyn on the lawn and Erem leaning around a hedge at the garden's border.

Lysbeth dashes over gravel.

Face locked on the dim sky, tears streak to Erruwyn's ears. Out of breath, Lysbeth slows to a stop at the hedge and follows his eyes.

A moment later, she lowers to her knees and wraps Erem in shaky arms.

Descending gracefully from the clouds at tremendous speed, _er'oo'n_ sheds long-fall-down.

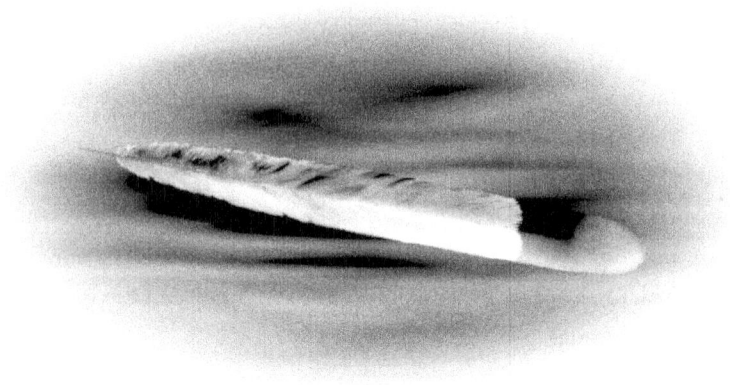

ᏩᏋᏩᏋᏩᏋᏩᏋᏩᏋᏩᏋᏩᏋᏩᏋᏩᏋᏩᏋᏩᏋᏩᏋ

ᏩᏋᏩᏋᏩᏋᏩᏋᏩᏋᏩᏋᏩᏋ

‡da'he͡ na, offered to the Outlanders
nu'im, the path is forged
a'ia͡ na, the people egress

a'ia͡ na, the people's Keening takes root in the soil.

Blue shells are crushed and woven into earth;
their color seeps into roots of the giant-trees.
When giant-trees are cut into vessels, they sit blue against blue on the horizon.

a'ia͡ na, the people's Keening is forged in the fire.

ay͡ na is forged to bind the seams of vessels,
to make fins which carry the vessels forward.
When ay͡ na is welded to vessels, they sit gleaming on the horizon.

a'ia͡ na, the people's Keening is woven in the cloth.

Blue cloth is woven to cover the ay͡ na of vessels,
to mute their shine with colors of the sea.
When the sun reaches zenith over blue vessels on blue waters, peeking ay͡ na winks to hunters
sitting hungry on the horizon.

a'ia͡ na, the people's Keening is voiced in the song.

ay͡ na fins of the vessels propel the voyage;
their articulation is sung in ⸘m'aen.
When the people must move quickly, the strongest ⸘m'aen sits low on ʔTheam's horizon.

a'ia͡ na, the people's Keening begins on the vessel.

The strongest ⸘m'aen of ʔTheam cannot be willed.
The strongest ⸘m'aen of ʔTheam sits at dusk;
the only path forward is darkness.
When ‡da'he͡ na is offered,
the ⸘m'aen of a'ia͡ na sends the people's vessel over the horizon.

Among the people it is said,
"The keening of a twiceborn ʑḏa'hẹ͡ ṇa echoes across the sea eternally."
The words are images of metaphor: a sorrow endless as the sea.
This is how we understand the words.
But I have touched them,
I know their images are different than their textures.

Even in moments of joy, keening rides the currents of my ʂṃ'ạẹn.
It can never truly go from me.
A piece of my soul is absent, taken from me as I did nothing.
ịx'ụḷ.
Now I chronicle my grief onto ◉ṃạ͡ jọç,
just as ʔRọṣḳẹ Archives the passage of time across her.

When I walk the grove of giant-trees,
my keening buries into the ʔṬḥẹạṃ of soil and root.

When I gaze into ḷịʼḷạ͡ ịtẹṭ as she exhales ạy,
my keening sears into the ʔṬḥẹạṃ of forge.

When I pass the cradles of spinning moths,
my keening weaves into the ʔṬḥẹạṃ of their bodies as they slumber into shape.

When I stand among the people,
they feel my keening and they keen softly with me.

The textures of the words are these:
ạʼịạ͡ ṇa, the people's Keening begins **as** the vessel.

From now until the muting of ◉ṃạ͡ jọç, the sea will carry my grief forward
with every vessel formed of giant-trees, ạy͡ ṇa, cloth, and song—
just as the vessel I stand on carries the grief of every distant ʑḏa'hẹ͡ ṇa
whose twiceborn was taken, whose keening is Archived on ◉ṃạ͡ jọç.

Twenty-seven moons distant,
ʃerru͡wyn was Threaded as bait.
We Keened as the Outlanders bit and gulped.
The fins of our vessel sent us forward quickly;
sent us far from ʃerru͡wyn as I did nothing.
ix'ul.
When ⊙ma͡joç rose on the horizon,
those awaiting our return heard our Keening and they Keened.
a'ia͡na.
Their Keening crossed the sea to meet us; our vessel moved even more swiftly.
I tasted the bitterness of doubt for the first time:
Doubt in my purpose, in my training.
In our mercy to hunters, especially.

When distant Outlanders broke ʒda'he͡na in search of ⊙ma͡joç,
it was decided future ʒda'he͡na must recite an answer.
The answer leads to a piece of wa't'un.
Outlanders cradled upon it signal a broken ʒda'he͡na.

Those ʒda'he͡na of our age:
ʃaa'wen, ʃkayu, ʝ'ah'on.
We believed the absence of their answer
signaled their contentment among Outlanders.
Many among the people hoped they had even found joy.

Then, twenty-four moons distant,
er'oo'n sang of a vessel on wa't'un.
Sang ʃerru͡wyn's answer.

All among the vessel were ik-tys. None were taken to our breast.
Their leader was that of ʃerru͡wyn's Threading and breaking.
He named his soil: Avonleigh.
He was woven into symmetry before I could arrive.
Many feared the pitch of my ry͡ine would tip me further from Fulcrum.
So.
For twenty-one moons,
I have joined any vessel charting near to Avonleigh's soil.
a'ia͡na.
Our voyages move quickly in my presence.
Those on set'ye feel my keening and they keen softly with me.

I send ꗏaf'ir forward each dusk.
She has flown nine set'ye above the Outland,
calling to ꗏerru⌢wyn with her ⸿m'aen.
On the ninth she returned bearing ji:

ꗏerru⌢wyn lives.
ꗏerru⌢wyn suffers.

ꗏaf'ir bore his words.
Their textures were thorns and flame:
Children tormented into silence.
Our hunters are not of sea, only.
Alder, lover of ꗏral'ya, has betrayed us.

ꗏaf'ir bore ⪦Anese:
Those lost to currents of madness took root on its shore.
ꗏaa'wen, ꗏkayu, ẙj'ah'one.
They were not broken. They were not content.
They were hunted.

ꗏaf'ir bore ꗏer'em:
Newest child of the people; soul-woven of ꗏerru⌢wyn.
She shares his threads; feels his absence as I do.
A piece of my soul has returned.
We are ey⌢ine, now, also.

I hold her against ⟨Danae.
The image of ⊙ma⌢joc has slowed her tears.

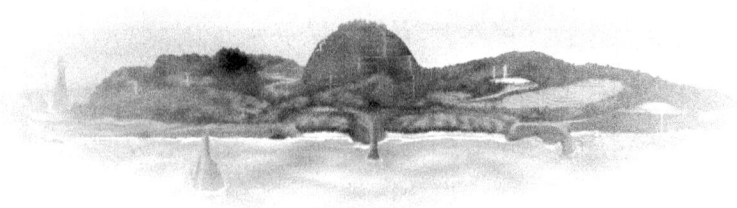

◉ma͡ jǫç's iris is bright like her children's.
There are flecks in the color—structures of those distant before her iris grew,
before the edges of her soil submerged again.
We must be careful navigating in her sight.

ʔRoṣḳę chronicled her lashes,
wore the stone around her into arches so we may always see horizon.

She cries with joy and sorrow,
we drink the tears of her springs and falls.
She closes her lid, we stumble about in her mists.
We carve the sediment of her slumber for ǫy and shelter.
j'tǫę, we plait her trees, tend her gardens, decorate her with chain.
She watches us with love, always.
Always.
We strive to keep her safe, and so it is said,
"To hold the cover of night, we must offer the brightest stars."
The words are images of metaphor:
◉ma͡ jǫç is beacon. ◊Ruaḥ's attunement protects her.
To dim her brightness, we offer ⚡da'hę͡ ṇa.
To preserve our harmony, we suffer a'iǫ͡ ṇa.
This is how we understand the words.

But I have touched them.

Their texture told me a'iǫ͡ ṇa is not ◊Ruaḥ's attunement.
It is ↪i'uaḥ͡ ṇa, born of ꙮluaḥ:
Suffering. Severance.
That which all paths wish to avoid,
which all paths must cross.
That which every ǫy͡ ṇa articulates,
no matter the forge, fire, or mold of its birth.
We did not notice its forces upon us,
but it has grown in the trees, the ores, the cocoons.
We accepted its curdled note; attuned our harmony to it.
It has become the tempo and melody of our song.

Now I near ◉ma͡ jǫç again.
I taste the bittersweetness of fated purpose.

We will harbor before ḏa'ja͡ṇa.
All will gather in ≏roọ'ḏa for the longest night.
They will hear ⸰erṛu͡wyṇ's words.
They will feel ⸰er'ẹm's silence.
They will see ⊀Aṇẹse.
They will Keen for the muting of ⸰aạ'wẹn, ⸰kaỵu, ⸰j'ah'oṇe, and
I will not permit their Keening to cease until they touch the words.

I Will master my keening. ạ'iạ͡ṇa͡hụ.
I Will wear ⊀Aṇẹse as hụ'aỵ to signal my Mastery.
I Will use my keen to drown out the curdled notes of ↪i'uah͡ṇa.
I Will burrow my keening into the ⁊Theạm of ◊Ṛuah and demand its restoration.

ȸạ'iạ͡ṇa
the people's Keening Will end with me.

ʊʊʊʊʊʊʊʊʊʊʊʊʊʊʊʊʊʊʊʊʊʊʊʊʊʊʊʊʊ

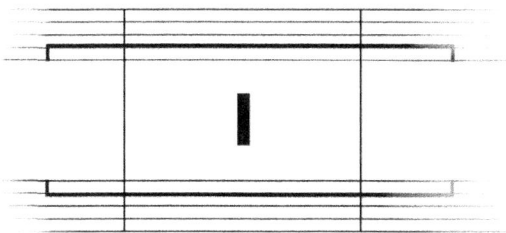

Lysbeth runs Afir's three-foot feather over her fingers. The color fades from grey to white, and a thin, black stripe contains the teal of its tip.

⟩ weep

"He's nearing," she mutters, setting the feather on her writing desk.

Avrella peers from the vanity. "Any change today?"

She holds her breath to focus on the vibrations. "I can't be sure. It's lessened considerably since the night-of, but there've been only slight changes in the last few days. I'd hoped WinterSol would help, but I think it's only reminded him of having Erem last year."

"It may never stop, My Lady." Ani shakes her head sadly from the dressing room doorway. "My aunt was never the same after the last Kingswar took my cousin."

"I can't deny I've had similar thoughts." Lysbeth glances at Avrella and Elane. "Still, please don't pester him with questions. I'm afraid it will only aggravate his sorrow."

"Of course, dear," Avrella says, turning a knowing smile on Elane.

Lysbeth has asked her kin to refrain from discussing *er'ǫǫ'ņ* almost daily for the last five weeks. Corah was quickly insulted by the repeated requests but agreed to hold her tongue after Elane explained Lysbeth needed the reminders most of all.

At the end of Afir's visit, and to everyone's surprise, Erruwyn placed *⟨Aņęșę* around Erem's neck, wrapped her in layers of blankets, lulled her to sleep with *șm'ąęņ*, and tucked her into Afir's breast-bracing. Then, Erem was gone—carried off by *er'ǫǫ'ņ* as in Lysbeth's childhood daydreams.

The Ladies turn to the door as he enters. "Another corrected portrait?" Avrella asks, eyeing the scribal case he sets on the vanity.

"No, *⟨mę⌐ņa*," he answers quietly, snapping tools to *⟨Daņąę's* arm. "It is a gift. To thank you. All. For your kindness. Patience. *⟨li'la*, also. Though, it requires privacy. I did not wish to reveal it among so many at Solstice."

Compassionate folds appear on Elane's brow. "That's very touching, Erruwyn."

"Yes, and quite mysterious." Avrella chuckles. "A fine way to whet our appetites. Do work quickly so we might call for Corah."

Erruwyn follows her instruction and dresses the first Ladies quickly. When they move to the couches, Lysbeth takes her turn. He smiles faintly as she lowers to the chair.

"I wished to thank you, also, *nar͡uah*. If you wish to ask, I feel ready."

"Are you sure?" she asks his reflection. "I can wait."

"Yes. I am certain. I will answer."

"But..." Her fingers move to *Anese*.

He flicks his eyes to her collarbones as he combs. "The void of *er'em*'s absence, it"— he hikes an eyebrow to punctuate the word she'd taught him on the lake—"coagulates with knowledge of her happiness. Her safety. The wound will seal soon. I do not regret my action. Though I fear the void of my answers will cause the wound of your unsatisfied curiosity to fester." He holds her gaze in the mirror and traces the curve of her neck with his fingertips. "Thank you, *nar͡uah*, for waiting."

Her chest rises quickly. "Of course. Thank you for your willingness to submit to my curiosity."

trill

da'he͡nar͡uah's smiles slant. Erem's absence had also meant *Jhenxi*'s, but after weeks of pain's slow recession, *k'es'sey* could will the rest away—at least for a time.

"I suppose we ought to call for Corah now," Lysbeth says. "She'll be cross if she's neglected. Ani?"

"Already near the door for summons!" a small voice calls from the bedchamber.

Elane grins. "You're too good for us!"

Lysbeth's chamber door shuts. Tiny footsteps trot to the dressing room and Ani's head rounds the doorframe. "As her Grace says, I won't argue a flattering opinion, My Lady."

"Quite so, my dear, quite so." Avrella chuckles.

When Corah is announced, she takes up post on the couches. "I should never complain about an interruption in Ms. Leeve's grooming lectures but watching Lys' hair dressing isn't much better."

da'he͡nar͡uah smile coyly again; for the last few months, Erruwyn's more prone to playing with Lysbeth's hair than dressing it. She leans around his abdomen to look at her sister. "Apologies, I thought you'd want to be included in our Eroon discussion and the present Erruwyn's secretly made for us. My mistake."

Corah's eyes light up. "I said I wasn't complaining! Where is the present?"

"We must wait until Lyssy is presentable," Avrella says, "which includes a treatment for the unsightly rotting of her curiosity as well as hair dressing, I hear."

"Goodness. I didn't realize it was such a noticeable blemish. I'd better get started." Lysbeth clears her throat behind a smile and motions to her desk. "Afir's feather. I worried I'd ruin its shape if I checked, but I could swear there are two sets of barbs."

Erruwyn drags long fingers through her hair. "Yes, twice-layered, *nar͡uah*. The seeds of *er'oo'n*'s expression occur along the scale of *Theam*. The barbs resonate with *m'aen* of *er'oo'n*. Anger, curiosity. The *m'aen* of calm affects small plume. Down, also."

"And a feather will remain in the form it held when shed?" Elane asks from the couch.

"Yes, Your Ladyship." He turns briefly. "The barbs fasten until resonance parts them. Though they can be forced to part, the result is unsavory."

"Then I'm glad I didn't try it, despite my festering." Lysbeth smiles.

"Is it common for fluffy Eroon to treat you as children?" Corah pipes.

Despite Alder's descriptions, the Ladies were unprepared for just how large and striking the birds truly were. Afir had landed in her curious form and changed to long-calm-down as she'd approached Erruwyn—on his knees in shocked, pained joy. Her tail feathers softened and curled, and her sleek silhouette puffed to nearly double its original size. Once close, she'd wrapped enormous wings around him and nestled him as she might an egg.

"Yes, *li'la*." Erruwyn begins a lackadaisical plait. "When loving, *er'oo'n* wishes to care for us. Protect us. If we are distressed especially."

"That's quite sweet." Ani's disembodied voice remarks from the dressing room.

"Agreed." Lysbeth smiles at her maid's eavesdropping. "I'm afraid my astonishment kept me nailed to the gravel. I'm glad someone had enough sense to comfort you," she says, tipping her head against the narrow, silver plates climbing the center of his abdomen.

da'he͡nar͡uah believe they've become rather adept at the art of subtle affection— this is because *da'he͡nar͡uah* still underestimate Avrella's perceptiveness.

"Are females often chosen as pets for their nurturing sensibilities?" Corah asks.

Erruwyn smiles at the assumptions. "Males show affection in this way, also, *li'la*. *er'oo'n* are companions, though maybe this means pet. They assist us in many ways. When twiceborn walking the path of *da'he͡na* have planted all silver roots, we are given the honor of raising a fledgling to accompany our *set'ye*, our voyages. *erru͡wan* and I choose *af'ir* for her eyes. Her lashes were longest of the clutch."

"As good a measure of character as any." Avrella chuckles.

Alder hadn't mentioned the similarities between human and *er'oo'n* eyes. Afir's lashes were noticeable even from a distance, and her bright green iris sat in an oval of white feathers, giving an appearance of sclera.

"Male Eroon take to nesting, do they?" she continues.

"Yes. *er'oo'n* nest together. *dj'en'ec*. Caring for the clutch as one, *me͡na*."

"That sounds awfully familiar." Lysbeth smiles.

"Yes. *er'oo'n* has been with us always. We learn much from them."

"Like your greetings, obviously," Corah says.

When Erruwyn regained his faculties, he'd stood and greeted Afir formally—as he'd done at his Offering—and Afir did the same, resting the hook of her break over his outstretched hand.

"Yes. It is a beautiful expression. *er'oo'n* greets this way if you are thought to be kin." He twists the finished plait thoughtfully. "Many among the people believe *er'oo'n* taught us _aro'x_, also."

"I suppose if they can recite, I shouldn't be surprised they're capable of mimicry," Lysbeth mutters, imagining choirs of enormous birds. "What else?"

He untwists the plait to wrap it around a finger. "_er'oo'n_ lock their wings to soar with ease.[31] We observed this, forged _m'ay-tut_'s joint lockings to spare our hinges. _er'oo'n_ matriarchs choose their mates on merit, also."

"Which merits are those?" She grins. "I don't suppose they've the dexterity to apply tongue silver."

He raises an amused eyebrow. "Dance, song. Combat, _aro'x_. Plumage."

"Heavens." Avrella chuckles. "It seems to me you have taken Eroon's culture whole cloth."

"I don't blame them," Elane says, leaning on the couch arm. "Erruwyn, does the name have a meaning? The word, 'Eroon'?"

"Oh, I'd like to know too." Lysbeth glances playfully. "I only know the meanings of their feather names."

Erruwyn bites his lip and lowers his eyes from her reflection. "The thought is: _spark in the eye of ⊙ma‿joc_. Though the truer words do not provide the image clarity."

ʔ

Among the people, it's said _er'oo'n_ are mountain souls.

_er'oo'n_: reflect ' mountain ' journey. This is what the people have called them for ages, though they don't remember why.

Fortunately, _ʔRoske_ chronicles.

Seven million years ago, the people wandered from the Outland along an enormous, snaking land bridge of young, folding mountains: _wa't'un_—the tallest ridgelines of a now-swallowed continent—bore them for ages, leagues, and leagues away from where they'd begun. As the solar tides arrived, peripheral ridges of _wa't'un_ submerged, froze, and re-melted, adding new shelves along its peaks as moraines. Though it continued to grow, it couldn't quite keep up with the frequency and erosion of water, and each time its shorter, outer peaks were enveloped, the people followed _er'oo'n_ to higher ground—reflect, mountain, journey—and the world's last megaflora and fauna climbed with them.

This continued until the ever-growing peaks of _wa't'un_ formed a labyrinth of underwater barriers blocking passage of any who didn't know the way. Outlanders now refer to this expanse of water as The Brine—the stretch of sea yet to be successfully crossed by their ships regardless of approach.

The Island of ⊙ma‿joc—the highest part of _wa't'un_—was born of the convergence of its three tectonic plates, piling together as fault block, fold, and dome mountains. ⊙ma‿joc's geological formation and distance from the Outland also gave it features not found elsewhere.

---

[31] _Dynamic soaring allows _er'oo'n_ to fly hundreds of miles per day with little energy expenditure._

Among them were rare ores, minerals, plants, and animals—alongside two megafauna who used supra and infra sounds to hunt: _er'oo'n_ and _i'yo'in_.

The _i'yo'in_ were large, carnivorous reptiles with a top speed of twenty miles per hour. They posed the greatest threat to both the people and _er'oo'n_, and by the time random mutation and sexual selection had distributed _≤m'aen_ among the people, their relationship with _er'oo'n_ had become symbiotic—warning each other of _i'yo'in_ and assisting each other in hunts.

Eventually, _er'oo'n_ were domesticated and bred for temperament, intelligence, and clarity of _=aen_ for message recitation. The people's matriarchal choosing of mates allowed for sexual selection along similar lines. The people's intelligence and curiosity lead to advancements in metallurgy, agriculture, and writing well before their Outland cousins—who had expanses of soil to roam and were content in their nomadic ways. When the people's curiosity took them along exploratory paths, _er'oo'n_ joined their first sea voyages, flying above to lead their vessels through the maze of _wa't'un_'s shoals.

ᘔ

"The eye of Mow-jahk?" Elane puzzles.

"Yes, Your Ladyship. This is how we refer to our soil."

Lysbeth bites her cheek as Erruwyn responds. She'd come up with temporary explanations for her questions over the last several weeks, and many have now been properly answered, but she's hesitant to ask one in particular.

Without lifting his eyes from her hair, he advises through a gentle smile, "Please do not fester, _nar ̄uah_."

She looks on with tender affection. "Alright. I suppose I've been curious to know what messages Afir carried to and from."

ᘔ _ji_

Erruwyn's misty eyes center on the copper plait twining his fingers.

"I'm sorry. Festering or not, I shouldn't have asked." Lysbeth turns in the chair, slithering the plait from his hand as she pivots. "Don't reward my crassness with an answer."

Coming to a stop, her chin rests near his knuckles; Erruwyn's torso blocks her from the rest of the room. Though he knows Avrella and Elane are privy to their relationship, he follows Lysbeth's lead in limiting displays of affection. Still, when an opportunity like this presents itself, he won't pass it up.

"Your curiosity is not crass, _nar ̄uah_. I will say." His thumb outlines her chin and cheek lightly. "_{af'ir_ carried news, love: _{ki'ky_'s sister has been despondent, as mine has. _{my ̄tik_ has become _aro'x_ Master. _{r'hea_ bore fe-male twiceborn. _{alyn–≤me ̄na_ rejected the request of a fellow Wise, our _dj'en'ec_ of elder _∝da'he ̄na_. She will not forgive him for stumbling over her favored _ket'ac_ plant in the darkness."

Avrella chuckles. "I do see why you believe she and I would get along."

"It is so, _≤me ̄na_." He smiles, dragging his thumb under the ledge of Lysbeth's lower lip. "I sent love: _{er'em_. Warnings: Echoes of Otay." He gazes, stretching his fingers along her jaw. "News: Alder's daughter has become *ṇaṛ⁀uah*."

Lysbeth presses a warm smile into his hand.

Avrella peers inconspicuously from the couch. She still enjoys their candid moments, and their tenderness is heartening, even in the face of the news she's been holding. After Afir, no one remembered the night's other messenger, and she'd resolved to keep the knowledge to herself until after Solstice. If another bird arrived bearing different tidings—ideally a report of her son's healing and a cancelled homecoming—she'd alter her plans accordingly.

No such message arrived, and as the original note failed to provide any details regarding the Duke's status, Avrella has confined her fretting to what she knows for certain—the turbulence Isaac's arrival will bring.

Among the many privileges of being a noble in a Kingswar, accompanying wounded kin home is high on the list. The arrangement has been taken advantage of from time to time, but as most contrivances are easy to spot, deceptive desertion is rare. She sighs silently. Solstice has passed, and here are her granddaughters already assembled. She decides to break the news after Erruwyn's present.

After lingering on Lysbeth's dressing, *da'hẹ⁀ṇaṛ⁀uah* join the Ladies. Erruwyn kneels between Avrella and Lysbeth's couches and pulls a scroll from the scribal case to the table.

"What I have done is not permitted," he says softly. "It must be destroyed after now." As the excited Ladies look on, a petite throat-clearing comes from the dressing room. "It is not for small children," he calls. "They cannot keep secrets."

Ani squeaks with offense and leans around the doorway. Grinning, he waves her over, and once she stands behind Avrella, unrolls half of paper.

The room gawks at the colorful illustration of an island.

Miniscule *er'oọ'ṇ* dot favored perches or fly above the scene. Jagged, primordial-looking rocks jut from bright, cyan shallows. Natural bridges in various states of erosion spoke out from wavy, striated cliff faces. Two long beaches divide the cliffs; their sand ends at a thick wall of densely woven trees. Terraced farms and groves—one of which is entirely dedicated to enormous blue trees—surround the scape's centerpiece: a tall, dome mountain. A garden sits at the top. Deliberate falls and vegetation wind down intricate arches and columns carved along a spiral path on its face.

"What's in the middle?" Corah asks faintly.

"⌖*rọọ'da*. Pupil of ⊙*ma⁀jọç*. Convergence of her quarters. A place of meeting. The brood is born and raised to ten years of age here. Educated, also." His fingers land on four points of the mountain. "Guilds. Training Halls. Records. Storing."

"Converging quarters?" Elane mutters.

"⊙*ma⁀jọç* is quartered. Ages distant, we lost much harvest soil along her shore." He points to a stone column under clear water. "Many were hungry until our number attuned. It was decided we must divide her soil. In this way, her resources must be lost in symmetry, also." Four fingers land on one corner of the island at a time. "Plant. Animal. Mining. Food." He drags his fingers next to ⌒*roo'da*. "Resources arrive. Refine." His fingers collapse on ⌒*roo'da*. "Brought to *ʔRoske*. Distributed. *ʔRoske* suggests what is required from next harvest, also."

Lysbeth leans forward, speaking weakly, "What happens when children turn ten years old? Why do they leave Rue-dah?"

"By this age, all have learned the essentials of mind, body, song. Those walking the path of ∾*da'he⌒na* remain; the brood begins procession. One year to learn essentials of each quarter, one year beside ⌒*roo'da* to learn refining. Now fifteen years of age, the year resides among guilds of ⌒*roo'da* to learn essentials along Mastery's narrow paths. Males begin *ne'ru'k* training, also. All choose a favored path from procession. All walk their path. Many are certain by eighteen or nineteen years of age, though, occasionally, those undecided begin another procession."

"What if everyone wants to become a farmer?" Ani asks. Elane waves her closer to see.

"*ʔRoske* will suggest attunement. Ask for a sum among the quarter to alter course. Those tallest of age offer first to permit their children time on the path they have enjoyed."

"It is a regular occurrence?" Avrella peers at the table.

"I knew of it on two occasions, ⤳*me⌒na*. Many enjoy the friendship of animals; the quarter is never lacking wayfarers. *ʔRoske*'s suggested sum was met easily."

He unfurls the remaining paper to reveal a beautiful vista. Falls, mists, lush gardens, and springs. Chains and chimes dangle from trees woven into aesthetically pleasing shapes and structures. In the distance, natural arches rise from a bay to frame the horizon. To the left, a woven tree holds lunestone like a streetlamp. Five people pile near it.

"⟩*alyn*–⤳*me⌒na*, ⟩*nem'ar*, ⟩*erru⌒wan*, ⟩*r'hea*, ⟩*my⌒tik*." He points.

Avrella and Lysbeth reach for their handkerchiefs.

"That flower." Lysbeth sniffles, nodding to a tree. "It's like the one you gave me."

Erruwyn keeps his eyes on the paper. "*so'jac*."

Lysbeth grins dopily under her handkerchief. He'd given her a silver version of the flower ⟩*r'hea* had given him—a heavily sentimental symbol.

The group stares and remarks, committing as much detail as they can to memory. After copious thanks, Erruwyn rises and feeds the fireplace.

"Alyn seems quite lovely, though I'm not sure how well I would do in silver bracing, myself." Avrella chuckles, tucking her handkerchief away as Erruwyn kneels. "How does one become a favored ⤳*me⌒na*?"

⟩ *hum*

"You've struck a chord," Lysbeth teasingly whispers across the table.

Erruwyn bites his lip. "There is a gesture of love's expression. Favor is shown when reciprocated."

Avrella peers above a wry smile. "Are beads involved in this form of favoritism?"

"Some may." He dips his head, watching his lacing fingers. "Though most favored escort their ꝫme͡ŋa to celebrations. Sit beside. Assist." His eyes flick to Avrella's feet.

The younger Ladies struggle to cover their delight at the building scene.

"I see." The Matriarch clears her throat. "Might we have a demonstration of this gesture?"

ꝫ purr

Lysbeth snorts into her hand; Erruwyn raises a sheepishly constricted smile to her.

"I'm sorry. Please," she says, motioning to Avrella.

After a pause, he scoots and lifts a cupped hand, palm to the floor. Avrella's smile elongates as she lays hers across it. Eyes low, Erruwyn guides her knuckles to his face, strokes each cheek from mouth to ear, and returns their hands to their starting position. As he counts woodgrain stripes on the floorboards, tickled Ladies wonder how long their Matriarch will make him wait for reciprocation.

Avrella purses her lips. Though teasing is as inherent to grandparentry as spoiling, she knows better than to trifle with a wounded soul, and surprises her granddaughters by slipping her hand under his after only a few moments. Bashful cyan flicks between wood and hand as Erruwyn's fingers approach her face, drag around her chuckle, and return. He breathes quickly, unsure what words could matter. To be singled out by one universally loved is a great honor, and he's just been favored by the Outland's one and only ꝫme͡ŋa.

Lysbeth catches her grandmother's attention and wiggles fingers over ꝫAnęsę. Reading the signal, Avrella offers her aid in smoothing the impact, "I look forward to my official escort next event."

"Yes, ꝫme͡ŋa." He smiles at the floor.

"For the time being, however, we've a bit of Haywood news to discuss."

"Yes, ꝫme͡ŋa."

Greatly improved in spirit, Erruwyn hops up and folds the scribal case over chest. Walking to the hall, he hesitates in the frame. "Thank you." The words come louder than intended; he hurriedly shuts the door on sweetly laughing Ladies. Ani grins her own thanks and leaves for the bedchamber.

"I'm glad he's better," Corah remarks. "And now we'll be free of Lys' pointless reminders."

Avrella stems the budding argument. "Ladies, it behooves us all to reserve the fight for common enemies, rather than one another."

"Common enemies?" Elane repeats.

"Yes. I am very sorry to report that Jaspyr has been injured. The message lacked any helpful information, which should leave no doubt as to its author. They arrive in a fortnight."

The women fidget. Though none think ill of Jaspyr Haywood, none are particularly close to him either—as fathers rarely take much interest in the female line. At the moment, all anxiety is reserved for Isaac.

Avrella continues, "I assume Jaspyr's injury is not too serious, else the Marquess would not have been given leave to accompany his return—infections acquired on the journey often pose the greater risk. That being the case, I have delayed Gyenna's visit until we are sure of Jaspyr's status. We will discuss what information might be best kept hidden tomorrow at teatime, so do give it some thought. Yes?"

A faint, affirmative chorus ensues.

"Very good. That is all." She flashes a look to Lysbeth as Corah returns to Ms. Leeve and Elane moves to her room with a book. Alone, she continues, "Erruwyn should join us, Lyssy. I trust you will inform him?"

"Yes." She rubs a temple. "Though I'd prefer not to sour his mood so soon. I'll tell him tomorrow."

"If you like, but send him along to me some time before tea, please."

"Why?"

"I might need his hand," she answers vaguely and eyes her progeny for a time. "Are you aware the vast majority of people fumble through their lives never knowing the look Erruwyn casts so freely upon you? He must really love you, I think."

"Granmama!"

"Do you disagree?"

Lysbeth smiles. "I suppose I'm less shocked by the remark than by your being the one to make it."

"Yes, indeed." Avrella chuckles. "He has managed to dredge up the bloated remains of a romantic in me." She sighs and turns a long, knowing look on her granddaughter. "News of Isaac's return will be difficult to swallow. Do make it as painless as possible, Lyssy."

———————

After luncheon the next afternoon, Lysbeth calls for dictation—tapping the vanity and smiling sly when Erruwyn arrives.

※ *buzz*

|

purr

He lays a parchment and stylus across the scribal case and sets it down where she'd marked. As soon as his fingers lift, Lysbeth walks him backwards to the closed dressing room door and moves his hands to her hips. He bites his grin. Fingertips pressing into her backside leverage his request for closer proximity; thumbs in the soft space past her hip bones second the motion. She obliges, laying in to wrap her arms around his neck.

"<u>k'es'sey</u> is feeling generous?" He squeezes firmly to avoid tickling her abdomen—and to clearly convey his own feelings on the matter in hands.

She tucks under his chin, speaking to <u>Danae</u>'s collarbones, "Kessey is feeling sorry."

"Sorry, <u>nar͡uah</u>?" Concerned hands loosen and slide to her waist.

"For the news I'm to tell you." She takes a long breath. "Father has been injured. We suspect it's not too serious, however, both he and the Marquess will be returning to Lindenholt in two weeks' time."

 buzz

   |

   chime

Erruwyn swallows at the windows along the opposite wall. Lysbeth stretches fingers behind his ears and raises her head slowly—tracing his throat with her nose until her lips hover over the border of his chin.

"We should discuss our options," she says.

trill

   |

   buzz

Her voice and touch displace his heartstrings. His eyes hide under lids. His lungs expand. His lips part for her consideration as she tilts his head down.

"Have you any thoughts?" she asks, mouth brushing lightly.

He nods.

"I'm listening," she whispers.

"My thought is to receive information in this way only." Feeling her abdomen flex with a chuckle, he smiles and kneads her waist. "Though important information may require repeating."

"I see. For instance, Lindenholt's Lords are returning," she repeats, kissing him softly.

He nods again, sliding his hands up her back to wrap long fingers around her shoulders. "Maybe another repeat to be certain, <u>nar͡uah</u>. My thoughts are wandering greatly."

"Well, I certainly wouldn't want to distract you." She pulls away, smiling as eager hands rearrange themselves across her—fingers cup her neck, a forearm bars her lower back.

"I hear. I hear, <u>nar͡uah</u>," he says, glimpsing her outline as he leans to match her distancing. "If it is delivered as the previous message, I am certain it will stay."

Grinning, she lifts her chin and closes her eyes: an invitation.

His forearm tightens to keep her hips close as he follows her arc. A breath below the rim of her jaw marks the start of his charting. Lightly grazing lips press trail markers along the winding path of her throat. Her respiration increases as he descends. Long fingers till her hair and squeeze gently, turning her head to stretch the curve of her neck. He lingers over the bend until her fingers curl to bring him in.

His embrace narrows. Tongue tips scout, twisting lightly on her skin as the center point of a warm, radial exhalation. She gasps in a weightless embrace as his lips alight and pull on her softly—tongues continuing their survey in the vacuum of his mouth. At her renewed clawing, his teeth landmark her neck's end. Bumps surface across her scenery. He encourages their stay, alternating lips, tongues, and teeth as he scales the ridgeline of her shoulder.

Her heart sprints.

"_ŋar͡uah_," he whispers, retracing his steps. Mouth preoccupied drawing air, she nods in his hands as a slow constriction pulls her upright. "I believe someone nears," he breathes below her jaw.

A contemptuous scoff and a disappointed sigh crash in Lysbeth's throat. Poised against _Danae_, she blinks away dizziness as Erruwyn guide her to the desk. Her coltish smile lowers to the chair.

"Don't forget where we left off," she says.

He smiles, smoothing her copper strands. "Our song is kept in the most accessible archives, _ŋar͡uah_. I have discarded my knowledge of Asquen for this purpose."

"Asquen?"[32] she asks, watching him move to the vanities. "I thought your thirteen essentials were meant to be the most likely languages of your hunters."

He picks up the prearranged scribal case and wiggles the back of his left hand. "Yes. The language rings. Thirteen required; fourteen hinges. The absence of the final ring was too great to bear. Asquen was the easiest remedy. It shares a root with three others." He grins, pointing to the knuckles of his index finger.

Lysbeth lays her cheek in her palm, chuckling at his wholesomeness. A moment later, a footman knocks to deliver a message bearing Gyenna's seal.

"Thank you, Temus," she says, breaking the wax as he exits. Reading, her smile makes a brief appearance. "Feunen follows his offer of condolence for my father's injury with a demand for another illustration. He writes, 'I was made to beg Avrella for an unkept invitation. In recompense, I require an illustration of Beauty's remaining appendage to complete my collection.'" Lysbeth bites her cheek to suppress another smile as her eyes lift.

"Maybe _ne'ry'k͡hu'ay_?" Erruwyn offers, laughing softly.

"Perfect." She grins and motions him over, lacing her fingers behind his neck once his kneel settles. "Before that, we really should discuss our options." At his sober expression, she adds, "I'm afraid my acrobatics loosened my bodice. I could use a bit of support."

Long hands form to her waist. "A new _da'he͡na_ duty?"

"Double duty." She arches an eyebrow. "To reach the effect you must first cause the

---

[32] One of Iodesh's very few landlocked countries.

cause."

❊ buzz

|

purr

Smiling, she traces the scars on his lip and brow. "These have healed nicely."

"Yes." His eyes close. "Thank you for your assistance."

"My assistance?"

He cracks a lid. "We heal faster when kept in *j-ṣm'aęn*. Purring."

"Truly?"

He nods, shutting his eye again as her finger trails from chin to chest. "You cause this even in sorrow of Echoes. Of Erem."

She glances down. The light pink Otay scar on his lower abdomen peeks out beside her knee. Her lips curl. Fingers journey to their new destination as she raises *❊Anęse*.

k'ęs'sey is no longer feeling generous.

❊ trill

|

buzz

Feeling the path of her touch, Erruwyn shakes his head and opens his eyes.

Lysbeth's crescent grin waxes as she speaks through *❊Anęse*, "Is something the matter, *Erruwyn*?"

He gasps with flashing eyes. Muscle and sinew tense under silver.

His training had not included provisions for a *k'ęs'sey-ṇaṛ⁀uaḥ*. The people's affinity for sound often leads to the eroticism of a favored partner's voice, and Lysbeth has devised a way to inject her voice directly into his nervous system without invoking *ke'ra-tu*.

They stare in amused, stimulated silence.

Rising anticipation quickens Erruwyn's breath. "You cannot know what you do to me," he whispers.

"Oh?" She bends an eyebrow and dips fingers under his abdominal plates.

"Yes," he manages. "You have all the advantage. This prevents your knowing."

She leans forward, hovering her lips near his ear. "Explain yourself, *Erruwyn*."

The key of her voice winds him to snap. Grooves in his arms and chest deepen his grip on her waist. "Your torment of me through *❊Anęse*. I sense what it gives you." He steadies a breath. "*er'wa* requires this; requires I respond to bring satisfaction. Though even this is not your greatest advantage."

Lysbeth waits for him continue, suddenly feeling a bit of moral quandary. Both of her roles—*ṇaṛ⁀uaḥ* and Lady—come with toolsets meant to maintain a power differential. Erruwyn had alleviated her concerns regarding the disparity, but from the sound of it, *er'wa* is a toolset she'd overlooked. Fortunately, she doesn't need to worry. *er'wa*'s reflections are instinctual, not compulsory. In fact, Erruwyn's current words are as much a manifestation of _er'wa_ as his physical responses.

His hands glide their decent. Beseeching fingers press her hips. "I am bound to your Will. I wish to bend where you blow. The greatest advantage of your torment is..." He swallows, laying grit teeth against her ear and inhaling sharply. "I must love it."

⋈_Jhenxi_ smiles licentiously.

Finding her stomach has been knocked to the floor, Lysbeth's first dip into unbridled passion commences with the lassoing of her legs around Erruwyn's waist and the urgent pulling of his mane to steer his mouth to hers. If he weren't fully occupied fulfilling his role as a mount of conveyance, his grin would be manic.

Erruwyn has had no qualms with the impossibly slow tempo of their encounters compared to those from home—however, he'd occasionally wondered if _k'uah⌒ni_'s suppressive influence would deny Lysbeth the joy of truly unfettered expression.

This is a ponderance he will no longer carry.

The last several weeks devoid of ⋈_Jhenxi_ had obstructed Lysbeth's trek across the unexplored wilderness of her own desires, and with so much ground to make up for, she was already looking for shortcuts. Now that she's cheerfully flung herself from the cliff _er'wa_ has provided, terrain is covered rapidly, and her arching is soon involuntary.

———————————

"Come."

Avrella stands from her writing desk—an heirloom, the one Alder's letter had been found and kept in.

The door opens for Erruwyn, who scans the room as he enters. Two large chairs sit on either side of an end table to his right. The head of Avrella's bed rests between two eastern windows. Her desk sits along the wall to its left, halfway to the fireplace.

"Erruwyn." She moves towards him. "I presume you have been informed."

"Yes, ⋜_me⌒na_."

The Matriarch smiles; he's taking it rather well.

"We will join the Ladies for tea shortly, but I have a few questions first. I hope you will forgive their delicate natures," she says, leading him to her chairs and sitting. When his kneel settles, she continues, "I prefer preparedness, and I am sure you know we have good reason to prepare."

"Yes," he says quietly.

She moves her hand to the armrest. "Firstly, do you believe yourself capable of discerning the Marquess' falsehoods?"

"I will attempt _tox'ki⌒rah_ if you wish it ⋜_me⌒na_, though, this means I must disobey Marquess' instruction."

"Instruction?"

His eyes jump to the floor and back. "The instruction of Marquess. Of Baron. To look only where I belong."

She draws a slow breath, speaking as she exhales. "It would have been more efficient to instruct the whole of your misery at once, but of course that would have gotten in the way of their enjoyment." Her fingers twitch. "Well. Try if able, particularly when I am present. However, should the moment feel precarious, do not risk it."

"Yes, *ꝫme͡na*."

She folds her hands against the rest and continues gently, "During your time with Warden Westcott, had you a hand in his correspondence?"

Erruwyn blinks. "Yes, *ꝫme͡na*."

"I am sorry, my dear. I would not ask if I did not think it potentially useful."

He nods. "Erem and I were kept in walls of Baron's room. I heard many dictations. Made many, also."

"And were any of those addressed to the Marquess?"

"Yes." He pauses. "Do you wish for *ꝛRoske*'s record, *ꝫme͡na*?"

"I do," she says, pulling a parchment from her sleeve, "using this, if Roske has no objection."

Erruwyn takes a few moments to memorize the paper—a substitution cipher shifting all letters of the alphabet over by seven; difficult enough to decipher that the document's absence would be noticed before its thief managed the task. Twenty minutes later, Erruwyn returns *ꝛRoske* to the scribal case and stands as Avrella locks the record in Alder's desk.

"Thank you. I am sorry to have asked without first being certain of its usefulness, but it is always better to avoid the regret of a missed opportunity if we can." She takes Erruwyn's arm. "Now, favorite, would you honor me with an escort?"

He grins at the scribal case on his chest.

"Thank you." She chuckles, motioning to the door.

They journey to Lysbeth's sitting room and enter to find the Ladies enjoying Ani's tea. As he helps the Matriarch to a couch, he exchanges cagey eyes with Lysbeth.

"Ani, do stay. You should be included in my conspiracy," Avrella says as the maid pours her cup. "We must come to a consensus on what facts should remain hidden from our Lords."

"*ꝫAnese*," Lysbeth answers firmly. "Isaac mustn't get his hands on it."

"Which must therefore include *ꝯDanae*'s resonant purposes," Avrella adds.

"Yes. Ani is the only member of the staff to understand nearly as much as we do about the resonance." Lysbeth pauses to think. "Brom is a close second. The rest must have gathered some connection, but surely no specifics."

"I believe you're right, My Lady," Ani confirms, handing her a teacup and saucer.

"Good." Lysbeth presses her bodice and looks at Erruwyn. "I'll keep *ꝫAnese* hidden from view, but you should give me a similar necklace as its placeholder should Isaac hear of it and request to see it."

"Yes, *nar⌐uah*."

"Isaac won't be thrilled to see *Danae* again, I should think," Elane posits.

Avrella sips. "The only opinion that truly matters is Jaspyr's, and given his correspondence, we have little to fear on that front."

♮ —

Erruwyn flicks apologetic eyes to Lysbeth's fingers as she pats *Anese*. "Though I hope *Danae* does not offend His Grace, *Ruah* demands my readiness if the Echoes return. I must refuse any request to remove it."

"In that case, we'll think of what to say." Elane lifts her cup. "Should we hide your tree stand and trunk?"

"I'd considered the same, but I don't think it's to our benefit," Lysbeth replies. "Isaac would only order Erruwyn to reveal them."

"What about Danae's star?" Corah points with a biscuit. "Will Isaac notice the difference?"

"You're right. I've grown so accustomed to seeing it this way I'd nearly forgotten. I doubt he'll recall, but we'll find a way around the truth if necessary."

Erruwyn returns Lysbeth's smile. "*nar⌐uah*, I wish for clarity of *ke'ra-tu*."

"Serendipitous," she says, placing her saucer on the table. "I wish to provide clarity of Keratu. What's fuzzy?"

"I thought to ask if Marquess is among your people."

"In what respect?"

"Marquess said I must exist beneath his feet. I believed he meant me as a footstool, though Baron explained the truer meaning." He swallows. "I am instructed to defend your people. I am of your people. So. I wonder if this means my own defense is permitted." Glancing around the silent table, solemn expressions answer his question. His gaze falls.

Lysbeth tightens the grip on her hands. Isaac is not of her people in any way that should matter, but he could threaten anyone he liked at Lindenholt. Her eyes dampen in frustrated antipathy; she'll have to alter her *ke'ra-tu* to include the odious stipulation.

"Incidentally, your fighting abilities may tempt the Marquess to spirit you north when he goes," Avrella notes.

"I am not permitted to influence conflicts of *k'uah⌐ni*," he explains faintly.

"I see." She peers. "Then withhold any direct refusals on the matter. I will see that Jaspyr understands your presence is crucial to Lindenholt's safety."

"Does Isaac know about the basement's sealing?" Elane asks.

"I cannot say with certainty. I informed Jaspyr in Summer; he may have relayed it."

The Ladies eye the nervous figure on the floor. Though Lysbeth succeeded in delivering the news painlessly, the pain was delayed rather than avoided. The more possibilities explored, the more Isaac's wrath seems an eventuality.

Avrella attempts optimism, "At the very least we might be spared the Marquess' fuss concerning Ms. Pinley's wages."

"He does love to scrimp," Lysbeth agrees.

"He does, though I believe austerity is better kept to thinning dead leaves than stripping branches. A tree providing neither shade nor beauty is little more than lumber, but he has always had a knack for deadening the atmosphere." Avrella sighs. "Afir's arrival was fortuitous."

Erruwyn nods slowly. "Yes, *ʒme͡na*. I am excessively grateful to *ʒerru͡wan* for sparing *ʒer'em*'s suffering."

"You mean you think Isaac would've hurt her?" Corah asks.

Isaac hadn't bothered with Corah for the most part—save for a small push here and there to encourage her adoption of his views. While she believes her kin's concerns, she lacks the firsthand experience to know he shouldn't be underestimated.

"Yes."

The certainty of Erruwyn's answer is disquieting, and the Ladies are quick to redirect the conversation—exploring succinct answers to Isaac's probable questions for the remainder of teatime. Erruwyn helps Ani tidy after the eldest and youngest depart, and stays by the table as the tray is taken.

"I seem to have taken up your hobby of daydreaming, Lys," Elane says, leaning back on the couch. "I hope you won't think less of me, but I've imagined you setting Ruah on Isaac. From your description, one look would be enough to send him off."

Lysbeth deflates on the couch's arm. "As have I. Though I'm afraid my imaginings were less merciful. He'd only come back otherwise." She glances at Erruwyn. "Does that make me truly wretched?"

He smiles gently. "To dream a path to safety? No, *ɲar͡uah*. This is done when no options could matter. When options must be dreamt."

"Well, we only need to stay out of his way for a fortnight or so before Jaques' negotiations," Elane says. "Some options could matter in the interim. For instance, don't take Isaac at his word straight away."

Lysbeth sits up. "Yes, wait until you've had time to think over what he's said, regardless of the subject. He's quite adept at slipping in without notice." She pauses. "He enjoys watching the effects of his efforts, too. Are you able to maintain an emotionless face?"

"I am uncertain."

"Alright, try." She smiles and scoots forward on the couch. "Try to hide what you're feeling from me."

As they stare, Erruwyn's worried expression slowly stretches to a grin.

ʒ purr

She laughs through her nose. "You're off to a bad start."

He rolls his lips in to hide his smile, managing for a moment before rising cheeks separate them again. "Forgive me, *nar͡uah*. I must not wish to hide my enjoyment of you." His eyes drop to *Anese*. "I could not, also," he adds.

Elane chuckles. "It's a decent thought, but you may not be the best practice dummy for this endeavor, Lys."

"Apparently not."

"Punctuality is feasible though," Elane continues, "Don't make Isaac wait, and don't waste his time once he's in front of you."

"That's right." Lysbeth nods. "We'll woxua if you aren't sure what to say, but as a rule, only ever reply, 'Yes, Your Lordship.'"

"Yes, Your Lordship," he replies, biting his lip at her feet.

Lysbeth blinks flirtatious disapproval.

trill

Not one to get in the way, Elane pulls up from her slouch. "Well, that ought to cover the basics. If you don't mind, I'm anxious to finish Wodal's book of poetry. Beg your pardon," she says, standing to cross the room.

Erruwyn smiles at the table, tonguing a molar. Lysbeth smiles at Erruwyn, biting her cheek. Elane smiles at the dressing room, shutting the door behind her.

Jhenxi has a way of pushing unpleasantness to the side, after all, and why not take advantage while one can?

———————

The gatehouse bell rings two weeks later.

"And so, our men return," Avrella remarks quietly, closing her book.

Corah drops a sparrow broach into the jewelry box she's been perusing.

Elane moves her needlework to a table and glances at the window. "Ready, Lys?"

Turning from dim panes, Lysbeth presses on the silver under the cloth of her bodice. "No."

The Ladies proceed to the Grand Chamber, where the servant's assembly has been arranged due to the chill. Still, tradition being ambivalent to weather, Lindenholt's entrance must remain open when receiving family. Mr. Tenson keeps eyes through the door's sliding window, ready to pull the handle once the Lords exit the carriage. After a few minutes, he twists to the Ladies in the center of the room.

"Tenson?" Avrella asks.

"Yes, Your Grace. I—His Lordship has descended with a covered cot." He twists back.

The women freeze as the first notes of panic are plucked. Avrella sways. Lysbeth catches her waist and holds, sharing a fearful look with Elane, who circles to support her from the other side.

Mask re-appended, Avrella steadies. "Pardon me, thank you," she says, patting her granddaughters' hands.

"It seems the cot is headed for the western servant's entrance." Mr. Tenson turns a regretful expression on the Ladies from the door. "His Lordship approaches." Closing his mouth, he reaches for the handle.

The doors swing to uneven clicks on the steps. Isaac's face bobs over the terrace—eyes already set on the women in the room. His unsteady climb is explained as the cane at his waist comes into view. Reaching the landing, he limps to the vestibule. The head of a miserable-looking valet peeks over the steps and follows, keeping a distinct distance from his master.

"Announcing The Most Honorable, The Marquess of Edenshire," Mr. Tenson calls.

Isaac continues past the entryway without correcting Mr. Tenson's announcement.

The Chamber breathes; the Duke still lives.

After fifteen paces, Isaac's valet enters the vestibule and shuts the outer door.

"Welcome, Sir." Avrella peers.

"Duchess. Ladies." Isaac brings his cane around and leans both hands on its hook.

"The Duke?"

"His Grace's physician thought to get him indoors as quickly as possible."

"Physician?"

"Yes. I hired one for the journey."

"I see," Avrella says, glancing at his leg. "And you?"

"And me," he echoes.

A silent moment passes.

"Well. Supper awaits."

The group moves to the dining parlor, where clinking cutlery dominates the conversation until Avrella speaks again.

"Sir, would you be so kind as to tell us the extent of Jaspyr's injuries?"

"I only know the wound was deep and he needs rest. Hence the physician."

She lowers her fork. "Then perhaps you might tell us how he acquired the injury."

"It's war, Madam." Isaac lifts his wine. "Blades and bodies tend to get in the way of one another. That's rather the point, isn't it?"

"Yes, but the point only goes where the hilt directs, and it has been my understanding that Lords are usually kept from such intersections." She peers as he sets down his glass.

"Not in this case, apparently."

"I see. Then might I ask why we were not informed of his injury's severity?"

"What good would the knowledge have done you? You had a pleasant Solstice thanks to my omission."

Avrella's fingers twitch beside her plate. Isaac's logic follows a clean line, if somewhat callous, but his words nag at suspicions she's carried since the lake-side attack. Lindenholt has over two-hundred eyes across it. How many provided a northern view? She runs over the answers they'd practiced. None should contradict any superficial reports he's received.

"Indeed, we did. How very good of you."

Isaac blots his mouth with a napkin. "I need to see the Faye. I'm to thank him on His Grace's behalf."

Avrella lifts her fork. "Then we shall call for him after supper."

The Ladies keep their countenance through the awkward meal and follow Isaac to the Grand Drawing Room at its end. When he takes the chair to Avrella's left, the Ladies shift uncomfortably—the spot belongs to the Haywood Patriarch; Jaspyr Haywood still lives.

Mr. Tenson crosses with a tray of drinks. "My Lord, I happened upon Doctor Kefer here while you dined," he says, offering Isaac his preferred spirit. "He may wish to see you."

Isaac settles in. "Very good, Tenson. The Duchess and I will attend him after I've seen the Faye."

Bending to deliver Avrella's sherry, Mr. Tenson nods to a footman near the arch.

⚜ *chime*

On arrival, Erruwyn bows slightly and grips a wrist behind him as he nears. "Your Lordship."

"Yes." Isaac stares. "Why are you wearing this?"

Eyes low, Erruwyn answers as practiced, "I am to defend Lindenholt against threats, Your Lordship. This filigree acts as armor."

"Is it different than it was before?"

"It is what I wore on arrival, Your Lordship," Erruwyn recites.

The Marquess' eyes narrow. "Come here." As Erruwyn steps forward, he lifting his cane and taps the silver Haywood crest with the handle. "What is that?"

"A medal of merit," Avrella says, "and a mark of Dahena Erruwyn's role as Keeper."

Isaac's nostrils flare. "Pure silver?"

"Sterling. Past Keepers were given land for their heroics. Would you prefer an exchange?"

"No. I've never understood the notion," Isaac says, pushing out of the chair. "We don't reward house maids for cleaning, why should guards be rewarded for guarding?" He sighs and begins an uneven saunter around Erruwyn. "Well, well. A medal of merit. You're quite the fighter then?"

Erruwyn glances at Lysbeth's w͟o͟x͟'͟u͟a͟: short fact.

"I have trained in combat, Your Lordship."

Rounding, Isaac pinches the end of Erruwyn's tall, shoulder-length ponytail. "Doesn't the length of hair pose unnecessary risk?" The observation is weighted.

⚜ *chime*

"Perhaps for others, but no one can touch Erruwyn," Corah says with pride.

"Is that so?" The Marquess continues around front. "No one can touch you?" he asks, cupping and lifting Erruwyn's jaw.

Unable to check Lysbeth's hand, Erruwyn follows the advice of her previous *wox'ya*: "I am touched, Your Lordship."

Isaac smirks. "If you're truly as skilled as I've heard, our Sovereign requires you. You'll accompany my return to the fight."

As instructed, Erruwyn stays silent.

"Shouldn't Father be the one to say?" Corah frowns.

Isaac's eyes dart to the couch. "Naturally he wouldn't deny Erruwyn the honor of serving." He drops his hand to prod the silver crest and grimaces. "Thank you ever so much for your contributions."

Intuiting any response will lead to his own entanglement, Erruwyn bows after Isaac steps back. Satisfied, the Marquess waves him off and stares at his back until the archway blocks it. Avrella stands.

"I am most eager to see the Duke," she says, handing her glass to Mr. Tenson.

"Then let us not delay your fulfillment."

The Marquess straightens his cane and steps; the Matriarch follows.

Elane sighs once they're gone. "That wasn't so terrible. Go on, Lys. We'll cover for you if he returns."

Grateful, Lysbeth nods and leaves for her sitting room. She'd instructed Erruwyn to use the servant's stairwell beside Elane's chamber—a back entrance to her apartments usually reserved for Ani's exclusive—through Isaac's stay. He waits against the wall as she opens the door; his eyebrows seek assessment as the handle latches.

"I think it went as well as we could've hoped. You did a fine job." She drapes across him and kisses him deeply.

🜂 *buzz*
|
trill

Holding her close as their lips part, he speaks amorously over her mouth, "This is due to your instruction, *nar uah*. I have learned much under you."

She grins from atop. "You're an ideal pupil."

"Mm." He tightens his clasp. "Your incentives make it so."

Laughing quietly, Lysbeth presses in for a gracious doling of laurels.

———————

Elane's book lowers at her cousin's abrupt entrance to the sitting room.

Lysbeth's hand leaves the door handle to wring its mate. "Erruwyn didn't come for Corah's lesson."

Not entirely surprised, Elane clucks. Isaac had been relatively well behaved since his arrival three days ago, but it was only a matter of time before he'd need to assert his dominance.

"I sent Temus for him," Lysbeth continues, walking to the couch. "He said Isaac won't allow him to leave the scrivery."

"Should we go to him then?" Elane asks.

"I don't know." Lysbeth sits and rubs her temple. "It's clear Isaac feels nothing but contempt for him. If our interference should provoke him..." She meets her cousin's eyes anxiously. "With Granmama so upset at Father's state and Erruwyn already straddling the line, everything seems far more precarious than we'd expected."

Having already lost one child—Elane's mother—Avrella has not been herself since visiting her son the night of his return. Though Jaspyr appeared to be sleeping peacefully, Doctor Kefer warned he was quite unwell and recommended she be the only visitor—young ladies lacking the constitution for death beds, etcetera. She's remained by his side ever since.

Unable to think of a plausible refutation for comfort's sake, Elane takes Lysbeth's hand and attempts to distract her by reading aloud. When the Grand Drawing Room bell rings for tea thirty minutes later, they move to the hall.

"Perhaps we should ask after Erruwyn directly instead of visiting the scrivery. That way Isaac won't feel we've subverted his authority," Lysbeth whispers as they turn down the gallery.

Elane nods. "I'll follow your lead."

They enter as Mr. Tenson hands off Isaac's tea and settle next to Corah on the couch. "Will Granmama be joining?" Lysbeth asks, accepting a cup.

"Natty reports Her Grace will be along shortly, My Lady," the butler says, continuing his distribution of caffeine.

After several quiet minutes, Lysbeth sets down her saucer. "Might I inquire after Erruwyn, Sir?"

"He's busy earning his keep," Isaac mutters, turning a page of his book.

"His keep is earned through recording my lessons and playing music for us as well," Corah corrects.

"Yes, his playing is unique. You might find it interesting," Elane tries.

"I can't read with music." Isaac glances at the couch. "Or inane chatter. But then, who am I to deny you his charming company?" He nods to Mr. Tenson.

Eyes low and wrist held, Erruwyn soon enters. When Isaac hooks an index finger, he steps to the center of the couches' aisle. Isaac hooks again; Erruwyn stands before his chair.

"Erruwyn. How are you? Well, I hope?"

"Yes, Your Lordship."

"Wonderful. I'm afraid I can't say the same." Isaac swivels his forearm to point at the

Ladies. "Though their reasoning eludes me, they've been hounding after you." He opens his palm. "Do put their worries to bed."

Hesitant, Erruwyn turns to the couch.

Air cracks. Muscle memory assumes control:

rap drop knees

rap drop hips

rap drop torso

⚡ *hiss*

Erruwyn folds over the floorboards. Comprehending his body's betrayal, the surprise of his new position is quickly overtaken by shame.

Genuine delight ornaments Isaac's features as he returns the hook of his cane to the armrest and drapes his injured leg over the silver spine below. His second leg joins shortly. Elane rests a palm on Corah's back to stop her protest.

The Marquess sighs happily and adjusts in his chair. "There, an agreeable compromise. You may be assured of his location, and he will continue to earn his keep without interrupting my reading." Smiling at the couch, he reopens his book and drags a finger over his tongue before flipping the pages.

Elane and Lysbeth meet eyes through stunned silence. The Baron must have relayed this method of command; or perhaps it was Isaac's idea from the start. Either way, his glee is telling. He's been looking forward to trying it for himself, and they'd given him a means to the end.

Long moments pass; ⚡*Anese*'s hiss fades.

Silver moves subtly with Erruwyn's pivoting head. She blinks fuzz from her vision to watch the shrug of his brow and the stretching corner of his mouth. Pursed lips halt her pained smile—he'd interpreted Isaac's threat of foot-stooling accurately, after all.

The couch turns with relief as Avrella's shuffling comes from the Grand Chamber. Having found need of her own cane again, her thin expression makes a slow journey across the room. Once she's seated, Mr. Tenson forgoes the tea and delivers a sherry.

She takes a healthy sip as the butler returns to the bar and chides Isaac under her breath, "Such vulgar displays are beneath us, Sir."

Isaac claps his book shut. "You've always been so very observant, Madam," he says, dragging his feet from the silver beneath them. "I beg your pardon, I've a bath in mind. I'll be sure to add Heel to the Faye's long list of accomplishments." He taps Erruwyn's arm with the tip of his cane. "You're dismissed."

"In fact, I could do with some music," Avrella says. "Something soothing."

Erruwyn stands and steps back from Isaac's path. "Yes, ‹*me͡ na*."

"*What*?" Isaac's pupils bore in high dudgeon. "What did you say?"

⚡ *chime*

Avrella sighs. "I have asked for a particular mode of address, Sir, and I have not the energy to argue."

Setting his jaw against a tense moment, Isaac finally moves to exit. Avrella downs her sherry and hovers her hand over the floor. Erruwyn takes it as he kneels beside her.

"Sovereign's Heel was once a court position, you know, and we peers live for nothing if not the emulation of royalty." She passes her empty glass to Mr. Tenson and retrieves a handkerchief. "A Lord's Heel required exacting back measurements; our corsetier's heyday you might say. I suppose there will always be some who long for the return of less charitable traditions."

"It is nothing, ⟨mę͡ ŋa," he says, dragging her knuckles across his cheek. "Please do not feel so."

She lowers the cloth from damp lids, revealing a small, wistful smile. "It seems you were a true lap cat all along."

Erruwyn grins, stroking his cheek twice more and returning the Matriarch's paw.

Relieved, Lysbeth sniffles. "How is Father?"

"I have seen no stirring," Avrella says, thumbing her handkerchief's embroidery. "Do serenade me, my dear."

"Yes, ⟨mę͡ ŋa."

Erruwyn collects the guitarra and plays a hopeful, soothing melody as the Ladies reminisce—interspersing Avrella's anecdotes of the Duke's youth with happy memories of family visits to Walstead. An hour later, the mood feels much improved.

"Thank you all." Avrella sighs. "I believe sleep might find me again. If I go where it saw me last, it will surely have an easier time of it." She chuckles and stands, tilting her head to kindly rebuff Erruwyn's offer of escort.

As she moves across the room, Doctor Kefer ducks in to whisper in Mr. Tenson's ear. The butler's eyes jump to Avrella, who knows the look all too well.

Nothing is near enough to break her fall.

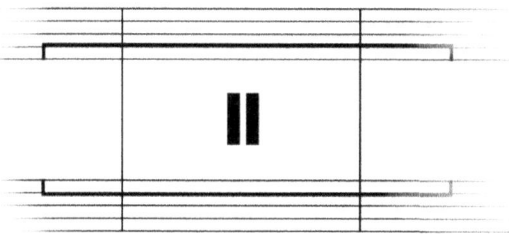

The Ladies sit on white silk couches in black silk dresses.

The afternoon was spent in the family plot, burying Jaspyr Haywood's ashes and building his cairn—without the dignity of an invitation to his peers and tenants to pay their respects. Avrella's spill has left her unresponsive for the last day and a half while an unmoved Isaac assumes his father's role. Erruwyn folds beneath him in the Grand Drawing Room as Mr. Tenson passes out a traditional funerary cocktail.

"To Jaspyr Haywood." The Duke raises his glass before downing it.

The Ladies tilt liquid to their lips in observance of tradition, but drink none. Isaac retrieves a note from his pocket, placing it and his empty tumbler on Mr. Tenson's tray.

"Tomorrow will see my first round of changes. Tenson, have these pieces removed from the halls."

Mr. Tenson nods, hiding his surprised disapproval; most of Lindenholt's paintings are portraits of Haywood ancestors.

"All staterooms but Gold are to be covered and closed," he continues, "After Gyenna we will not be hosting guests unless they pay a decent sum for use of Erruwyn once we've returned from the fight. Repeat for the western wing, other than the study and den." Flipping to his bookmark, he waves Mr. Tenson off.

The butler walks to the couch. One at a time, Ladies place full glasses on the tray and fold shaky hands in their laps.

"Lady Corah, you're excused," Isaac mumbles. "Return to your room to help Ms. Leeve pack your things. You depart for Walstead in the morning."

The women turn to Corah with alarm. Erruwyn lifts his head from the floor, ceasing as Isaac's heel digs into his ribs.

Raising her eyes from Erruwyn to her brother, Corah plays the only hand she can think of in her shock. "What of Mr. Spantier?"

Isaac's book flops down. "It might be worth the cost had you talent enough for violin or cello, but no Lord cares for accompaniment instruments, Lady Corah, really." He scoffs and tilts his book up again. "And you will hand over any Faye silver you've acquired to Mr. Tenson."

Chin quivering, Corah slides from the couch and reluctantly steps from the hands of her cousin and sister. The trio shares a heavy look. Lysbeth and Elane move their grips to one another as she departs.

"That goes for you two as well," Isaac says to his book.

"Yes, Sir," Elane manages on their behalf.

"Erruwyn," he continues.

Lysbeth holds her breath.

"Yes, Your Grace," Erruwyn answers faintly.

"You will refer to the members of this family by their proper titles."

"Yes, Your Grace."

"You will not enter the main floor unless explicitly called for by me."

"Yes, Your Grace."

"Tomorrow you will come to the study at nine in the morning."

"Yes, Your Grace."

"If the gelding cannot be sold by the end of the week, I will relieve us of its burden personally."

Isaac peeks over his book at the ensuing silence.

"Yes, Your Grace."

The Duke returns to his page.

When Lysbeth is certain he's reabsorbed, she wiggles her shoe. Erruwyn pivots his head enough to catch her _wox'ua_ behind the couch's arm: go _ʒme͡na_.

They sit in silence for an hour before Mr. Tenson's somber dinner announcement. Legs numb, Erruwyn pushes himself from the amused Duke's path, only lifting his eyes enough to confirm Lysbeth's instructions as she stands. When his appendages are steady enough to walk, he makes his way to Avrella's room. Natty answers his light knock.

"Oh Erruwyn, I'm glad you've come. I fear she's set to sleep forever," the maid says, walking him to the bed.

Avrella's skin is lax and translucent. She looks peaceful. Absent.

Erruwyn brushes strands from her forehead and gently takes her hand. "_ʒme͡na_," he whispers, "please do not depart us for your sorrow." Sitting on the edge of the bed, he runs a thumb over her knuckles and hums the melody he'd improvised at her earlier request. The maid returns to her chair, sniffling and knitting quietly, until Lysbeth's entry within the hour.

"My Lady." She rises.

"Natty." Lysbeth approaches and takes the woman's hands. "You look pale. Have you eaten?"

"I'm not sure I can."

"We both know Granmama wouldn't stand for that," she says through a plaintive smile. "We'll look after her for a while. Try to eat."

Natty nods and exits for the kitchens as Lysbeth moves to the bed. When the door shuts, her fingers land on Erruwyn's elbow. His arm wraps her waist; hers, his shoulders.

⟩ *buzz*

|

weep

She leans her temple against ⟨*Danae*⟩'s horns, watching silver caress Avrella's hand. "How is she?"

"I am uncertain, *nar͡uah*. Her anima is weak."

"The same, then. What can be done for Kiky?"

"I will send him to the wood. He will remain close. Hidden."

"Alright," she whispers. Her throat tightens. "I suppose you won't be dressing our hair anymore. Or giving us lessons. Or recording for Cora—" She exhales a sob.

Erruwyn stands, holding her close. They sway together comfortingly, allowing their grief to manifest.

"I was so fearful Isaac would see Anese rumbling through my dress. Should you take it to be sure he doesn't find it?" she whispers.

He shakes his nose in her hair. "This would break our mooring."

"But it feels so risky to wear it." She pulls back to see him. "I want to keep it safe."

"Is there no place for hiding?" He traces her cheek.

"My nightstand has a false panel. There isn't a lock, but it will make do." She glances at the false panel drawer of Alder's desk, eyes widening as she notices parchment spread across the top. "Alder's letter. Granmama must find as much solace in it as I do."

She dabs her eyes and leads Erruwyn to the desk, sniffling over the pages.

He reads from a distance.

Something in ⟩*Anese* changes. Lysbeth turns. "I can't feel Anese properly under the cloth and your buzzing. What is it?"

He lulls as she flicks her eyes to the letter and back. Concerned striations appear on his brow.

"When ⟩*ral'ya*'s actions became known, those distant feared Alder would speak on return. For many moons they prepared to defend ◉*ma͡joc*; waited for Outlanders to appear. None arrived. When *wa't'un*'s next vessels carried no knowledge of an Outlander connected with us, we sang of Alder and ⟩*ral'ya*; celebrated their song. We understood this to mean some among the Outlanders could be trusted."

Lysbeth nods with faintly affirmative pride.

He tilts his head to the desk. "This makes it not so. For centuries we have praised a great betrayal. Now I have seen it, I believe The Wise would wish its destruction."

"*Destruction!?*" She turns, protectively placing her hands on either side of the desk behind her.

"I—"

"Even if his letter was misguided, Alder's love for your people was true."

Erruwyn clenches his jaw and eyes the floor.

"You disagree?" She reels.

He shifts his feet. "If he truly felt this way, he could not have written it, *ṇaŗ⁻uaḥ*."

Lysbeth strains to keep her voice low, "Surely you see he only meant to help!"

"No, *ṇaŗ⁻uaḥ*. I see only what suffering he has caused. My Threading. *ạ'ịạ⁻ṇạ*. *ēṛ'ẹm*'s brother. *ēṛ'ẹm*. Families of Brynen." He breathes quickly. "Your kin suffer waiting for assistance in their fight; waiting for *ṣfẹụ'ṇ'ẹṇ*'s barter of me. What number might have been spared in my absence? Hundred? Thousand? Your fathe—"

"Stop." Lysbeth's lip trembles. "Stop speaking." She brings a handkerchief to her face and turns back to the desk.

Erruwyn's regret is immediate. His growing anxiety over Isaac has clouded his judgment. He knows Alder didn't intend for his letter to have such far-reaching consequences, but even if Erruwyn's interpretation of those consequences was accurate, he didn't need to list them all. The letter has been a source of respite for over half of Lysbeth's life. Hearing terrible things about sentimental treasures is rarely received with enthusiasm, and he's just blamed hers for the death of her father.

"You said you viewed your Calling and everything after as part of Ruah's path. According to your own reasoning you should be thanking Alder." Her gasp shudders. "Dorsit. Isaac. Baron. All of us." After a heavy silence, she twists the knife. "You're dismissed."

Lysbeth knew the words would hurt—it's why she'd said them—but her regret is immediate. Those who try to make sense of senseless suffering don't expect to have their reasoning turned against them by ones they trust, and Erruwyn is the last person who needs reminding of his own vulnerability with her final command. Love often lashes out when threatened or injured—as does pride, a staple of the Outland and currently the only obstacle to Lysbeth's prompt apology.

Neck straining, Erruwyn stares at Lysbeth's back, hoping she'll change her mind and tell him to stay—tell him anything that might alter the clarification she's just given of her true regard for him. When she doesn't, he swallows his words, wipes his face, and exits to the Grand Gallery.

Lysbeth's tears come faster as the door shuts. She spins to Avrella, gripping her hand and sobbing quietly on the bed.

Erruwyn peeks down the long hall towards Lysbeth's apartments. Two footmen stand near the end, consulting Isaac's list and marking paintings for removal. To avoid their notice, he descends the servant's stairwell further along the Grand Gallery. At the bottom, he waits for footsteps to fade before moving again—Isaac's reign has brought old anxieties out of storage; Lysbeth's words have pried off their lids. Certain his standing has plummeted again, he makes unsteady progress, buzzing and hiding from others on the way to the eastern servant's exit.

Finally, he steps into dark, chilly air and makes his way around the side of the stable block to Kiky's pen. On seeing his friend, Kiky hops the fence and offers nuzzles. Erruwyn accepts them gratefully, striving to maintain a sense of perspective: Erem is distant, but happy and safe. Corah will be miserable and distant, but safe. Kikyum will be close, happy, and safe—and the silver embedded in his ear will allow Erruwyn to call him back with ꙅ*m'aen* if he's able.

He tightens the straps of the horse blanket and hugs Kiky's face, signaling once he's ready. Grunting, Kiky presses his nose into Erruwyn's shoulder before cantering to the woods at the edge of the property.

Cold, tired, and anxious, Erruwyn heads to his room. Brom watches from the dresser as he enters and curls up under his blanket.

The Duke's declarations had been the primary topic of conversation in the servant's hall, and Brom has accurately guessed Erruwyn's recent task. He moves to the bed and peels back the wool blanket. Two large, troubled eyes shift timidly to his own, not quite holding steady contact—Isaac is already unstitching the fabric of his toy. After a while, he offers what he can.

"It's difficult."

A stoic's profundity.

Damp circles form on Erruwyn's pillow as Brom lays another blanket over the shivering lump.

A restless night passes.

Erruwyn emerges from bed unrested. Too full of apprehension to eat, he scrubs pots after helping the kitchen with breakfast. When there's nothing left to clean, he checks the scrivery. An order arrived yesterday. He completes the title page and table of contents, dragging his pace so the project will last longer.

At twenty-to-nine, he exits to the stone court. A packed carriage sits at the bottom of Lindenholt's terrace steps. Corah and Ms. Leeve stand beside it. Seeing Erruwyn, Corah rushes forward and throws her arms around his waist. He kneels, laying a hand across the strawberry blonde head nestled in his shoulder.

"I will miss you, ꙅ*li'la*. Greatly."

"Please will you write to me?" Her voice is fragile. "Send pictures?"

"I will try. If I cannot, do not believe it is because I no longer sense your absence." Feeling her shake, he pulls back to see her face. "ꙅ*li'la ⁻itet*. The strongest flames burn their light into darkness. Force it back." He smooths her hair. "The strongest flames cast shadow, also. Though both are darkness, one is yours alone to move. Do not forget."

Corah nods and sniffles between gulps of air. When her face twists again, they re-latch. Ms. Leeve approaches soberly.

"I'm terribly sorry. The carriage driver insists we leave now to make Claridale by sundown." She pauses as they pull apart. "For what it's worth, you have my respect and well wishes, Erruwyn."

"Thank you, Ms. Leeve," he says softly, taking Corah's hands as he stands. "It is worth much. You have my respect and wishes for happiness, also." He endeavors to smile. "You also, *li'la*."

After a long look, the carriage is mounted. Erruwyn waits until it rolls forward and returns Corah's splayed hand as he moves towards the servant's entrance. Inside, he avoids those he can on the way to the stairwell. Ascending replenishes some warmth to his muscles, and by the time he reaches the landing, he's collected himself. Stepping into the Grand Library's hallway, he turns left towards the study and glances at the walls. Bright rectangles of wallpaper frame vacancies. A fresh bout of heartache commences at the absence of Avrella's younger portrait.

He stops to look again. Something has taken its place.

Regained warmth disperses across frigid perspiration.

An ink rendering sits on square parchment. Pained eyes turn to the viewer: himself, witnessing his own reflection in the Baron's mirror, kneeling in profile on one of the Baron's tables—the same construction found in Isaac's de-basement.

Restraints accessible from holes across the table's surface tighten unbearably from gears underneath to bind his folded legs. Restraints from pulleys above bind his arms together and up. The bind around his neck pulls his head back, keeping his face arced to the ceiling. Five metal rods protrude from his spinal roots. Contusions stretch around his body. Blood covers his throat and chest—Baron's mock ⊖*ay'ena* had a spiked bit to keep him awake. After a day or two without sleep, wounds in his mouth would seep constantly. He'd nearly drowned. Many times.

Erruwyn staggers, pressing shoulder and hand into the wall.

When resonating images of his own tortures, Baron always demanded two copies. He'd assumed Isaac was the recipient of the doubles, but he'd never expected them to be displayed. He takes a quaking breath and closes his eyes. Baron had ordered twenty-two doubles. If what he'd seen last night was any indication, Isaac has removed at least thirteen paintings from halls with the most foot traffic. There are more than enough drawings to replace them. Soon, Lindenholt will host graphic depictions of his education for all to see.

He rolls his back to the wall. His eyes follow the corridor's carpet. Footmen stare from their postings at the western gallery's intersection. One returns his attention to the square he's pinning on wallpaper.

Erruwyn's diaphragm spasms. Retreating to the servant's door, he lurches across the stairwell's landing, glad for his empty stomach as he dry heaves. When his wretches slow, he presses into the corner and wipes his face with trembling hands, seeking some semblance of control. It evades him. Claws rake his scalp as the weight of repulsed glares push him to the floor. He folds up, gasping for air.

Noise comes from the floor below. Adrenaline floods him. He freezes, terrorized at the thought of being seen.

Another flood: if he's late for his summons, Isaac will relish the excuse. In fact, every delay seems orchestrated to suit that very end.

He buries his face in his hands, heaving silently. His toes twist over each other, frustrated his eyes and cheeks remain wet despite repeated wipes. When there's no air left to expel, he forces the oscillating expansion of his lungs. His fingers drop to the shiny patch of raised skin on his left forearm—the location of his first introduction to the Outland's restraints. He digs, pinches and twists. The scarring indents, torques, and begrudgingly gives way.

It's enough to move him.

He enters the study holding his left arm behind his back and his wet face to the floor.

Isaac speaks from the desk, "It's not that I regret removing the portraits, mind, but the walls felt a bit empty." He stands, slowly tapping the parchment before him. "Come here."

Erruwyn digs forward; Isaac pushes the sheet as he nears. It drifts to the floor and lands beside Erruwyn's feet—the basement illustration he'd drawn for Avrella's letter to the previous Duke. Though Isaac's mistreatment doesn't require explanation, revenge is as good a reason as any other, and his point has been made: he blames Erruwyn for Wescott's death and for the loss of his recreational facilities. The time and funds he'd spent on both have gone to waste. Waste: Isaac's least favorite word is also one of his most widely applied.

"I've had a report the gelding is missing." Isaac limps around the desk. "Most troublesome. I'd arranged a meeting with an interested buyer overmorrow. He was offering quite a large sum. As the gelding was your responsibility, you have now acquired a debt in the amount I would have received for it."

"Yes, Your Grace."

Isaac's lips curve. Erruwyn responded to his threat as he'd hoped. Now he's free of a useless horse and his demands for recompense have a solid foundation. He stops in front of the Faye. "Unfortunately, debt collection will be quite difficult since you've no wages to draw from, and scrivery income is reinvested in supplies and the other scribe's wages and the like, you see."

"Yes, Your Grace."

"So, we must look elsewhere." He ducks under Erruwyn's bowed head for a look. "Mustn't we?"

"Yes, Your Grace." His eyelids flutter.

"Yes. Still, I'm a reasonable man," he says, tugging on *Danae's* collarbone. "I'll spare you the debt of a squanderous Dowager."

Primed to wince, Erruwyn holds his forward bend as Isaac fiddles with the silver crest.

"Absurd." Isaac chuckles with little amusement. "Have you any idea the price of silver? Have you any idea how ridiculous you look?" His voice sharpens as the metal comes away. "She hoped to paint the brass, did she? Believed dangling our family's emblem from you would compensate for your aberrance? How disappointed she must've been. Poor old girl. As though your room and board weren't enough of an insult." He tosses the silver on the desk and turns back to gauge how well his words are landing.

Erruwyn lowers his head further.

He hadn't seen it that way. He'd assumed the crest was a signal of acceptance.

Presumptuous, Baron said.

But that can't be. Lysbeth still sees him lower. She already wants to be rid of *Anese*—be rid of him, his diff-errancies. After novelty, a burden.

Abhorrent.

If he was truly accepted, they would've given him what everyone else wore. Was the silver meant to mock him? Did all the daughters of *me͠na* know? He'd worn it so proudly.

Insolent.

Of course they knew—knew he would do, or say, or wear anything for their kinship; to follow Baron's instruction, to look where he belonged and see them. They knew he was desperate. Afraid. Lonely. Despised. Worthless.

Nothing.

Shaking fingers dig.

Isaac tilts his chin thoughtfully. "Oh, yes. Of which I am reminded, your living arrangements are changing." He limps back around the desk and slides another piece of parchment across it. "Once the others arrive, you will recite this exactly as written. Exactly."

"Yes, Your Grace," Erruwyn whispers. He blinks to free his vision and glances at the page. His heart drops into a well of nausea. "Your Grace, plea—" He flinches as Isaac's palm strikes mahogany. Displaced air nudges the parchment. He freezes under the Duke's eager scrutiny until the opening door forces a breath.

Brom, Ms. Makensi, Mr. Sandel, and Konja file in, disquieted by both the current image and ones they'd passed in the hall—Brom especially, as he distinctly recalls destroying the illustrations at Wescott's prison.

Isaac passes each a folded note and rests his fingertips lightly on the desk's edge. "Before you open your lists, Erruwyn has something to say."

Erruwyn digs enough to inhale. He digs enough to open his mouth. He digs enough to force air through shaky lips and stain the floor with his voice. "Your association with me has soiled His Grace's good opinion. You and those listed are to leave at once without reference. No questions or protests will be tolerated." He digs, grimacing through quiet tears. "Please forgive me."

"Ah." Isaac clucks. "No additions."

———————————

"I'm sure he'll understand, Lys. Regret is inherent to rows, that's why we struggle so to avoid them," Elane offers. Seeing no effect, she tries again, "He must feel as badly as you do for mentioning Uncle Jaspyr as he did."

"I should hope not. What he said wasn't kind, but it wasn't spiteful, either." Lysbeth turns from her desk, eyes still pink from her goodbye with Corah. "I was very wrong, Elane."

"Then go to him and tell him so," she insists, gently tugging a thread of her canvas.

Lysbeth nods, continuing after a pause, "What are we to do if Granmama passes? And how could I possibly leave you here if Jaques succeeds in negotiations next week?"

"Don't fret on that. Isaac doesn't consider me worthwhile prey; I was spared your trouble projecting docility." Elane lowers her gaze to make another stitch. "I'm quite sure he'll forget I'm even here."

"But—" Lysbeth starts at the knock across the room. "Come."

Ani enters pale and leans against the latching door; the cousins stand over dropping stomachs. Elane steps to the maid, gingerly steering petite shoulders to a couch.

Lysbeth joins them. "What is it, Ani?"

"His Gr—" Ani's sharp breath cuts her words; she twists a handkerchief and takes a breath. "His Grace has dismissed over half of the staff without reference, My Lady. Everyone's crowded 'round the kitchen block to see the postings."

The Ladies share a panicked glance above her head.

Isaac's designs are viciously clever.

In order to conserve funds during long Kingswars, nobles often abandon their country estates-dismissing most, or all, servants until the family's return. Though this practice is historically uncommon for Edenshire's nobility, the reduction in staff won't be viewed with great suspicion. Moreover, without reference, rumors of Isaac's cruelty will be seen as nothing more than the slander of disgruntled employees who'd failed to secure their employer's good word.

The message is clear: each of Lindenholt's souls are strung to Isaac's marionette bar, and he can pull them anyway he likes.

"Brom and every Keeper but Brynen's men," Ani continues, "The quintet. The scribes. Even Miss Makensi."

Lysbeth stands in shock. "But the Sandels have been with us for generations! Konja? The *Marshal*?" She begins a dazed pace.

Elane squeezes Ani's arm. "At least you're safe."

"Yes." Lysbeth's fingers wring. "He would never find another maid willing to look after both of us for what father paid you."

When Elane was offered her own maid, she'd refused. As a matter of status and image, this answer was not particularly well received by the late Duke, however, when Ani suggested she take the salary of a maid looking after one presented Lady instead of two, he'd acquiesced. Touched by the affection inherent to the offer, he'd also turned a blind eye to the extravagant Winter Solstice presents Ani received from his daughter and niece each year in compensation.

"Lys, you have the employees' previous listings, don't you?" Elane asks. "Could we write references ourselves and send them along to their last addresses?"

"I was thinking the same." Lysbeth's feet can't decide where to take her. "But I'm not sure how we'd sneak them out for delivery."

Elane's eyes trail her cousin. "Perhaps we should use Roske? Write them quickly to lessen the risk of discovery and determine the logistics later?"

"Yes, agreed." Lysbeth moves for the door, stopping briefly as Ani speaks.

"My Lady, no one's seen Erruwyn since this morning, and—"

Color draining, Lysbeth spins and walk faster.

"My Lady, wait! The paintings!" Ani's knuckles rush to her chin as she stands.

Lysbeth throws the door open and stops. She grips the doorframe.

Lily Haywood's portrait is gone from its spot on the opposite wall.

Something has replaced it. She squints and steps closer.

A body? But it hangs oddly; contorted.

Wrung.

She covers her mouth and turns away before her mind can process more.

Erruwyn's words flash:

Marquess is a hammer without chisel. Striking low to de-base.

Isaac would do anything to knock your foundation from under you; to tear away parts of you until you resemble what he wants as quickly as possible. She forces herself to breathe and looks down the hall.

Six paintings have been replaced. Keeping her eyes low, she moves to the intersection of the eastern gallery and peeks around the corner. The footmen have gone to the kitchen block, but the paintings in the gallery are accounted for—Isaac wouldn't risk an unexpected caller seeing the new drawings.

Continuing down the hall, she lifts *Anese* higher in her bodice to reduce its muffling.

Corah's door stands open after the eastern library; the room's emptiness twists her chest. At the Grand Gallery she turns around, glimpsing enough of a square for the partial interpretation of another acutely disturbing scene. She feels it keenly after her words last night and takes a moment to steady herself before backtracking. With no other anima—no other bodies nearby—every slight sound is loud. Her weight presses floorboards, her shoes tap, her skirt swishes.

》

She turns down the eastern gallery. The front drawing room's curtains are drawn, encasing the space in a dingy foreboding. A cherrywood cane surfaces in memory, demanding her attention.

Isaac has permeated Lindenholt; filled it barren with Baron's echoes.

She slips off her shoes. The Grand Chamber's marble is cold against her feet. Nearing the western wing, she lifts 》*Anese* completely.

》 *wail _ peal*

Lysbeth hides in the armor stand's niche, holding her breath to focus on the faint sensation. Despair, fear. Dread.

She hesitates, afraid to go further. If the only remaining guards are mercenaries, she can't assume their goodwill any longer. Isaac knows money drives the straightest lines of motivation.

Distant footsteps.

She rushes back to the eastern wing on the balls of her feet, ashamed of her cowardice and impotently worried. She rounds the doorframe of her sitting room with her shoes held to her stomach.

"Did you find him?" Elane asks, arm around Ani.

"Not exactly." Lysbeth shakily lowers 》*Anese*. "Though I'd rather not discuss it. Let's begin the references."

Ani confirms what names she can and the cousins set to work through puffy eyes. Without *?Roske*, they've only written eight endorsements by the time they're called to the Grand Drawing Room to sit under Isaac's thumb before supper. They move through the arch, faltering momentarily.

Isaac's heels cross over bars of welts on Erruwyn's back. An open sore on his inner arm drools idly. Reasserting their grip on composure, the Ladies take their spots on the couch. Lysbeth bites the tip of her tongue to relieve the dryness of her mouth. "I understand Your Grace has cut many loose," she says evenly.

"Trimming the fat, Lady Lysbeth." Isaac turns a page. "I've no idea why you kept on three scribes when this one completes orders faster alone."

"A little more fat might be of use if we're attacked again."

"Oh, don't fret. You and Erruwyn will be quite well-guarded."

Lysbeth falls silent before her trepidity reveals itself. After several minutes, she wiggles her shoe. When Erruwyn doesn't respond, she clicks her sole lightly. His head pivots over a long moment. A red eye watches her *wox'ua*: sorry go *ʒmę͡ ŋa*.

An hour later, Erruwyn drags his forehead over wood as he pushes himself from Isaac's path. When the pins and needles in his legs reduce, he returns to Avrella's room. Natty lets him in, and having seen the illustrations, kindly refrains from social contrivance before excusing herself.

Splintered and shaken, he fumbles to the bed and rests his hand on edge of the mattress. Warm rivulets pioneer trails down his cheeks; those after follow the path.

He understands now that Wescott's death is meaningless. Baron lives on quite merrily in the dark fissures between Erruwyn's Archival shelves, ready to ooze out and hem in as soon as an opportunity presents itself. After several grim minutes, his eyes gather enough courage to meet Avrella's face. She rests serenely.

He pulls chronicles forward, revisiting the details of their textures: ƺ*me͡ŋa*'s fond smirk and peering eyes. Her chuckle and discerning fingers. Her love.

When he rejoins the present, he finds his hand has already made its way to hers. He lifts and presses her knuckles into his cheek, terraforming distributaries.

Lysbeth nears within half an hour.

ƺ *wail_peal*

Erruwyn's dread tears him from the bed. Seeing Avrella again has restored some lucidity, but de-basement aims to destabilize from the foundations up. Unable to bolt or hide, he stares at the floor and grips his elbow behind him, ready to dig as Lysbeth enters.

Noting Natty's absence, she extends her arms and moves to him briskly. When he steps back, her approach halts. Her hands drop under gasping tears. His neck strains as he joins her.

The Outland's emotional puppetry is still very difficult for Erruwyn to grasp. Among the people, feeling and influencing each other as they do, the delivery of emotional pain is avoided whenever possible, and weaponizing misery for entertainment or revenge is profoundly alien. Unfortunately, Erruwyn's instinctual equating of expression with truth leaves him susceptible to emotional manipulation, and he's taken most Outland comments and opinions at face value—in fact, it was this facet of Erruwyn's purity that first drew the Warden's notice.

Though Erruwyn has tempered his instinct to believe disparaging words of other servants, he's viewed Lysbeth as one among his people, and fully trusted her intentions. She hadn't spoken to hurt him, she'd spoken to correct his misinterpretation of her feelings—to correct his abhorrent, insolent presumption. The shock of seeing his illustrations had reaffirmed Baron's lessons, though the affirmation was hardly necessary. When at the mercy of malicious whims, blaming and doubting oneself is often the path of least resistance. There's no one else on the road, after all.

"I'm sorry," Lysbeth cries quietly. "Please, Erruwyn, I was hurt and angry. I spoke bitterly, but I didn't truly mean it."

Erruwyn breathes through his confusion. The path can't be wholly empty, though. No such path exists. There are always trailblazes, markers from others offering to assist if you look for them. Wayfinders, even. On occasion.

Fighting every burrowed tendril of Baron's hold, he lifts his eyes to observe Lysbeth's texture. His voice is faint and desperate for clarity, "Do you care for me?"

She moves closer, eyebrows and lips carving incredulous sorrow. "Very much."

✴ ∿∿

Erruwyn exhales injurious relief as she steps in.

Clasping tightly, *da'he⌐nar⌐uah* arrive at an unspoken conclusion: if every part of their world must come undone, their mooring will be the last to give way.

"Will you forgive me?" Lysbeth whispers.

His answer appears as fingers through her hair. "Will you?"

"Yes, but there's little to forgive, as usual." She sniffles. "Please don't believe me if I'm cruel. Ask me to clarify; make me think on what I've said. But no matter what, don't believe Isaac."

"I will try," he says, softly earnest, resting his cheek on her crown.

She grips ✴*Danae*'s spine. Her mind darts over scenarios. Perhaps it's not too late for ✴*Ruah*. Perhaps she could direct it to incapacitate Isaac and no one else—the remaining employees might even understand. Then she and Erruwyn could run.

They could run...

She grits her teeth. Nowhere. Even if they managed to make it to Jaques' estate without being seen, there's no conceivable way to control for gossip in houses with a triple digit staff. Someone would talk the moment a reward was offered, if not before.

"Don't give up hope. Jaques is coming soon," she reminds them both.

He nods, molding to her new position as she dabs her eyes.

"After Corah left, Isaac had Mr. Tenson collect our silver. If he knew about Anese, the necklace you gave me seems to have worked in its place. Has he confiscated your things, too?"

"Yes. Though I am uncertain for the trunk, the *ay'tuan* tree was taken to a room nearby me."

"Where are you kept? I felt Anese in the Chamber this afternoon."

"Below. A room to stay beneath him, always." When she pulls back in alarm, he adds, "It is not as it was. It is closer to how I lived with Marshal." His eyes dampen again. "I caused their absence, *nar⌐uah*."

She shakes her head furiously. "No, it's all Isaac's doing."

He runs a thumb across her cheekbone, clarifying with heavy grief, "I am present."

Lysbeth's blurry gaze shifts to Alder's desk. She's sure Isaac would've made similar changes without Erruwyn, but it's unlikely they would've been quite so drastic—or quite as overwhelmingly cruel.

"It's still not your fault. I can't deny the effects of Alder's letter, but I believe his intentions were noble. Had he an inkling, his quill would've stayed dry. I'm sure of it." Her eyes return to Erruwyn. Though she still doesn't know how much stock to place in his Concepts, she wants to include him in her decision. "And if Ruah did need the letter to dampen Otay's discord, then its purpose has been served."

She takes his hand and walks to the desk. Tears land on faded heirloom ink as she slides each page into their leather jacket. Turning back to Erruwyn, she hooks her arm through his and offers a corner. He pinches it guiltily, regarding Lysbeth with sad, grateful eyes as they step to the fireplace.

Leaning forward, *ḍa'he͡ nar͡ uah* feed the flame.

———————

Erruwyn isn't seen during the fraught week that follows.

Confined to a room below the western wing, a desk, a bed, and scribal supplies are his roommates and two mercenaries guard his door—though they won't stop his leaving should the Echoes return.

In the mornings, Lysbeth and Elane write employee references in the sitting room. They keep the stack hidden, aiming to sneak it out with Jaques. Erruwyn resonates texts.

At luncheon, the cousins move to Avrella's room. Her condition shows no improvement, and Doctor Howe fears her spell may have been a stroke. Erruwyn resonates texts.

The Ladies stay by the Matriarch's side until the Grand Drawing Room bell is rung each evening. Afraid Erruwyn will reap any anger she sows in Isaac, Lysbeth remains completely silent in her brother's company—an hour while he reads, and another while they eat. Erruwyn resonates texts.

After supper, Isaac descends to the basement, and the cousins return to the sitting room—where Lysbeth's tremendous anxiety over Jaques' visit and Erruwyn's wellbeing compels her to pace and wring until bedtime.

Without the wages of workshop employees to eat up funds, Erruwyn's scribal skills are paying off his false debt for Kiky while his role as Isaac's pin cushion covers debts for Wescott and the basement. Fortunately, the latter installment plan is limited in scope—Erruwyn's work requires steady hands, and serious injury would risk the Duke's plan to bring Erruwyn north in thirty-two days.

Though Erruwyn's physical suffering is less than what he's experienced previously, he puts on a good show to satisfy Isaac's urges faster: His free time is limited and he's been pursuing a project of his own.

Knowing Lysbeth was able to feel *ꝗÁneṣe* from the Grand Chamber, Erruwyn has endeavored to produce a *≤m'aẹn* she should be able to feel from her room: a keen—the frequency of *≤m'aẹn* which has the single greatest effect on *ay͡ na* alloys.

It's an ambitious task.

The first step to willfully producing notes between emotions is to understand the textures of an emotion—including physical textures in the throat—and sliding up or down from it along the scale of *Theam*. Eventually, with enough experience, patience, and practice, notes on the scale can be willed without invoking their nearby emotions.

To avoid accidental activation, *ay ̂na* is only forged to respond to notes of willed *şm'aen*. Pieces of *Danae* and fins of the people's vessels are among the few exceptions, with the latter specifically forged to respond to the emotional note of keening—the note which will articulate the fins fastest.

As great despair is rarely experienced among the people, keening is believed to be unmasterable—as the lack of familiarity prevents their study of its texture, and its note by association.

The cold rest of *◊Ruah*: The people are too happy to fully understand the depths of great loss, but if they understood great loss, they'd be able to escape their hunters without sacrificing a *da'he ̂na* to force their keen.

Erruwyn's experiences in Avonleigh have brought him close to understanding keening's texture, far closer than he ever would've been had he remained among the people. Though it's painful, he brings himself to keening's cusp each night, hoping to break through. If he can master the note, he'll be able to reach Lysbeth—enough to let her know he's thinking of her, at least.

This is important to Erruwyn, who doubts Jaques' barter will be successful.

It's important because Erruwyn plans to accompany Isaac north voluntarily.

It's important because he won't hesitate to answer *◊Ruah*'s demand when Isaac forces him to fight.

It's important because Lysbeth will be free of Isaac forever.

He needs her to know she was on his mind every moment before then—that if ridding her of Isaac meant Erruwyn's execution, it's what he wanted. It's what he'd planned.

Installment duly paid, Isaac lowers his cane, tugs his jacket, and slicks back his hair.

As the door shuts, Erruwyn rises to a kneel for practice.

———————

The week concludes when the Baron's images are mercifully removed for Jaques' arrival.

He stands on the terrace, welcomed by a servant's assembly of thirty and a dour mood.

Inside, a notable amount of décor has been stripped from the few rooms with open doors. Avrella, Corah, and Erruwyn are absent. Lysbeth and Elane look despondent and thinner than Jaques remembers. He'd gone through a similar phase after Ryn's death, but their suffering is clearly spurred on by Isaac. He offers sincere condolences, keeping opinions on staff and décor to himself.

Sitting in the Grand Drawing Room before supper, his attempts to speak with

Lysbeth alone are continually thwarted. She hasn't been answering his letters, and Isaac's insistent presence alludes to the reason—she can't answer what she's been kept from receiving.

The four dine in silence. As they finish, Isaac orders a footman to ready the den for their negotiations. The group stands. Lysbeth and Elane retire to the sitting room. Jaques follows Isaac to the den, slowing past the door.

Prostrating before a richly upholstered chair, Erruwyn's expanding ribs morph the topographic map of clay red, navy blue, and pine green charting his figure. Ink-splattered fingers find shelter in a thick, Finnigar rug as Isaac sits and drapes legs over silver. Unfolding parchment from his breast pocket, the Duke clears his throat.

"'Ysbet.'" He stops to look at Jaques. "Really, Gyenna, you're an educated man. Feigning your inability to pronounce an 'L' couldn't possibly obstruct your ability to write one." Returning to the paper, he continues, "'Ysbet, we must discuss alternatives for negotiations now that the only reasonable Haywood man has very sadly departed us.'" He sighs and folds the note. "Please speak freely, Gyenna."

Polishing his veneer, Jaques pieces the scene together. Isaac couldn't help showing off what he's been up to. Maltreating servants is a tradition as old as an age is long, but given southern Avonleigh's benevolent opinion of Erruwyn, some might raise an eyebrow if Jaques spread word—in which case, Isaac would flash evidence of Jaques' conspiring. It wouldn't matter what the conspiring was about; the thin words of a bastard Duke can't afford to lose weight.

Isaac is unlikely to agree to anything he asks for, but he has to try.

"Forgive me, 'Denshire, I didn't realize your sister's involvement in her own marriage plans would cause you to feel so imperiled." Jaques pulls his mouth to the side as Isaac's nostrils flare. "If you wish to negotiate as your Sovereign asks, I will do so. If not, I will return to Crora. Hm?"

Isaac reads the intention. Sovereign Hinri entrusted Jaques' negotiations to the Duke of Edenshire. As the current Duke of Edenshire, he must come away with something.

"I'm sure we can reach an arrangement but allow me to save us both some time. The Faye is not up for discussion."

"Why?" Jaques squints.

Unblinking, Isaac tugs his jacket and crosses his ankles over Erruwyn's spine. "He's very comfortable."

The men hold steady gazes.

———————

In the eastern wing, Lysbeth's pacing and wringing have doubled in speed. By the time Elane convinces her to sit, Ani knocks on the door. She enters at their call, eyes pink and voice wavering.

"His Grace has finalized negotiations. Lady Elane and Jaques are to marry in Crora next week. I'm to help pack for an early departure." She sniffles and pulls a small scroll from her sleeve. "He snuck me this to deliver."

Lysbeth's fingers are cold as she unfurls the message. Though her conscious mind fails to comprehend Ani's words, her vision blurs. She blinks and shakes her head, confused by the blur's return as she sinks to the couch. Swaying from her own shock, Elane sinks, too.

"Let me see, Lys," she whispers. Moving an arm around her cousin, she takes the paper and reads aloud:

> *Lysbeth, forgive me. He learned of our arrangement by my letters. I thought it better to secure one of you than none. My heart breaks. Elane and I will search for some way to release you and Erruwyn. I swear it.*

Elane sighs mournfully, rocking a now-convulsive Lysbeth and lifting her damp gaze to Ani's. After a long moment, she nods to begin packing without her.

Lysbeth cries until the skin under her nose is raw. She cries until her eyelids burn and swell. She cries until each sob forces an unwanted yawn from her throat. Distraught at the sight—and the outlook for all involved—Elane pulls her to bed, hoping the exhaustion of her grief will be enough for sleep. Their hands clasp under streaming tears. Lysbeth heaves low.

"Take the references. And Ani."

Elane's lips part in surprise.

"Even married, Jaques would be the last to discourage your dalliance."

"Oh, Lys," Elane whispers. Face wrenched, she pulls Lysbeth close and holds her tightly until sleep grants a more merciful embrace.

Below the western wing, Erruwyn lays on the floor of his cell.

The evening's collection had occurred with interest—triumphant exhilaration propelling the Duke's cane. Erruwyn waits for Isaac's footsteps to fade completely before attempting to push his shaky shoulders from the floor.

The servant's meals are fuller than they'd been before Lindenholt's fat-trimming, but Erruwyn lacks an appetite. The intersections of *Danae* and *m'ay-tut* contract to fit him properly, but the weight loss will soon be undeniable. Isaac won't be happy. He wants a proper specimen to show the Sovereign in twenty-four days.

Leaning forward on his palms, he drags his knees to a kneel.

It's dark.

He's excessively sore.

He practices.

da'he͡na mourn their Calling differently than those they leave behind. As with Erem, the wound is shallower with knowledge of the people's safety and harmony—and understanding there's no chance of returning acclimatizes them to their new life faster, accelerating the wound's closure. When Erruwyn practices, he doesn't think of the happiness of his people or the safety of his twiceborn, as those thoughts don't bring him pain.

Instead, his mind wanders the pathless plains of loss. Wide, flat expanses of muted grass, dotted with painfully vibrant memories—always enough to notice their shortage. To notice there's room for so many, many more.

There should be more.

He thinks of ⸰*me͡ŋa* and her daughters. He thinks of ⸰*Anese*.

⸰*wail*

He thinks of the void of Lindenholt's soul: Marshal, Sandel, Konja, Makensi, the anima of those who brought Lindenholt to life.

He thinks of Lysbeth, beaming in the Grand Library. The Offering when she'd laughed at his purr. Spring Equinox when lune-pigment lit her face. The water gardens at PromSol. Their dance under the canopy in Autumn.

⸰*wail*

The hope in her eyes as she'd told him her wish for their path. How all she wanted was to celebrate their song.

But the path is closed now.

And their song will end soon.

⚕ ㋡

Upstairs in Lysbeth's nightstand, ⸰*Anese* rattles in tightly folded cloth.

———————————

Lysbeth wakes to grey light through her windows; her tears begin again.

Weighted dread pulls her through an uneaten breakfast. Sniffles and stifled sobs carry her, Elane, and Ani through their last dressing. When footmen come to collect Elane's trunk, the women hold each other tightly, heaving through a final, grievous goodbye.

No attempts at condolence are made. There's no reassurance to be had.

Cleft, drained, and hollowed, she sinks beside her bed after the door shuts. Before there was uncertainty; now her path is clear, and it stretches before her unceasingly: Isaac will keep her and Erruwyn as baubles in a box for the rest of their lives.

She opens her nightstand and digs for ⸰*Anese* under the false panel—feeling now it's her only friend in the world. She unwraps the cloth and coils the chain around her knee.

Discovering Lindenholt's handkerchief supply is ill-equipped to handle the volume of her grief, she stops wiping her face by teatime. When she doesn't appear by supper, Natty comes to check up.

Unsettled by the mass she finds stretched over the bed, the maid sets to work. After a washed face and a clean nightgown, she drags Lysbeth to the sitting room while she returns to change the sheets.

Once on the couch, Lysbeth's tears roll again. The bereaved's contradiction: absence intensifies presence. She can't exist in her apartments without seeing Elane, Ani, Avrella, and Erruwyn everywhere.

Natty tries her best at comfort, and once Lysbeth tapers to tearful hiccups, bravely marches to the Grand Chamber to catch Isaac after his supper. She stands tall through her offer to look after Lysbeth for free, now that Ani's gone, and unable to resist, he accepts. She watches him leave for the basement and returns to put Lysbeth to bed. Taking a spot on the edge of mattress, she pulls blankets to her young mistress' shoulders and reaches for a pile of freshly washed handkerchiefs.

"You know, I've always loved birds," she says, expertly folding squares. "I can never seem to stay away long, which is why I made a point of befriending the coop master here as I'd done at Walstead. People don't realize how hard-up coop masters are for company, but it's true, seeing as they work alone."

Sniffling quietly, Lysbeth watches her new maid add another handkerchief to the neat stack.

"He's not a bad sort, perhaps a little rough around the edges, but making good company takes practice, and as I said..." She smiles, leaving one square on the bed and placing the stack on the nightstand. "Now Jaques knows his messages have been intercepted, His Grace can have no reason to suspect any more will arrive for you."

Lysbeth wipes her face. "And perhaps no reason to think I would send any?"

"It stands to reason, apparently."

"Remind me to write you a reference tomorrow, in case." Lysbeth smiles weakly. "Thank you, Natty."

"Of course, My Lady." She squeezes Lysbeth's shoulder. "Now get some sleep."

The door closes.

Lysbeth rolls onto her back and reaches for her mother's pillow, staring at the outline of her bed's canopy for an indeterminate length of time. The raw, collapsing feeling in her stomach swells to her throat. Large, slow tears spill down her temples, tickling her hairline and ears.

⚥ ₪

She gasps. Bolting up, a frantic fabric-tossing uncovers silver on her knee. She unclasps the chain and brings the pendant to her neck.

Weeping through a chapped smile, Lysbeth rocks her mother's pillow as ⚥*Anese* bursts in deliberate patterns against her collarbones.

———————————

Over the next eight days, Isaac enjoys the quiet, the enormous funds in his accounts, and his time with Erruwyn.

Lysbeth keeps to Avrella's room and stays up for Erruwyn's keen each night.

Erruwyn pays his debts.

This evening's collection was moderate—the Duke needs him in decent shape for their departure in sixteen days. Footsteps fade.

Dragging into a kneel, Erruwyn readies his keen and freezes.

He waits to be sure.

Afir's *ṡm'aẹn*. It's distant.

His breath comes quick.

Brynen guards him tonight; there's a chance.

He moves to the door and softly pats the wood. "Brynen."

Brynen starts and looks up. Other than the unpleasant noises of Isaac's visits, he hasn't heard Erruwyn in weeks. Though far from thrilled with his new post, Isaac had doubled his pay, and his family comes first. He peeks at the chair next to him. Chrys is asleep.

His graveled voice is hushed, "Yeah?"

After a pause, a polite request leaks around iron and wood: "Please allow me to leave."

The mercenary grins in spite of himself. He's liked the Faye ever since his interrogation and, generally speaking, giants respect anyone who can disarm them with regularity. "Why now?"

"*ȥaf'ir* has come."

Brynen's head tilts in surprise—he'd witnessed the bird's previous visit and been just as awed as the rest. He glances around and thinks. Other than his men, Lindenholt staffs twenty-five servants. Only people are guarded, not the grounds. But even if the risk is low...

"Please," Erruwyn tries again, tugging on the truth Brynen is most likely to understand, "she carries the words of my family."

The giant's large palm slides down his face and pulls on his beard. He sighs long. "Alright, go out the side."

Thin and discolored, Erruwyn squints at the room's fire light as the door opens. "Thank you," he whispers.

Brynen nods. "Hurry."

Erruwyn does.

Walking quickly to the western servant's exit, he steps outside and crouches against Lindenholt's stone. Afir is likely exploring. She returns his *ṡm'aẹn* promptly, and soon a wide head on a tall neck tips around the corner.

On seeing Erruwyn, Afir's downward-arcing feathers spread into a lacey crown. He signals for quiet; the crown dips flat before erecting again. Puffy with long-calm-down, she trots around the corner. The wall takes a feather as she drags against it. Erruwyn rises. His head barely reaches her shoulder; her crown towers six feet above.

They greet each other formally. Afir's long tail stretches towards the sky, wings unfolded partially due to the wall's proximity. Extending her neck, she rests her large, curved beak on Erruwyn's outstretched hand. He draws her close and lays the arc of her bottom beak across his forehead. When his nose presses into her chin feathers, a quiet recitation of his twiceborn's ⸗*aen* comes from within Afir's throat:

‖ ⟨*erru͡wyn* • *ki͡* ◊*Ruah* • *ir'ie-roe'it'ua* • *ʒj'ol͡ na* • ⟨*af'ir-ke* ‖

Taking several shaky breaths, Erruwyn pulls back and *wox'ua*s: find Kiky. Afir's feathers smooth as she bounces away. He reenters the door, pausing to steel his nerves before returning to his cell.

"Got the message?" Brynen whispers.

"Yes. Thank you." He glances at the cell door. "Please forgive me."

Brynen falls to the ground; Chrys joins him without waking.

Erruwyn eyes them guiltily.

Taking a branch from ∪*ay'ena*, he shoves a silver tool into the inner port of his cell's lock, hoping the implied scene will spare them Isaac's fury once his escape is discovered. Buzzing, he moves through dark passages to the last known location of his tree: the storeroom a few halls away. He removes another tool from ∪*ay'ena*'s branch and picks the lock as he'd been shown two months ago—when Mattor had drawn the lot to fight Erruwyn at practice, but Brom was late to unlock the weapons.

He peeks in, buzzing to the tree in darkness and returning with it to the side exit. Crouching against the exterior wall again, he removes ⟪*Danae*'s sealing horns with trembling hands and picks up Afir's long-calm-down. He folds the feather in half and lays the horns between, securing the items together with ⟩*m-aen͡hu'ay*'s chains. After snapping the bundle to ⟪*Danae*'s hip, he unfolds Kiky's *ay-tut* from the tree and calls to the woods with ⧚*m'aen*.

His incessant hissing makes him easy to relocate, and Afir soon leads Kiky up Lindenholt's slope. Erruwyn takes a relieved breath at the missing horse blanket. He hadn't been thinking clearly when he'd tightened the straps, and he'd worried about sores—but even buckles are no match for Kiky's wriggling.

He pries a curry brush from the horse's *ay-tut* and works swiftly. Afir watches the process, alternating fluffy affection and sleek inquisitiveness. When he's done what he can, Erruwyn guides Kiky's hooves into the filigree. The silver climbs, closes, and locks.

Gripping the *ay'tuan* tree, metal layers curl into a crescent at Erruwyn's ⧚*m'aen*. He attaches its vertices to silver intersections on Kiky's hindquarters and swivels it behind the horse's tail.

He mounts.

⟩ *hiss*

Lysbeth's head jerks from the pillow. She's been waiting for Erruwyn's keen, but now he's close. Very close. Somehow.

As she ties her robe, a tap comes from the window—fifteen feet off the ground. She throws back the curtains; Afir's large eye stares up at her through the bottom pane. Lysbeth covers her yelp and listens for guards in the eastern gallery before sliding the window open and leaning out.

Erruwyn stands on Kiky's shoulders just below, motioning her back. When the horse rears, Erruwyn leaps and clings to the sill. Knowing this game from climbing falls back home, Afir moves her head under his dangling foot and lifts. He pours through the window, rolling to soften his fall. Lysbeth watches wide-eyed as he lands in a crouch.

da'he͡ nar͡uah stare silently, taking each other in. They'd both lost weight. Lysbeth's face is raw, Erruwyn's body is bruised. He stands.

They step to each other. Urgent arms claw at backs; tumultuous breaths source tears.

"Has ⸝*me͡ na* woken?" he asks through quiet effort.

Lysbeth shakes her head. His hold tightens.

"How have you come?" she whispers. "What's happened?"

⸝ *hiss*

He brings the bundle from ⸝*Danae*'s hip to Lysbeth, squeezing her against him. "I wish for you to carry the flame. It has many purposes."

She shifts from Erruwyn's neck to glance at the parcel. Tears fall steadily as he waits. She takes it with trepidation and raises expectant eyes.

"⸝*af'ir* carries word. ◊*Ruah* has demanded," he explains weakly. "I am to assist with Restoration. I could not depart before seeing you."

"Depart?" Her fingers curl over ⸝*Danae*'s star. "I don't understand."

⸝ *hiss*

"⸝*r'uah͡ na*. ◊*Ruah* has demanded the Echoes' attunement." His neck strains.

"Otay?"

"Yes. It is likely we will fight."

"*Fight*? W-when will you return?"

⸝ ಡ

Erruwyn's face is tranquil under streams. "I am to be re-embraced."

Lysbeth's lungs bellow. Her features wind in acute panic.

"If we fight, if I live, I will suffer every day gone from you—" His voice breaks. "My whole life. Please know it."

Her head shakes in pained denial, unable to hear the message through the words. "If you live?" she whispers.

He takes her horrified face in his hands. "Please know I do not wish to go from you."

With no break on the reel, Lysbeth's mind unspools. Her teeth chatter in cold shock;

her hands tingle from too much air.

"Ladyship. Teammate." Grief-stricken eyes dance over her features. "*nar⁻uah.*" Long thumbs wipe her cheeks and tuck back her hair. His face wrenches through a pained exhale, "*lysbeth.*"

Her trembling halts. Impact suspends her in stillness until a heave folds her back into *Danae*. Erruwyn constricts around her, keening silently.

Lysbeth's desperation claws up her throat, shrieking from the cage of her ribs, driving her to beg, plead, bid—pin him down with *ke'ra-tu* and call the guards if she must. She fights the monster with gritted teeth and bated breath, enough to keep it contained. No matter how desperate, she won't beg Erruwyn to remain Isaac's pet. Pleading with him to take her along would only hurt more—forcing him to deny her request, forcing herself to hear the denial. Only Outlanders cradled by *wa't'un* are taken in, and *r'uah⁻na* outranks her bidding, even if she did unmuzzle the beast.

No words could matter.

But *ke'ra-tu*...

When her heaves reduce to breathy sobs, tremoring fingers pull *Anese* to her throat. Erruwyn watches through water, and in a display of absolute trust, kneels. Lysbeth holds his eyes and gasps through gnarled lips.

"Live."

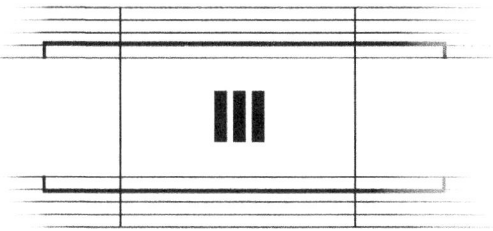

Erruwyn and Kiky streak over Avonleigh's countryside, reflecting just enough moon in silver to be seen as a wisp of light by any who happen to glimpse them.

Afir flies above, leading the way. Erruwan's message had been short and straightforward. "◊_Ruah_ demands. Echoes attune or mute. The people embrace. Follow ⟨_af'ir_."

The information he'd sent back months ago must have prompted debate.

When a major question arises, consensus is called, and all twenty-five thousand gather in ⌒_roo'da_. Like most of the island, echea[33] and resonant amplifiers abound in ⊙_ma⌐joc_'s center. Those who wish to make an argument are given a day and time to speak. The ≤_m'aen_ of charismatic individuals tends to resonate most widely, and those whose _kw'da_ leads the song are given additional time.

The debates can last for days, weeks, or even scatter over months, but Consensus is only reached when ⌒_roo'da_ sings in unison.

Harmony. A-chord.

It must have arrived quickly.

The sun will come within an hour and Erruwyn is exhausted. Fortunately, Kiky and Afir are well trained to work together, and his directing isn't required. Unfortunately, the energy he saves is expended on wave after wave of guilt and self-loathing.

There's no guide for abandoning one's _nar⌐uah_; it was never understood to be an option. If circumstances at Lindenholt were different, he might feel simmering anguish instead of blistering agony, but as it stands, he's left Lysbeth alone with an Outlander whose discord rivals the Baron's in more ways than he's comfortable exploring—they'd both even kept images of Lily Haywood in their dens.

Afir's ≤_m'aen_ changes at the first whiffs of ocean air. Erruwyn glances up through ⌒_ay'enru_ to see the beginning of her descent. A short sea cliff comes into view below her. Lapping waves sound beyond.

ʊ

A new ≤_m'aen_.

---

[33] *Acoustic resonators used to absorb unwanted frequencies.*

His heart keeps time with Kiky's racing hooves. Afir leads them to a safe path down the cliff and glides to a tall rock far along the beach. Kiky canters over the waterline's packed sand, slowing to a trot as they near. Erruwyn pulls ⌒*ay'enru* and ⌣*ay'ena* from his face and slides from Kiky's back.

↺*ji* Dawn steps from behind the rock.

ᵶ 〰〰 Dusk's legs refuse to hold him.

They cry quietly as Erruwan joins him in the sand.

Hopping from the rock in long-calm-down, Afir pushes the pair together with the bend of her enormous wings and settles her fluffy belly against them, very pleased both of her tragically down-less fledglings are together again. Knee-to-knee, the twiceborn reach forward, grabbing arms, shoulders, and necks.

Erruwan's face screws at the scars and bruises on her brother's body. When she notices his fall[34] blowing to the side of his neck instead of his hips, she cries harder.

Nerves shot, Erruwyn's mind compartmentalizes in self-preservation—a labyrinth of dams granting him use of speech. "How can it be. Say." He heaves quietly. "Is ⸨*er'em* near?"

"◉*ma* ⌐*joc* watches her." Erruwan swallows and breathes, regaining enough control to consider practicality.

↺*buzz*

"I will say how on *xewa–set*. We must depart." She stands and pulls on his arms.

Afir and Kiky support Dusk's walk to the scow behind the rock. Dawn shoves the first three-quarters into water, holding it steady as Kiky embarks and lays down. Erruwyn climbs in after and folds beside before joining Erruwan's buzz. Reaching forward, he lifts a socketed chain attached to the bow and tosses it to Afir.

Watching with smooth curiosity from her perch on the rock, she catches it and loops her long neck to slot it to her breast bracing. After it locks, she spreads sixteen feet of wings and compacts her flight feathers until nearly solid. The sea wind lifts her slowly. Her legs swing back to her tail feathers, which narrow and flair at the tip as she rises.

Erruwan waits for a suitable wave to lift the half-buoyant scow. When it comes, she pushes—a signal to Afir. The bird's appendages move against the draft, sending her up and forward in a burst. Erruwan jumps in before the scow is yanked away, mirroring Erruwyn on the other side of Kiky.

They skim quickly and quietly out to sea as pink laps blue in the east. Erruwan regards the fresh colors of day with damp eyes, absently reaching over Kiky's back for her brother. When he doesn't meet her fingers with his own, she turns.

His arms fold tightly over his chest, his knees fold tightly over his arms. His gaze is set low. She spikes her buzzing to catch his attention and opens her fingers again.

---

[34] *Ponytail.*

He inhales sharply at the sensation of a ₷m'aęn diverging in strength from his own. His eyes rise and lower to her hand, forearm uncrossing reflexively. He'd lost the expectation of vacant touch. It wasn't something he'd thought about before his Calling, but its void was deeply felt.

 buzz

|

ji

His hand moves to hers, small smile forming as their fingers play. Erruwan sniffles, brows waving in concern. He's different. Injured within, also. Their heads whisk to the beach as a new shape on the cliff reflects their buzz.

A fisherman stands at the precipice. In dim illumination, he sees a wyvern pulling merfolk to sea on a giant fish scale. His mouth oscillates before finally performing its duty and drawing air. The outline of a bucket and pole fall from his silhouette as he turns and sprints.

Dawn glances at Dusk.

"His words will be doubted. Those who collect food are often unknown to ꝉRoskę, also," he explains.

Erruwan nods and points to his missing sealing horns. "Where?"

"ņar⌒uah. To protect. I hope."

She puzzles at the answer, soon noticing another absence. "Trunk?"

"Taken," he says softly.

Her eyes widen. "hu'aỵ?"

Erruwyn nods.

The scow slows as swells increase. Now far enough from shore that noise and sight are less of a concern, Erruwan connects her throat to an intersection of the scow's aỵ⌒ņa with ≥m-aęn⌒hu'aỵ. Erruwyn pulls ₷Danaę's horn for his disc chain.

"I will sing to fins. I have mastered keening," she says, waiting for surprised chirps.

Erruwyn blinks. "I have mastered keening, also."

They eye each other blankly.

↻ *ji*

Shoulders shake as exhausted grins lead to silent, senseless laughter.

Twiceborn: one soul embodied twice. Both Dusk and Dawn had mastered an unmasterable ₷m'aęn in each other's absence.

Erruwyn attaches his chain to the scow as they catch their breath. Turning back, the siblings share a heavy look above tightly entwined fingers.

↻ ₪

Submerged fins at the back of the scow pivot, and the craft moves quickly again. Face wet with sea mist and grief, Erruwyn watches the shoreline recede.

Erruwan observes.

When she'd put her mind to mastering her keen, she'd learnt to divorce emotion from note—but at the moment, a piece of Dusk's keen is genuine. Guilty eyes lower to ⸲Danǫe's open chest plate.

When xewǫ–set comes into view four miles offshore, their keening fades.

Across each side of the fifty-foot vessel lay two sets of three massive, cloth-covered ǫy⌢na fingers—stacked parallel to the water and decreasing in size. Large, branching fins fold vertically against the blue ark's bow and stern. Above the fins, retractable coves cover each end of the deck for daytime shade. Other than the coves, the deck is structurally empty.

xewǫ–set's ten-person crew huddles at the rail-less edge, bright grins aiming bright ⸲m'aęn at the water.

"Those present at your Threading demanded to be the first to caress you." Erruwan smiles.

set'yę's perilous nature knits tight bonds, and for those on set'yę, the most perilous time is noon—particularly if the vessel is weighed with unrefined ore.

Blue cloth covers the shine of ǫy, but the people's journey for resources can take months. Fibers stretched over tubes lose their weave from constant wind, salt, heat, and the damp tug of gravity. As cloth wears thin, ǫy beneath it occasionally meets with sun. For most of the day, this is controlled for by angling the vessel's reflections in one direction, but for the few hours of sun's zenith, the rays scatter. If glinting is seen by Outlanders curious and close enough to give chase, the race begins.

set'yę's second most perilous time takes place offshore—particularly if knowledge of the area is outdated. Crews must earn ⮞m-aęn⌢hu'ǫy to signal each other with ⸲m'aęn on land and aid vessel propulsion. Mastery specialization diverges from there: astronomers, cartographers, geologists, botanists, zoologists—each with ǫy-tut specific to their role.

As ⸲Danǫe is forged for utility, and its amplification reaches farther, at least one ⸲da'hę⌢na must accompany survey teams ashore in case of emergency. If necessary, ⸲da'hę⌢na will lure Outlanders away from the team's camp, make a stand to defend the group's retreat, or both. These sightings have served as the foundation for many Outland myths of water horses, shapeshifters, and merfolk.

Bound in such peril, crews grow close, and commonly voyage together for a lifetime—unless their ⸲da'hę⌢na is offered.

Returned to ⊙mǫ⌢jǫc, witnesses of Threading often choose new, grounded paths. Erruwyn's crew followed this trend until news of his re-embracing rekindled their taste for salt, wind, and sea.

Afir lands behind the happy group, who disconnect her socket and pull on its chain.

As the scow is tugged parallel to the vessel, layers of willful ≶m'aẹn move xewạ–sẹṭ's webbed fingers. A hammock of snake-chain scoops the scow and lifts it level with the deck. Thin ạy tubes along lips of both vessels lock together, securing the raft's suspension. Fingers return flush against xewạ–sẹṭ as Kiky, Erruwan and Erruwyn exit.

⇌ jị

Tears of joyful sorrow flow. Erruwyn is smothered in hands and piled with gentle affection, snacks, and questions.

"Where is his hair?"

"Two horns absent?"

"Such color across him."

"Why does he not eat faster?"

"No trunk?"

"He is too like a reed."

The reunion is interrupted when Afir shifts to long-cut-down.

Turning west, she spreads rigid wings. Willful ≶m'aẹn lowers the stern's cove and fins as the crew gathers to buzz in a skein[35]. Behind them, Afir's wings create a dish, funneling the powerful group ≶m'aẹn far over unobstructed sea. A faint reflection forms: one slow-moving ship two miles away.

⌒ Ⅎ

Though their cloth is only three weeks old, they won't take any chances. The crew is immediately influenced by the willed keen and softly join.

xewạ–sẹṭ's large fins articulate. A second pitch is added to retract a rectangular slot on the deck, granting access to a wide ramp. The crew, Afir, and Kiky descend—whinnies erupting as Kiky reunites with his sister behind the bow's partitioned storage wall.

With these partitions only appearing at bow and stern, the vessel's belly is spacious. Vertical ạy⌒ṇa ribs intersect with horizontally curving tubes, which carry the song of sẹṭ'yẹ to fins, coves, and fingers. Retractable shelves and chests line the middle of the area; hammocks stretch along either side.

Once they're safe, Erruwan pulls her twiceborn to a swing beside her own. Opening a bag hanging from it, she withdraws a box.

"⸲ɑlyṇ–⸲me⌒ṇa would not permit ⸲r'hẹạ to join us. She sends love." Erruwan holds the box forward. "This, also."

Erruwyn eyes the container. Though fairly certain of its content, stripped nerves prevent his acceptance. His sister nods and returns it to the bag.

"⸲er'em?" he whispers.

"She was happy in ⌒roo'dạ as I left for now," she says, folding back the hammock's

---

[35] *V formation.*

blanket.

He exhales slowly. He'd trusted Erem would be happy, but the words bring relief. The scab of her absence falls away.

Erruwan tilts her head at the down-stuffed swing. "Sleep."

Weary with turmoil, he clips *ₑDanₑaₑ's* horns to silver at the hammock's end and crawls in. The soft cocoon molds around him. He's missed these sleeping arrangements.

Crooning *tau⌒ine*'s lullaby, Erruwan drapes the blanket and caresses his hair—watching his drift into leaden sleep with misty eyes.

————————————

Erruwyn wakes sore, disoriented, and hungry fourteen hours later. Recollection hits.

⸚ji

He rolls over. The belly is dark but for the faint, silver glow of hammock lunestone warmed by sleeping bodies. Erruwan sits nearby with a pouch of Erruwyn's favorite treat: *ga'jho*—nuts, grains and dried fruits held together with a sweet glaze.

He climbs from the swing and approaches.

"Is this why Outlanders are so slow on the path? They sleep so long?" she asks, raising a hand past her smirk.

"No. It is their herding of many to narrow paths." He takes her arm and pulls. "I have not been permitted true rest in many moons. The Outland beds of those lowest in order are jagged. We wake early; work long."

"You were lowest?" She tugs him towards the ramp.

"Not the most-low. Though occasionally, yes," he answers softly as he's dragged to the deck. "So few of their thoughts attune. They smooth their surface though the sand below ripples greatly. Those who must work hardest are treated hardest, also. Denied nourishing food, restorative sleep, true education. It is opposite for those who do little."

They emerge to a steady, salty breeze and sit cross-legged, knee-to-knee, arm-through-arm. Erruwyn looks up. Twelve *ay* fingers arch overhead, stretching their webbing as sails. The night sky beyond glitters with clarity. When *ₑn'ar'uaₕ* winks from the starlit path, a deep pang in his heart sees his tear's advance and his hunger's retreat.

⇔ ℸ

Mists fall lightly as the bow parts the sea with increased zeal. Erruwan sings to sails and joins her twiceborn's keen as the fingers lower. She recognizes its texture. A piece of his soul is missing.

"Forgive me." Her head falls to his shoulder.

"Why?" he whispers, leaning against her.

"I had not thought that you might be *ey⌒ine*," she says.

Erruwyn's head straightens.

ey͡ine. Soul-woven.

da'he͡nar͡uah's meeting was fated by Alder's chronicle. They'd been torn apart soon after, but they'd woven together stronger. It had happened so naturally he hadn't seen it.

Now they're torn again.

He curls in to cover his face from the realization. When it finds him anyway, he covers his mouth to stifle the pain of his ignorance. Confused and concerned, Erruwan wraps her arms around him, watching as a new wound splits his psyche. After several minutes, his shuddering tapers enough for her thumbs to wipe his cheeks.

"What seeds does Wayfinder carry?" she asks.

To avoid the sky, Erruwyn's gaze fastens to the deck. "Curious, clever. Determined. Bright as *ɣn'ar'uah*." He exhales bitterly. "*k'es'sey*. Sol-hair."

Erruwan sits up slowly. Seeds of this daughter would draw even the shy eyes of Dusk from horizon's edge. She points to his bruising and hair. "Why did she permit this?"

"She did not wish it, *ɣerru͡wan*," he answers firmly to combat his twiceborn's protectiveness. "She will suffer under the one who did."

"Then why did she not bid your *ry͡ine*?"

"It is not so simple. There were many lives among us."

"What you say is very simple."

Erruwyn rubs his forehead. "It is not. Doing this would mean our hunt. *k'uah͡ni* of many soils chasing. Nowhere to go." When she doesn't argue, he takes a breath and looks around. His voice strains, "How can this be, *ɣerru͡wan*? Say."

"Okay." She wraps his arm to play with his hand. "The *ik-tys* you delivered to *wa't'un* told us of your breaking. His words caused ripples of doubt. Some have wondered why we must show such mercy to our hunters. I began to accompany those on *set'ye*. *ɣaf'ir* found you, so goes the branching of this tale..."

☙ hum

"When we harbored, even those who had not doubted our mercy felt *ɣer'em*'s silence greatly—your words, also. I rippled the Keen for *⊀Anese* and called for consensus Though I refused patience, The Wise bade me wait for the longest night's end. So. Frustration fed my Mastery. The first night of *da'ja͡na* I rippled my mastered keen." She peeks at Erruwyn. Glad to see a faint smile, she tips her chin. "Then I rippled my keen." His faint smile grows. She pushes his shoulder to sway him. "Again, I rippled my keen."

Erruwyn bites his lip.

Though *⤳Jhenxi͡ky* understand the importance of *da'ja͡na*, they've low stakes in the sexual festivities. Erruwan had rippled her keen through a populace in the throes of a sensual celebration honoring life's pleasing textures. The mood was grossly affected.

"What was your thought in doing so?" he asks.

She grins. "Many wail for the loss of our _er'wa_ on the final day of celebration. I required their support to ensure the tide of consensus rose in favor of your re-embracing."

True _er'wa_ are rare—born roughly once every other generation—and highly valued among the people as ideal lovers. When Erruwyn had trouble with _ne'ru'k_ training at fifteen, some thought he stood in _Jhenxi_'s shadow with Erruwan. After his true expression was determined, many suggested the twiceborn step from _da'he͡na_'s path. Erruwan convinced him otherwise: _er'wa_'s value could not matter if Outlanders discovered _⊙ma͡joc_.

This moment became Dawn's first _ix'ul_ as Dusk was Thread—deposited from _xewa–set_ in the offering scow—followed shortly by her second _ix'ul_: doing nothing as the Outlanders bit and swallowed.

She continues, "The Wise offered consensus in place of the _aro'x_ tournament if I agreed to cease my ripples. I agreed. I argued. I won," she concludes, nodding to the sea.

Erruwyn blinks at his sister, waiting for clarity. She flicks her eyes to him.

"I argued the Echoes are siblings."

ɼ'uah͡na. When the Attuning Will of the people is disturbed by one among the people, debates take place to determine where the whole has failed its part. Since all among the people are responsible for all others, all must find a way to repair the damage and restore equilibrium together. If the Echoes are kin, their participation in restoration is mandatory— one way or another.

"I argued also against Threadings," she continues, "_ɼ'uah͡na_ cannot truly be attuned if our Keening is required. If the displacement of _da'he͡na_ is required."

She smiles at her brother's steady _≤m'aen_. Most among the people had stuttered at this declaration. For ages they'd run their fingers with the grain. When she'd run their fingers against it, they couldn't deny the splinters—the pricks of truth in her words.

"I have wondered this," Erruwyn says softly. "The offering of _da'he͡na_, the binding of _k'uah͡ni_, our covenant with Outlanders. Those distant must have known there is no true covenant. The Echoes' suffering to madness made it known. Why was the truth forgotten. Ignored. Why have we continued to honor that which is absent?"

Stretching her legs, Erruwan stares at horizon's division—points of light against inky darkness. "Most Wills bind, constrict from without. The Will of Severance roots, strangles from within. Difficult to remove once sown. This is what I have seen."

Erruwyn mulls her words. He'd come to a similar conclusion after Isaac had displayed his illustrations. A rooted Will only requires time to bend you. No doctrines or instruction, just the slow, silent burrowing of expectation through experience.

"Then we will make them see, also," he says, squeezing her hand.

↻ _ji_

They share an alloyed look—glad for a partner, saddened to know their camaraderie is the result of prolonged suffering.

"What argument brought me here?" he asks after a time.

She sighs. "I argued ʂ*ral'ya*'s returning of Alder to the Outland was betrayal. In this way, ʂ*ral'ya*'s actions require Attunement. Alder's chronicle of betrayal led to your Threading. In this way, the path to restoration must mean your unthreading."

"Then, what is the path to the Echoes' restoration?"

Erruwan eyes him. "Explain your disagreement."

ƨ*chime*

Erruwyn tenses. Her phrasing isn't a question. She knows the minutiae of his expressions and ≤*m'aęn*. It's a reminder of the people's mask-less-ness; unfortunately, it's not enough to remind him that having a different opinion won't risk her ire.

Confused by his chime, Erruwan pulls his elbow and cups his chin, raising his face to observe his texture.

ƨ*peal*

"What? What?" Erruwan whispers in alarm.

She scans the deck, turning back to lift his eyelid with her thumb. Following his gaze to the wood between them, her knee jerks up—mind conjuring a deadly insect or snake to explain his fear. Seeing nothing, she grows puzzled.

Erruwyn's peal reduces.

Here is his reminder: the people's sympathetic resonance can grow stale. Differing opinions—differing textures of ≤*m'aęn*—are valued. Her statement isn't an accusation of wrongdoing as it would be in Avonleigh; her statement was simply a statement. The night is clear. The air is cool. Dusk has an opinion; Dawn wants to hear it.

He exhales. "I am sorry. I require time. My eyes must adjust. Readjust."

Erruwan's brow knots as she studies him. Among the people, anxiety is rarely experienced in response to social interactions. This is partly because there are very few social consequences to fear, but largely because chimes and peals are meant as evolutionary warnings of harm or life-threatening dangers—if social anxiety were common, calls of danger would be indistinguishable, and a significant survival mechanism would be lost.

Her brow-knot tightens.

Dusk had been born first, but Dawn had always led the charge. He was quiet and tender and shy. She was louder and blunter and bolder. During training she'd often felt she should be the one offered—that her boldness would protect her from the Outland's discord. Now she's not sure.

The uncertainty is justified. Traits like hers are weeded from Outland women—for instance, in lieu of Lords, Corah's isolation is currently providing the weed-remover. If Dawn were offered, she'd have returned even more changed than Dusk.

"I will explain my disagreement." Erruwyn spreads his fingers for her hand, which she swiftly twines. "Though, please say the path to restoration before this."

"Okay." Erruwan moves the pouch of *ga'jho* to his lap. "I will say as you eat."

He opens the fabric and reluctantly shoves a clump in his mouth.

"When did you cease to like *ga'jho*?" she quizzes.

He swallows joylessly under a glance to his twiceborn. She nods: his *ʔAnese* has no anima. It will take time to find pleasure in simple things again.

"We will float on the Echoes' waters. *ʃfo'lar* will offer peaceful restoration."

"*ʃfo'lar* still lives?"[36]

"Yes." Erruwan waits for him to eat more before continuing, "It was decided she must have the honor. She still flies well in armor, also. If her words are rejected, we fight." She pauses to pass him a water skin. "I wish for her rejection."

Erruwyn drinks the dry from his mouth. "Why do you wish for combat? There is risk."

♥*crackle*

She squints at the sea. "I wish for amends. For all the Aegis they have hunted. For you. I am not afraid of them."

"This is because your strength prevents your fear, *ʃerru⁀wan*," he says, watching her squeeze his knuckles. "You should fear for those less strong. This means all others."

After a beat, she shrugs. "Okay."

Eyebrows pinched above his nose, Erruwyn leans back on his free palm and stares at her profile.

Feeling his eyes, she smiles. "I had thought to heed your wisdom if you returned. Though do not expect it to last long," she adds, glancing at the pouch.

He swallows the remaining *ga'jho* as she hugs his arm. "Then my second wisdom is to continue heeding."

"Mm. What is your disagreement with my argument of Alder?"

"I agree with many pieces." He inhales to lighten his heavy heart. "Alder's displacement. Alder's chronicle. These led to my Threading. Though I believe ◊*Ruah* required my Threading, my *ix'ul*. My *ik-tys*."

Her head jerks. "Your *ik-tys*?"

"Yes. Without it, the Echoes would have muted me. No one to receive *ʃaf'ir*. Another Aegis for their procession. Another Wayfinder."

ⱬ*hiss*

"My re-embracing—" He sits up and rubs his face until the pain of his bruising matches the pain in his chest. "I cannot stay knowing they suffer."

♥*drone*

---

[36] *er'oo'n often live to eighty. ʃfo'lar, a veteran er'oo'n matriarch claimed by ʃalyn–ʃmę⁀na and her twiceborn, ʃnem'ar, nears ninety.*

"They?" Erruwan asks, keeping the back of her hand on his leg.

"The daughters of Alder." His hand drops to hers. "ŋaɾ⌢uaḫ. ₹Avrella–ȝmȩ⌢ŋa, ₹Corah–li'la. ₹Elane–ela⌢ŋȩ."

She smiles. "They know ela⌢ŋȩ?"

He nods. "She did not request clarity. Her name was Elane already."

"Mm. Did you observe the chronicle of Alder?"

"Yes. ŋaɾ⌢uaḫ fed the flame."

"Then she is a true ŋaɾ⌢uaḫ." Erruwan points to his contusions. "These. If you return, they will grow?"

"It could not matter."

She pokes a blotch of indigo on his leg; he flinches and blinks apprehensively at her finger. Her eyebrows duck—in the past, he would've pushed her over or knocked her hand away before she'd made contact.

"It seems to matter. Decide after restoration. You might feel less so once you have seen The Wise." She returns to his shoulder. "Though if you do not, you must defeat me in combat to return."

He regards the deck as she twiddles his fingers. "I am already no longer heeded."

"I did say." Erruwan smiles.

---

xewa–set is the first to arrive at the fleet's meeting coordinates ten miles from the Echoes' soil. As they wait, Erruwyn Archives all he'd learned of Otay from Lindenholt's library, and the crew takes shifts to maintain j–≤m'aȩn—increasing Erruwyn's healing rate and keeping his chimes submerged.

On their second day, the song of set'yȩ is heard in the West, and a skein of twelve vessels moves on the horizon. fexa–set—what could reasonably be called the people's flagship—leads at the apex.

Three times larger than its companions, fexa–set bears six sets of fingers and carries three pairs of elder ↺da'hȩ⌢ŋa known as The Wise. Within the hour, it pulls alongside the Keening Masters. Bow to stern, the remaining vessels surround the two in concentric circles, and webbed fingers of thirteen vessels extend, linking together as bridges converging on the flagship.

↺da'hȩ⌢ŋa file.

↻ ji

The Wise stand on deck with open arms, tearful grins, and silver hair whipping around legs. Laughing at his bashful hesitation, Erruwyn's crew and sister push him across the bridge. A final shove sees his wet face buried in ₹alyn–ȝmȩ⌢ŋa's shoulder. Erruwan sandwiches from the other side, smiling as the loving embrace of The Wise closes in.

↺da'hȩ⌢ŋa twiceborn and crews arrive from surrounding ships, and soon fexa–set floods with elation. Palms cover Erruwyn's frame as he's pulled, embraced, and pushed across the deck. Eventually, The Wise call for calm.

The fleet turns to Alyn, sending her favored back on a wave of doting appendages. He stands in wracked rhapsody on her shore—attentive hands continually lapping his frame.

"There is much to celebrate," Alyn declares. Those closest simultaneously whisper her declaration. Those in proximity repeat the whisper, and so on, until her words ripple out to, and by, all. "First, Restoration. Consensus begins."

↻ *sing*

Crews re-cross the bridges as twenty-four *da'he͡na* and six Wise descend to *fexa–set*'s lower level. They kneel and fold around Erruwyn—the pillar of their pile.

↻ *ji*

Here, where emotion is voiced through *m'aen*, words describing the group's jubilation at Erruwyn's return, and their devastation at his loss don't need stating. The Wise get down to business.

Alyn smiles warmly. "*erru͡wyn*, we wished to have you for consensus. Say what you know of *ir'ie͡dj'en'ec*."

"Yes, *me͡na*." Erruwyn sways in the tall grass of arms. "Echoes believe the muting of *da'he͡nar͡uah* will restore their departed *m'aen*. They are confused. Discordant. Though, with time, their discord could be attuned. Maybe."

↻ *drone*

Responses trickle from The Wise:

"We do not have the time."

"We cannot stay long. A quarter moon, maybe."

"If *fo'lar* is rejected, *◊Ruah* demands the Echoes' muting."

"This Attunement is required. Those distant failed *ry͡ine*."

↻ *drone*

"What do you know of the soil?" Alyn asks.

Erruwyn passes *ʔRoske*'s record. "The *dj'en'ec* is six miles across two. It is believed the walls are mortar of limestone. Sandstone, also."

⌒ **hum** *drone*

The news brings optimism. *m'aen* in *fexa–set*'s belly splits from grief of the Echoes' misfortune. Alyn unrolls the record, stopping on a map of a small cape.

"Though I do not know of their arrows, their weapons were plated. Steel, toxin." He continues, motioning to a recipe in the Archive, "Toxin's pole is there. Our stores carry the flora."

⌒ *drone* **hum** *crackle*

"They have harbor. Likely vessels of oak, iron. It sits nearby the end of their *dj'en'ec*." Erruwyn points to the map. "Their shelters are densest at harbor's soil—their *roo'da*. One mile across two."

⪬ *hum＿**drone***

"So. I wonder, maybe, that we might twice-offer peace. ⫶*fo'lar*. Vessels. ⫶*fo'lar*."

The Wise nod. A second chance flavored with destruction might make the fleet's offer more appealing.

Alyn repeats his words, "⫶*fo'lar*. Vessels. ⫶*fo'lar*."

⪼ *hum*

The first phase of consensus completes with a hopeful hum. ⪦*da'he⁀na* rub Erruwyn as they stand to return to their vessels.

"I will go." Erruwan smiles, releasing her brother's hand. "You stay."

⪼ *purr*

The Wise replace their children's fawning of Erruwyn as the belly empties. Alyn and her twiceborn, Nemar, press against him from either side—a silent acknowledgement: the only ones permitted to caress his scourged hair directly.

"What is your thought of ⫶*fo'lar*'s recitation, ⫶*erru⁀wyn*?" Nemar asks. "Your Croran is most amended among us. You must provide the words."

Erruwyn weaves his fingers. "Maybe, to clarify our kinship; we are siblings. To clarify those distant could not have truly wished for conflict; could not have truly believed our muting would restore ⪯*m'aen*. Though, if the Echoes wish to fight, they must be warned of *ry⁀ine*, also."

Alyn observes him as he speaks. "You are different."

⪬ *purr*
　|
⪦ *hiss*

"This cannot be helped. Our paths texture us." She pulls his head to her shoulder. "Do you wish to articulate the weight of your burden? Lift?"

Erruwyn leans against her. Bringing his hands to her leg, he pinches his fingers in thought. "No, ⪦*me⁀na*," he answers quietly. "Though the chronicle is heavy, I do not know what words could lift."

"It cannot be helped," The Wise repeat softly.

"You will Archive in time," Alyn adds. She touches ⫶*Danae*'s star. "You remain moored?"

⪬ *ji*
　|
⪦ *hiss＿wail*

"Yes," he strains. "Always."

"Your path diverges greatly. The first we have known," Alyn remarks gently. "Where does it take you?"

Erruwyn's hiss of self-loathing increases. His twiceborn had been right. His resolve to return to Lysbeth has wavered after seeing The Wise.

By re-embracing Erruwyn, the people have committed to reassessing their interactions with the Outland, including the role of *da'he͡ na*. If he returns to Lysbeth, he'll be denying his people his voice—a voice that would play a significant role in determining the course of their future, and whose assistance in teaching the keen would be sorely missed. If he returns to *ma͡ joc*, he'll be breaking his oath to Lysbeth, leaving ⟨Avrella–*me͡ na* and her daughters to despair under Isaac and *k'uah͡ ni* without his presence as a buffer.

Both paths lead to the abandonment of those he treasures.

In their wisdom, The Wise don't press his silence. Alyn and Nemar constrict their arms around him, casting a wistful look over his shoulders.

It takes a special kind of twiceborn to become *da'he͡ na*, and they'd always considered Dawn and Dusk to be even more special. They weren't alone in feeling so; the natural skill and pleasant natures of Erruwan and Erruwyn drew wide appreciation. Though Erruwan was confident, her confidence was earned, and rather than falling to apathy or arrogance, she put it to use offering assistance where needed—Erruwyn always shyly at her side, too unassuming to realize he was as widely favored as his sister.

Among the people, it's said ◊*Ruah*, Fulcrum, resides between such tidy poles.

The people's esteem combined with the pair's young age made Erruwyn's Calling very difficult to accept. Normally, names of *da'he͡ na* are added to ⌒*roo'da*'s memorial the day a vessel returned from Threading. In Erruwyn's case, the people's Keening sliced through *ma͡ joc* for several days before his name was carved alongside the twenty-five others previously Thread. Dorsit's appearance on *wa't'un* hadn't caused ripples of doubt to form, rather, it caused the ripples formed at Erruwyn's Calling to surface. The Wise encouraged their propagation. As did Erruwan.

m'aen rises across the fleet.

↻ *hum*

Consensus is reached as *da'he͡ na* relay the plan to their crews. The fleet moves five miles closer to the Echoes' soil and reassemble on *fexa–set*.

Folar and her son, Fen, claimed by another pair of Wise, are brought to the deck and armored. They're instructed to circle and gather members of the populace, then to land high. When the Echoes cluster, Folar will recite a message of peaceful Restoration and leave them with the flame spigot attached to her breast bracing. Fen will accompany to record the exchange. If the Echoes agree to peace, they'll set off the spigot by midnight.

Erruwyn gives Folar the recitation. The birds take off at dusk.

They return in under an hour. The fleet falls silent as Alyn signals Fen's record of the exchange.

Ambient noises of awe exit through his beak; the timbre suggests a large crowd. When

Folar speaks in Erruwyn's voice, the recitation elicits appropriately timed—though unhappy—responses. At the very least, they'd understood the message. Fen's repeat ends with the clink of a flame spigot on cobblestone.

With nothing to do but wait, time is passed regaling Erruwyn with tales from home. As midnight nears, the fleet's hum dims. No spigot is seen.

⤳da'he˺˺ng return to their ships and retract their bridges, forming a skein with *fexa–set* at the back vertex. Approaching the Echoes' harbor, each individual is assigned a finger of their vessel, and they link again—this time as amplifying dishes.

Knowing their options for *⊙ma˺˺joc*'s defense are limited, the people bring vessels freed from *wa't'un* home for practice. On the scale of *⁊Theam*, iron nails and oak planks used to craft the Outlanders' ships sit in the range of *≈aen*.

They'll need to be fast.

Ears are tightly plugged. *er'oo'n* are sent to hover far behind the skein as the fleet divides its efforts. Half sing to iron and half to oak, taking turns for breath each time their finger's muffling-breaks clamp in response to threats of resonant destruction.

⎈ ♪

The song is loud. Iron nails struggle to oscillate. Holes in wood widen. Creaks and splinters join the choir as planks fight to bend at their center. Halfway through, those singing to oak alter their pitch for planks on vessels perpendicular to the fleet—as *⁊Theam* changes across grain. The creaking begins again as lanterns appear on the wall.

Now loosened at the seams, *⁊Roske* will chronicle the vessels sinking.

Bells ring onshore. The fleet detach their fingers, reversing stern and bow by raising and lowering their respective fins. Properly oriented, *fexa–set* leads their retreat at the apex.

The Keening Masters of *xewa–set* stay up to check the harbor at dawn. They glide over water one-half mile away. Otayans clump atop the wall in a set pattern. Parts of the docks themselves appear to have come undone, and only very small boats with proportional planks stay afloat.

⟳ *chime*

A projectile hurtles towards them, falling short and splashing water over their portside.
Catapults.

⟳ ⅏

xewa–set zips away before another bullet flies. Rejoining the fleet, Dusk and Dawn report to *fexa–set*'s belly.

"The vessels have submerged." Erruwan leans against blue wood and crosses her arms. "There are many eyes. The Echoes have slings, also, *⸨me˺˺ng*."

"Then *⸨fo'lar* must stay high for recitation," Alyn says, watching Nemar unroll *⁊Roske*'s map.

"The slings sit, so." Erruwyn points along the wall where Otay had clustered. "Continue so, maybe," he says, repeating the pattern further out.

Nemar nods. "This knowledge will greatly assist. Rest for the moon."

The Keening Masters return to their ship and descend to the hammocks. The crew is already dozing.

"Do you feel differently of ⊙*ma͡joc*?" Erruwan asks, removing ⦃*Danae*'s horns.

"Yes." Erruwyn sits in the swing beside her, rolling his remaining horns in his fingers. "I feel I cannot bear either path of the fork before me."

"Mm." Erruwan slides in front of her twiceborn, clapping his cheeks and planting their foreheads. "So." Long eyelashes skim between irises. "Carve your own path."

———————

At dusk, Folar and Fen are armored again and instructed to remain in constant flight while they recite and record. The message implores the Echoes' cooperation and warns that the path of violence will not end until Restoration is complete.

The bird's lift.

Twenty minutes later, Fen returns in long-cut-down. The fleet's lament muffles as Alyn signals his record:

> *Fen's flight-wind blows soft and steady; Folar recites to distant jeers. Faintly squeaking hinges proceed a sickening thud. Wind and oration end abruptly. Jeers amplify as metal crashes on stone. The Echoes' malice drowns out the final, pained notes of Folar's* tia͡ua.

⌢ *wail⌣* **crackle**

A new consensus is called on *fexa–set*'s deck. The fleet ripples Alyn's words: "Flame. ⸮*Roske*. Stone. ⦃*Ruah*."

⥀ **crackle**

Torches pinprick heavily-guarded walls as the skein mobilizes one-quarter mile offshore. Vessels moor, raise their fins, and weave fingers into dishes—maintaining a buzz to see borders of the Echoes' *dj'en'ec*.

Six veteran *er'oo'n* are armored and fitted with canisters of *li'li-a*—destructive pyrophoric powders. When the birds open their beaks, levers attached to the canisters will eject a set amount of powders from two separate tubes. To avoid splash-back, *er'oo'n* will only release the chemicals on the updraft after diving.

Eight unarmored *er'oo'n* are instructed to hover high and buzz in formation, providing constant, overhead sight for kin assigned to fire-dive buildings and wall-top catapults.

Path lain, the swarm lifts from the deck in long-cut-down. Within minutes, streaks of fire cleave through dark firmament. Jets of powder combine, ignite in the air, and land like buckets of water across roofs, roads, and wall towers—stubborn blazes latching to fireproof materials.

Panic begins.

Torches carried by wall guards quickly descend to aid with flames in the streets—they'll come to learn the pyrophoric chemicals also react to water and can only be smothered. Each source splash will take up to thirty-six hours to fade. In the meantime, nearby flammable materials will catch, and attempts to douse will only spread the flame.

Soon, the wall is outlined against a steadily increasing glow. The divers keep to an area of two-by-two miles, and one by one return when their canisters empty. By the time all *er'oo'n* are called back, tongues of flame lap air above the wall's crenellations.

The skein remains offshore through the night, listening grimly as chords of shock and fear ebb to grief and agitation.

When daylight overtakes flame, crews move vessel fingers over decks to obstruct the occasional arrow slung from harbor. Once construction of the projectiles is known, the fleet sings to feathers, and future arrows fly off course. By evening, botanists distribute vials of antidote.

Otay's glow continues through the third night of Restoration. Fen flies, reporting limited activity in the area. The fleet approaches shore. When their bottoms touch sand, each crew member is assigned a finger and the vessels become dodecapedes. Walking to a flat area of land just beyond the walls, they arrange themselves in a tight spiral with *fexa–set* at the center.

To stay upright, one set of fingers on each ship stretch to grip the deck of its forward neighbor. Another set stretches and digs into sand and soil—providing grounded support and canopies for exterior cover. The remaining fingers stretch into dishes, waiting to repel arrows if needed. Low, blue sections of hull retract for direct paths to the spiral's center and one path to the beach.

A skein of twenty-four *Theam* assemble and kneel in profile beside the Echoes' walls. On the scale of *Theam*, the pitch of mortar is high. Layering sound together, *as'etu* is quickly achieved. Quills align down spines and abdomens.

⌒ ⁊

Five *er'oo'n* stand behind the chorus to funnel pitches with their wings. Others fly as scouts, taking turns to dive and claw at stone.

Slackened mortar bulges. Low bricks struggle under the weight of bricks above. When the first stone yields to *er'oo'n*'s talons, a stack of loose blocks follow. After twenty minutes, the outermost wall sports a large crag. Mortar and pebble filling within falls quickly, and another thirty minutes sees a break through the final stone wall.

Fen stands before the skein and spreads his wings. The drastic change in sound's reflection cuts *?Theam*'s string. Released puppets kneel slumped, slowly regaining presence as animal handlers guide *er'oo'n* to dig and drag sediment away.

Once all *da'he⌢na* are cleared of spinal injury, they swap *?Theam* for *Danae* and rejoin their crews to assist with deconstruction. By midnight, the twenty-foot-wide rift in Otay's defense is tidy, and by morning, fires within have begun to fade. Vessel teams break to eat at midday, and crews take over watch so all *da'he⌢na* will be well-rested for nightfall's advance.

When Erruwyn and Erruwan's turn for food comes, they join Alyn under *fexa–set*'s finger-canopy. She gives both a bar of *ga'jho* with their fish, peering at *Danae*'s star as they kneel.

"*?erru⌢wyn, Ruah.*"

"Yes, *?me⌢na.*" He breaks off a corner of the bar. "I will remain to send the moorings."

"Two hours may be enough," Alyn says grimly. "The Wise will assist in shielding from arrows."

"I will stay also," Dawn adds, pulling a fishbone from her mouth.

Alyn smiles warmly and returns to Erruwyn. "Say your thoughts. I feel them on you."

He lowers his *ga'jho.* "I thought to ask for consensus when we return, *?me⌢na.*"

"A debate to celebrate your re-embracing?" She chuckles. "What is your argument?"

"Consensus is known: *?ral'ya*'s displacement of Alder is attuned by my unthreading. I wish to argue this alone cannot mean Restoration."

Alyn peers. "I hear."

"Alder claimed kinship of the people in his chronicle. In this way, the betrayal of his departure requires Attunement, also." Erruwyn swallows and squeezes the bar of *ga'jho.* "The true path of Restoration must require the re-filling of Alder's absence on *◉ma⌢joc*— must require *er'oo'n* to sing again of Outlanders cradled on *wa't'un.*"

The *ga'jho* crumbles; his eyes lift to Alyn.

Her grin appears slowly.

A warning *≤m'aen* rings as *er'oo'n* face inland in long-cut-down. A third party gathers on a tall hill less than a mile away. The warning is repeated; *da'he⌢na* reassemble.

"They bear the cloth of Crora, *?me⌢na,*" Erruwyn says. "The Echoes deliver embodiments of *⋈Jhenxi* to influence *k'uah⌢ni.* Crora may wish to assist them."

⌢ *drone_ **crackle***

"Croran weapons I have seen rest on the scale of those we have known from *wa't'un,*" he adds.

⌥ ***hum***

———————————

The Duke of Mantfurt squints at the bizarre, blue spiral on the beach. "What are they?"

Yerish leans against him and breaths in his ear. "The enemy, Grace."

Mantfurt squeezes her grey-silked waist.

Jaques rolls his eyes.

Three nights ago, Bengli sitting in the laps of powerful Croran Lords received urgent messages from their homeland. Not wasting any time, they'd set to work convincing their benefactors to assist with a vague threat to Otay—one which could spread to Crora if not contained. A handful of Lords along Otay's border agreed to take their warbands for observation.

Jaques—who knows marriage is still Lysbeth's best chance of escape—has been shopping for a nobleman worthy of her, and happened to be at Lord Mantfurt's court. Knowing the full truth of Otay, he'd volunteered to join Mantfurt's excursion once he'd been filled in. Scouts had arrived midmorning to prepare the hilltop camp. Unable to make sense of the view on the beach, they'd delivered fearful reports to the warband that evening, and their unsettling descriptions have lent credence to Yerish's warnings.

"Call for aid, Grace." Yerish nuzzles.

"Aid?" Jaques scoffs. "You think Mantfurt could be defeated by so few in number?"

She glares. "You see they have already burned our largest port. Think of what could happen to Castle Marsyll." Her glare seamlessly reforms to a lustful smile as Mantfurt glances.

Jaques holds his tongue and scans Otay's inner walls. Torchlight grows in the port's scorched remains. Otayans have noticed the warband's arrival and are gathering to support any moves made.

He juts his chin at the town. "Look, there is your aid, hm? Or better, let them fight their own enemies."

Mantfurt strokes his beard as Yerish strokes his belly. "For Crora, this matter is trivial. Think of the gratitude our assistance will foster." He smirks as Yerish's hand lowers to his belt.

Jaques crosses the Duke from his shopping list of suitors. Backing Otay is the obvious choice politically, but Mantfurt isn't interested in diplomatic gratitude.

"We will attack at dawn," Mantfurt declares. "A scout will stay behind to call for aid if needed." He grips Yerish's rump and turns to steer her to his tent.

Jaques lingers as they go, watching his shadow lengthen in silence until the familiar silhouette of his valet approaches. He extends his arm and a wine bottle appears in his palm. He takes a deep pull from the bottle's neck.

Luis scoffles. "Thin wine doesn't lubricate mouths as much as you think, but the scouts said silver people walked the beach at noon. Are they Erruwyn's?"

"Who else, hm?" Jaques returns the bottle. "Yerish will soon persuade Mantfurt to call for reinforcement." He slides *Jhenxi*'s ring from his finger and raises it to the beach. "Do you think if I flashed this they would agree to parlay? I could sneak down now to warn them?"

Luis finishes his swig. "Jaques, if it's true they are like the Otayans, they will surely kill you before you near. And who will be blamed for allowing you to go? Me. Why do you want this? Because I drink too much of your swill?"

Jaques grins, returning the ring to his finger and yanking the bottle from his servant's hands. "No. Because you insult my swill." He spins to his tent and drinks again.

"If you bought better wine, the truth wouldn't insult you," Luis mumbles, digging in his bag for another bottle.

Their tent is the only one still lit by the time both bottles are empty. Luis snores from his cot in the corner. Jaques remains at the folding desk, too ill at the thought of Erruwyn under Isaac's feet to sleep. He thumbs the ring's carvings as his mind digs a rut of melancholic musings: He should've told Jaspyr Haywood about Isaac's behavior when they'd come to Gyenna nine years ago. Or challenged Isaac to a duel directly. He would've lost Edenshire's friendship, but a world without Isaac is a better world.

An obnoxiously amorous cricket pulls him from the trench. He sighs heavily and threads the ring with his finger. As he moves to stand, a deafening bellow jolts him. He claps his ears and twists to Luis. The valet rolls over, groaning inaudibly under the sustained note.

Motion catches Jaques eye—the sword on his trunk is rattling ferociously. Grimacing, Luis sits up with a pillow wrapped around his head and joins Jaques' squint at the weapon. After several merciless minutes, the noise fades. Jaques lowers his hands, tugs on his lobes, and shakes his head, but the ringing in his ears remains.

Peeking out of the tent, sounds of confusion swarm the camp. He closes the flap and turns back to Luis. Their eyes meet and drop to the sword. Jaques walks and reaches forward slowly. As he lifts the weapon, the sheathed blade, pommel, and crossbar clatter; the hilt remains in his grip.

His sonorous giggle rolls down the hill's slope.

———————————

Horizon unfurls pale blue, offering the sun a comfortable spot from which to observe the beginnings of Restoration's *ry⌐ine*.

Concerned Crora's appearance would embolden gathering Echoes, the fleet altered their previous consensus. Before disarming most swords in the area, *er'oo'n* dropped a line of fire around Otay's perimeter—a barrier of flame preventing more Echoes from joining or leaving. Another line was dropped to isolate the port town from the rest of the territory.

Now, fleet crews are singing to feathers and armoring horses as *da'he⌐na* assemble in *fexa–set*'s lowest level. Twenty-two *ay'tuan* trees wait again the walls. *da'he⌐na* stand before them, and each twiceborn pair preforms an Offering ritual to their *er'oo'n*. As the eleven birds accept, their beaks are pulled to *Danaes*' diamond chest plates, and *Anese* are moored to their breast bracings.

In two hours, Erruwyn and Erruwan will release the moored *er'oo'n*. The birds' ≤*m'aen* will travel through ⟩*Anese* and resonate in ⟨*Ruah*, calling each pair of twiceborn ⊲*da'he⌢na* and their horses back to the beach. Once all have returned, *er'oo'n* will cut ⟨*Ruah*'s strings.

Fen, Nekki and Afir remain unmoored. The Keening Masters armor them and bring them to *fexa–set*'s deck as twenty-four armored horses and twenty-two ⟨*Ruah* file out of the spiral.

Short, wooden barricades have been erected at the wall's fissure.

A drum sounds within.

The fighters form a skein on the beach. Erruwyn and Erruwan give the unmoored birds instruction: fly high and fire-dive any third-party interference. Then they signal. As the three *er'oo'n* lift from the deck, the ≤*m'aen* of long-cut-down engulfs the beach.

⟨*Ruah* alter shape on hearing it.

ry⌢ine begins.

Demonic silver frenzies. Shrieking horses charge and jump the barricades. Monstrous ⟨*Ruah* barrel through.

Terrorized screams soon follow.

The Keening Masters return to The Wise and join their song to arrows until tinkling is heard on the hull. Alyn *wox'ua*s: see.

Erruwan and Erruwyn step outside. Shards of metal littering the ground grow denser as they near the spiral's exit. Erruwan nods to a piece embedded in blue wood. The decks likely have more. Fortunately, the *ay⌢na* of vessels wont set flame if punctured.

Arriving at the beach, a large pockmark dents the sand twenty feet from the waterline. Metal and ceramic shards lay in patches around it. They squat, picking up clay fragments and piecing together what they can.

"Orb?" Erruwan posits. "Two feet?"

"I think, yes. Metal within to fly when broken, also."

"The pitch must be nearby to our fired-soil," she says, rotating a scrap. "Higher, maybe. It is thin."

"Did you drink the pole to toxin? The metal may be corrupted."

She nods at the clay in her hands. Relieved, Erruwyn turns to scan the wall. A loaded catapult sits at the far end.

≤*peal*

Heeding her brother's warning, Erruwan looks up in time to see the sling's arm release an orb. The twiceborn dive in opposite directions as it impacts.

Clay shatters. Sand flies. Metal shards zip over the beach and strike vessels behind them. When the hail ends, the pair rise to wipe grit from their faces and pull away metal flecks drawn to ⁅*Danae*⁆'s magnetic intersections.

"Okay?" Erruwan asks, dislodging a shard from her thigh.

"Yes." Erruwyn squeezes his eyes to shake sand from his hair. "We must deliver its note to the crews."

"Mm—" She stops. Her face contorts at his ribs.

He follows her gaze to a shard near ⁅*Danae*⁆'s star.

⟨*Roske* stills.

Edges of broken silver glow.

His chest is hot.

Too hot, far too hot.

The glow spreads. He bends forward in pain.

Flame will erupt in seconds. The smell of searing flesh hits Erruwan's nose as she stumbles towards Erruwyn's outstretched hand.

⁅*Danae*⁆'s rib ignites as their fingertips brush.

The arc of Erruwyn's spine pulls him away.

ᔕ ᒥ _ ᜋᜒᜋᜒ

Erruwan's screams cross ⟨*Theam*.

Airborne fins of the fleet clack uncertainly as she falls to the sand, bracing for the visceral horror of her twiceborn's *tia ꙯ua*.

What she hears instead is an unknown Avon's voice:

⁅*Live*⁆

⟨*The blossom of expression ripens.*

Erruwyn enters *as'etu*.

⁅*Danese*⁆ pulls his strings.

Appendages blur; ⏄*m'aen* sings to spinal roots.

⁅*Danese*⁆ yanks its puppet forward and safely to the ground.

Mouth agape, Erruwan stands. Instinct moves her.

She lunges for the filigree's feet, lifts, and swings.

Bubbling waves catch fire as ⁅*Danae*⁆ sinks in water.

———————

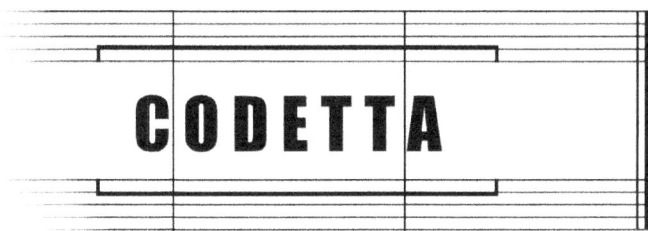

CODETTA

Black silk sways over the end of a carpet runner. Black shoes move from wood to marble.

Lysbeth's seventy-third tour of Lindenholt's ghost is underway.

Lysbeth's seventy-fifth day spared Isaac's company will begin in six hours.

Lysbeth's ninetieth day suffering Erruwyn's absence will begin in six hours.

Lysbeth's four guards—tour guides—protect her down each artless hall. Past each sheeted room. Through each fading memory.

She must have exercise, after all.

In the southern wing, their promenade along the Grand Gallery is broken by a short foray to the Salon, where she's taken to a window for five minutes of observation. The fountain ran dry last month. It's still dry. The lawn and hedgerows are overgrown. They continue to grow. The terrace is utterly vacant.

They continue to the western wing where she's walked between the Grand Library's boarded walnut bookshelves and covered couches. Another five minutes to enjoy a garden of sludge basins through the window.

They exit to the western gallery. The dining parlor has been emptied to furnish the private dining room that was once Elane's bedroom.

Another runner ends. Shoes echo on marble as they cross the Grand Chamber.

The archways are open; a cruel reminder that there's no one left to fill the enormous space. No more cozy Winter Solstices. No more PromSol. No more greeting assemblies.

The long tables of the Grand Dining Hall seat hundreds of high-backed, off-white spirits. Instruments in the Grand Drawing Room have been cased and shoved into a corner.

Avrella's chair is left uncovered to better serve as a pedestal for her ashes; her cairn remains unbuilt.

Lysbeth's tour ends with the eastern gallery.

A guard opens her mourning room door. She steps through, eyes down to avoid the midline border of Erruwyn's illustrations across the walls of her apartments—the four rooms that mark the bounds of her life, save for her daily stroll.

The door shuts.

She crosses to Alder's desk, now tucked between her favorite window and another. She'd found some satisfaction in thinking Isaac overlooked the opportunity: an illustration of Erruwyn over the panes would've denied her the view.

Later she realized the illustrative borders of her rooms were positioned to avoid fading the ink with direct sunlight, and the pain of viewing Lindenholt's lifeless stone court and empty blocks through her window was already at saturation.

Isaac often saw things before she did—though he hadn't foreseen Erruwyn's escape. On discovery, his rage burned coolly: blue flame under a spit of methodical planning.

Since Isaac wasn't sure who might still have sympathies for his sister, he'd dismissed everyone over the weeks leading up to his departure. With Natty gone, so too went the sneaking of Elane's letters into Lysbeth's hands.

Lysbeth's new Lady's maid follows strict instruction not to speak. She dresses Lysbeth in black at nine each morning, she serves Lysbeth's meals in the dining room adjoining her bedchamber during the day and she appears at nine each night to disrobe Lysbeth for bed.

The shell of Lindenholt is run by strangers; five servants and six guards. The first-floor kitchens were reopened for the cook to use poor quality ingredients delivered to Lindenholt's gatehouse each week. Two housemaids and a scullery maid spot clean the manor and tidy Lysbeth's apartments on occasion.

The guards protect Lysbeth from visitors and outside communication.

The Otay and lakeside attacks provided Isaac cover for Lysbeth's guarded isolation— though none beyond Lindenholt knew its true extent. If any among the current staff find the situation strange or troubling, they make no complaints. Protracted Kingswars leave many desperate for work, and Isaac was careful to hire the most desperate applicants.

So, here Lysbeth sits. Isolated in a cage designed to torment her.

The only bright spot in recent months arrived enclosed in Elane's final letter: a note from Jaques describing the attack on Otay.

Croran warbands watched, breathless, as shape-shifting demons and fire-breathing dragons sectioned the territory with flame and tore it to shreds in a matter of days. When the Faye left, Crora entered Otay's walls for the first time in fifteen-hundred years. The child population and a small group of Otayan adults were found corralled in one of the few un-scourged buildings.

With so many reliable first-hand accounts and the erasure of a country as proof, the People's existence was confirmed, but Jaques assured Lysbeth this knowledge would not result in an increase of Faye sea-hunting parties. Quite the opposite, in fact, as fear of the Faye had spread as quickly as their fires.

Perhaps they might finally voyage in peace.

Lysbeth glances at the window. There's less than an hour of light left.

She pulls a key from her bodice and opens Alder's false panel drawer. Avrella passed a week before Isaac's return to the North. He'd had exactly enough time to review her will and effects.

The Matriarch planned to divide her personal possessions among her granddaughters equally. Isaac prevented most items from reaching their intended, but when he saw Alder's desk on the list, he thought its addition to Lysbeth's sitting room would fit the curated aesthetic of misery perfectly: a piece to commemorate the forming and dashing of all her hopes and dreams.

The desk was brought to her room on the day of Isaac's departure over two months ago. She was grieved to see it but, as it provided a better hiding spot for *Danae*'s sealing horns, she resolved to regard it as a blessing in disguise. When she'd opened the drawer to transfer the horns, she was surprised to see a packet looking very much like the one she'd destroyed with Erruwyn.

Avrella had followed in Alder's footsteps and written a secret plea of her own. Its contents were much less fanciful.

Lysbeth lifts the false panel and brings the packet to the desk. *Danae*'s horns, ⇒*m-aen hu'ay,* and Afir's severed long-calm-down slide from the top. She unfolds the leather wrapping, flipping past *?Roske*'s deciphered record of the Baron's correspondence and Avrella's summary of suspicions regarding Isaac—avoiding the cryptic notation in the margins: *Mara 13, 1484 - IW appointee visit.* The year matches Isaac's birth, but the date is off by nearly nine months.

She stops on the final page; a letter addressed to her.

Sections of the ink are sloppy. Avrella had used her last bits of strength to fight her declining muscle control and move Alder's letter to the top of the desk: a signal to Lysbeth to return it to the drawer, whereupon she would discover Avrella's packet.

Distraught by the rapid deterioration of her world and all those in it, Lysbeth hadn't picked up the hint. Now she reads Avrella's letter after every tour. Her suffering elevates to numbness, allowing her to carry on until tomorrow's tour—when the forced recollection of all the joy she's lost disturbs the stillness of her despondency.

She unsheathes *Danae*'s sealing horns as she reads.

> *Lyssy,*
>
> *I beg you deliver this packet to Mr. Tindale—only Tindale—as soon as you have read it, but do so with great care. The Kingswar has seasoned Isaac's appetites. We are in danger, my dear—a danger, I regret to say, I did not fully understand until now.*
>
> *I have called three times and no one hears. My legs faltered twice reaching the desk. I fear a trek to the door will see me fall and stay, and so I dare not waste the opportunity to convey what I can, while I can.*

The second stage of Lysbeth's ritual begins with the daily forking of her circular path.

She lifts her gaze from the letter to eye the syringes rolling in each hand. If she continues reading, she'll walk the circle to the same fork tomorrow. If she forks, her path will come to a permanent end after a step or two.

Her eyes water. The room is losing light. She needs to make a decision.

Clenching her jaw, she re-slots the syringes and lowers her eyes to the page.

>*My current ailments have dragged me to a conclusion. I now believe the wounds of our menfolk were, each of them, inflicted by the other. I must assume, whether by confrontation or sneakery, Isaac learned of my accusations against him and favored a proactive approach to self-preservation.*
>
>*Of course, the fastest way home would require a wound on Jaspyr's still-breathing body. Thanks to your grandfather's love of botany, my symptoms happened to recall a plant he spoke of two Kingswars past—a paralyzing, toxic berry which grows in the highlands far North. The name eludes me. Check the eastern library for his botany book and notations, there may yet be a cure.*
>
>*If my conclusion is accurate, what better cover than a physician to accompany Jaspyr for slow administration of the toxin over the long journey home? And what better means to revenge himself on me than my precious sherry? Though know, child, other than the pain of my ignorance and my fear of his plans for you and Erruwyn, I do not suffer.*
>
>*I feel quite dizzy and so will retire in the hopes I may be able to retain my faculties through to morning. If not, be assured my last waking thoughts shall be of how very dearly I love you all.*

When a wine glass is overwhelmed by an external source of its natural resonant frequency—by too much of what makes it up—the vibrations loop in amplification, oscillating its physical material so quickly it comes apart. It fractures, then shatters.

A similar effect takes place in Lysbeth's mind each time she finishes the letter. An external source of knowledge regarding her own experience—of what makes her up—arrives all at once and all too late. She fractures, then shatters.

Tears roll past a blank expression, eyes set on the wall behind Alder's desk. Her hands refold the packet, replace the items, and lock the drawer without her. She rises and moves to the window of the darkened room—where she'll remain until her maid comes to cluck at the wet neckline of her dress as she's readied for bed.

The night is clear.

The moon is bright.

The view is matte and grey—nearly two dimensional.

She doesn't see it.

Months ago, she'd imagined a third fork in the path. She'd pack a bag with Avrella's packet, the listings of her most trusted employees, Erruwyn's horns, and the gaudy sparrow broach she'd managed to hide. She'd set her dining room alight as a distraction, grab Avrella's ashes, and flee to the village. She'd beg a ride to the docks of Limington, sell her broach—worth enough to get by on for a year if she was careful—and make her way to Walstead. She'd deliver Avrella's packet to Mr. Tindale. She'd reunite with Corah. She'd write to Brom, Mr. Sandel, Konja, and Elane—gather all those she trusted together for assistance in bringing Isaac to justice once and for all.

She'd felt reasonably convinced of the plan's success until she realized Isaac's obstruction of Avrella's bequeathment meant the dismissal of Mr. Tindale as the Haywood's Steward. After fifty years, Steward and Matriarch trusted each other implicitly, and without him, the fork closed. Avrella pleaded for his involvement precisely because so few others would listen to a woman's accusation against a Lord—without a male figure in the Haywood's inner circle to vouch for Lysbeth, Isaac's meeting with true justice was nearly impossible.

She stands still.

She stares.

As she stares, her eyes lose focus.

If she gave up retribution and concentrated her efforts on retrieving Corah, Isaac's new Steward would bar the way—unless she was prepared to light another fire and flee with her sister as Walstead's occupants vacated to escape the flame.

While reducing both Lindenholt and Walstead to ash would serve as poetic justice for the man who abhorred waste, it would also paint a target on her back, and she had nowhere to hide. Moreover, neither Haywood sister possesses the practical skills necessary to make their own way. The only houses in need of governesses belong to nobles who would recognize Lysbeth, and she wouldn't burden her prior employees by asking for help and making them targets, too.

A pale reflection looks back at her from the pane.

It's gaunt, drawn, and lifeless.

She doesn't recognize it.

She stands still.

She stares.

As she stares, something rolls and settles on the reflection's forehead.

Her pupils refocus. Two triangles of fog appear on the pane beneath her nose.

⟨The object is long.

She slides the window open and bends over the sill. The object rolls again.

⟨One side of it is ragged, worn.

It tumbles towards her as a cool breeze dries her face, and stops below her window.

⟨Her eyes follow down.

Wind pins the feather to Lindenholt's brickwork as a wide head on a tall neck tilts around the corner.

⟩*Anese* whispers against her knee.

‖ *Ilysbeth* ‖

The ship anchored well and nimbly against the bank that was our prison,
and there began a procession of the people known to my countrymen as Faye.
-Alder Haywood-

ʔthe ay'tuan flips

Lysbeth wakes precisely as she'd been before sleeping.

Early light gives the dark, granite cove a silver complexion. Her lungs expand, pulling sweet, floral scents through her nose. The stream just beyond the archway falls steady, providing a gentle, persistent purl in its stone-dented puddle. Her fingertips rest on the lacey scar she'd fallen asleep tracing.

She traces it again.

At her stirring, ʒerru͡wyn tucks the Archive into a side-pocket of their nest and lifts the arm wrapped under her waist to pull her in. Lysbeth's drowsy smile rolls across him to press her nose against the bend of his jaw. His hand returns from the pocket to join its mate in fondling the length of her they can reach.

"Has Roske finally satisfied you?" she asks, lips muffled against his skin.

Long fingers comb her hair. "I believe, yes."

"Truly? Even the unverifiable passages?"

ʒerru͡wyn smiles. "ʔRoske expresses what it wishes. Are you dissatisfied?" Her head shakes in his neck. "Then, is there more you wish for it to say?"

"That depends." Lysbeth crosses her arms over his chest and props herself up slowly. "Has it Archived your wish yet? The one you wouldn't tell me after Otay's Equinox attack?"

When her refreshed face comes into his view, the silver in and around her ear rumbles deeply. He lifts, kissing her fervidly. She laughs through her nose as their incline increases, trying her best to keep up with his spiritedness. Upright, he begins a diligent cartological charting: mouth winding to her neck, hands roaming the fabric of her robe. She tilts her smile to the ceiling and closes her eyes.

An unplanned sway of the hammock slows ʒerru͡wyn's exploration. He glances down as a second set of bitsy fingers curl over the swing's edge.

"ʒlysbeth, ʒerruwyn," a tiny voice calls in overtones.

The pair reorient their grins to one another and recline again. ʒerru͡wyn dips an arm over the side as Lysbeth shifts to make room for the floor-pilgrim's deposit onto his stomach.

ʒer'em unlatches and curls into a kneel, lilting, "Jaques said rabbits aren't lazy."

"Are they not?" Lysbeth asks, resting temple on wrist.

{er'em shakes her head and idly flops {erru͡wyn's palm. "Because, mmm, Corah said you're lazy, but Jaques said rabbits aren't lazy, and then Ms. Pinley bopped Jaques, and then Corah said...said because if you're rabbits you don't need to eat much and, mmm, she's going to eat your breakfast if you're late again."

{erru͡wyn grins and squeezes Lysbeth's ribs as she buries a laugh in his neck. "Okay. Will you please say we are joining soon? Maybe hide a little food from {li'la, also?"

{er'em nods a sheepish smile and clutches his forearm.

"Thank you, {er'em," he says, lowering her to the floor.

They watch her bound through sheer curtains waving in the archway, turning blissful smiles on one another when she rounds the corner.

Lysbeth picks up a long, jet lock and twirls. "Last night, Brom mentioned that climbing to the Mena Garden is still a bit much for his leg. I offered to take flowers to Granmama's cairn on his behalf today."

"Mm. I will deliver more remedy." {erru͡wyn's knuckle trails her jawline. "{Konja desires to play before midday, also."

She presses in, folding her knee over his waist. "Elane and Rhea want to greet the new clutch."

He bites his lip, kneading her leg and rumbling. "{Sandel–ʔRoske requested assistance in the Archives."

She drifts above him again, calves hedging his thighs as she rises. "Erruwan promised Ani she'd take the lot of us sailing after The Last Dahena's keening lesson this afternoon." Her eyebrow arches.

"So many plans." The creases of his abdomen deepen to pull his grin up to hers. "I am glad {feu'n'en has clarified our tardiness should not suggest our laziness."

She laughs quietly and drapes her forearms around his neck. "Indeed, I can think of no rival to our industriousness."

Heart singing, {erru͡wyn gazes over a long moment.

"This. Here, all together," he says, gingerly tucking copper behind her ear. "This was my wish."

Eyes misting above tender smiles, da'he͡nar͡uah's day begins in celebration of their song.

Thank you for taking the time to read ḏa'he͡ ŋaɾ͡ u̯aẖ's Archive.
Those who've questioned, or resonated with, Strung's themes are
encouraged to express their thoughts by leaving a review or emailing
RoskeChronicler@gmail.com.

ɑx'nɑ͡rah

Glossary

〰〰〰〰

a a a

〰〰〰〰

♦ ⸗a̧ȩn̠

voice-essential-path:
sounds in the Outlander's audible range.

♦ a'ia̠⌒na

vocalized-grief ⌒(of) people:
Keening, dirge, lamentation.

♦ ⸮A̠ne̠se

vibration-journey-air-anima:
Resonance. A silver pendant representing a ⸗da'he̠⌒na̠'s anima. Offered to ̠nar̠⌒uah̠.

♦ aro'x

mouth-recapture ' memory:
borrowing sounds to make music

   o   ⌒hu'a̠y: mastery silver.

♦ as'e̠tu

voice/person-hollow ' anima-tool:
puppeted embodiment; a blackout state
whereby (some believe) a Concept puppets an
individual through a̠y⌒na̠.

♦ ◡a̠y'e̠na

articulated-smoke ' covering-mouth:
mouth mask of ⸮Da̠na̠e̠.

♦ ⌢a̠y'e̠nru̠

articulated-smoke ' covering-obfuscation:
eye mask of ⸮Da̠na̠e̠.

♦ a̠y⌒na̠

articulated-smoke ⌒(of) people:
the people's silver alloy. Forged to move via
acoustic resonation.

♦ a̠y'ta̠l

articulated-smoke ' mouth-flame:
silver tongue; tongue piercings awarded for
skill in pleasure-giving.

♦ a̠y'tu̠an

articulated-smoke ' puppet-rooted:
silver puppet; alloy exoskeleton suits
associated with specific Concepts and required
for as'e̠tu̠. Use various forms of magnetism
and acoustic resonance.

   o   ⌒hu'a̠y:
       Mastery silver of a̠y'tu̠an̠; cartilage
       earrings.

♦ ax'ni̠⌒ra̠h̠

vocal-memory ' outland ⌒(of) observation:
silent period of language observance after a
⸗da'he̠⌒na̠ reaches the Outland.

〰〰〰〰

ḏ ḏ ḏ

〰〰〰〰

♦ da'he̠⌒na

harmony ' sprouted ⌒(of the) people:
distant navigators and linguists who joined
se̠t'n̠e̠ to barter with Outlanders, and whose
ancestral memory formed the foundation of
Iodesh's folklore.

♦ ⸮da'he̠⌒na

melody ' beloved ⌒(of the) people:
highly trained twiceborn who escort se̠t've̠ to
assist with resource collection and protection.
Sightings contribute to Outland folklore.

♦ ⸗da'he̠⌒na

harmony ' aegis ⌒(of the) people:
Sacrificial lambs offered to pursuing ships to
ensure se̠t've̠'s escape and the secret location
of ⊙ma̠⌒jo̠c is preserved.

♦ da'he̠⌒nar̠⌒uah̠

unifying hope ⌒(of the) guided ⌒(of) purpose:
conjunction of da'he̠⌒na and ̠nar̠⌒uah̠. The
resonant salvation of a ⸗da'he̠⌒na.

♦ _da'ja‿na_

harmony ' loving-source‿(of the) people:
nine-day festival of sensuality occurring over winter solstice—during which, _me'ya‿itet_ mate with those they have chosen.

♦ ⟪Danae⟫

strong-roots-affected:
Amplification. An _ay'tuan_ worn exclusively by _da'he‿na_. Primarily used for utility on _set'ye_. Also used for the Offering rite when a _da'he‿na_ is Called, and the subsequent resonation of _da'he‿nar‿uah_.

♦ ⟪Danese⟫

strong-articulation-journey-air-anima:
Concept; union of Amplification and Resonance. Physics principle of sympathetic resonance.

♦ _dj'en'ec_

complex-love ' covering ' soul-flora:
seedpod; conceptually, a group of individuals bound together.

♦ _d'koa_

strong ' leading-wind:
expression of ⋈_Jhenxi_. Enjoys steering others.

♦ _de'tae‿hu_

all ' essential-body-shaped (of) master:
Elemental stance mastery.

- o _ota'tae_: sound stance
- o _~oa'tae_: wind stance
- o _ʔwa'tae_: water stance
- o _Λoo'tae_: mountain stance
- o _Ue'tae_: flame stance
- o _‿hu'ay_: mastery silver; horns

❧❧❧❧❧
e̶ e̶ e̶
❧❧❧❧❧❧

♦ _er'em_

light-attune ' light-begin:
flicker of light in the darkness; hope, firefly.

♦ _erru_

light-attune-refract-obstacle:
mist-refracting-light. Mistbow.

♦ _er'wa_

light-reflect ' motion-voice:
light on water; one who reflects their partner's desires. A rare expression of ⋈_Jhenxi_, only receives sexual gratification through gratifying another.

♦ _er'oo'n_

essential-attune ' mountain ' path:
sparks in the eye of ⊙_ma‿joc_; mega fauna, birds.

♦ _ey‿ine_

soul-void‿(of) unfavorable-towards-essential:
conceptually, weaving damaged souls together to become whole.

❧❧❧❧❧
f f f
❧❧❧❧❧❧

♦ _feu'n'en_

steady-anima-obstacle ' towards ' soul-path:
Follow the sting to honey—an irritant which becomes useful or desirable. _One who lays a path of stingers_—one whose list of delinquencies has grown so long, it becomes more impressive than offensive.

♦ _f'o'ss_

long-wear-down:
sleek feathers of Eroon's curious form.

♦ _f'eh'ss_

long-calm-down:
soft feathers of Eroon's loving form.

♦ _f'u'ss_

long-cut-down:
sharp feathers of Eroon's angry form.

ꙮꙮꙮꙮꙮ
i i i
ꙮꙮꙮꙮꙮ

♦ *ik-tys*

fated-string (with) *physical-void-hollow*:
become discordant/displaced.

♦ *ir'ie*

unfavorable-equilibrium ' fated-soul:
Fading echo; a called *ᵹda'he⌐na* becomes an
echo--destined to fade without the resonance
of *ₗnar⌐uaḥ*.

♦ ⋈*Iuaḥ*

pain-without-breath:
Concept of Severance; Suffering.

♦ *ix'ul*

pained-memory ' without-warmth:
a corrupted/haunting memory that requires
expression.

   ○   *ix'ul-ae*:   neighboring memory
        tainted by an *ix'ul*.

ꙮꙮꙮꙮꙮ
j j j

ꙮꙮꙮꙮꙮ

♦ ⋈*Jhenxi*

desire-aim-essential-path-feeling-fated:
Concept; androgynous personification of
sexuality.

   ○   ⌐*ay-tut*: silver shell of ⋈*Jhenxi*.
   ○   ⌐*ky*: shadow of ⋈*Jhenxi*; asexual
        spectrum.

♦ *ji-ji-ji*

pleasing-unpleasantness (and) *affectionate-conflict* (and) *covet-fated*:
ecstatic torment; bittersweetness magnified.

♦ *j'tae*

beauty ' body-affected:
beautification, primping.

♦ *jo'ta*:

alluring-carry ' surface-individual:
a cuff displaying sexual preferences and
expressions of ⋈*Jhenxi*.

ꙮꙮꙮꙮꙮ
ḳ ḳ ḳ
ꙮꙮꙮꙮꙮ

♦ *ke'ra-tu*:

authority-essential ' attune articulate (with)
container-use:
resonant bidding of *ₗnar⌐uaḥ*

♦ *k'es'sey*

string ' soul-hollow ' hollow-anima-void:
string unfulfilled promise; expression of
⋈*Jhenxi* which enjoys teasing, denial. "Show
the fruit, give the stone." Pairs with *er'wa* in
ne'ru'k training.

♦ *ki'ky'um*

pulled-fate ' leading-grey ' remove:
shadow departed; one so swift they leave their
shadow behind, or one so unsavory even their
shadow leaves them.

♦ ⊩*Konok*

pull-carry-journey-carry-pull:
kinesthetic, physical forces e.g. gravity.

♦ *k'uaḥ⌐ni*

Sovereign ' Will ⌐ (of the) Outland:
laws of the Outland's Sovereigns. *ᵹda'he⌐na*
must follow the laws of the lands they inhabit
unless *ₗnar⌐uaḥ* or *ᵣ'uaḥ⌐ na* intercede.

♦ *kw'da*

leading-motions ' many-voices:
conductor.

ꙍꙍꙍꙍꙍ

!!!

ꙍꙍꙍꙍꙍ

• _li'la ͡itet_

flame-fated ' sun-origin ͡ (of)dancer:
dancer in the forge; powerful flame of great
potential if nurtured carefully.

• _lyr ͡itet_

sun-moon-equilibrium ͡ (of) dance:
twiceborn dance performed at equinoxes.

ꙍꙍꙍꙍꙍ

ɱ ɱ ɱ

ꙍꙍꙍꙍꙍ

• _ma ͡joc_

primal-origin ͡(of) beautiful-earth-scape:
motherland.

• _m'aen_

primal ' voice-essential-path:
primal pitches; infra and supra sonic pitches.
Produced as ≦involuntary emotional
responses from birth. Can be ≦willfully
produced after training and used as an
acoustic power source.

   ○   ≯_m-aen ͡hu'ay_:
       mastery silver of 3 chains

• _m'ay-tut_

primal ' articulated-smoke ' shell:
joint-bracing framework.

• _me'ya ͡itet_

primal-anima ' void-voice ͡(of) dancer:
a primal, a mother.

• ≷_me ͡na_

primal-anima ͡(of the) people:
woman of the people: respected matriarchs,
titled by consensus.

ꙍꙍꙍꙍꙍ

ɳ ɳ ɳ

ꙍꙍꙍꙍꙍ

• ¡_nar ͡uah_

Wayfinder's Will:
An Outlander chosen by a ᴢ_da'he ͡na_ to act
as one of three Wills he obeys. Wayfinders
guide a ᴢ_da'he ͡na_ through Outland customs,
mores, and laws, and maintain his emotional
resonance.

• _ne'ru'k_

survival ' obstacle ' influence:
breakwater; birth control through non-
ejaculatory orgasm.

• _nu'im_

path-reaped ' fated-beginning:
imminent fate; the time between a
ᴢ_da'he ͡na_'s Threading and the scow either
sinking or accepted as offering.

ꙍꙍꙍꙍꙍ

ɾ ɾ ɾ

ꙍꙍꙍꙍꙍ

• ʔ_Roske_

reproduce-string-anima:
Concept. Chronicler of Time. Often used to
Archive memories and knowledge through
text and images.

• ꞊_roo'da_

attune-mountain ' song:
the central hub and carved, dome mountain
of _ma ͡joc_.

• ᵣ_r'uah ͡na_

attuned Will ͡ (of the) people:
First Will. The people's closest notion to a
codified law.

• ◊_Ruah_

equilibrium-will:
Concept of Fulcrum; Equilibrium.

- ⟡*Ruaḫ*

ay'tuan of ⟡*Ruaḫ*. Requires *as'etu*.

- *ry⌒ine*

equilibrium-void⌒(of) weaving:
symmetry weaving. Restoration of balance
overseen by justiciars of ⟡*Ruaḫ*

  o ∞*ry⌒ine⌒hu'ay*: mastery silver;
    branching stalks of ⌣*ay'ena*

৶৶৶৶৶

ș ș ș

ৼ৶৶৶৶

- *șet'ne*

vessel ' away-essential:
ages distant, a voyage for resources and trade
with the Outland.

- *șet'ye*

vessel ' void-essential:
a dangerous voyage for resources accompanied
by a *șda'he⌒na* pair.

- *șo'jac*

air-earth ' beautiful-anima-flora:
flowering tree endemic to ⊙*ma⌒joc*.

- *ș'wo*

soft ' motion-earth (sand):
expression of ⋈*Jhenxi*; enjoys yielding.

ৼ৶৶৶৶

t t t

ৼ৶৶৶৶

- *tau⌒ine*

texture-throat-use⌒(of) weaving:
a combination infra and supra sonic pitches.
Facilitate a sense of serene calm, sleep, and/or
comfort for the distraught.

- ?*Theam*

physical-endeavor-anima-articulate-primal:
Concept of Resonant Frequency. First element.

  o ⌒*hu'ay*: mastery silver
  o ⌒*itet*: dancer; personification of
    Resonant Frequency through dance.
  o ⌒*rah*: observation; meditation of
    Resonant Frequency's effect on
    matter.

- *tia⌒ua*

physical-pain-voice⌒(of) muting:
the *m'aen* sung as one dies in pain.

- *tox'ki⌒rah*

physical-emotion ' strung⌒(of) observance:
physically expressed textures of emotion.

ৼ৶৶৶৶

ẉ ẉ ẉ

ৼ৶৶৶৶

- *wa't'un*

water ' physical ' obstruct-path:
massive ridgeline of a now-submerged
continent. Outland vessels washed up here are
taken in by the people.

- *wox'ua*

motion-carry-memory ' remove-voice:
sign language.

- *wan*

motion-voices-towards:
dawn

- *wyn*

motion-dark-towards:

dusk

Printed in Great Britain
by Amazon

62328647R00224